Victor Hugo, Newton Crosland, Frederick Lokes Slous

Dramatic Works of Victor Hugo

Vol. 1

Victor Hugo, Newton Crosland, Frederick Lokes Slous

Dramatic Works of Victor Hugo
Vol. 1

ISBN/EAN: 9783337376420

Printed in Europe, USA, Canada, Australia, Japan

Cover: Foto ©Andreas Hilbeck / pixelio.de

More available books at **www.hansebooks.com**

DRAMATIC WORKS OF VICTOR HUGO.

TRANSLATED BY

FREDERICK L. SLOUS,

AND

MRS. NEWTON CROSLAND,

Author of " The Diamond Wedding, and other Poems," " Hubert Freeth's Prosperity,"
" Stories of the City of London," etc.

————+————

HERNANI.
THE KING'S DIVERSION.
RUY BLAS.

PROFUSELY ILLUSTRATED WITH ELEGANT

WOOD ENGRAVINGS.

VOLUME V.

NEW YORK:

P. F. COLLIER, PUBLISHER:

CONTENTS.

· EDITOR'S PREFACE.

S the Translator of "Hernani" and "Ruy Blas," I may be permitted to offer a few remarks on the three great dramas which are now presented in an English form to the English-speaking public. Each of these works is preceded by the Author's Preface, which perhaps exhausts all that had to be said of the play which follows—from his own original point of view. It is curious to contrast the confident egotism, the frequent self-assertion, and the indignation at repression which mark the prefaces to "Hernani" and "Le Roi s'Amuse" with the calm dignity of the very fine dramatic criticism which introduces the reader to "Ruy Blas." But when the last-named tragedy was produced, Victor Hugo's fame was established and his literary position secure; he no longer had need to assert himself, for if a few enemies still remained, their voices were but as the buzzing of flies about a giant. Trusting that the Author's Prefaces will be carefully read, I will endeavor only to supplement what is said in them.

"Hernani" belongs emphatically to the romantic school, and to the period in European literature when the bonds of olden custom in all the arts were being broken—often for good results, though not always. Hernani is a rebel, and called a bandit throughout the play—but he is a rebel noble, sworn to avenge his father's wrongs, and his band may fairly be supposed to have been recruited from a disaffected army. He is a young lover as ardent as Romeo, with less trust and more jealousy, and Doña Sol corresponds in some respects to Juliet. Yet it is well to mark the difference between the man's love and the woman's, as the great poet has faithfully shown it. With Doña Sol her love is her "sole existence." It is because Hernani refuses when urged to subdue his master passion, vengeance, and thus be released from his pledge, that the play becomes a tragedy. Not until too late for life and happiness is his vengeance overcome by the magnanimity of Charles.

One of the admirable characteristics of this work is that all the personages portrayed are such distinct individuals that any one knowing the play tolerably well would, there is little doubt, identify any line that might be quoted, apportioning it to the right speaker. But this power of distinctly and forcibly delineating his characters is one of Hugo's never-failing attributes, and is shown hardly less in the subordinate courtiers who play their part in the drama, than in the leading personages. Don Carlos may not be quite the Charles the Fifth of history, but he is something greater—a poet's fine creation.

It seems to me that the old man, Ruy Gomez, is one of the most subtle conceptions which a great poet ever vivified. He is a man who has reached sixty years of age in the enjoyment of unsullied fame and the noblest repute—a man to whom the preservation of what was called Castilian honor was beyond all other duties, all other happiness. The scene of the Portraits must warm every noble nature to pathetic sympathy; and yet when we have finished the play we discover of how little worth was that chivalry of Spain which "Cervantes laughed away"—how completely was it a mere form—a code of set rules—not what chivalry surely ought to be, an influence springing from Christianity and capable of being adapted to all circumstances.

Such was not the chivalry of Don Ruy Gomez de Silva, Duke de Pastrana, when crossed and thwarted in his heart's desire. Tempted then by furious passions he fell. There was no chivalry in his Shylock-like holding of Hernani to his bond.

I think there are two or three brief sentences in the Fifth Act, which are like flashes of lurid lightning by which we see the depths of the malignity which rages in the heart of the old Duke—depths which it would have taken an inferior writer half a page to describe.

Perhaps, however, the finest portion of this work is the Fourth Act, which includes the magnificent monologue of Charles the Fifth before the tomb of Charlemagne. A translator must be very incompetent if his rendering of this speech does not stir the pulse of the reader who remembers that it embodies the ideas of a noble despot in the days when despotism was the only form of government. And this brings one to the point of what has often been said about Victor Hugo being untranslatable.

It cannot be denied that in a certain sense all poetry of the first order must be untranslatable. It is scarcely possible that any phrase of another language can be quite so happy as that into which the molten thought of genius first flowed. Neither is it likely, if possible, that the melody of the first inspiration can find a complete equivalent in a strange tongue. But surely the language of Shakespeare and Milton, of Pope and of Byron, and of our living Victorian poets is not so poor that it cannot express subtle thoughts precisely, eloquent pleadings with fervor, and poetical imagery with force and grace!

Shakespeare must be as untranslatable—in the sense to which I have alluded—as undoubtedly is Victor Hugo. Yet the French know something of our greatest poet even through translations. Byron also is tolerably familiar to them, not to mention lesser lights. It may seem a paradox, but I think it is only a truth, to say that the greater a poet is, the more capable are his works of translation; and for this reason.

They contain the larger store of deep thought, which, like pure gold, may be put into the crucible and melted into a new shape. Smaller poets do not supply this precious substance, and so what little charm they have evaporates in the necessary treatment.

It has, I believe, been said by one or two detracting critics that Victor Hugo is, for a great writer, deficient in humor. He is generally too terribly in earnest to be turned aside to make fun on slight provocation; but the manner in which Don Carlos, in the First Act of "Hernani," mystifies the proud Duke surely belongs to the richest vein of comedy; and of sarcasm there is abundance throughout the play.

It would occupy too much space to relate half the amusing stories associated with the first production of "Hernani." The great actress, Mdlle. Mars—though more than fifty years of age—personated the heroine to perfection; but she did not in the first instance like her part, nor did she appreciate the play until success enabled her to do so. Certainly she could not have comprehended the work in its entireness, or she would not have raised the objection she did to a certain line in the Third Act, Scene the Fourth. In her egotism she probably looked on Hernani as a common bandit, instead of a rebel Lord defying a King. It is a powerful scene in which Hernani had been lamenting that he had only a dole of misery to offer to his love, and Doña Sol exclaims:

"Vous êtes mon lion superbe et généreux!"
("You are my lion generous and superb!")

And time after time, at rehearsal, Mdlle. Mars halted at this passage, shaded her eyes with her hand, and pretended to look round for the author—though she knew perfectly well where he was seated in the orchestra—and then would inquire if M. Hugo were present. "I am here, Madam," Hugh would reply—and then would ensue a dialogue but slightly varied on each occasion.

It is Dumas, who attended many of these rehearsals, that tells the story :

"Do you really like that line?" the actress would say.

"Madam, I so wrote it."

"So you stick to your *lion?*"

"Find me something better, and I will alter it."

"That is not for me to do," retorted the actress. "I am not the author."

"Well, then, Madam, as that is the case, let us leave it as it is."

A little more argument, but next day all had to be gone over again. And when Mdlle. Mars declared that it was a dangerous line, which would certainly be hissed, the author replied that this would only be the case if she did not deliver it with her usual power. At last she ventured to suggest that instead of "mon lion" Doña Sol should say "Monseigneur," and wondered what objection there could be to the substitution.

"Only," replied Hugo, "that *mon lion* elevates the verse, and *Monseigneur* lowers it,"—adding, "I would rather be hissed for a good verse than applauded for a bad one."

In fact these vexatious interruptions were so irritating to the poet, that towards the close of one of the rehearsals, he asked to speak to Mdlle. Mars, and told her that he wished her to give back the part. The actress turned pale; she was accustomed to be urgently solicited to undertake characters, but never before had she been required to give one up. She apologized, and the little quarrel was in a measure made up; though she preserved a cold, discontented manner which chilled the other actors; happily, however, she did exert all her powers when the hour for their display arrived.

On the first night that "Hernani" was performed, a significant incident showed the effect that it produced. The monologue of Charles the Fifth, in the Fourth Act, was received with thunders of applause; and while the tumult was unabated, it was intimated to Victor Hugo that he was wanted. It was a little man with eager eyes who wished to speak to him.

"My name is Mame," said the stranger, "I am the partner of M. Baudoin the publisher—but we cannot talk here—can you spare me a minute outside the theatre?"

They passed into the street, when the little man continued:—

"M. Baudoin and I have witnessed the performance—we should like to publish 'Hernani,' will you sell it?"

"What will you give?" said the author.

"Six thousand francs."

Victor Hugo suggested that he should wait till the performance was over, but M. Mame desired to conclude the business at once, notwithstanding Hugo's generous reminder that the success at the close might be less complete than it appeared at present.

"That is true," said the publisher, "but it may be greater. At the second act I meant to offer you two thousand francs; at the third I advanced to four thousand; and now at the fourth I offer you six. If I wait till the fifth act is over I fear I should offer you ten thousand."

Victor Hugo was so amused that he could not help laughing, and promised that the matter should be arranged the next morning. But this little delay did not suit the impatient publisher, who had the money in his pocket, and wished to settle the affair at once. So the pair entered a tobacconist's shop, where stamped paper and pen and ink were procured, and the bargain duly made; one exceedingly acceptable to the poet, who was then very poor, and had but fifty francs in his possession.

In the author's preface to "Le Roi s'Amuse" he eloquently defends himself from the charge of having produced an immoral play. Certainly in this work vice is neither really triumphant nor made for one moment attractive, and yet, as the translator forcibly observes, there can be little wonder that after one representation its performance was prohibited.

It was intimated to the Author that "Le Roi s'Amuse" was suppressed because it contained a verse that was looked upon as an insult to the Citizen King Louis Philippe. Victor Hugo denied emphatically any such intention, and as for long years afterwards the Orleans family remained on the most familiar and friendly terms with him, it is difficult to suppose that they believed in the accusation. And just as Hugo had refused from Charles the Tenth an addition to his pension in consideration of the suppression of "Marion de Lorme"—so now, after the performance of "Le Roi s'Amuse" had been prohibited, on being taunted by the Ministerial journals with receiving his original pension of two thousand francs, he threw it up, declining to take another sou. It is true also that in his preface he speaks contemptuously of the government—but the fact remains—testified anew in the recently published volume, "Choses Vues"—that Hugo continued the intimate associate of the King and the Orleans princes. Few readers will blame the censor for prohibiting the play, though they may differ concerning the verity of his alleged motives—and for pastime may sharpen their wits in seeking to find the clue to the puzzle.

I look upon it as a curious coincidence that the "Lady of Lyons" in London, and "Ruy Blas" in Paris, should have been produced in the same year. Both dramas turn on the incident of a man of humble station loving a woman greatly his superior in social rank, and winning her affections in an assumed character; and quite possibly both plays were suggested by the true story of Angelica Kauffman, who was entrapped into a marriage with a valet, believing him to be a foreign nobleman. But save in the one circumstance no two works can be more dissimilar than these are. The English like plays to end happily, or at any rate, for only the repulsive villains to suffer, and the cleverly constructed yet highly melodramatic "Lady of Lyons" hit the taste of the town exactly. Two great artists, Macready and Helen Faucit, embodied Lord Lytton's creations in so poetical a manner, that they assumed a dignity which inferior actors must fail to give them. The love was pure, and there was repentance with atonement before the happy climax. Besides, the difference between the gardener's son and the merchant's daughter was not so outrageously great, as to shut out the hope of its being spanned. The audience was deeply, pathetically touched—the play was effective in the highest degree—and the acting supremely fine—but every one felt that things would come right at last.

Not so with "Ruy Blas." Near the close of the first act, at scene the third, we know perfectly well that it is a tragedy before us. The fatal words of the hero overheard by the remorseless Don Salluste unloose the stream which is to carry him to perdition :—

> "Oh ! mon âme au demon ! Je la vendrais, pour être
> Un des jeunes seigneurs que, de cette fenêtre,
> Je vois en ce moment."

> "My soul
> Is given over, I would sell it might
> I thus become like one of those young lords
> That from this window I behold."

It is a realization of the mediæval legend. He has his wish and his heart's desire, but in consequence wave after wave arises to bear him on to his doom. To those who will read between the lines, Ruy Blas is surely full of the noblest and most Christian teaching. We pity, it is true, the sorely tried and tempted, but we know as a fact in ethics—and therefore a truth to be upheld in Art—that retribution must follow wrong-doing. And as Victor Hugo may be considered the greatest dramatist since Shakespeare, he knew well that his work must be a tragedy. But it is so supreme and perfectly moulded a work of art because he has, in its proper place, brightened the drama with rich comedy. In this he resembles our own great poet. The wonderful manner in which the character of Don Cæsar is sustained and revealed through dialogues flashing with wit, and incidents only to have been conceived by a real humorist—proclaims the master.

Surely there is consummate art in separating the third from the fifth act by a series of scenes, which, though keeping the motive of the play well in view, gives the spectator rest from the culminating excitement of the one, before witnessing the struggle and pathos of the other. Never let the moralist forget that in the end Ruy Blas is the conqueror—conquering even himself, and saving the poor outraged Queen. But the death penalty is inevitable, for Nemesis is never absent from the " personages " of Hugo's dramas.

And now I beg leave to say a very few words of myself. If these translations of mine should prove the last work of a pen that for nearly fifty years has been busy in many departments of literature, I hope I shall be justified in the estimation of thoughtful readers. There is such a glow of eternal youth about Hugo's works, that I rather rejoice at finding myself capable of being fascinated by them. The world is always young! Somewhere always noble natures are aspiring, and young hearts beating with their first awakening to a master passion. To faithfully portray the struggles of the heart is one of the poet's missions, and surely in depicting in " Hernani " and " Ruy Blas," love and revenge, ambition and loyalty, remorse and despair, the noblest teaching is embodied—teaching that appeals to many natures more forcibly in the manner in which it is here presented than in a more solemn and didactic form. I do not deny that here and there a daring thought may displease timid readers—but let them rather turn to those eternal truths which are the basis, the life and spirit of all religious creeds, and which shine luminously in the poetry of Victor Hugo. Let us thank him for the jewels he gives us, and not bring a lens through which to search for the flaws!

Ever is Victor Hugo the defender of the weak and oppressed,

the scorner of selfishness and vice, the teacher of self-sacrifice in the cause of duty, and the upholder of the dignity of woman. It may be that in these matter-of-fact days we require such teaching quite as much as did mankind in the ages which were called darker, and there is little doubt that the greatest of French poets reaches many hearts that have proved insensible to weaker influences.

CAMILLA CROSLAND.

October, 1887.

HERNANI:

A TRAGEDY IN FIVE ACTS.

(15)

AUTHOR'S PREFACE TO THE FIRST
EDITION OF HERNANI, 1830.

NLY a few weeks since, the Author of this drama wrote, concerning a poet who died before maturity, as follows :—

"* * * At this moment of literary turmoil and contention, whom should we the more pity, those who die, or those who wrestle? Truly it is sad to see a poet of twenty years old pass away, to behold a broken lyre, and a future that vanishes; but, is not repose also some advantage? Are there not those around whom calumnies, injuries, hatreds, jealousies, secret wrongs, base treasons incessantly gather; true men, against whom disloyal war is waged; devoted men, who only seek to bestow on their country one sort of freedom the more, that of art and intelligence; laborious men, who peaceably pursue their conscientious work, a prey on one side to the vile stratagems of official censure, and on the other exposed too often to the ingratitude of even those for whom they toil; may not such be permitted sometimes to turn their eyes with envy towards those who have fallen behind them, and who rest in the tomb? *Invideo*, said Luther, in the cemetery of Worms, *invideo quia quiescunt*.

"What does it signify? Young people, take heart. If the present be made rough for us, the future will be smooth. Romanticism, so often ill-defined, is only—and this is its true definition if we look at it from its combative side—liberalism in literature. This truth is already understood by nearly all the best minds, and the number is great; and soon, for the work is well advanced, liberalism in literature will not be less popular than in politics. Liberty in Art, liberty in Society, behold the double end towards which consistent and logical minds should tend; behold the double banner that rallies the intelligence—with but few exceptions, which will become more enlightened—of all the young who are now so strong and patient; then, with the young, and at their head the choice spirits of the generation which has preceded us, all those

(17)

sagacious veterans, who, after the first moment of hesitation and examination, discovered that what their sons are doing to-day is the consequence of what they themselves have achieved, and that liberty in literature is the offspring of political liberty. This principle is that of the age, and will prevail. The *Ultras* of all sorts, classical and monarchical, will in vain help each other to restore the old system, broken to pieces, literary and social; all progress of the country, every intellectual development, every stride of liberty will have caused their scaffolding to give way. And, indeed, their efforts at reaction will have been useful. In revolution every movement is an advance. Truth and liberty have this excellence, that all one does for and against them serves them equally well. Now, after all the great things that our fathers have done, and that we have beheld, now that we have come out of the old social form, why should there not proceed a new out of the old poetic form? For a new people, new art. In admiring the literature of Louis the Fourteenth's age, so well adapted to his monarchy, France will know well how to have its own and national literature of the nineteenth century, to which Mirabeau gave its liberty, and Napoleon its power."—*Letter to the Publishers of the Poems of M. Dovalle.*

Let the author of this drama be pardoned for thus quoting himself. His words have so little the power of impressing, that he often needs to repeat them. Besides, at present it is perhaps not out of place to put before readers the two pages just transcribed. It is not this drama which can in any respect deserve the great name of *new art* or *new poetry*. Far from that; but it is that the principle of freedom in literature has advanced a step; it is that some progress has been made, not in art, this drama is too small a thing for that, but in the public; it is that in this respect at least one part of the predictions hazarded above has just been realized.

There is, indeed, some danger in making changes thus suddenly, and risking on the stage those tentative efforts hitherto confided to paper, which endures everything; the reading public is very different from the theatrical public, and one might dread seeing the latter reject what the former had accepted. This has not been the case. The principle of literary freedom already comprehended by the world of readers and thinkers, has not been less fully accepted by that immense crowd, eager for the pure enjoyment of art, which every night fills the theatres of Paris. This loud and powerful voice of the people, likened to the voice of God, declares that henceforth poetry shall bear the same device as politics: TOLERATION AND LIBERTY.

Now let the poet come! He has a public.

And whatever may be this freedom, the public wills that in the State it shall be reconciled with order, and in literature with art. Liberty has a wisdom of its own, without which it is not complete.

That the old rules of D'Aubignac should die with the old customs of Cujas is well; that to a literature of the court should succeed a literature of the people is better still; but, above all, it is best that an inner voice should be heard from the depths of all these novelties. Let the principle of liberty work, but let it work well. In letters, as in society, not etiquette, not anarchy, but laws. Neither red heels * nor red caps.

This is what the public wants, and it wishes rightly. As for us, in deference to that public which has accepted with so much indulgence an attempt which merits so little, we give this drama now as it has been represented. Perhaps the day will come when the author will publish it as he conceived it,† indicating and discussing the modifications to which he had to submit. These critical details may be neither uninstructive nor uninteresting, though they seem trifling at present—freedom in art is admitted, the principal question is settled; why pause to dwell on secondary questions? We shall return to them some day, and also speak of them in detail, demolishing by evidence and reason this system of dramatic censure —which is the only obstacle to the freedom of the theatre now that it no longer exists in the public mind. We shall strive at all risks and perils, and by devotion to art, to expose the thousand abuses of this petty inquisition of the intellect, which has, like the other holy office, its secret judges, its masked executioners, its tortures, its mutilations, and its penalty of death. We will tear away, if we can, those swaddling clothes of the police, in which it is shameful that the theatre should be wrapped up in the nineteenth century.

At present there is only place for gratitude and thanks. To the public it is that the author addresses his own acknowledgments, and he does so from the depths of his heart. This work, not from its talent, but for conscience' and freedom's sake, has been generously protected from enmities by the public, because the public is also itself always conscientious and free. Thanks, then, be rendered to it, as well as to that mighty youthful band which has brought help and favor to the work of a young man as sincere and independent as itself. It was for youth above all that he labored, because it would be a great and real glory to be applauded by the leading young men, who are intelligent, logical, consistent, truly liberal in literature as well as politics—a noble generation, that opens wide its eyes to look at the truth, and to receive light from all sides.

As for his work, he will not speak of it. He accepts the criticisms which it has drawn forth, the most severe as well as the

---

* Red heels, typical of the aristocracy; red caps, of liberty—or anarchy.— TRANS.

† This day has long since come, and the translation of Hernani, which is now offered to English readers, is from the unmutilated edition of 1836.—TRANS.

most kindly, because he may profit by all. He dares not flatter himself that every one can at once have understood this drama, of which the *Romancero General* is the true key. He would willingly ask persons whom this work has shocked, to read again *Le Cid, Don Sanche, Nicomède*, or rather all Corneille and all Molière, those great and admirable poets. Such reading, however much it might show the immense inferiority of the author of *Hernani*, would perhaps render them more indulgent to certain things which have offended them in the form, or the motive, of this drama. In fact, the moment is perhaps not yet come to judge it. *Hernani* is but the first stone of an edifice which exists fully constructed in the author's mind, the whole of which can alone give value to this drama. Perhaps one day it will not be thought ill that his fancy, like that of the architect of Bourges, puts a door almost Moorish to his Gothic Cathedral.

Meanwhile, what he has done is but little, and he knows it. May time and power to proceed with his work not fail him ! It will but have worth when it is completed. He is not one of those privileged poets who can die or break off before they have finished without peril to their memory ; he is not of those who remain great even without having completed their work—happy men, of whom one may say what Virgil said of Carthage traced out :—

> Pendent opera interrupta minæque
> Murorum ingentes.

March 9th, 1830.

PERSONAGES OF THE DRAMA.

HERNANI.
DON CARLOS.
DON RUY GOMEZ DE SILVA.
DOÑA SOL DE SILVA.
THE KING OF BOHEMIA.
THE DUKE OF BAVARIA.
THE DUKE OF GOTHA.
THE BARON OF HOHENBOURG.
THE DUKE OF LUTZELBOURG.
DON SANCHO.
DON MATIAS.
DON RICARDO.
DON GARCIE SUAREZ.
DON FRANCISCO.
DON JUAN DE HARO.
DON PEDRO GUSMAN DE LARA.
DON GIL TELLEZ GIRON.
DOÑA JOSEFA DUARTE.
JAQUEZ.

A Mountaineer.
A Lady.
First Conspirator.
Second Conspirator.
Third Conspirator.

Conspirators of the Holy League, Germans and
Spaniards, Mountaineers, Nobles, Soldiers,
Pages, Attendants, etc.

SPAIN, A.D. 1519.

HERNANI.

ACT FIRST: THE KING.

SCENE 1.—SARAGOSSA. *A Chamber. Night: a lamp on the table.*

DOÑA JOSEFA DUARTE, *an old woman dressed in black, with body of her dress worked in jet in the fashion of Isabella the Catholic.* DON CARLOS.

DOÑA JOSEFA, *alone. She draws the crimson curtains of the window, and puts some armchairs in order. A knock at a little secret door on the right. She listens. A second knock.*

DOÑA JOSEFA.

Can it be he already?   [*Another knock.*

     'T is, indeed,

At th' hidden stairway.   [*A fourth knock.*

     I must open quick.

[*She opens the concealed door.* DON CARLOS *enters, his face muffled in his cloak, and his hat drawn over his brows.*

Good evening to you, sir!

[*She ushers him in. He drops his cloak and reveals a rich dress of silk and velvet in the Castilian style of* 1519. *She looks at him closely, and recoils astonished.*

     What now?—not you,

Signor Hernani! Fire! fire! Help, oh help!

DON CARLOS (*seizing her by the arm*).

But two words more, Duenna, and you die!

[*He looks at her intently. She is frightened into silence.*

Is this the room of Doña Sol, betrothed

(23)

To her old uncle, Duke de Pastrana?
A very worthy lord he is—senile,
White-hair'd and jealous. Tell me, is it true
The beauteous Doña loves a smooth-faced youth,
All whiskerless as yet, and sees him here
Each night, in spite of envious care? Tell me,
Am I informed aright?

> *[She is silent. He shakes her by the arm.*
> Will you not speak?

DOÑA JOSEFA.   '

You did forbid me, sir, to speak two words.

DON CARLOS.

One will suffice. I want a yes, or no.
Say, is thy mistress Doña Sol de Silva?

DOÑA JOSEFA.

Yes, why?

DON CARLOS.

> No matter why. Just at this hour
The venerable lover is away?

DOÑA JOSEFA.

He is.

DON CARLOS.

And she expects the young one now?

DOÑA JOSEFA.

Yes.

DON CARLOS.

Oh, that I could die!

DOÑA JOSEFA.

> Yes.

DON CARLOS.

> Say, Duenna,
Is this the place where they will surely meet?

DOÑA JOSEFA.

Yes.

DON CARLOS.

Hide me somewhere here.

Doña Josefa.
                You?

Don Carlos.
                    Yes, me.

Doña Josefa.
                        Why?

Don Carlos.
No matter why.

Doña Josefa.
I hide you here!

Don Carlos.
                Yes, here.

Doña Josefa.
No, never!

Don Carlos (*drawing from his girdle a purse and a dagger*).
        Madam, condescend to choose
Between a purse and dagger.

Doña Josefa (*taking the purse*).
                    Are you then
The devil?

Don Carlos.
        Yes, Duenna.

Doña Josefa (*opening a narrow cupboard in the wall*).
            Go—go in.

Don Carlos (*examining the cupboard*).
This box!

Doña Josefa (*shutting up the cupboard*).
        If you don't like it, go away.

Don Carlos (*re-opening cupboard*).
And yet!   [*Again examining it.*
        Is this the stable where you keep
The broom-stick that you ride on?
            [*He crouches down in the cupboard with difficulty.*
                    Oh! oh! oh!

Doña Josefa (*joining her hands and looking ashamed*).
A man here!

    Don Carlos (*from the cupboard, still open*).
         And was it a woman then
Your mistress here expected?

            Doña Josefa.
                    Heavens! I hear
The step of Doña Sol! Sir, shut the door!
Quick—quick!
        [*She pushes the cupboard door, which closes.*

      Don Carlos (*from the closed cupboard*).
           Remember, if you breathe a word
You die!

        Doña Josefa (*alone*).
       Who is this man? If I cry out,
Gracious! there's none to hear. All are asleep
Within the palace walls—Madam and I
Excepted. Pshaw! the other'll come. He wears
A sword; 'tis his affair. And Heav'n keep us
From powers of hell. [*Weighing the purse in her hand.*
         At least no thief he is.

Enter Doña Sol *in white.* (Doña Josefa *hides the purse.*)

Scene 2.—Doña Josefa; Don Carlos, *hidden ;* Doña Sol:
    afterwards Hernani.

         Doña Sol.
   Josefa!

        Doña Josefa.
     Madam?

        Doña Sol.
      I some mischief dread,
For 'tis full time Hernani should be here.
        [*Noise of steps at the secret door.*

He's coming up; go—quick! at once, undo
Ere he has time to knock.

> [JOSEFA *opens the little door. Enter* HERNANI *in
> large cloak and large hat; underneath, costume
> of mountaineer of Aragon—gray, with a cuirass
> of leather; a sword, a dagger, and a horn at
> his girdle.*

DOÑA SOL (*going to him*).
                    Hernani! Oh!

HERNANI.

Ah, Doña Sol! it is yourself at last
I see—your voice it is I hear. Oh, why
Does cruel fate keep you so far from me?
I have such need of you to help my heart
Forget all else!

DOÑA SOL (*touching his clothes*).
                    Oh! Heav'ns! your cloak is drench'd!
The rain must pour!

HERNANI.
          I know not.

DOÑA SOL.
                    And the cold—

You must be cold!

HERNANI.
          I feel it not.

DOÑA SOL.
                    Take off

This cloak then, pray.

HERNANI.
                    Doña, beloved, tell me,
When night brings happy sleep to you, so pure
And innocent—sleep that half opes your mouth,
Closing your eyes with its light finger-touch—
Does not some angel show how dear you are
To an unhappy man, by all the world
Abandoned and repulsed?

DOÑA SOL.

Sir, you are late;
But tell me, are you cold?

HERNANI.

Not near to you.
Ah! when the raging fire of jealous love
Burns in the veins, and the true heart is riven
By its own tempest, we feel not the clouds
O'erhead, though storm and lightning they fling forth!

DOÑA SOL.

Come, give me now the cloak, and your sword too.

HERNANI (*his hand on his sword*).
No. 'Tis my other love, faithful and pure.
The old Duke, Doña Sol—your promised spouse,
Your uncle—is he absent now?

DOÑA SOL.

Oh, yes;
This hour to us belongs.

HERNANI.

And that is all!
Only this hour.! and then comes afterwards!—
What matter! For I must forget or die!
Angel! one hour with thee—with whom I would
Spend life, and afterwards eternity!

DOÑA SOL.

Hernani!

HERNANI.

It is happiness to know
The Duke is absent. I am like a thief
Who forces doors. I enter—see you—rob
An old man of an hour of your sweet voice
And looks. And I am happy, though, no doubt
He would deny me e'en one hour, although
He steals my very life.

DOÑA SOL.

Be calm.
[*Giving the cloak to the Duenna.*

Josefa!

This wet cloak take and dry it. [*Exit* Josefa.

[*She seats herself, and makes a sign for* Hernani *to draw near.*

Now come here.

Hernani (*without appearing to hear her*).
The Duke, then, is not in the mansion now?

Doña Sol.

How grand you look!

Hernani.
He is away?

Doña Sol.
Dear one,
Let us not think about the Duke.

Hernani.
Madam,
But let us think of him, the grave old man
Who loves you—who will marry you! How now?
He took a kiss from you the other day.
Not think of him!

Doña Sol.
Is't that which grieves you thus?
A kiss upon my brow—an uncle's kiss—
Almost a father's.

Hernani.
No, not so; it was
A lover's, husband's, jealous kiss. To him—
To him it is that you will soon belong.
Think'st thou not of it! Oh, the foolish dotard,
With head drooped down to finish out his days!
Wanting a wife, he takes a girl; himself
Most like a frozen spectre. Sees he not,
The senseless one! that while with one hand he
Espouses you, the other mates with Death!
Yet without shudder comes he 'twixt our hearts!
Seek out the grave-digger, old man, and give
Thy measure.

Who is it that makes for you
This marriage? You are forced to it, I hope?

DOÑA SOL.

They say the king desires it.

HERNANI.

King! this king!
My father on the scaffold died condemned
By his; * and, though one may have aged since then—
For e'en the shadow of that king, his son,
His widow, and for all to him allied,
My hate continues fresh. Him dead, no more
We count with; but while still a child I swore
That I'd avenge my father on his son.
I sought him in all places—Charles the King
Of the Castiles. For hate is rife between
Our families. The fathers wrestled long
And without pity, and without remorse,
For thirty years! Oh; 'tis in vain that they
Are dead; their hatred lives. For them no peace
Has come; their sons keep up the duel still.
Ah! then I find 'tis thou who hast made up
This execrable marriage! Thee I sought—
Thou comest in my way!

DOÑA SOL.

You frighten me!

HERNANI.

Charged with the mandate of anathema,
I frighten e'en myself; but listen now:
This old, old man, for whom they destine you,
This Ruy de Silva, Duke de Pastrana,
Count and grandee, rich man of Aragon,

---

* It is questionable if the author really meant the father of Charles the Fifth, Philip the Handsome, son of the Emperor of Germany, though Philip was for a short time Regent, in consequence of the mental incapacity of his wife Joanna. Possibly, taking a poetical license, Victor Hugo wished to indicate the grandfather, King Ferdinand. They were equally capable of exercising tyranny and oppression, and Philip was powerful in Spain long before he became Regent; he, however, died too young for the animosity to have raged so many years as the text implies.—TRANS.

In place of youth can give thee, oh! young girl,
Such store of gold and jewels that your brow
Will shine 'mong royalty's own diadems;
And for your rank and wealth, and pride and state,
Queens many will perhaps envy you. See, then,
Just what he is. And now consider me.
My poverty is absolute, I say.
Only the forest, where I ran barefoot
In childhood, did I know. Although perchance
I too can claim illustrious blazonry,
That's dimm'd just now by rusting stain of blood.
Perchance I've rights, though they are shrouded still,
And hid 'neath ebon folds of scaffold cloth,
Yet which, if my attempt one day succeeds,
May, with my sword from out their sheath leap forth.
Meanwhile, from jealous Heaven I've received
But air, and light, and water—gifts bestowed
On all. Now, wish you from the Duke, or me,
To be delivered? You must choose 'twixt us,
Whether you marry him, or follow me.

DOÑA SOL.

You, I will follow!

HERNANI.

'Mong companions rude,
Men all proscribed, of whom the headsman knows
The names already. Men whom neither steel
Nor touch of pity softens; each one urged
By some blood feud that's personal. Wilt thou
Then come? They'd call thee mistress of my band,
For know you not that I a bandit am?
When I was hunted throughout Spain, alone
In thickest forests, and on mountains steep,
'Mong rocks which but the soaring eagle spied,
Old Catalonia like a mother proved.
Among her hills—free, poor, and stern—I grew;
And now, to-morrow if this horn should sound,
Three thousand men would rally at the call.
You shudder, and should pause to ponder well.
Think what 'twill prove to follow me through woods

And over mountain paths, with comrades like
The fiends that come in dreams! To live in fear,
Suspicious of a sound, of voices, eyes:
To sleep upon the earth, drink at the stream,
And hear at night, while nourishing perchance
Some wakeful babe, the whistling musket balls.
To be a wanderer with me proscribed,
And when my father I shall follow—then,
E'en to the scaffold, you to follow me !

DOÑA SOL.

I'll follow you.

HERNANI.

   The Duke is wealthy, great
And prosperous, without a stain upon
His ancient name. He offers you his hand,
And can give all things—treasures, dignities,
And pleasure——

DOÑA SOL.

   We'll set out to-morrow. Oh !
Hernani, censure not th' audacity
Of this decision. Are you angel mine
Or demon ? Only one thing do I know,
That I'm your slave. Now, listen : wheresoe'er
You go, I go—pause you or move I'm yours.
Why act I thus? Ah! that I cannot tell;
Only I want to see you evermore.
When sound of your receding footstep dies
I feel my heart stops beating; without you
Myself seems absent, but when I detect
Again the step I love, my soul comes back,
I breathe—I live once more.

HERNANI (embracing her).

     Oh ! angel mine !

DOÑA SOL.

At midnight, then, to-morrow, clap your hands
Three times beneath my window, bringing there
Your escort. Go ! I shall be strong and brave.

HERNANI.

Now know you who I am ?

DOÑA SOL.

Only my lord.
Enough—what matters else?—I follow you.

HERNANI.

Not so. Since you, a woman weak, decide
To come with me, 'tis right that you should know
What name, what rank, what soul, perchance what fate
There hides beneath the low Hernani here.
Yes, you have willed to link yourself for aye
With brigand—would you still with outlaw mate?

DON CARLOS (*opening the cupboard*).
When will you finish all this history?
Think you 'tis pleasant in this cupboard hole?
    [HERNANI *recoils, astonished.* DOÑA SOL *screams and*
        takes refuge in HERNANI'S *arms, looking at* DON
        CARLOS *with frightened gaze.*

HERNANI (*his hand on the hilt of his sword*).
Who is this man?

DOÑA SOL.
Oh, heavens, help!

HERNANI.
                                        Be still,
My Doña Sol! you'll wake up dangerous eyes.
Never—whatever be—while I am near,
Seek other help than mine.
    (*To* DON CARLOS.)   What do you here?

DON CARLOS.
I?—Well, I am not riding through the wood,   ✎
That you should ask.

HERNANI.
                            He who affronts, then jeers,
May cause his heir to laugh.

DON CARLOS.
                                Each, Sir, in turn.
Let us speak frankly. You the lady love,
And come each night to mirror in her eyes
Your own. I love her too, and want to know

Who 'tis I have so often seen come in
The window way, while I stand at the door.

HERNANI.

Upon my word, I'll send you out the way
I enter.

DON CARLOS.

As to that we'll see. My love
I offer unto Madam. Shall we then
Agree to share it? In her beauteous soul
I've seen so much of tenderness, and love,
And sentiment, that she, I'm very sure,
Has quite enough for ardent lovers twain.
Therefore to-night, wishing to end suspense
On your account, I forced an entrance, hid,
And—to confess it all—I listened too.
But I heard badly, and was nearly choked;
And then I crumpled my French vest—and so,
By Jove! come out I must!

HERNANI.

Likewise my blade
Is not at ease, and hurries to leap out.

DON CARLOS (*bowing*).

Sir, as you please.

HERNANI (*drawing his sword*).

Defend yourself!

[DON CARLOS *draws his sword.*

DOÑA SOL.

Oh, Heaven!

DON CARLOS.

Be calm, Señora.

HERNANI (*to* DON CARLOS).

Tell me, Sir, your name.

DON CARLOS.

Tell me yours!

HERNANI.

It is a fatal secret,
Kept for my breathing in another's ear,

Some day when I am conqueror, with my knee
Upon his breast, and dagger in his heart.

DON CARLOS.

Then tell to me this other's name.

HERNANI.
To thee
What matters it? On guard! Defend thyself!
[*They cross swords. Doña Sol falls trembling into
a chair. They hear knocks at the door.*

Doña Sol (*rising in alarm*).

Oh Heavens! there's some one knocking at the door!
[*The champions pause. Enter Josefa, at the little
door, in a frightened state.*

HERNANI (*to Josefa*).

Who knocks in this way?

Doña Josefa (*to Doña Sol*).
Madame, a surprise!
An unexpected blow. It is the Duke
Come home.

Doña Sol (*clasping her hands*).
The Duke! Then every hope is lost!

Doña Josefa (*looking round*).

Gracious! the stranger out! and swords, and fighting!
Here's a fine business!
[*The two combatants sheathe their swords. Don
Carlos draws his cloak round him, and pulls
his hat down on his forehead. More knocking.*

HERNANI.
What is to be done?
[*More knocking.*

A Voice (*without*).

Doña Sol, open to me.
[*Doña Josefa is going to the door, when Hernani
stops her.*

HERNANI.
Do not open.

Doña Josefa (*pulling out her rosary*).
Holy St. James! now draw us through this broil!

[*More knocking.*

Hernani (*pointing to the cupboard*).
Let's hide!

Don Carlos.
What! in the cupboard?

Hernani.
Yes, go in;
I will take care that it shall hold us both.

Don Carlos.
Thanks. No; it is too good a joke.

Hernani (*pointing to secret door*).
Let's fly
That way.

Don Carlos.
Good night! But as for me I stay
Here.

Hernani.
Fire and fury, Sir, we will be quits
For this. (*To Doña Sol.*) What if I firmly barr'd the
door?

Don Carlos (*to Josefa*).
Open the door.

Hernani.
What is it that he says?

Don Carlos (*to Josefa, who hesitates bewildered*).
Open the door, I say.

[*More knocking. Josefa opens the door, trembling.*

Doña Sol.
Oh, I shall die!

Scene 3.—*The same, with Don Ruy Gomez de Silva, in black;
white hair and beard. Servants with lights.*

Don Ruy Gomez.
My niece with two men at this hour of night!
Come all! The thing is worth exposing here.

(*To* Doña Sol.) Now by St. John of Avila, I vow
That we three with you, madam, are by two
Too many.   (*To the two young men.*) My young Sirs,
    what do you here?
When we'd the Cid and Bernard—giants both
Of Spain and of the world—they travelled through
Castile protecting women, honoring
Old men. For them steel armor had less weight
Than your fine velvets have for you. These men
Respected whitened beards, and when they loved,
Their love was consecrated by the Church.
Never did such men cozen or betray,
For reason that they had to keep unflawed
The honor of their house. Wished they to wed,
They took a stainless wife in open day,
Before the world, with sword, or axe, or lance
In hand. But as for villains such as you,
Who come at eve, peeping behind them oft,
To steal away the honor of men's wives
In absence of their husbands, I declare,
The Cid, our ancestor, had he but known
Such men, he would have plucked away from them
Nobility usurped, have made them kneel,
While he with flat of sword their blazon dashed.
Behold what were the men of former times
Whom I, with anguish, now compare with these
I see to-day ! What do you here? Is it
To say, a white-haired man's but fit for youth
To point at when he passes in the street,
And jeer at there? Shall they so laugh at me,
Tried soldier of Zamora? At the least
Not yours will be that laugh.

Hernani.
But Duke——

Don Ruy Gomez.
Be still !
What ! You have sword and lance, falcons, the chase,
And songs to sing 'neath balconies at night,
Festivals, pleasures, feathers in your hats,

Raiment of silk—balls, youth, and joy of life;
But wearied of them all, at any price
You want a toy, and take an old man for it.
Ah, though you've broke the toy, God wills that it
In bursting should be flung back in your face!
Now follow me!

HERNANI.
Most noble Duke——

DON RUY GOMEZ.
                                        Follow—
Follow me, sirs. Is this alone a jest?
What! I've a treasure, mine to guard with care,
A young girl's character, a family's fame.
This girl I love—by kinship to me bound,
Pledged soon to change her ring for one from me.
I know her spotless, chaste, and pure. Yet when
I leave my home one hour, I—Ruy Gomez
De Silva—find a thief who steals from me
My honor, glides unto my house. Back, back,
Make clean your hands, oh base and soulless men,
Whose presence, brushing by, must serve to taint
Our women's fame! But no, 'tis well. Proceed.
Have I not something more? [*Snatches off his collar.*
                        Take, tread it now
Beneath your feet. Degrade my Golden Fleece.
                        [*Throws off his hat.*
Pluck at my hair, insult me every way,
And then, to-morrow through the town make boast
That lowest scoundrels in their vilest sport
Have never shamed a nobler brow, nor soiled
More whitened hair.

DOÑA SOL.
My lord——

DON RUY GOMEZ (*to his servants*).
                        A rescue! grooms!
Bring me my dagger of Toledo, axe,
And dirk.   [*To the young men.*
        Now follow—follow me—ye two.

Don Carlos (*stepping forward a little*).
Duke, this is not the pressing thing just now ;
First we've to think of Maximilian dead,
The Emperor of Germany.

> [*Opens his cloak, and shows his face, previously hidden by his hat.*

Don Ruy Gomez.
> Jest you !
Heavens, the King !

Doña Sol.
> The King !

Hernani.
> The King of Spain !

Don Carlos (*gravely*).
Yes, Charles, my noble Duke, are thy wits gone ?
The Emperor, my grandsire, is no more.
I knew it not until this eve, and came
At once to tell it you and counsel ask,
Incognito, at night, knowing you well
A loyal subject that I much regard.
The thing is very simple that has caused
This hubbub.

> [Don Ruy Gomez *sends away servants by a sign,
> and approaches* Don Carlos. Doña Sol *looks
> at* The King *with fear and surprise.* Hernani
> *from a corner regards him with flashing eyes.*

Don Ruy Gomez.
> But oh, why was it the door
Was not more quickly opened ?

Don Carlos.
> Reason good.
Remember all your escort. When it is
A weighty secret of the state I bear
That brings me to your palace, it is not
To tell it to thy servants.

Don Ruy Gomez.
> Highness, oh !
Forgive me, some appearances——

Don Carlos.
                                        Good father,
Thee Governor of the Castle of Figuère
I've made. But whom thy governor shall I make?

Don Ruy Gomez.
Oh, pardon——

Don Carlos.
                        'Tis enough. We'll say no more
Of this. The Emperor is dead.

Don Ruy Gomez.
                                        Your Highness's
Grandfather dead!

Don Carlos.
                        Ay! Duke, you see me here
In deep affliction.

Don Ruy Gomez.
                Who'll succeed to him?

Don Carlos.
A Duke of Saxony is named. The throne
Francis the First of France aspires to mount.

Don Ruy Gomez.
Where do the Electors of the Empire meet?

Don Carlos.
They say at Aix-la-Chapelle, or at Spire,
Or Frankfort.

Don Ruy Gomez.
                But our King, whom God preserve!
Has he not thought of Empire?

Don Carlos.
                                        Constantly.

Don Ruy Gomez.
To you it should revert.

Don Carlos.
                        I know it, Duke.

Don Ruy Gomez.
Your father was Archduke of Austria.
I hope 'twill be remembered that you are

Grandson to him, who but just now has changed
Th' imperial purple for a winding-sheet.

Don Carlos.

I am, besides, a citizen of Ghent.

Don Ruy Gomez.

In my own youth your grandfather I saw.
Alas! I am the sole survivor now
Of all that generation past. All dead!
He was an Emperor magnificent
And mighty.

Don Carlos.

Rome is for me.

Don Ruy Gomez.

Valiant, firm,
And not tyrannical, this head might well
Become th' old German body.

[*He bends over* The King's *hands and kisses them.*]

Yet so young.
I pity you indeed, thus plunged in such
A sorrow.

Don Carlos.

Ah! the Pope is anxious now
To get back Sicily—the isle that's mine;
'Tis ruled that Sicily cannot belong
Unto an Emperor; therefore it is
That he desires me Emperor to be made;
And then, to follow that, as docile son
I give up Naples too. Let us but have
The Eagle, and we'll see if I allow
Its wings to be thus clipp'd!

Don Ruy Gomez.

What joy 'twould be
For this great veteran of the throne to see
Your brow, so fit, encircled by his crown!
Ah, Highness, we together weep for him,
The Christian Emperor, so good, so great!

Don Carlos.

The Holy Father's clever. He will say—
This isle unto my States should come; 'tis but

A tatter'd rag that scarce belongs to Spain.
What will you do with this ill-shapen isle
That's sewn upon the Empire by a thread ?
Your Empire is ill-made ; but quick, come here,
The scissors bring, and let us cut away !—
Thanks, Holy Father, but if I have luck
I think that many pieces such as this
Upon the Holy Empire will be sewn !
And if some rags from me are ta'en, I mean
With isles and duchies to replace them all.

DON RUY GOMEZ.

Console yourself, for we shall see again
The dead more holy and more great. There is
An Empire of the Just.

DON CARLOS.

    Francis the First
Is all ambition. The old Emperor dead,
Quick he'll turn wooing. Has he not fair France
Most Christian ? 'Tis a place worth holding fast.
Once to King Louis did my grandsire say—
If I were God, and had two sons, I'd make
The elder God, the second, King of France.

      [*to* DON RUY GOMEZ.
Think you that Francis has a chance to win ?

DON RUY GOMEZ.

He is a victor.

DON CARLOS.

    There'd be all to change—
The golden bull doth foreigners exclude.

DON RUY GOMEZ.

In a like manner, Highness, you would be
Accounted King of Spain.

DON CARLOS.

     But I was born
A citizen of Ghent.

DON RUY GOMEZ.

    His last campaign
Exalted Francis mightily.

DON CARLOS.

The Eagle
That soon perchance upon my helm will gleam
Knows also how to open out its wings.

DON RUY GOMEZ.
And knows your Highness Latin?

DON CARLOS.

Ah, not much.

DON RUY GOMEZ.
A pity that. The German nobles like
The best those who in Latin speak to them.

DON CARLOS.
With haughty Spanish they will be content,
For trust King Charles, 'twill be of small account,
When masterful the voice, what tongue, it speaks.
To Flanders I must go. Your King, dear Duke,
Must Emperor return. The King of France
Will stir all means. I must be quick to win.
I shall set out at once.

DON RUY GOMEZ.

Do you then go,
Oh Highness, without clearing Aragon
Of those fresh bandits who, among the hills,
Their daring insolence show everywhere?

DON CARLOS.
To the Duke d'Arcos I have orders giv
That hevshould quite exterminate the band.

DON RUY GOMEZ.
But is the order given to its Chief
To let the thing be done?

DON CARLOS.

Who is this Chief—
His name?

DON RUY GOMEZ.

I know not. But the people say
That he's an awkward customer.

Don Carlos.

                    Pshaw! I know
That now he somewhere in Galicia hides;
With a few soldiers, soon we'll capture him.

Don Ruy Gomez.

Then it was false, the rumor which declared
That he was hereabouts?

Don Carlos.

                    Quite false. Thou canst
Accommodate me here to-night.

Don Ruy Gomez (*bowing to the ground*).

                    Thanks! Thanks!
Highness! (*He calls his servants.*)
          You'll do all honor to the King,
My guest.
    [*The servants re-enter with lights. The* Duke
      *arranges them in two rows to the door at the
      back. Meanwhile* Doña Sol *approaches* Her-
      nani *softly.* The King *observes them.*

Doña Sol (*to* Hernani).

To-morrow, midnight, without fail
Beneath my window clap your hands three times.

Hernani (*softly*).

To-morrow night.

Don Carlos (*aside*).

               To-morrow!
    [*Aloud to* Doña Sol, *whom he approaches with
      politeness.*
                    Let me now
Escort you hence, I pray.
    [*He leads her to the door. She goes out.*

Hernani (*his hand in his breast on dagger hilt*).

               My dagger true!

Don Carlos (*coming back, aside*).

Our man here has the look of being trapp'd.
    [*He takes* Hernani *aside.*
I've crossed my sword with yours; that honor, sir,
I've granted you. For many reasons I

Suspect you much, but to betray you now
Would shame the king: go therefore freely.   E'en
I deign to aid your flight.

Don Ruy Gomez (*coming back, and pointing to* Hernani).
                              This lord—who's he?

Don Carlos.
One of my followers, who'll soon depart.
    [*They go out with servants and lights, the* Duke *pre-
        ceding with waxlight in his hand.*

Scene 4.—Hernani *alone.*

Hernani.
One of thy followers!   I am, oh King!
Well said.   For night and day and step by step
I follow thee, with eye upon thy path
And dagger in my hand.   My race in me
Pursues thy race in thee.   And now behold
Thou art my rival!   For an instant I
'Twixt love and hate was balanced in the scale.
Not large enough my heart for her and thee ;
In loving her oblivious I became
Of all my hate of thee.   But since 'tis thou
That comes to will I should remember it,
I recollect.   My love it is that tilts
Th' uncertain balance, while it falls entire
Upon the side of hate.   Thy follower !
'Tis thou hast said it.   Never courtier yet
Of thy accursed court, or noble, fain
To kiss thy shadow—not a seneschal
With human heart abjured in serving thee ;
No dog within the palace, trained the King
To follow, will thy steps more closely haunt
And certainly than I.   What they would have,
These famed grandees, is hollow title, or
Some toy that shines—some golden sheep to hang
About the neck.   Not such a fool am I.
What I would have is not some favor vain,
But 'tis thy blood, won by my conquering steel—

Thy soul from out thy body forced—with all
That at the bottom of thy heart was reached
After deep delving. Go—you are in front—
I follow thee. My watchful vengeance walks
With me, and whispers in mine ear. Go where
Thou wilt I'm there to listen and to spy,
And noiselessly my step will press on thine.
No day, shouldst thou but turn thy head, oh King,
But thou wilt find me, motionless and grave,
At festivals; at night, should'st thou look back,
Still wilt thou see my flaming eyes behind.

                        [*Exit by the little door.*

SECOND ACT: THE BANDIT.

SARAGOSSA.

SCENE 1.—*A square before the Palace of* SILVA. *On the left the high walls of the Palace, with a window and a balcony. Below the window a little door. To the right, at the back, houses of the street. Night. Here and there are a few windows still lit up, shining in the front of the houses.*

DON CARLOS, DON SANCHO SANCHEZ DE ZUNIGA COMTE DE MONTEREY, DON MATIAS CENTURION MARQUIS D'ALMU-NAN, DON RICARDO DE ROXAS LORD OF CASAPALMA.

All four arrive, DON CARLOS *at the head, hats pulled down, and wrapped in long cloaks, which their swords inside raise up.*

    DON CARLOS (*looking up at the balcony*).
Behold ! We're at the balcony—the door.
My heart is bounding.
                [*Pointing to the window, which is dark.*
                  Ah, no light as yet.
        [*He looks at the windows where light shines.*
Although it shines just where I'd have it not,
While where I wish for light is dark.

DON SANCHO.
Your Highness,
Now let us of this traitor speak again.
And you permitted him to go!

DON CARLOS.
'Tis true.

DON MATIAS.
And he, perchance, was Major of the band.

DON CARLOS.
Were he the Major or the Captain e'en,
No crown'd king ever had a haughtier air.

DON SANCHO.
Highness, his name?

DON CARLOS (*his eyes fixed on the window*).
Muñoz—— Fernan——
(*With gesture of a man suddenly recollecting.*)
A name
In i.

DON SANCHO.
Perchance Hernani?

DON CARLOS.
Yes.

DON SANCHO.
'Twas he.

DON MATIAS.
The chief, Hernani!

DON SANCHO.
Cannot you recall
His speech?

DON CARLOS.
Oh, I heard nothing in the vile
And wretched cupboard.

DON SANCHO.
Wherefore let him slip
When there you had him?

DON CARLOS (*turning round gravely and looking him in
the face.*)
     Count de Monterey,
You question me !
   [*The two nobles step back, and are silent.*
     Besides, it was not he
Was in my mind. It was his mistress, not
His head, I wanted. Madly I'm in love
With two dark eyes, the loveliest in the world,
My friends ! Two mirrors, and two rays ! two flames !
I heard but of their history these words :
"To-morrow come at midnight." 'Twas enough.
The joke is excellent ! For while that he,
The bandit lover, by some murd'rous deed
Some grave to dig, is hindered and delayed,
I softly take his dove from out its nest.

DON RICARDO.
Highness, 'twould make the thing far more complete
If we, the dove in gaining, killed the kite.

DON CARLOS.
Count, 'tis most capital advice. Your hand
Is prompt.

DON RICARDO (*bowing low*).
    And by what title will it please
The King that I be Count ?

DON SANCHO.
     'Twas a mistake.

DON RICARDO (*to* DON SANCHO).
The King has called me Count.

DON CARLOS.
     Enough—enough !
      (*to* DON RICARDO.)
I let the title fall ; but pick it up.

DON RICARDO (*bowing again*).
Thanks, Highness.

Don Sancho.

A fine Count—Count by mistake!

[The King *walks to the back of the stage, watching
eagerly the lighted windows. The two lords talk
together at the front.*

Don Matias (*to* Don Sancho).

What think you that the King will do, when once
The beauty's taken?

Don Sancho (*looking sideways at* Don Ricardo).

Countess she'll be made;
Lady of honor afterwards, and then,
If there's a son, he will be King.

Don Matias.

How so?—
My Lord! a bastard! Let him be a Count.
Were one His Highness, would one choose as king
A Countess' son?

Don Sancho.

He'd make her Marchioness
Ere then, dear Marquis.

Don Matias.

Bastards—they are kept
For conquer'd countries. They for viceroys serve.

[Don Carlos *comes forward.*

Don Carlos (*looking with vexation at the lighted windows*).

Might one not say they're jealous eyes that watch?
Ah! there are two which darken; we shall do.
Weary the time of expectation seems—
Sirs, who can make it go more quickly?

Don Sancho.

That
Is what we often ask ourselves within
The palace.

Don Carlos.

'Tis the thing my people say
Again with you. [*The last window light is extinguished.*
The last light now is gone.

(*Turning towards the balcony of* Doña Sol, *still dark.*)

Oh, hateful window! When wilt thou light up?
The night is dark; come, Doña Sol, and shine
Like to a star! (*to* DON RICARDO).
>   Is 't midnight yet?

>   DON RICARDO.
>   Almost.

>   DON CARLOS.
Ah! we must finish, for the other one
At any moment may appear.
>   [*A light appears in* DOÑA SOL'S *chamber. Her shadow
>   is seen through the glass.*
>   My friends!
A lamp! and she herself seen through the pane!
Never did daybreak charm me as this sight.
Let's hasten with the signal she expects.
We must clap hands three times. An instant more
And you will see her. But our number, perhaps,
Will frighten her. Go, all three out of sight
Beyond there, watching for the man we want.
'Twixt us, my friends, we'll share the loving pair,
For me the girl—the brigand is for you.

>   DON RICARDO.
Best thanks.

>   DON CARLOS.
>   If he appear from ambuscade,
Rush quickly, knock him down, and, while the dupe
Recovers from the blow, it is for me
To carry safely off the darling prize.
We'll laugh anon. But kill him not outright,
He's brave, I own;—killing's a grave affair.
>   [*The lords bow and go.* DON CARLOS *waits till they
>   are quite gone, then claps his hands twice. At
>   the second time the window opens, and* DOÑA
>   SOL *appears on the balcony.*

Scene 2.—Don Carlos. Doña Sol.

Doña Sol (*from the balcony*).
Hernani, is that you?

Don Carlos (*aside*).
           The devil! We must
Not parley!   [*He claps his hands again.*

Doña Sol.
I am coming down.
[*She closes the window, and the light disappears.
The next minute the little door opens, and she
comes out, the lamp in her hand, and a mantle
over her shoulders.*

Doña Sol.
           Hernani!
[Don Carlos *pulls his hat down on his face, and
hurries towards her.*

Dona Sol (*letting her lamp fall*).
Heavens! 'Tis not his footstep!
[*She attempts to go back, but* Don Carlos *runs to
her and seizes her by the arm.*

Don Carlos.
           Doña Sol!

Doña Sol.
'Tis not his voice! Oh, misery!

Don Carlos.
           What voice
Is there that thou could'st hear that would be more
A lover's? It is still a lover here,
And King for one.

Doña Sol.
The King!

Don Carlos.
           Ah! wish, command,
A kingdom waits thy will; for he whom thou
Hast vanquish'd is the King, thy lord—'tis Charles,
Thy slave!

DOÑA SOL (*trying to escape from him*).
To the rescue! Help, Hernani! Help!

DON CARLOS.
Thy fear is maidenly, and worthy thee.
'Tis not thy bandit—'tis thy King that holds
Thee now!   .

DOÑA SOL.
Ah, no. The bandit's you. Are you
Not 'shamed? The blush unto my own cheek mounts
For you. Are these the exploits to be noised
Abroad? A woman thus at night to seize!
My bandit's worth a hundred of such kings!
I do declare, if man were born at level
Of his soul, and God made rank proportional
To his heart, he would be king and prince, and you
The robber be!

DON CARLOS (*trying to entice her*).
Madam!——

DOÑA SOL.
Do you forget
My father was a Count?

DON CARLOS.
And you I'll make
A Duchess.

DOÑA SOL (*repulsing him*).
Cease! All this is shameful;—go!
[*She retreats a few steps.*
Nothing, Don Carlos, can there 'twixt us be.
My father for you freely shed his blood.
I am of noble birth, and heedful ever
Of my name's purity. I am too high
To be your concubine—too low to be
Your wife.

DON CARLOS.
Princess!

DOÑA SOL.
Carry to worthless girls,
King Charles, your vile addresses. Or, if me

You treat insultingly, I'll show you well
That I'm a woman, and a noble dame.

Don Carlos.

Well, then but come, and you shall share my throne,
My name—you shall be Queen and Empress——

Doña Sol.

No.

It is a snare. Besides, I frankly speak,
Since, Highness, it concerns you. I avow
I'd rather with my king, Hernani, roam,
An outcast from the world and from the law—
Know thirst and hunger, wandering all the year,
Sharing the hardships of his destiny—
Exile and warfare, mourning hours of terror,
Than be an Empress with an Emperor!

Don Carlos.

Oh, happy man is he!

Doña Sol.

What! poor, proscribed!

Don Carlos.

'Tis well with him, though poor, proscribed he be,
For he's beloved!—an angel watches him!
I'm desolate. You hate me, then?

Doña Sol.

I love
You not.

Don Carlos (*seizing her violently*).

Well, then, it matters not to me
Whether you love me, or you love me not!
You shall come with me—yes, for that my hand's
The stronger, and I will it! And we'll see
If I for nothing am the King of Spain
And of the Indies!

Doña Sol (*struggling*).

Highness! Pity me!
You're King, you only have to choose among
The Countesses, the Duchesses, the great

Court ladies, all have love prepared to meet
And answer yours; but what has my proscribed
Received from niggard fortune? You possess
Castile and Aragon—Murcia and Léon,
Navarre, and still ten kingdoms more. Flanders,
And India with the mines of gold you own,
An empire without peer, and all so vast
That ne'er the sun sets on it. And when you,
The King, have all, would you take me, poor girl,
From him who has but me alone.

[*She throws herself on her knees. He tries to draw her up.*

DON CARLOS.

Come—come!

I cannot listen. Come with me. I'll give
Of Spain a fourth part unto thee. Say, now,
What wilt thou? Choose.

DOÑA SOL (*struggling in his arms*).

For mine own honor's sake
I'll only from your Highness take this dirk.

[*She snatches the poignard from his girdle.*

Approach me now but by a step!

DON CARLOS.

The beauty!

I wonder not she loves a rebel now.

[*He makes a step towards her. She raises the dirk.*

DOÑA SOL.

Another step, I kill you—and myself.

[*He retreats again. She turns and cries aloud.*

Hernani! Oh, Hernani!

DON CARLOS.

Peace!

DOÑA SOL.

One step,
And all is finished.

DON CARLOS.

Madam, to extremes
I'm driven. Yonder there I have three men
To force you—followers of mine.

HERNANI (*coming suddenly behind him*).
But one

You have forgotten.

[THE KING *turns, and sees* HERNANI *motionless behind him in the shade, his arms crossed under
the long cloak which is wrapped round him, and
the brim of his hat raised up.* DOÑA SOL *makes
an exclamation and runs to him.*

SCENE 3.—DON CARLOS, DOÑA SOL, HERNANI.

HERNANI (*motionless, his arms still crossed, and his
fiery eyes fixed on the* KING).
Heaven my witness is,

That far from here it was I wished to seek him.

DOÑA SOL.

Hernani! save me from him.

HERNANI.
My dear love,

Fear not.

DON CARLOS.
Now what could all my friends in town

Be doing, thus to let pass by the chief
Of the Bohemians? Ho! Monterey!

HERNANI.

Your friends are in the hands of mine just now,
So call not on their powerless swords; for three
That you might claim, sixty to me would come
Each one worth four of yours. So let us now
Our quarrel terminate. What! you have dared
To lay a hand upon this girl! It was
An act of folly, great Castilian King,
And one of cowardice!

DON CARLOS.
Sir Bandit, hold!

There must be no reproach from you to me!

HERNANI.

He jeers! Oh, I am not a king; but when
A king insults me, and above all jeers,

My anger swells and surges up, and lifts
Me to his height. Take care! When I'm offended,
Men fear far more the reddening of my brow
Than helm of king. Foolhardy, therefore, you
If still you're lured by hope.   [*Seizes his arm.*
                    Know you what hand
Now grasps you? Listen. 'Twas your father who
Was death of mine. I hate you for it. You
My title and my wealth have taken. You
I hate. And the same woman now we love.
I hate—hate—from my soul's depths you I hate.

DON CARLOS.

That's well.

HERNANI.

          And yet this night my hate was lull'd.
Only one thought, one wish, one want I had—
'Twas Doña Sol! And I, absorbed in love,
Came here to find you daring against her
To strive, with infamous design! You—you,
The man forgot—thus in my pathway placed!
I tell you, King, you are demented! Ah!
King Charles, now see you're taken in the snare
Laid by yourself: and neither flight nor help
For thee is possible. I hold thee fast,
Besieged, alone, surrounded by thy foes,
Bloodthirsty ones, what wilt thou do?

DON CARLOS (*proudly*).

                    Dare you
To question me!

HERNANI.

          Pish! pish! I would not wish
An arm obscure should strike thee. 'Tis not so
My vengeance should have play. 'Tis I alone
Must deal with thee. Therefore defend thyself.
                    [*He draws his sword.*

DON CARLOS.

I am your lord, the King. Strike! but no duel.

HERNANI.

Highness, thou may'st remember yesterday
Thy sword encountered mine.

DON CARLOS.

                              I yesterday
Could do it. I your name knew not, and you
Were ignorant of my rank. Not so to-day.
You know who I am, I who you are now.

HERNANI.

Perchance.

DON CARLOS.

No duel. You can murder. Do.

HERNANI.

Think you that kings to me are sacred ? Come,
Defend thyself.

DON CARLOS.

You will assassinate

Me then ?

[HERNANI *falls back. The* KING *looks at him with
eagle eyes.*

Ah ! bandits, so you dare to think
That your most vile brigades may safely spread
Through towns—ye blood-stained, murderous, miscreant
    crew—
But that you'll play at magnanimity !
As if we'd deign th' ennobling of your dirks
By touch of our own swords—we victims duped.
No, crime enthralls you—after you it trails.
Duels with you ! Away ! and murder me.

[HERNANI, *morose and thoughtful, plays for some
instants with the hilt of his sword, then turns
sharply towards the* KING *and snaps the blade
on the pavement.*

HERNANI.

Go, then.

[*The* KING *half turns towards him and looks at him
haughtily.*

We shall have fitter meetings. Go.
Get thee away.

DON CARLOS.
'Tis well. I go, Sir, soon
Unto the Ducal Palace. I, your King,
Will then employ the magistrate. Is there
Yet put a price upon your head?

HERNANI.
Oh, yes.

DON CARLOS.
My master, from this day I reckon you
A rebel, trait'rous subject; you I warn.
I will pursue you everywhere, and make
You outlaw from my kingdom.

HERNANI.
That I am
Already.

DON CARLOS.
That is well.

HERNANI.
But France is near
To Spain. There's refuge there.

DON CARLOS.
But I shall be
The Emperor of Germany, and you
Under the empire's ban shall be.

HERNANI.
Ah, well!
I still shall have the remnant of the world,
From which to brave you—and with havens safe
O'er which you'll have no power.

DON CARLOS.
But when I've gained
The world?

HERNANI.
Then I shall have the grave.

DON CARLOS.
Your plots
So insolent I shall know how to thwart.

HERNANI.
Vengeance is lame, and comes with lagging steps,
But still it comes.

Don Carlos (*with a half laugh of disdain*).
                    For touch of lady whom
The bandit loves!

        Hernani (*with flashing eyes*).
                    Dost thou remember, King,
I hold thee still? Make me not recollect
Oh, future Roman Cæsar, that despised
I have thee in my all too loyal hand,
And that I only need to close it now
To crush the egg of thy Imperial Eagle!

            Don Carlos.
Then do it.

            Hernani.
        Get away.
        [*He takes off his cloak, and throws
            it on the shoulders of the* King.
        Go, fly, and take
This cloak to shield thee from some knife I fear
Among our ranks. [*The* King *wraps himself in the cloak.*
            At present safely go,
My thwarted vengeance for myself I keep.
It makes 'gainst every other hand thy life
Secure.

            Don Carlos.
        And you who've spoken thus to me
Ask not for mercy on some future day.
                    [*Exit* Don Carlos.

        Scene 4.—Hernani. Doña Sol.

        Doña Sol (*seizing* Hernani's *hand*).
Now let us fly—be quick.

            Hernani.
                It well becomes
You, loved one, in the trial hour to prove
Thus strong, unchangeable, and willing e'en
To th' end and depth of all to cling to me;
A noble wish, worthy a faithful soul!

But Thou, oh God, dost see that to accept
The joy that to my cavern she would bring—
The treasure of a beauty that a king
Now covets—and that Doña Sol to me
Should all belong—that she with me should 'bide,
And all our lives be joined—that this should be
Without regret, remorse—it is too late.
The scaffold is too near.

DOÑA SOL.
What is't you say?

HERNANI.
This King, whom to his face just now I braved,
Will punish me for having dared to show
Him mercy. He already, perhaps, has reached
His palace, and is calling round him guards
And servants, his great lords, his headsmen——

DOÑA SOL.
Heavens!
Hernani! Oh, I shudder. Never mind,
Let us be quick and fly together then.

HERNANI.
Together! No; the hour has passed for that.
Alas! When to my eyes thou didst reveal
Thyself, so good and generous, deigning e'en
To love me with a helpful love, I could
But offer you—I, wretched one!—the hills,
The woods, the torrents, bread of the proscribed,
The bed of turf, all that the forest gives;
Thy pity then emboldened me—but now
To ask of thee to share the scaffold! No,
No, Doña Sol. That is for me alone.

DOÑA SOL.
And yet you promised even that!

HERNANI (*falling on his knees*).
Angel!
At this same moment, when perchance from out
The shadow Death approaches, to wind up
All mournfully a life of mournfulness,

I do declare that here a man proscribed,
Enduring trouble great, profound—and rock'd
In blood-stained cradle—black as is the gloom
Which spreads o'er all my life, I still declare
I am a happy, to-be-envied man,
For you have loved me, and your love have owned!
For you have whispered blessings on my brow
Accursed!

        DOÑA SOL (*leaning over his head*).
      Hernani!

           HERNANI.
          Praiséd be the fate
Sweet and propitious that for me now sets
This flower upon the precipice's brink! (*Raising himself.*)
'Tis not to you that I am speaking thus;
It is to Heaven that hears, and unto God.

           DOÑA SOL.
Let me go with you.

           HERNANI.
         Ah, 'twould be a crime
To pluck the flower while falling in the abyss.
Go: I have breathed the perfume—'tis enough.
Remould your life, by me so sadly marred.
This old man wed; 'tis I release you now.
To darkness I return. Be happy thou—
Be happy and forget.

           DOÑA SOL.
         No, I will have
My portion of thy shroud. I follow thee.
I hang upon thy steps.

        HERNANI (*pressing her in his arms*).
          Oh, let me go
Alone! Exiled—proscribed—a fearful man
Am I.
[*He quits her with a convulsive movement, and is going.*

      DOÑA SOL (*mournfully, and clasping her hands*).
      Hernani, do you fly from me!

HERNANI (*returning*).

Well, then, no, no. You will it, and I stay.
Behold me! Come into my arms. I'll wait
As long as thou wilt have me. Let us rest,
Forgetting them.   [*He seats her on a bench.*
          Be seated on this stone.
               [*He places himself at her feet.*
The liquid light of your eyes inundates
Mine own. Sing me some song, such as sometimes
You used at eve to warble, with the tears
In those dark orbs. Let us be happy now,
And drink; the cup is full. This hour is ours,
The rest is only folly. Speak and say,
Enrapture me. Is it not sweet to love,
And know that he who kneels before you loves?
To be but two alone? Is it not sweet
To speak of love in stillness of the night
When nature rests? Oh, let me slumber now,
And on thy bosom dream. Oh, Doña Sol,
My love, my darling!   [*Noise of bells in the distance.*

DOÑA SOL (*starting up frightened*).
               Tocsin!—dost thou hear?
The tocsin!

HERNANI (*still kneeling at her feet*).
          Eh! No, 'tis our bridal bell
They're ringing.
     [*The noise increases. Confused cries. Lights at all
     the windows, on the roofs, and in the streets.*

DOÑA SOL.
          Rise—oh, fly—great God! the town
Lights up!

HERNANI (*half rising*).
A torchlight wedding for us 'tis!

DOÑA SOL.
The nuptials these of Death, and of the tombs!
               [*Noise of swords and cries.*

HERNANI (*lying down on the stone bench*).
Let us to sleep again.

A Mountaineer (*rushing in, sword in hand*).
The runners, sir.
The alcadés rush out in cavalcades
With mighty force. Be quick—my Captain,—quick.

[HERNANI *rises.*

DoÑa Sol (*pale*).
Ah, thou wert right !

The Mountaineer.
Oh, help us !

Hernani (*to* Mountaineer).
It is well—
I'm ready.   (*Confused cries outside.*)
Death to the bandit !

Hernani (*to* Mountaineer).
Quick, thy sword——
(*To* DoÑa Sol.)
Farewell !

DoÑa Sol.
'Tis I have been thy ruin ! Oh,
Where canst thou go ? (*Pointing to the little door.*)
The door is free. Let us
Escape that way.

Hernani.
Heavens ! Desert my friends !
What dost thou say ?

DoÑa Sol.
These clamors terrify.
Remember, if thou diest I must die.

Hernani (*holding her in his arms*).
A kiss !

DoÑa Sol.
Hernani ! Husband ! Master mine !

Hernani (*kissing her forehead*).
Alas ! it is the first !

DoÑa Sol.
Perchance the last !

[HERNANI *exit. She falls on the bench.*

THIRD ACT: THE OLD MAN.

THE CASTLE OF SILVA.

In the midst of the Mountains of Aragon.

SCENE 1.—*The gallery of family portraits of Silva; a great hall of which these portraits—surrounded with rich frames, and surmounted by ducal coronets and gilt escutcheons—form the decoration. At the back a lofty gothic door. Between the portraits complete panoplies of armor of different centuries.*

DOÑA SOL, *pale, and standing near a table.*

DON RUY GOMEZ DE SILVA, *seated in his great carved oak chair.*

DON RUY GOMEZ.

At last the day has come!—and in an hour
Thou'lt be my Duchess, and embrace me! Not
Thine Uncle then! But hast thou pardoned me?
That I was wrong I own. I raised thy blush,
I made thy cheek turn pale. I was too quick
With my suspicions—should have stayed to hear
Before condemning; but appearances
Should take the blame. Unjust we were. Certes
The two young handsome men were there. But then—
No matter—well I know that I should not
Have credited my eyes. But, my poor child,
What would'st thou with the old?

DOÑA SOL (*seriously, and without moving*).
                                        You ever talk
Of this. Who is there blames you?

DON RUY GOMEZ.
                        I myself,
I should have known that such a soul as yours

Never has galants; when 'tis Doña Sol,
And when good Spanish blood is in her veins.

Doña Sol.

Truly, my Lord, 'tis good and pure ; perchance
'Twill soon be seen.

Don Ruy Gomez (*rising, and going towards her*).

Now list. One cannot be
The master of himself, so much in love
As I am now with thee. And I am old
And jealous, and am cross—and why? Because
I'm old ; because the beauty, grace, or youth
Of others frightens, threatens me. Because
While jealous thus of others, of myself
I am ashamed. What mockery ! that this love
Which to the heart brings back such joy and warmth,
Should halt, and but rejuvenate the soul,
Forgetful of the body. When I see
A youthful peasant, singing blithe and gay,
In the green meadows, often then I muse—
I, in my dismal paths, and murmur low :
"Oh, I would give my battlemented towers,
And ancient ducal donjon, and my fields
Of corn, and all my forest lands, and flocks
So vast which feed upon my hills, my name
And all my ancient titles—ruins mine,
And ancestors who must expect me soon,
All—all I'd give for his new cot, and brow
Unwrinkled. For his hair is raven black,
And his eyes shine like yours. Beholding him
You might exclaim : A young man this ! And then
Would think of me so old." I know it well.
I am named Silva. Ah, but that is not
Enough ; I say it, see it. Now behold
To what excess I love thee. All I'd give
Could I be like thee—young and handsome now !
Vain dream ! that I were young again, who must
By long, long years precede thee to the tomb.

Doña Sol.

Who knows?

Don Ruy Gomez.

And yet, I pray you, me believe,
The frivolous swains have not so much of love
Within their hearts as on their tongues. A girl
May love and trust one; if she dies for him,
He laughs. The strong-winged and gay-painted birds
That warble sweet, and in the thicket trill,
Will change their loves as they their plumage moult.
They are the old, with voice and color gone,
And beauty fled, who have the resting wings
We love the best. Our steps are slow, and dim
Our eyes. Our brows are furrowed,—but the heart
Is never wrinkled. When an old man loves
He should be spared. The heart is ever young,
And always it can bleed. This love of mine
Is not a plaything made of glass to shake
And break. It is a love severe and sure,
Solid, profound, paternal,—strong as is
The oak which forms my ducal chair. See then
How well I love thee—and in other ways
I love thee—hundred other ways, e'en as
We love the dawn, and flowers, and heaven's blue!
To see thee, mark thy graceful step each day,
Thy forehead pure, thy brightly beaming eye,
I'm joyous—feeling that my soul will have
Perpetual festival!

Doña Sol.

Alas!

Don Ruy Gomez.

And then,
Know you how much the world admires, applauds,
A woman, angel pure, and like a dove,
When she an old man comforts and consoles
As he is tott'ring to the marble tomb,
Passing away by slow degrees as she
Watches and shelters him, and condescends
To bear with him, the useless one, that seems
But fit to die? It is a sacred work
And worthy of all praise—effort supreme

Of a devoted heart to comfort him
Unto the end, and without loving perhaps,
To act as if she loved. Ah, thou to me
Wilt be this angel with a woman's heart
Who will rejoice the old man's soul again
And share his latter years, and by respect
A daughter be, and by your pity like
A sister prove.

DOÑA SOL.

                   Far from preceding me,
'Tis likely me you'll follow to the grave.
My lord, because that we are young is not
A reason we should live. Alas! I know
And tell you, often old men tarry long,
And see the young go first, their eyes shut fast
By sudden stroke, as on a sepulchre
That still was open falls the closing stone.

DON RUY GOMEZ.

Oh cease, my child, such saddening discourse,
Or I shall scold you. Such a day as this
Sacred and joyous is. And, by-the-by,
Time summons us. Are you not ready yet
For chapel when we're called? Be quick to don
The bridal dress. Each moment do I count.

DOÑA SOL.

There is abundant time.

DON RUY GOMEZ.

                   Oh no, there's not.
(*Enter a* PAGE.)
What want you?

THE PAGE.

                   At the door, my lord, a man—
A pilgrim—beggar—or I know not what,
Is craving here a shelter.

DON RUY GOMEZ.

                   Let him in
Whoever he may be. Good enters with
The stranger that we welcome. What's the news

From th' outside world? What of the bandit chief
That filled our forests with his rebel band?

THE PAGE.

Hernani, Lion of the mountains, now
Is done for.

DOÑA SOL (*aside*).

God!

DON RUY GOMEZ (*to the Page*).

How so?

THE PAGE.

The troop's destroyed.
The King himself has led the soldiers on.
Hernani's head a thousand crowns is worth
Upon the spot; but now he's dead, they say.

DOÑA SOL (*aside*).

What! Without me, Hernani!

DON RUY GOMEZ.

And thank Heaven!
So he is dead, the rebel! Now, dear love,
We can rejoice; go then and deck thyself,
My pride, my darling. Day of double joy.

DOÑA SOL.

Oh, mourning robes!   [*Exit* DOÑA SOL.

DON RUY GOMEZ (*to the Page*).

The casket quickly send
That I'm to give her.   [*He seats himself in his chair.*
'Tis my longing now
To see her all adorned Madonna like.
With her bright eyes, and aid of my rich gems,
She will be beautiful enough to make
A pilgrim kneel before her. As for him
Who asks asylum, bid him enter here,
Excuses from us offer; run, be quick.
                    [*The* PAGE *bows and exit.*
'Tis ill to keep a guest long waiting thus.
        [*The door at the back opens.* HERNANI *appears disguised as a Pilgrim. The* DUKE *rises.*

Scene 2.—Don Ruy Gomez. Hernani.

(Hernani *pauses* at the threshold of the door.)

HERNANI.

My lord, peace and all happiness be yours!

Don Ruy Gomez (*saluting him with his hand*).
To thee be peace and happiness, my guest!
[Hernani *enters. The* Duke *reseats himself.*
Art thou a pilgrim?

HERNANI (*bowing*).
Yes.

Don Ruy Gomez.
No doubt you come
From Armillas?

HERNANI.
Not so. I hither came
By other road, there was some fighting there.

Don Ruy Gomez.
Among the troop of bandits, was it not?

HERNANI.
I know not.

Don Ruy Gomez.
What's become of him—the chief
They call Hernani? Dost thou know?

HERNANI.
My lord,
Who is this man?

Don Ruy Gomez.
Dost thou not know him then?
For thee so much the worst! Thou wilt not gain
The good round sum. See you a rebel he
That has been long unpunished. To Madrid
Should you be going, perhaps you'll see him hanged

HERNANI.
I go not there.

Don Ruy Gomez.
A price is on his head
For any man who takes him.

HERNANI (*aside*).
> Let one come!

DON RUY GOMEZ.
Whither, good pilgrim, goest thou?

HERNANI.
> My lord,
I'm bound for Saragossa.

DON RUY GOMEZ.
> A vow made
In honor of a Saint, or of Our Lady?

HERNANI.
Yes, of Our Lady, Duke.

DON RUY GOMEZ.
> Of the Pillar?

HERNANI.
Of the Pillar.

DON RUY GOMEZ.
> We must be soulless quite
Not to acquit us of the vows we make
Unto the Saints. But thine accomplished, then
Hast thou not other purposes in view?
Or is to see the Pillar all you wish?

HERNANI.
Yes. I would see the lights and candles burn,
And at the end of the dim corridor
Our Lady in her glowing shrine, with cope
All golden—then would satisfied return.

DON RUY GOMEZ.
Indeed, that's well. Brother, what is thy name?
Mine, Ruy de Silva is.

HERNANI (*hesitating*).
> My name——

DON RUY GOMEZ.
> You can
Conceal it if you will. None here has right
To know it. Cam'st thou to asylum ask?

HERNANI.

Yes, Duke.

DON RUY GOMEZ.

Remain, and know thou'rt welcome here.
For nothing want; and as for what thou'rt named,
But call thyself my guest. It is enough
Whoever thou may'st be. Without demur
I'd take in Satan if God sent him me.

[*The folding doors at the back open. Enter* DOÑA
SOL *in nuptial attire. Behind her Pages and
Lackeys, and two women carrying on a velvet
cushion a casket of engraved silver, which they
place upon a table, and which contains a jewel
case, with Duchess's coronet, necklaces, bracelets,
pearls, and diamonds in profusion.* HERNANI,
breathless and scared, looks at DOÑA SOL *with
flaming eyes without listening to the* DUKE.

SCENE 3.—*The Same :* DOÑA SOL, PAGES, LACKEYS,
WOMEN.

DON RUY GOMEZ (*continuing*).
Behold my blessed Lady—to have prayed
To her will bring thee happiness.

[*He offers his hand to* DOÑA SOL, *still pale and grave.*
Come then,
My bride. What! not thy coronet, nor ring!

HERNANI (*in a voice of thunder*).
Who wishes now a thousand golden crowns
To win ?

[*All turn to him astonished. He tears off his Pilgrim's robe, and crushes it under his feet,
revealing himself in the dress of a Mountaineer.*
I am Hernani.

DOÑA SOL (*joyfully*).
Heavens! Oh,
He lives !

HERNANI (*to the Lackeys*).
See! I'm the man they seek.

(*To the* Duke.)

You wished

To know my name—Diego or Perez?
No, no! I have a grander name—Hernani.
Name of the banished, the proscribed. See you
This head? 'Tis worth enough of gold to pay
For festival.   (*To the Lackeys.*)

I give it to you all.

Take ; tie my hands, my feet. But there's no need,
The chain that binds me 's one I shall not break.

Doña Sol (*aside*).

Oh misery!

Don Ruy Gomez.

Folly! This my guest is mad—
A lunatic!

Hernani.

Your guest a bandit is.

Doña Sol.

Oh, do not heed him.

Hernani.

What I say is truth.

Don Ruy Gomez.

A thousand golden crowns—the sum is large.
And, sir, I will not answer now for all
My people.

Hernani.

And so much the better, should
A willing one be found. (*To the Lackeys.*)

Now seize, and sell me!

Don Ruy Gomez (*trying to silence him*).
Be quiet, or they'll take you at your word.

Hernani.

Friends, this your opportunity is good.
I tell you, I'm the rebel—the proscribed
Hernani!

Don Ruy Gomez.

Silence!

Hernani.

I am he!

TRIBOULET AND THE COURTIERS.

The King's Diversion.—Act III., Scene

DOÑA SOL (*in a low voice to him*).
Be still!

HERNANI (*half turning to* DOÑA SOL).
There's marrying here! My spouse awaits me too.
(*To the* DUKE.)
She is less beautiful, my Lord, than yours,
But not less faithful. She is Death. (*To the Lackeys.*)
Not one
Of you has yet come forth!

DOÑA SOL (*in a low voice*).
For pity's sake!

HERNANI (*to the Lackeys*).
A thousand golden crowns. Hernani here!

DON RUY GOMEZ.
This is the demon!

HERNANI (*to a young Lackey*).
Come! thou'lt earn this sum,
Then rich, thou wilt from lackey change again
To man. (*To the other Lackeys, who do not stir.*)
And also you—you waver. Ah,
Have I not misery enough?

DON RUY GOMEZ.
My friend,
To touch thy life they'd peril each his own.
Wert thou Hernani, or a hundred times
As bad, I must protect my guest,—were e'en
An Empire offered for his life—against
The King himself; for thee I hold from God.
If hair of thine be injured, may I die. (*To* DOÑA SOL.)
My niece, who in an hour will be my wife,
Go to your room. I am about to arm
The Castle—shut the gates. [*Exit, followed by servants.*

HERNANI (*looking with despair at his empty girdle*).
Not e'en a knife!
[DOÑA SOL, after the departure of the DUKE, takes
a few steps, as if to follow her women, then
pauses, and when they are gone, comes back to
HERNANI <i>with anxiety.</i></div>

Scene 4.—Hernani. Doña Sol.

Hernani *looks at the nuptial jewel-case with a cold and apparently indifferent gaze; then he tosses back his head, and his eyes light up.*

Hernani.

Accept my 'gratulations! Words tell not
How I'm enchanted by these ornaments.
                    [*He approaches the casket.*
This ring is in fine taste,—the coronet
I like,—the necklace shows surpassing skill.
The bracelet's rare—but oh, a hundred times
Less so than she, who 'neath a forehead pure
Conceals a faithless heart. [*Examining the casket again.*
                    What for all this
Have you now given? Of your love some share?
But that for nothing goes! Great God! to thus
Deceive, and still to live and have no shame!
                    [*Looking at the jewels.*
But after all, perchance, this pearl is false,
And copper stands for gold, and glass and lead
Make out sham diamonds—pretended gems!
Are these false sapphires and false jewels all?
If so, thy heart is like them, Duchess false,
Thyself but only gilded. [*He returns to the casket.*
                    Yet no, no!
They all are real, beautiful, and good,
He dares not cheat, who stands so near the tomb.
Nothing is wanting.
                    [*He takes up one thing after another.*
                    Necklaces are here,
And brilliant earrings, and the Duchess' crown
And golden ring. Oh marvel! Many thanks
For love so certain, faithful and profound.
The precious box!

Doña Sol (*She goes to the casket, feels in it, and draws forth a dagger*).
                    You have not reached its depths.
This is the dagger which, by kindly aid

Of patron saint, I snatched from Charles the King
When he made offer to me of a throne,
Which I refused for you, who now insult me.

HERNANI (*falling at her feet*).
Oh, let me on my knees arrest those tears,
The tears that beautify thy sorrowing eyes.
Then after thou canst freely take my life.

DOÑA SOL.
I pardon you, Hernani. In my heart
There is but love for you.

HERNANI.
                    And she forgives—
And loves me still! But who can also teach
Me to forgive myself, that I have used
Such words? Angel, for heaven reserved, say where
You trod, that I may kiss the ground.

DOÑA SOL.
                            My love!

HERNANI.
Oh no, I should to thee be odious.
But listen. Say again—I love thee still!
Say it, and reassure a heart that doubts.
Say it, for often with such little words
A woman's tongue hath cured a world of woes.

DOÑA SOL (*absorbed, and without hearing him*).
To think my love had such short memory!
That all these so ignoble men could shrink
A heart, where his name was enthroned, to love
By them thought worthier.

HERNANI.
                    Alas! I have
Blasphemed! If I were in thy place I should
Be weary of the furious madman, who
Can only pity after he has struck.
I'd bid him go. Drive me away, I say,
And I will bless thee, for thou hast been good
And sweet. Too long thou hast myself endured,
For I am evil; I should blacken still

Thy days with my dark nights. At last it is
Too much; thy soul is lofty, beautiful,
And pure; if I am evil, is't thy fault?
Marry the old duke then, for he is good
And noble. By the mother's side he has
Olmédo, by his father's Alcala.
With him be rich and happy by one act.
Know you not what this generous hand of mine
Can offer thee of splendor? Ah, alone
A dowry of misfortune, and the choice
Of blood or tears. Exile, captivity
And death, and terrors that environ me.
These are thy necklaces and jewelled crown.
Never elated bridegroom to his bride
Offered a casket filled more lavishly,
But 'tis with misery and mournfulness.
Marry the old man—he deserves thee well!
Ah, who could ever think my head proscribed
Fit mate for forehead pure? What looker-on
That saw thee calm and beautiful, me rash
And violent—thee peaceful, like a flower
Growing in shelter, me by tempests dash'd
On rocks unnumber'd—who could dare to say
That the same law should guide our destinies?
No, God, who ruleth all things well, did not
Make thee for me. No right from Heav'n above
Have I to thee; and I'm resigned to fate.
I have thy heart; it is a theft! I now
Unto a worthier yield it. Never yet
Upon our love has Heaven smiled; 'tis false
If I have said thy destiny it was.
To vengeance and to love I bid adieu!
My life is ending; useless I will go,
And take away with me my double dream,
Ashamed I could not punish, nor could charm.
I have been made for hate, who only wished
To love. Forgive and fly me, these my prayers
Reject them not, since they will be my last.
Thou livest—I am dead. I see not why
Thou should'st immure thee in my tomb.

Doña Sol.

Ingrate!

Hernani.

Mountains of old Aragon! Galicia!
Estremadura! Unto all who come
Around me I bring misery! Your sons,
The best, without remorse I've ta'en to fight,
And now behold them dead! The bravest brave
Of all Spain's sons lie, soldier-like, upon
The hills, their backs to earth, the living God
Before; and if their eyes could ope they'd look
On heaven's blue. See what I do to all
Who join me! Is it fortune any one
Should covet? Doña Sol, oh! take the Duke,
Take hell, or take the King—all would be well,
All must be better than myself, I say.
No longer have I friend to think of me,
And it is fully time that thy turn comes,
For I must be alone. Fly from me then,
From my contagion. Make not faithful love
A duty of religion! Fly from me,
For pity's sake. Thou think'st me, perhaps, a man
Like others, one with sense, who knows the end
At which he aims, and acts accordingly.
Oh, undeceive thyself. I am a force
That cannot be resisted—agent blind
And deaf of mournful mysteries! A soul
Of misery made of gloom. Where shall I go?
I cannot tell. But I am urged, compelled
By an impetuous breath and wild decree;
I fall, and fall, and cannot stop descent.
If sometimes breathless I dare turn my head,
A voice cries out, "Go on!" and the abyss
Is deep, and to the depths I see it red
With flame or blood! Around my fearful course
All things break up—all die. Woe be to them
Who touch me. Fly, I say! Turn thee away
From my so fatal path. Alas! without
Intending I should do thee ill.

Doña Sol.

Great God !

Hernani.

My demon is a formidable one.
But there's a thing impossible to it—
My happiness. For thee is happiness.
Therefore go seek another lord, for thou
Art not for me. If Heaven, that my fate
Abjures, should smile on me, believe it not :
It would be irony. Marry the Duke !

Doña Sol.

'Twas not enough to tear my heart, but you
Must break it now ! Ah me ! no longer then
You love me !

Hernani.

Oh ! my heart—its very life
Thou art ! The glowing hearth whence all warmth comes
Art thou ! Wilt thou then blame me that I fly
From thee, adored one?

Doña Sol.

No, I blame thee not,
Only I know that I shall die of it.

Hernani.

Die ! And for what ? For me ? Can it then be
That thou should'st die for cause so small ?

Doña Sol (bursting into tears).

Enough.
[She falls into a chair.

Hernani (seating himself near her).
And thou art weeping ; and 'tis still my fault !
And who will punish me? for thou I know
Wilt pardon still ! Who, who can tell thee half
The anguish that I. suffer when a tear
Of thine obscures and drowns those radiant eyes
Whose lustre is my joy. My friends are dead !
Oh, I am crazed—forgive me—I would love
I know not how. Alas ! I love with love
Profound. Weep not—the rather let us die !

Oh that I had a world to give to thee!
Oh, wretched, miserable man I am!

Doña Sol (*throwing herself on his neck*).
You are my lion, generous and superb!
I love you.
Hernani.
Ah, this love would be a good
Supreme, if we could die of too much love!

Doña Sol.
Thou art my lord! I love thee and belong
To thee!

Hernani (*letting his head fall on her shoulder*).
How sweet would be a poignard stroke
From thee!

Doña Sol (*entreatingly*).
Fear you not God will punish you
For words like these?

Hernani (*still leaning on her shoulder*).
Well, then, let Him unite us!
I have resisted: thou would'st have it thus.
[*While they are in each other's arms, absorbed and
gazing with ecstasy at each other, Don Ruy
Gomez enters by the door at the back of the
stage. He sees them, and stops on the thresh-
hold as if petrified.*

Scene 5.—Hernani. Doña Sol. Don Ruy Gomez.

Don Ruy Gomez (*motionless on the threshold, with arms
crossed*).
And this is the requital that I find
Of hospitality!
Doña Sol.
Oh Heavens—the Duke!
[*Both turn as if awakening with a start.*

Don Ruy Gomez (*still motionless*).
This then's the recompense from thee, my guest?
Good duke, go see if all thy walls be high,

And if the door is closed, and archer placed
Within his tower, and go the castle round
Thyself for us ; seek in thine arsenal
For armor that will fit—at sixty years
Resume thy battle-harness—and then see
The loyalty with which we will repay
Such service ! Thou for us do thus, and we
Do this for thee ! Oh, blessed saints of Heaven !
Past sixty years I've lived, and met sometimes
Unbridled souls; and oft my dirk have drawn
From out its scabbard, raising on my path
The hangman's game birds : murd'rers I have seen
And coiners, traitorous varlets poisoning
Their masters ; and I've seen men die without
A prayer, or sight of crucifix. I've seen
Sforza and Borgia ; Luther still I see,
But never have I known perversity
So great that feared not thunder bolt, its host
Betraying ! 'Twas not of my age—such foul
Black treason, that at once could petrify
An old man on the threshold of his door,
And make the master, waiting for his grave,
Look like his statue ready for his tomb.
Moors and Castilians ! Tell me, who's this man ?

> (*He raises his eyes and looks round on the portraits on the wall.*)

Oh you, the Silvas who can hear me now,
Forgive if, in your presence by my wrath
Thus stirr'd, I say that hospitality
Was ill advised.

> HERNANI (*rising*).
> Duke——

> DON RUY GOMEZ.
> Silence !
> [*He makes three steps into the hall looking at the portraits of the* SILVAS.
> Sacred dead !

My ancestors ! Ye men of steel, who know
What springs from heav'n or hell, reveal, I say,

Who is this man? No, not Hernani he,
But Judas is his name—oh, try to speak
And tell me who he is! (*Crossing his arms.*)
　　　　　　　　In all your days
Saw you aught like him? No.

HERNANI.

　　　　　　My lord——

DON RUY GOMEZ (*still addressing the portraits*).

　　　　　　　　　　See you
The shameless miscreant? He would speak to me,
But better far than I you read his soul.
Oh, heed him not! he is a knave—he'd say
That he foresaw that in the tempest wild
Of my great wrath I brooded o'er some deed
Of gory vengeance shameful to my roof.
A sister deed to that they call the feast
Of Seven Heads.* He'll tell you he's proscribed,
He'll tell you that of Silva they will talk
E'en as of Lara. Afterwards he'll say
He is my guest and yours. My lords, my sires,
Is the fault mine? Judge you between us now.

HERNANI.

Ruy Gomez de Silva, if ever 'neath
The heavens clear a noble brow was raised,
If ever heart was great and soul was high,
Yours are, my lord ; and oh, my noble host,
I, who now speak to you, alone have sinn'd.
Guilty most damnably am I, without
Extenuating word to say. I would
Have carried off thy bride—dishonor'd thee.

---

* This allusion is to the seven brothers who were slain by the treachery of their uncle Ruy Velasquez. According to a note prefixed by Lockhart to the ballad on this subject, "After the seven Infants were slain, Almanzor, King of Cordova, invited his prisoner, Gonzalo Gustio, to feast with him in his palace; but when the Baron of Lara came in obedience to the royal invitation, he found the heads of his sons set forth in chargers on the table. The old man reproached the Moorish king bitterly for the cruelty and baseness of this proceeding, and suddenly snatching a sword from the side of one of the royal attendants, sacrificed to his wrath, ere he could be disarmed and fettered, thirteen of the Moors who surrounded the person of Almanzor."—TRANS.

'Twas infamous. I live; but now my life
I offer unto thee. Take it. Thy sword
Then wipe, and think no more about the deed.

DOÑA SOL.

My lord, 'twas not his fault—strike only me.

HERNANI.

Be silent, Doña Sol. This hour supreme
Belongs alone to me; nothing I have
But it. Let me explain things to the Duke.
Oh, Duke, believe the last words from my mouth,
I swear that I alone am guilty. But
Be calm and rest assured that she is pure,
That's all. I guilty and she pure. Have faith
In her. A sword or dagger thrust for me.
Then throw my body out of doors, and have
The flooring washed, if you should will it so.
What matter?

DOÑA SOL.

Ah! I only am the cause
Of all; because I love him.
[DON RUY *turns round trembling at these words, and*
fixes on DOÑA SOL *a terrible look. She throws*
herself at his feet.
Pardon! Yes,
My lord, I love him!

DON RUY GOMEZ.

Love him—you love him!
(*To* HERNANI.)
Tremble!   [*Noise of trumpets outside. Enter a* PAGE.
What is this noise?

THE PAGE.

It is the King,
My lord, in person, with a band complete
Of archers, and his herald, who now sounds.

DOÑA SOL.

Oh God! This last fatality—the King!

THE PAGE (*to the* DUKE).
He asks the reason why the door is closed,
And order gives to open it.

DON RUY GOMEZ.
Admit
The King.   [*The* PAGE *bows and exit.*

DOÑA SOL.
He's lost!
[DON RUY GOMEZ *goes to one of the portraits—that
of himself and the last on the left ; he presses
a spring, and the portrait opens out like a door,
and reveals a hiding-place in the wall. He turns
to* HERNANI.
Come hither, sir.

HERNANI.
My life
To thee is forfeit; and to yield it up
I'm ready. I thy prisoner am.
[*He enters the recess.* DON RUY *again presses the
spring, and the portrait springs back to its
place looking as before.*

DOÑA SOL.
My lord,
Have pity on him!

THE PAGE (*entering*).
His Highness the King!
[DOÑA SOL *hurriedly lowers her veil. The folding-
doors open. Enter* DON CARLOS *in military
attire, followed by a crowd of gentlemen equally
armed with halberds, arquebuses, and cross-bows.*

Scene 6.—Don Ruy Gomez. Doña Sol *veiled*, Don Carlos *and*
Followers.

Don Carlos *advances slowly, his left hand on the hilt of his*
sword, his right hand in his bosom, and looking at the
Duke *with anger and defiance. The* Duke *goes before the*
King *and bows low. Silence. Expectation and terror on*
all. At last the King, *coming opposite the* Duke, *throws*
back his head haughtily.

DON CARLOS.

How comes it then, my cousin, that to-day
Thy door is strongly barr'd? By all the Saints
I thought your dagger had more rusty grown,
And know not why, when I'm your visitor,
It should so haste to brightly shine again
All ready to your hand.
(Don Ruy Gomez *attempts to speak, but the* King
continues with an imperious gesture.)
Late in the day
It is for you to play the young man's part!
Do we come turban'd? Tell me, are we named
Boabdil or Mahomet, and not Charles,
That the portcullis 'gainst us you should lower
And raise the drawbridge?

Don Ruy Gomez (*bowing*).
Highness——

Don Carlos (*to his gentlemen*).
Take the keys
And guard the doors.
[*Two officers exeunt. Several others arrange the*
soldiers in a triple line in the hall from the King
to the principal door. Don Carlos *turns again*
to the Duke.
Ah! you would wake to life
Again these crushed rebellions. By my faith,
If you, ye Dukes, assume such airs as these
The King himself will play his kingly part,
Traverse the mountains in a warlike mode,

And in their battlemented nests will slay
The lordlings !

DON RUY GOMEZ (*drawing himself up*).
Ever have the Silvas been,
Your Highness, loyal.

DON CARLOS (*interrupting him*).
Without subterfuge
Reply, or to the ground I'll raze thy towers
Eleven ! Of extinguished fire remains
One spark—of brigands dead the chief survives,
And who conceals him? It is thou, I say !
Hernani, rebel-ringleader, is here,
And in thy castle thou dost hide him now.

DON RUY GOMEZ.
Highness, it is quite true.

DON CARLOS.
Well, then, his head
I want—or if not, thine. Dost understand,
My cousin ?

DON RUY GOMEZ.
Well, then, be it so. You shall
Be satisfied.
[DOÑA SOL *hides her face in her hands and sinks into
the arm-chair.*

DON CARLOS (*a little softened*).
Ah ! you repent. Go seek
Your prisoner.
[*The* DUKE *crosses his arms, lowers his head, and remains some moments pondering. The* KING *and*
DOÑA SOL, *agitated by contrary emotions, observe
him in silence. At last the* DUKE *looks up, goes
to the* KING, *takes his hand, and leads him with
slow steps towards the oldest of the portraits,
which is where the gallery commences to the right
of the spectator.*

DON RUY GOMEZ (*pointing out the old portrait to the* KING).
This is the eldest one,
The great forefather of the Silva race,

Don Silvius our ancestor, three times
Was he made Roman consul.
    (*Passing to the next portrait.*)
       This is he
Don Galceran de Silva—other Cid !
They keep his body still at Toro, near
Valladolid; a thousand candles burn
Before his gilded shrine. 'Twas he who freed
Leon from tribute o' the hundred virgins.*
    (*Passing to another.*)
Don Blas—who, in contrition for the fault
Of having ill-advised the king, exiled
Himself of his own will. (*To another.*)
       This Christoval !
At fight of Escalon, when fled on foot
The King Don Sancho, whose white plume was mark
For general deadly aim, he cried aloud,
Oh, Christoval ! And Christoval assumed
The plume, and gave his horse. (*To another.*)
      This is Don Jorge,
Who paid the ransom of Ramire, the King
Of Aragon.

DON CARLOS (*crossing his arms and looking at him from head
      to foot*).
    By heavens now, Don Ruy,
I marvel at you ! But go on.

    DON RUY GOMEZ.
      Next comes
Don Ruy Gomez Silva, he was made
Grand Master of St. James, and Calatrava.
His giant armor would not suit our heights.
He took three hundred flags from foes, and won
In thirty battles. For the King Motril
He conquer'd Antequera, Suez,
Nijar ; and died in poverty. Highness,
Salute him.

---

 * A yearly tribute exacted by the Moors after one of their victories. One of
the fine Spanish ballads translated by Lockhart is on this subject.—TRANS.

[*He bows, uncovers, and passes to another portrait.
The* King *listens impatiently, and with increasing anger.*

Next him is his son, named Gil,
Dear to all noble souls. His promise worth
The oath of royal hands. (*To another.*)
                              Don Gaspard this,
The pride alike of Mendocé and Silva.
Your Highness, every noble family
Has some alliance with the Silva race.
Sandoval has both trembled at, and wed
With us. Manrique is envious of us : Lara
Is jealous. Alencastre hates us. We
All dukes surpass, and mount to Kings.

Don Carlos.
                              Tut ! tut !
You're jesting.

Don Ruy Gomez.
                Here behold Don Vasquez, called
The Wise. Don Jayme surnamed the Strong. One day
Alone he stopped Zamet and five score Moors.
I pass them by, and some the greatest.
        [*At an angry gesture of the* King *he passes by a
        great number of portraits, and speedily comes
        to the three last at the left of the audience.*
                                      This,
My grandfather, who lived to sixty years,
Keeping his promised word even to Jews.
        (*To the last portrait but one.*)
This venerable form my father is,
A sacred head. Great was he, though he comes
The last. The Moors had taken prisoner
His friend Count Alvar Giron. But my sire
Set out to seek him with six hundred men
To war inured. A figure of the Count
Cut out of stone by his decree was made
And dragged along behind the soldiers, he,
By patron saint, declaring that until
The Count of stone itself turned back and fled,

He would not falter; on he went and saved
His friend.

DON CARLOS.

I want my prisoner.

DON RUY GOMEZ.

This was

A Gomez de Silva. Imagine—judge
What in this dwelling one must say who sees
These heroes——

DON CARLOS.

Instantly—my prisoner!

DON RUY GOMEZ.

[*He bows low before the* KING, *takes his hand, and
leads him to the last portrait, which serves for
the door of* HERNANI'S *hiding-place.* DOÑA SOL
*watches him with anxious eyes. Silence and ex-
pectation in all.*

This portrait is my own. Mercy! King Charles!
For you require that those who see it here
Should say, " This last, the worthy son of race
Heroic, was a traitor found, that sold
The life of one he sheltered as a guest!"

[*Joy of* DOÑA SOL. *Movement of bewilderment in
the crowd. The* KING *disconcerted moves away
in anger, and remains some moments with lips
trembling and eyes flashing.*

DON CARLOS.

Your Castle, Duke, annoys me, I shall lay
It low.

DON RUY GOMEZ.

Thus, Highness, you'd retaliate,

Is it not so?

DON CARLOS.

For such audacity

Your towers I'll level with the ground, and have
Upon the spot the hemp-seed sown.

DON RUY GOMEZ.

I'd see

The hemp spring freely up where once my towers

Stood high, rather than stain should eat into
The ancient name of Silva. (*To the portraits.*)
     Is 't not true?
I ask it of you all.

DON CARLOS.
    Now, Duke, this head,
'Tis ours, and thou hast promised it to me.

DON RUY GOMEZ.
I promised one or other. (*To the portraits.*)
     Was 't not so?
I ask you all? (*Pointing to his head.*)
   This one I give. (*To the* KING.)
     Take it.

DON CARLOS.
Duke, many thanks: but 'twould not do. The head
I want is young; when dead the headsman must
Uplift it by the hair. But as for thine,
In vain he'd seek, for thou hast not enough
For him to clutch.

DON RUY GOMEZ.
    Highness, insult me not.
My head is noble still, and worth far more
Than any rebel's poll. The head of Silva
You thus despise!

DON CARLOS.
   Give up Hernani!

DON RUY GOMEZ.

Have spoken, Highness.

DON CARLOS. (*To his followers.*)
    Search you everywhere
From roof to cellar, that he takes not wing——

DON RUY GOMEZ.
My keep is faithful as myself; alone
It shares the secret which we both shall guard
Right well.

Don Carlos.
I am the King!

Don Ruy Gomez.
Out of my house,
Demolished stone by stone, they'll only make
My tomb,—and nothing gain.

Don Carlos.
Menace I find
And prayer alike are vain. Deliver up
The bandit, Duke, or head and castle both
Will I beat down.

Don Ruy Gomez.
I've said my word.

Don Carlos.
Well, then.
Instead of one head I'll have two.
(*To the* Duke d'Alcala.)
You, Jorge,
Arrest the Duke.

Doña Sol (*she plucks off her veil and throws herself
between the* King, *the* Duke, *and the* Guards).
King Charles, an evil king
Are you!

Don Carlos.
Good heavens! Is it Doña Sol
I see?

Doña Sol.
Highness! Thou hast no Spaniard's heart!

Don Carlos (*confused*).
Madam, you are severe upon the King.
[*He approaches her, and speaks low.*
'Tis you have caused the wrath that's in my heart.
A man approaching you perforce becomes
An angel or a monster. Ah, when we
Are hated, swiftly we malignant grow!
Perchance, if you had willed it so, young girl,
I'd noble been—the lion of Castile;
A tiger I am made by your disdain.

You hear it roaring now. Madam, be still!

[Doña Sol *looks at him.   He bows.*

However, I'll obey. (*Turning to the* Duke.)

Cousin, may be

Thy scruples are excusable, and I

Esteem thee. To thy guest be faithful still,

And faithless to thy King. I pardon thee.

'Tis better that I only take thy niece

Away as hostage.

Don Ruy Gomez.

Only!

Doña Sol.

Highness! Me!

Don Carlos.

Yes, you.

Don Ruy Gomez.

Alone! Oh, wondrous clemency!

Oh, generous conqueror, that spares the head

To torture thus the heart! What mercy this!

Don Carlos.

Choose 'twixt the traitor and the Doña Sol;

I must have one of them.

Don Ruy Gomez.

The master you!

[Don Carlos *approaches* Doña Sol *to lead her
     away.   She flies towards the* Duke.

Doña Sol.

Save me, my lord! (*She pauses.—Aside.*)

Oh misery! and yet

It must be so. My Uncle's life, or else

The other's!—rather mine! (*To the* King.)

I follow you.

Don Carlos (*aside*).

By all the Saints! the thought triumphant is!

Ah, in the end you'll soften, princess mine!

[Doña Sol *goes with a grave and steady step to the
     casket, opens it, and takes from it the dagger,
     which she hides in her bosom.* Don Carlos *comes
     to her and offers his hand.*

DON CARLOS.

What is 't you're taking thence ?

DOÑA SOL.

Oh, nothing !

DON CARLOS.

Is 't

Some precious jewel ?

DOÑA SOL.

Yes.

DON CARLOS (*smiling*).

Show it to me.

DOÑA SOL.

Anon you'll see it.

[*She gives him her hand and prepares to follow
him.* DON RUY GOMEZ, *who has remained motionless and absorbed in thought, advances a few
steps crying out.*

DON RUY GOMEZ.

Heavens, Doña Sol !

Oh, Doña Sol ! Since he is merciless,
Help ! walls and armor come down on us now !
(*He runs to the* KING.)
Leave me my child ! I have but her, oh King !

DON CARLOS (*dropping* DOÑA SOL'S *hand*).

Then yield me up my prisoner.

[*The* DUKE *drops his head, and seems the prey of
horrible indecision. Then he looks up at the
portraits with supplicating hands before them.*

Oh, now

Have pity on me all of you !

[*He makes a step towards the hiding-place,* DOÑA
SOL *watching him anxiously. He turns again
to the portraits.*

Oh hide

Your faces ! They deter me.

[*He advances with trembling steps towards his own
portrait, then turns again to the* KING.

Is't your will ?

Don Carlos.
Yes.

[*The* Duke *raises a trembling hand towards the spring.*

Doña Sol.
Oh God !

Don Ruy Gomez.
No !

[*He throws himself on his knees before the* King.
In pity take my life !

Don Carlos.
Thy niece !

Don Ruy Gomez (*rising*).
Take her, and leave me honor then.

Don Carlos (*seizing the hand of the trembling* Doña Sol).
Adieu, Duke.

Don Ruy Gomez.
Till we meet again !

[*He watches the* King, *who retires slowly with* Doña
Sol. *Afterwards he puts his hand on his dagger.*
May God

Shield you !

[*He comes back to the front of the stage panting,
and stands motionless, with vacant stare, seeming neither to see nor hear anything, his arms
crossed on his heaving chest. Meanwhile the*
King *goes out with* Doña Sol, *the suite following two by two acccording to their rank. They
speak in a low voice among themselves.*

Don Ruy Gomez (*aside*).
Whilst thou go'st joyous from my house,
Oh, King, my ancient loyalty goes forth
From out my bleeding heart.

[*He raises his head, looks all round, and sees that
he is alone. Then he takes two swords from a
panoply by the wall, measures them, and places
them on a table. This done, he goes to the portrait, touches the spring, and the hidden door
opens.*

SCENE 7.—DON RUY GOMEZ.   HERNANI.

DON RUY GOMEZ.

Come out.

[HERNANI *appears at the door of the hiding-place.* DON
RUY GOMEZ *points to the two swords on the table.*

Now choose.

Choose, for Don Carlos has departed now,
And it remains to give me satisfaction.
Choose, and be quick.   What, then! trembles thy hand?

HERNANI.

A duel!   Oh, it cannot be, old man,
'Twixt us.

DON RUY GOMEZ.

Why not?   Is it thou art afraid?
Or that thou art not noble?   So or not,
All men who injure me, by hell I count
Noble enough to cross their swords with mine.

HERNANI.

Old man——

DON RUY GOMEZ.

Come forth, young man, to slay me, else
To be the slain.

HERNANI.

To die, ah yes!   Against
My will thyself hast saved me, and my life
Is yours.   I bid you take it.

DON RUY GOMEZ.

This you wish?

(*To the portraits.*)

You see he wills it.   (*To* HERNANI.)

This is well.   Thy prayer
Now make.

HERNANI.

It is to thee, my lord, the last
I make.

DON RUY GOMEZ.

Pray to the other Lord.

HERNANI.

No, no,
To thee. Strike me, old man—dagger or sword—
Each one for me is good—but grant me first
One joy supreme. Duke, let me see her ere
I die.

DON RUY GOMEZ.

See her!

HERNANI.

Or at the least I beg
That you will let me hear her voice once more—
Only this one last time!

DON RUY GOMEZ.
Hear her!

HERNANI.

Ah well,
My lord, I understand thy jealousy,
But death already seizes on my youth.
Forgive me. Grant me—tell me that without
Beholding her, if it must be, I yet
May hear her speak, and I will die to-night.
I'll grateful be to hear her. But in peace
I'd calmly die, if thou wouldst deign that ere
My soul is freed, it sees once more the soul
That shines so clearly in her eyes. To her
I will not speak. Thou shalt be there to see,
My father, and canst slay me afterwards.

DON RUY GOMEZ (*pointing to the recess still open*).
Oh, Saints of Heaven! can this recess then be
So deep and strong that he has nothing heard?

HERNANI.
No, I have nothing heard.

DON RUY GOMEZ.
I was compelled
To yield up Doña Sol or thee.

HERNANI.
To whom?

DON RUY GOMEZ.

The King.

HERNANI.

Madman! He loves her.

DON RUY GOMEZ.

Loves her! He!

HERNANI.

He takes her from us! He our rival is!

DON RUY GOMEZ.

Curses be on him! Vassals! all to horse—
To horse! Let us pursue the ravisher!

HERNANI

Listen! The vengeance that is sure of foot
Makes on its way less noise than this would do.
To thee I do belong. Thou hast the right
To slay me. Wilt thou not employ me first
As the avenger of thy niece's wrongs?
Let me take part in this thy vengeance due;
Grant me this boon, and I will kiss thy feet,
If so must be. Let us together speed
The King to follow. I will be thine arm.
I will avenge thee, Duke, and afterwards
The life that's forfeit thou shalt take.

DON RUY GOMEZ.

And then.

As now, thou'lt ready be to die?

HERNANI.

Yes, Duke.

DON RUY GOMEZ.

By what wilt thou swear this?

HERNANI.

My father's head.

DON RUY GOMEZ.

Of thine own self wilt thou remember it?

HERNANI (*giving him the horn which he takes from his girdle*).
Listen! Take you this horn, and whatsoe'er
May happen—what the place, or what the hour—

Whenever to thy mind it seems the time
Has come for me to die, blow on this horn
And take no other care; all will be done.

Don Ruy Gomez (*offering his hand*).
Your hand!   [*They press hands.*
(*To the portraits.*)
And all of you are witnesses.

FOURTH ACT.

The Tomb. Aix-la-Chapelle.

Scene 1.—*The vaults which enclose the Tomb of Charlemagne
at Aix-la-Chapelle.* Great arches of Lombard architecture, with semicircular columns, having capitals of birds
and flowers. At the right a small bronze door, low and
curved. A single lamp suspended from the crown of
the vault shows the inscription:* CAROLVS MAGNVS. It
is night. One cannot see to the end of the vaults, the
eye loses itself in the intricacy of arches, steps, and
columns which mingle in the shade.

Don Carlos, Don Ricardo de Roxas, Comte de Casapalma,
lanterns in hand, and wearing large cloaks and
slouched hats.

Don Ricardo (*hat in hand*).
This is the place.

---

* Charlemagne was buried, as Palgrave says, with circumstances of "ghastly
magnificence." The embalmed corpse was seated "erect in his curule chair,
clad in his silken robes, ponderous with broidery, pearls and orfrey, the imperial
diadem on his head, his closed eyelids covered, his face swathed in the dead-
clothes, girt with his baldric, the ivory horn slung in his scarf, his good sword
'Joyeuse' by his side, the gospel-book open on his lap, musk and amber, and
sweet spices poured around, his golden shield and golden sceptre pendant
before him."

Charlemagne died, A.D. 814. Twice or thrice, however, at long intervals,
his tomb was opened; and three hundred years before the time of Charles
the Fifth the remains were placed in a costly chest, which is still preserved
in the Cathedral of Aix-la-Chapelle.—Trans.

DON CARLOS.

    Yes, here it is the League
Will meet; they that together in my power
So soon shall be. Oh, it was well, my lord
Of Trèves th' Elector—it was well of you
To lend this place; dark plots should prosper best
In the dank air of catacombs, and good
It is to sharpen daggers upon tombs.
Yet the stake's heavy—heads are on the game,
Ye bold assassins, and the end we'll see.
By heaven, 'twas well a sepulchre to choose
For such a business, since the road will be
Shorter for them to traverse. (*To* DON RICARDO.)
      Tell me now
How far the subterranean way extends?

DON RICARDO.

To the strong fortress.

DON CARLOS.

    Farther than we need.

DON RICARDO.

And on the other side it reaches quite
The Monastery of Altenheim.

DON CARLOS.

     Ah, where
Lothaire was overcome by Rodolf. Once
Again, Count, tell me o'er their names and wrongs.

DON RICARDO.

Gotha.

DON CARLOS.

  Ah, very well I know why 'tis
The brave Duke is conspirator: he wills
For Germany, a German Emperor.

DON RICARDO.

Hohenbourg.

DON CARLOS.

    Hohenbourg would better like
With Francis hell, than Heaven itself with me.

DON RICARDO.

Gil Tellez Giron.

DON CARLOS.

Castile and our Lady!
The scoundrel!—to be traitor to his king!

DON RICARDO.

One evening it is said that you were found
With Madame Giron. You had just before
Made him a baron; he revenges now
The honor of his dear companion.

DON CARLOS.

This, then, the reason he revolts 'gainst Spain?
What name comes next?

DON RICARDO.

                              The Reverend Vasquez,
Avila s Bishop.

DON CARLOS.

                    Pray does he resent
Dishonor of his wife!

DON RICARDO.

                          Then there is named
Guzman de Lara, who is discontent,
Claiming the collar of your order.

DON CARLOS.

                                        Ah!
Guzman de Lara! If he only wants
A collar he shall have one.

DON RICARDO.

                              Next the Duke
Of Lutzelbourg. As for his plans, they say——

DON CARLOS.

Ah! Lutzelbourg is by the head too tall.

DON RICARDO.

Juan de Haro—who Astorga wants.

DON CARLOS.

These Haros! Always they the headsman's pay
Have doubled.

Don Ricardo.
That is all.

Don Carlos.
Not by my count.
These make but seven.

Don Ricardo.
Oh, I did not name
Some bandits, probably engaged by Trèves
Or France.

Don Carlos.
Men without prejudice of course,
Whose ready daggers turn to heaviest pay,
As truly as the needle to the pole.

Don Ricardo.
However, I observed two sturdy ones
Among them, both new comers—one was young,
The other old.

Don Carlos.
Their names?
[Don Ricardo *shrugs his shoulders in sign of ignorance.*
Their age then say?

Don Ricardo.
The younger may be twenty.

Don Carlos.
Pity then.

Don Ricardo.
The elder must be sixty, quite.

Don Carlos.
One seems
Too young—the other, over old ; so much
For them the worse 'twill be. I will take care—
Myself will help the headsman, be there need.
My sword is sharpened for a traitor's block,
I'll lend it him if blunt his axe should grow,
And join my own imperial purple on
To piece the scaffold cloth, if it must be
Enlarged that way.   But shall I Emperor prove?

DON RICARDO.

The College at this hour deliberates.

DON CARLOS.

Who knows? Francis the First, perchance, they'll name,
Or else their Saxon Frederick the Wise.
Ah, Luther, thou art right to blame the times
And scorn such makers-up of royalty,
That own no other rights than gilded ones.
A Saxon heretic! Primate of Trèves,
A libertine! Count Palatine, a fool!
As for Bohemia's king, for me he is.
Princes of Hesse, all smaller than their states!
The young are idiots, and the old debauched,
Of crowns a plenty—but for heads we search
In vain! Council of dwarfs ridiculous,
That I in lion's skin could carry off
Like Hercules; and who of violet robes
Bereft, would show but heads more shallow far
Than Triboulet's. See'st thou I want three votes
Or all is lost, Ricardo? Oh! I'd give
Toledo, Ghent, and Salamanca too,
Three towns, my friend, I'd offer to their choice
For their three voices—cities of Castile
And Flanders. Safe I know to take them back
A little later on.

(DON RICARDO *bows low to the* KING, *and puts on his hat.*)
You cover, Sir!

DON RICARDO.

Sire, you have called me thou (*bowing again*).
                    And thus I'm made
Grandee of Spain.

DON CARLOS (*aside*).

          Ah, how to piteous scorn
You rouse me! Interested brood devour'd
By mean ambition. Thus across my plans
Yours struggle. Base the Court where without shame
The King is plied for honors, and he yields,
Bestowing grandeur on the hungry crew. (*Musing.*)
God only, and the Emperor are great,

Also the Holy Father! for the rest,
The king and dukes, of what account are they?

DON RICARDO.

I trust that they your Highness will elect.

DON CARLOS.

Highness—still Highness! Oh, unlucky chance!
If only King I must remain.

DON RICARDO (*aside*).

By Jove,
Emperor or King, Grandee of Spain I am.

DON CARLOS.

When they've decided who shall be the one
They choose for Emperor of Germany,
What sign is to announce his name?

DON RICARDO.

The guns.
A single firing will proclaim the Duke
Of Saxony is chosen Emperor;
Two if 'tis Francis; for your Highness three.

DON CARLOS.

And Doña Sol! I'm crossed on every side.
If, Count, by turn of luck, I'm Emperor made,
Go seek her; she by Cæsar might be won.

DON RICARDO (*smiling*).

Your Highness pleases.

DON CARLOS (*haughtily*).

On that subject peace!
I have not yet inquired what's thought of me.
But tell me when will it be truly known
Who is elected?

DON RICARDO.

In an hour or so,
At latest.

DON CARLOS.

Ah, three votes; and only three!
But first this trait'rous rabble we must crush.

And then we'll see to whom the Empire falls,
[*He counts on his fingers and stamps his foot.*
Always by three too few! Ah, they hold power.
Yet did Cornelius know all long ago:
In Heaven's ocean thirteen stars he saw
Coming full sail towards mine, all from the north.
Empire for me—let's on! But it is said,
On other hand, that Jean Trithème Francis
Predicted! Clearer should I see my fate
Had I some armament the prophecy
To help. The Sorcerer's predictions come
Most true when a good army—with its guns
And lances, horse and foot, and martial strains,
Ready to lead the way where Fate alone
Might stumble—plays the midwife's part to bring
Fulfilment of prediction. That's worth more
Than our Cornelius Agrippa or
Trithème. He, who by force of arms expounds
His system, and with sharpen'd point of lance
Can edge his words, and uses soldiers' swords
To level rugged fortune—shapes events
At his own will to match the prophecy.
Poor fools! who with proud eyes and haughty mien
Only look straight to Empire, and declare
"It is my right!" They need great guns in files
Whose burning breath melts towns; and soldiers, ships,
And horsemen. These they need their ends to gain
O'er trampled peoples. Pshaw! at the cross roads
Of human life, where one leads to a throne
Another to perdition, they will pause
In indecision,—scarce three steps will take
Uncertain of themselves, and in their doubt
Fly to the Necromancer for advice
Which road to take. (*To* Don Ricardo.)
     Go now, 'tis near the time
The trait'rous crew will meet. Give me the key.
   Don Ricardo (*giving key of tomb*).
Sire, 'twas the guardian of the tomb, the Count
De Limbourg, who to me confided it,
And has done everything to pleasure you.

DON CARLOS.

Do all, quite all that I commanded you.

DON RICARDO (*bowing*).

Highness, I go at once.

DON CARLOS.

The signal then
That I await is cannon firing thrice?

. (DON RICARDO *bows and exit.*)

[DON CARLOS *falls into a deep reverie, his arms
crossed, his head drooping; afterwards he raises
it, and turns to the tomb.*

SCENE 2.

DON CARLOS (*alone*).

Forgive me, Charlemagne! Oh, this lonely vault
Should echo only unto solemn words.
Thou must be angry at the babble vain
Of our ambition at your monument.
Here Charlemagne rests! How can the sombre tomb
Without a rifting spasm hold such dust!
And art thou truly here, colossal power,
Creator of the world? And canst thou now
Crouch down from all thy majesty and might?
Ah, 'tis a spectacle to stir the soul
What Europe was, and what by thee 'twas made.
Mighty construction with two men supreme
Elected chiefs to whom born kings submit.
States, duchies, kingdoms, marquisates and fiefs—
By right hereditary most are ruled,
But nations find a friend sometimes in Pope
Or Cæsar: and one chance another chance
Corrects: thus even balance is maintained
And order opens out. The cloth-of-gold
Electors, and the scarlet cardinals.
The double, sacred 'senate, unto which
Earth bends, are but paraded outward show,
God's fiat rules it all. One day HE wills

A thought, a want, should burst upon the world,
Then grow and spread, and mix with every thing,
Possess some man, win hearts, and delve a groove
Though kings may trample on it, and may seek
To gag;—only that they some morn may see
At diet, conclave, this the scorned idea,
That they had spurned, all suddenly expand
And soar above their heads, bearing the globe
In hand, or on the brow tiara. Pope
And Emperor, they on earth are all in all,
A mystery supreme dwells in them both,
And Heaven's might, which they still represent,
Feasts them with kings and nations, holding them
Beneath its thunder-cloud, the while they sit
At table with the world served out for food.
Alone they regulate all things on earth,
Just as the mower manages his field.
All rule and power are theirs. Kings at the door
Inhale the odor of their savory meats,
Look through the window, watchful on tip-toe,
But weary of the scene. The common world
Below them groups itself on ladder rungs.
They make and all unmake. One can release,
The other surely strike. The one is Truth,
The other Might. Each to himself is law,
And is, because he is. When—equals they
The one in purple, and the other swathed
In white like winding-sheet—when they come out
From Sanctuary, the dazzled multitude
Look with wild terror on these halves of God,
The Pope and Emperor. Emperor! oh, to be
Thus great! Oh, anguish, not to be this Power
When beats the heart with dauntless courage fill'd!
Oh, happy he who sleeps within this tomb!
How great, and oh! how fitted for his time!
The Pope and Emperor were more than men,
In them two Romes in mystic Hymen joined
Prolific were, giving new form and soul
Unto the human race, refounding realms
And nations, shaping thus a Europe new,

And both remoulding with their hands the bronze
Remaining of the great old Roman world.
What destiny! And yet 'tis here he lies?
Is all so little that we come to this!
What then? To have been Prince and Emperor,
And King—to have been sword, and also law;
Giant, with Germany for pedestal—
For title Cæsar—Charlemagne for name:
A greater to have been than Hannibal
Or Attila—as great as was the world.
Yet all rests here! For Empire strive and strain
And see the dust that makes an Emperor!
Cover the earth with tumult, and with noise,
Know you that one day only will remain—
Oh, madd'ning thought—a stone! For sounding name
Triumphant, but some letters 'graved to serve
For little children to learn spelling by.
How high so e'er ambition made thee soar,
Behold the end of all! Oh, Empire, power,
What matters all to me! I near it now
And like it well. Some voice declares to me
Thine—thine—it will be thine. Heavens, were it so!
To mount at once the spiral height supreme
And be alone—the key-stone of the arch,
With states beneath, one o'er the other ranged,
And kings for mats to wipe one's sandall'd feet!
To see 'neath kings the feudal families,
Margraves and Cardinals, and Doges—Dukes,
Then Bishops, Abbés—Chiefs of ancient clans,
Great Barons—then the soldier class and clerks,
And know yet farther off—in the deep shade
At bottom of th' abyss there is Mankind—
That is to say a crowd, a sea of men,
A tumult—cries, with tears, and bitter laugh
Sometimes. The wail wakes up and scares the earth,
And reaches us with leaping echoes, and
With trumpet tone. Oh, citizens, oh, men!
The swarm that from the high church towers seems now
To sound the tocsin! (*Musing.*)
                    Wondrous human base

Of nations, bearing on your shoulders broad
The mighty pyramid that has two poles,
The living waves that ever straining hard
Balance and shake it as they heave and roll,
Make all change place, and on the highest heights
Make stagger thrones, as if they were but stools.
So sure is this, that ceasing vain debates
Kings look to Heaven! Kings look down below,
Look at the people!—Restless ocean, there
Where nothing's cast that does not shake the whole;
The sea that rends a throne, and rocks a tomb—
A glass in which kings rarely look but ill.
Ah, if upon this gloomy sea they gazed
Sometimes, what Empires in its depths they'd find!
Great vessels wrecked that by its ebb and flow
Are stirr'd—that wearied it—known now no more!
To govern this—to mount so high if called,
Yet know myself to be but mortal man!
To see the abyss—if not that moment struck
With dizziness bewildering every sense.
Oh, moving pyramid of states and kings
With apex narrow,—woe to timid step!
What shall restrain me? If I fail when there
Feeling my feet upon the trembling world,
Feeling alive the palpitating earth,
Then when I have between my hands the globe
Have I the strength alone to hold it fast,
To be an Emperor? Oh, God, 'twas hard
And difficult to play the kingly part.
Certes, no man is rarer than the one
Who can enlarge his soul to duly meet
Great Fortune's smiles, and still increasing gifts.
But I! Who is it that shall be my guide,
My counsellor, and make me great?

              [*Falls on his knees before the tomb.*
                       'Tis thou,

Oh, Charlemagne! And since 'tis God for whom
All obstacles dissolve, who takes us now
And puts us face to face—from this tomb's depths
Endow me with sublimity and strength.

Let me be great enough to see the truth
On every side. Show me how small the world
I dare not measure—me this Babel show
Where, from the hind to Cæsar mounting up,
Each one, complaisant with himself, regards
The next with scorn that is but half restrained.
Teach me the secret of thy conquests all,
And how to rule. And show me certainly
Whether to punish, or to pardon, be
The worthier thing to do.

                              Is it not fact
That in his solitary bed sometimes
A mighty shade is wakened from his sleep,
Aroused by noise and turbulence on earth ;
That suddenly his tomb expands itself,
And bursts its doors—and in the night flings forth
A flood of light? If this be true indeed,
Say, Emperor ! what can after Charlemagne
Another do ! Speak, though thy sovereign breath
Should cleave this brazen door. Or rather now
Let me thy sanctuary enter lone !
Let me behold thy veritable face,
And not repulse me with a freezing breath.
Upon thy stony pillow elbows lean,
And let us talk. Yes, with prophetic voice
Tell me of things which make the forehead pale,
And clear eyes mournful. Speak, and do not blind
Thine awe-struck son, for doubtlessly thy tomb
Is full of light. Or if thou wilt not speak,
Let me make study in the solemn peace
Of thee, as of a world, thy measure take,
Oh giant, for there's nothing here below
So great as thy poor ashes. Let them teach,
Failing thy spirit.   [*He puts the key in the lock.*
                    Let us enter now.   [*He recoils.*
Oh, God, if he should really whisper me !
If he be there and walks with noiseless tread,
And I come back with hair in moments bleached !
I'll do it still.   [*Sound of footsteps.*
          Who comes ? who dares disturb

Besides myself the dwelling of such dead!
> [*The sound comes nearer.*

My murderers! I forgot! Now enter we.
[*He opens the door of the tomb, which shuts upon him.*
(*Enter several men walking softly, disguised by large cloaks and hats.*)

Scene 3.—The Conspirators.

(*They take each others' hands, going from one to another and speaking in a low tone.*)

First Conspirator (*who alone carries a lighted torch*).
Ad augusta.

Second Conspirator.
Per angusta.

First Conspirator.
> The Saints

Shield us.

Third Conspirator.
The dead assist us.

First Conspirator.
> Guard us, God!
> [*Noise in the shade.*

First Conspirator.
Who's there?

A Voice.
Ad augusta

Second Conspirator.
> *Per angusta.*
[*Enter fresh* Conspirators—*noise of footsteps.*

First Conspirator *to* Third.
See! there is some one still to come.

Third Conspirator.
> Who's there?

(Voice *in the darkness.*)
Ad augusta.

THIRD CONSPIRATOR.

Per angusta.

(*Enter more* CONSPIRATORS, *who exchange signs with their
hands with the others.*)

FIRST CONSPIRATOR.

'Tis well.

All now are here. Gotha, to you it falls
To state the case. Friends, darkness waits for light.

[*The* CONSPIRATORS *sit in a half circle on the tombs.
The* FIRST CONSPIRATOR *passes before them, and
from his torch each one lights a wax taper
which he holds in his hand. Then the* FIRST
CONSPIRATOR *seats himself in silence on a tomb
a little higher than the others in the centre of
the circle.*

DUKE OF GOTHA (*rising*).

My friends ! This Charles of Spain, by mother's side
A foreigner, aspires to mount the throne
Of Holy Empire.

FIRST CONSPIRATOR.

But for him the grave.

DUKE OF GOTHA (*throwing down his light and crushing it
with his foot*).

Let it be with his head as with this flame.

ALL.

So be it.

FIRST CONSPIRATOR.

Death unto him.

DUKE OF GOTHA.

Let him die.

ALL.

Let him be slain.

DON JUAN DE HARO.

German his father was.

DUKE DE LUTZELBOURG.

His mother Spanish.

DUKE OF GOTHA.

Thus you see that he
Is no more one than other. Let him die.

A CONSPIRATOR.

Suppose th' Electors at this very hour
Declare him Emperor!

FIRST CONSPIRATOR.

Him! oh, never him!

DON GIL TELLEZ GIRON.

What signifies? Let us strike off the head,
The Crown will fall.

FIRST CONSPIRATOR.

But if to him belongs
The Holy Empire, he becomes so great
And so august, that only God's own hand
Can reach him.

DUKE OF GOTHA.

All the better reason why
He dies before such power august he gains.

FIRST CONSPIRATOR.

He shall not be elected.

ALL.

Not for him
The Empire.

FIRST CONSPIRATOR.

Now, how many hands will't take
To put him in his shroud?

ALL.

One is enough.

FIRST CONSPIRATOR.

How many strokes to reach his heart?

ALL.

But one.

FIRST CONSPIRATOR.

Who, then, will strike?

ALL.

All! All!

FIRST CONSPIRATOR.

The victim is
A traitor proved. They would an Emperor choose,
We've a high-priest to make. Let us draw lots.

> [*All the* CONSPIRATORS *write their names on their
> tablets, tear out the leaf, roll it up, and one
> after another throw them into the urn on one of
> the tombs. Afterwards the* FIRST CONSPIRATOR
> says,*

Now let us pray.

(*All kneel, the* FIRST CONSPIRATOR *rises and says,*)
Oh, may the chosen one
Believe in God, and like a Roman strike,
Die as a Hebrew would, and brave alike
The wheel and burning pincers, laugh at rack,
And fire, and wooden horse, and be resigned
To kill and die. He might have all to do.

> [*He draws a parchment from the urn.*

ALL.

What name?

FIRST CONSPIRATOR (*in low voice*).
Hernani!
HERNANI (*coming out from the crowd of* CONSPIRATORS).
I have won, yes won!
I hold thee fast! Thee I've so long pursued
With vengeance.

DON RUY GOMEZ (*piercing through the crowd and taking*
HERNANI *aside*).
Yield—oh yield this right to me.

HERNANI.

Not for my life! Oh, Signor, grudge me not
This stroke of fortune—'tis the first I've known.

DON RUY GOMEZ.

You nothing have! I'll give you houses, lands,
A hundred thousand vassals shall be yours

In my three hundred villages, if you
But yield the right to strike to me.

HERNANI.

No—no.

DUKE OF GOTHA.

Old man, thy arm would strike less sure a blow.

DON RUY GOMEZ.

Back! I have strength of soul, if not of arm.
Judge not the sword by the mere scabbard's rust.
(*To* HERNANI.)
You do belong to me.

HERNANI.

My life is yours,
As his belongs to me.

DON RUY GOMEZ (*drawing the horn from his girdle*).

I yield her up,
And will return the horn.

HERNANI (*he trembles*).

What life! my life
And Doña Sol! No, I my vengeance choose.
I have my father to revenge—yet more,
Perchance I am inspired by God in this.

DON RUY GOMEZ.

I yield thee Her—and give thee back the horn!

HERNANI.

No!

DON RUY GOMEZ.

Boy, reflect.

HERNANI.

Oh, Duke, leave me my prey.

DON RUY GOMEZ.

My curses on you for depriving me
Of this my joy.

FIRST CONSPIRATOR.   (*To* HERNANI.)
Oh, brother, ere they can

Elect him—'twould be well this very night
To watch for Charles.

HERNANI.

Fear nought, I know the way
To kill a man.

FIRST CONSPIRATOR.

May every treason fall
On traitor, and may God be with you now.
We Counts and Barons, let us take the oath
That if he fall, yet slay not, we go on
And strike by turn unflinching till Charles dies.

ALL (*drawing their swords*).
Let us all swear.

DUKE OF GOTHA (*to* FIRST CONSPIRATOR).

My brother, let's decide
On what we swear.

DON RUY GOMEZ (*taking his sword by the point and raising
it above his head*).

By this same cross.

ALL (*raising their swords*).

And this
That he must quickly die impenitent.
[*They hear a cannon fired afar off. All pause and
are silent. The door of the tomb half opens,
and* DON CARLOS *appears at the threshold. A
second gun is fired, then a third. He opens
wide the door and stands erect and motionless
without advancing.*

SCENE 4.—*The* CONSPIRATORS *and* DON CARLOS. *Afterwards*
DON RICARDO; SIGNORS. GUARDS, *The* KING OF BOHEMIA.
The DUKE OF BAVARIA, *afterwards* DOÑA SOL.

DON CARLOS.
Fall back, ye gentlemen—the Emperor hears.
[*All the lights are simultaneously extinguished. A
profound silence.* DON CARLOS *advances a step
in the darkness, so dense, that the silent, motionless* CONSPIRATORS *can scarcely be distinguished.*

Silence and night! From darkness sprung, the swarm
Into the darkness plunges back again!
Think ye this scene is like a passing dream,
And that I take you, now your lights are quenched,
For men's stone figures seated on their tombs?
Just now, my statues, you had voices loud,
Raise, then, your drooping heads, for Charles the Fifth
Is here. Strike. Move a pace or two and show
You dare. But no, 'tis not in you to dare.
Your flaming torches, blood-red 'neath these vaults,
My breath extinguished; but now turn your eyes
Irresolute, and see that if I thus
Put out the many, I can light still more.

> [*He strikes the iron key on the bronze door of the
> tomb. At the sound all the depths of the
> cavern are filled with soldiers bearing torches
> and halberts. At their head the* Duke d'Alcala,
> *the* Marquis d'Almuñan, *etc.*

Come on, my falcons! I've the nest—the prey.

(To Conspirators.)

I can make blaze of light, 'tis my turn now,
Behold! (*To the* Soldiers.)
> Advance—for flagrant is the crime.

Hernani (*looking at the Soldiers*).
Ah, well! At first I thought 'twas Charlemagne,
Alone he seemed so great—but after all
'Tis only Charles the Fifth.

Don Carlos (*to the* Duke d'Alcala).
> Come, Constable
Of Spain, (*To* Marquis d'Almuñan.)
> And you Castilian Admiral,
Disarm them all.
> [*The* Conspirators *are surrounded and disarmed.*

Don Ricardo (*hurrying in and bowing almost to the ground*).
> Your Majesty!

Don Carlos.
> Alcadé
I make you of the palace.

DON RICARDO (*again bowing*).

Two Electors,
To represent the Golden Chamber, come
To offer to your Sacred Majesty
Congratulations now.

DON CARLOS.

Let them come forth.

(*Aside to* DON RICARDO.)

The Doña Sol.

[RICARDO *bows and exit. Enter with flambeaux and
flourish of trumpets the* KING OF BOHEMIA *and the*
DUKE OF BAVARIA, *both wearing cloth of gold,
and with crowns on their heads. Numerous followers. German nobles carrying the banner of
the Empire, the double-headed Eagle, with the
escutcheon of Spain in the middle of it. The
Soldiers divide, forming lines between which the*
ELECTORS *pass to the* EMPEROR, *to whom they bow
low. He returns the salutation by raising his hat.*

DUKE OF BAVARIA.

Most Sacred Majesty
Charles, of the Romans King, and Emperor,
The Empire of the world is in your hands—
Yours is the throne to which each king aspires !
The Saxon Frederick was elected first,
But he judged you more worthy, and declined.
Now then receive the crown and globe, oh King—
The Holy Empire doth invest you now,
Arms with the sword, and you indeed are great.

DON CARLOS.

The College I will thank on my return.
But go, my brother of Bohemia,
And you Bavarian cousin.—Thanks : but now
I do dismiss you—I shall go myself.

KING OF BOHEMIA.

Oh ! Charles, our ancestors were friends. My Sire
Loved yours, and their two fathers were two friends—
So young ! exposed to varied fortunes ! say,

Oh Charles, may I be ranked a very chief
Among thy brothers? I cannot forget
I knew you as a little child.

DON CARLOS.

Ah, well—
King of Bohemia, you presume too much.
[*He gives him his hand to kiss, also the* DUKE OF
BAVARIA, *both bow low.*
Depart. [*Exeunt the two* ELECTORS *with their followers.*

THE CROWD.
LONG LIVE THE EMPEROR!

DON CARLOS (*aside*).
So 'tis mine,
All things have helped, and I am Emperor—
By the refusal though of Frederick
Surnamed the Wise!

(*Enter* DOÑA SOL *led by* RICARDO.)
DOÑA SOL.
What, Soldiers!—Emperor!
Hernani! Heavens, what an unlooked-for chance!

HERNANI.
Ah! Doña Sol!

DON RUY GOMEZ (*aside to* HERNANI).
She has not seen me.
[DOÑA SOL *runs to* HERNANI, *who makes her recoil
by a look of disdain.*

HERNANI.
Madam!

DOÑA SOL (*drawing the dagger from her bosom*).
I still his poignard have!

HERNANI (*taking her in his arms*).
My dearest one!

DON CARLOS.
Be silent all. (*To the* CONSPIRATORS.)
Is't you remorseless are?
I need to give the world a lesson now,

The Lara of Castile, and Gotha, you
Of Saxony—all—all—what were your plans
Just now ? I bid you speak.

HERNANI.

                        Quite simple, Sire,
The thing, and we can briefly tell it you.
We 'graved the sentence on Belshazzar's wall.

   [He takes out a poignard and brandishes it.
We render unto Cæsar Cæsar's due.

DON CARLOS.

Silence !

     (*To* DON RUY GOMEZ.
And you ! You too are traitor, Silva !

DON RUY GOMEZ.

Which of us two is traitor, Sire ?

HERNANI (*turning towards the* CONSPIRATORS).

     Our heads
And Empire—all that he desires he has.

     (*To the* EMPEROR.)
The mantle blue of kings encumbered you ;
The purple better suits—it shows not blood.

DON CARLOS (*to* DON RUY GOMEZ).

Cousin of Silva, this is felony,
Attaining your baronial rank. Think well,
Don Ruy—high treason !

DON RUY GOMEZ.

     Kings like Roderick
Count Julians make.*

DON CARLOS (*to the* DUKE D'ALCALA).

    Seize only those who seem
The nobles,—for the rest !——

---

* Roderick, the last Gothic King, by craft and violence dishonored Florinda,
the daughter of Count Julian, who, in revenge, invited the Saracens into Spain,
and assisted their invasion, A.D. 713. Their army was commanded by Tarik, who
gave the name Gibel-al-Tarik, or mountain of Tarik, to the place where he
landed—a name corrupted to Gibraltar. So incensed were the Spaniards against
the hapless Florinda, that they abolished the word as a woman's name, reserving it henceforth for dogs.—TRANS.

[Don Ruy Gomez, *the* Duke de Lutzelbourg, *the*
Duke of Gotha, Don Juan de Haro, Don Guzman de Lara, Don Tellez Giron, *the* Baron
of Hohenbourg *separate themselves from the
group of* Conspirators, *among whom is* Hernani. *The* Duke d'Alcala *surrounds them with
guards.*

Doña Sol (*aside*).
Ah, he is saved!

Hernani (*coming from among the* Conspirators).
I claim to be included! (*To* Don Carlos.)
Since to this
It comes, the question of the axe—that now
Hernani, humble churl, beneath thy feet
Unpunished goes, because his brow is not
At level with thy sword—because one must
Be great to die, I rise. God, who gives power,
And gives to thee the sceptre, made me Duke
Of Segorbé and Cardona, Marquis too
Of Monroy, Albaterra's Count, of Gor
Viscount, and Lord of many places, more
Than I can name. Juan of Aragon
Am I, Grand Master of Avis—the son
In exile born, of murder'd father slain
By king's decree, King Charles, which me proscribed,
Thus death 'twixt us is family affair;
You have the scaffold—we the poignard hold.
Since heaven a Duke has made me, and exile
A mountaineer,—since all in vain I've sharpen'd
Upon the hills my sword, and in the torrents
Have tempered it,   [*He puts on his hat.*
(*To the* Conspirators.)
Let us be covered now,
Us the Grandees of Spain. (*They cover.*)
(*To* Don Carlos.)
Our heads, oh! King,
Have right to fall before thee covered thus.
(*To the* Prisoners.)
Silva, and Haro—Lara—men of rank

And race make room for Juan of Aragon.
Give me my place, ye Dukes and Counts—my place.
(*To the* Courtiers *and* Guards.)
King, headsmen, varlets—Juan of Aragon
Am I. If all your scaffolds are too small
Make new ones. (*He joins the group of* Nobles.)

Doña Sol.
Heavens !

Don Carlos.
                              I had forgotten quite
This history.

Hernani.
              But they who bleed remember
Far better. Th' evil that wrong-doer thus
So senselessly forgets, forever stirs
Within the outraged heart.

Don Carlos.
                    Therefore, enough
For me to bear this title, that I'm son
Of sires, whose power dealt death to ancestors
Of yours !

Doña Sol (*falling on her knees before the* Emperor).
              Oh, pardon—pardon ! Mercy, Sire,
Be pitiful, or strike us both, I pray,
For he my lover is, my promised spouse,
In him it is alone I live—I breathe ;
Oh, Sire, in mercy us together slay.
Trembling—oh Majesty !—I trail myself
Before your sacred knees. I love him, Sire,
And he is mine—as Empire is your own.
Have pity ! (Don Carlos *looks at her without moving.*)
              Oh what thought absorbs you ?

Don Carlos.
                                        Cease.
Rise—Duchess of Segorbé—Marchioness
Of Monroy—Countess Albaterra—and (*To* Hernani.)
Thine other names, Don Juan ?

HERNANI.

Who speaks thus,
The King?

DON CARLOS.

No, 'tis the Emperor.

DOÑA SOL.

Just Heav'n!

DON CARLOS (*pointing to her*).

Duke Juan, take your wife.

HERNANI (*his eyes raised to heaven, DOÑA SOL in his arms*).

Just God!

DON CARLOS (*to DON RUY GOMEZ*).

My cousin,
I know the pride of your nobility,
But Aragon with Silva well may mate.

DON RUY GOMEZ (*bitterly*).

'Tis not a question of nobility.

HERNANI (*looking with love on DOÑA SOL and still holding
her in his arms*).

My deadly hate is vanishing away.

[*Throws away his dagger.*

DON RUY GOMEZ (*aside, and looking at them*).

Shall I betray myself? Oh, no—my grief,
My foolish love would make them pity cast
Upon my venerable head. Old man
And Spaniard! Let the hidden fire consume,
And suffer still in secret. Let heart break
But cry not;—they would laugh at thee.

DOÑA SOL (*still in HERNANI's arms*).

My Duke!

HERNANI.

Nothing my soul holds now but love!

DOÑA SOL.

Oh, joy!

DON CARLOS (*aside, his hand in his bosom*).

Stifle thyself, young heart so full of flame,
Let reign again the better thoughts which thou

So long hast troubled. Henceforth let thy loves,
Thy mistresses, alas!—be Germany
And Flanders—Spain (*looking at the banner*).
                    The Emperor is like
The Eagle his companion, in the place
Of heart, there's but a 'scutcheon.

HERNANI.
                    Cæsar you!

DON CARLOS.
Don Juan, of your ancient name and race
Your soul is worthy (*pointing to* DOÑA SOL).
                    Worthy e'en of her.
Kneel, Duke.
        [HERNANI *kneels.* DON CARLOS *unfastens his own*
            Golden Fleece and puts it on HERNANI's *neck.*
            Receive this collar.
        [DON CARLOS *draws his sword and strikes him three*
            times on the shoulder.
                    Faithful be,
For by St. Stephen now I make thee Knight.
                    [*He raises and embraces him.*
Thou hast a collar softer and more choice;
That which is wanting to my rank supreme,—
The arms of loving woman, loved by thee.
Thou wilt be happy—I am Emperor. (*To* CONSPIRATORS.)
Sirs, I forget your names. Anger and hate
I will forget. Go—go—I pardon you.
This is the lesson that the world much needs.

THE CONSPIRATORS.
Glory to Charles!

DON RUY GOMEZ (*to* DON CARLOS).
                    I only suffer then!

DON CARLOS.
And I!

DON RUY GOMEZ.
                    But I have not like Majesty
Forgiven!

Hernani.
Who is't has worked this wondrous change?

All. Nobles, Soldiers, Conspirators.
Honor to Charles the Fifth, and Germany!

Don Carlos (*turning to the tomb*).
Honor to Charlemagne! Leave us now together.

[*Exeunt all.*

Scene 5.—Don Carlos (*alone*).

[*He bends towards the tomb.*

Art thou content with me, oh, Charlemagne!
Have I the kingship's littleness stripped off?
Become as Emperor another man?
Can I Rome's mitre add unto my helm?
Have I the right the fortunes of the world
To sway? Have I a steady foot that safe
Can tread the path, by Vandal ruins strewed,
Which thou hast beaten by thine armies vast?
Have I my candle lighted at thy flame?
Did I interpret right the voice that spake
Within this tomb? Ah, I was lost—alone
Before an Empire—a wide howling world
That threatened and conspired! There were the Danes
To punish, and the Holy Father's self
To compensate—with Venice—Soliman,
Francis, and Luther—and a thousand dirks
Gleaming already in the shade—snares—rocks;
And countless foes; a score of nations, each
Of which might serve to awe a score of kings
Things ripe, all pressing to be done at once.
I cried to thee—with what shall I begin?
And thou didst answer—Son, by clemency!

FIFTH ACT.

The Nuptials.

Scene 1.—Saragossa. *A terrace of the palace of Aragon. At the back a flight of steps leading to the garden. At the right and left, doors on to a terrace which shows at the back of the stage a balustrade surmounted by a double row of Moorish arches, above and through which are seen the palace gardens, fountains in the shade, shrubberies and moving lights, and the Gothic and Arabic arches of the palace illuminated. It is night. Trumpets afar off are heard. Masks and Dominoes, either singly or in groups, cross the terrace here and there. At the front of the stage a group of young lords, their masks in their hands, laugh and chat noisily.*

Don Sancho Sanchez de Zuñiga, Comte de Monteret, Don Matias Centurion, Marquis d'Almuñan, Don Ricardo de Roxas, Comte de Casapalma, Don Francisco de Sotomayor, Comte de Valalcazar, Don Garcie Suarez de Carbajal, Comte de Penalver.

Don Garcie.
Now to the bride long life—and joy—I say !

Don Matias (*looking to the balcony*).
All Saragossa at its windows shows.

Don Garcie.
And they do well. A torch-light wedding ne'er
Was seen more gay than this, nor lovelier night,
Nor handsomer married pair.

Don Matias.
Kind Emp'ror !

DON SANCHO.

When we went with him in the dark that night
Seeking adventure, Marquis, who'd have thought
How it would end?

DON RICARDO (*interrupting*).
I, too, was there.   (*To the others.*)
Now list.

Three galants, one a bandit, his head due
Unto the scaffold; then a Duke, a King,
Adoring the same woman, all laid siege
At the same time.   The onset made—who won?
It was the bandit.

DON FRANCISCO.
Nothing strange in that,
For love and fortune, in all other lands
As well as Spain, are sport of the cogg'd dice.
It is the rogue who wins.

DON RICARDO.
My fortune grew
In seeing the love-making.   First a Count
And then Grandee, and next an Alcadé
At court.   My time was well spent, though without
One knowing it.

DON SANCHO.
Your secret, sir, appears
To be the keeping close upon the heels
O' the King.

DON RICARDO.
And showing that my conduct's worth
Reward.

DON GARCIE.
And by a chance you profited.

DON MATIAS.
What has become of the old Duke? has he
His coffin ordered?

DON SANCHO.
Marquis, jest not thus
At him! For he a haughty spirit has;

And this old man loved well the Doña Sol.
His sixty years had turned his hair to gray,
One day has bleached it.

DON GARCIE.
Not again, they say,
Has he been seen in Saragossa.

DON SANCHO.
Well?
Wouldst thou that to the bridal he should bring
His coffin?

DON FRANCISCO.
What's the Emperor doing now?

DON SANCHO.
The Emperor is out of sorts just now,
Luther annoys him.

DON RICARDO.
Luther!—subject fine
For care and fear! Soon would I finish him
With but four men-at-arms!

DON MATIAS.
And Soliman
Makes him dejected.

DON GARCIA.
Luther—Soliman
Neptune—the devil—Jupiter! What are
They all to me? The women are most fair,
The masquerade is splendid, and I've said
A hundred foolish things!

DON SANCHO.
Behold you now
The chief thing.

DON RICARDO.
Garcie's not far wrong, I say.
Not the same man am I on festal days.
When I put on the mask in truth I think
Another head it gives me.

Don Sancho (*apart to* Don Matias).
Pity 'tis
That all days are not festivals!

Don Francisco.
Are those
Their rooms?

Don Garcie (*with a nod of his head*).
Arrive they will, no doubt, full soon.

Don Francisco.
Dost think so?

Don Garcie.
Most undoubtedly!

Don Francisco.
'Tis well.
The bride is lovely!

Don Ricardo.
What an Emperor!
The rebel chief, Hernani, to be pardoned—
Wearing the Golden Fleece! and married too!
Ah, if the Emperor had been by me
Advised, the gallant should have had a bed
Of stone, the lady one of down.

Don Sancho (*aside to* Don Matias).
How well
I'd like with my good sword this lord to smash,
A lord made up of tinsel coarsely joined;
Pourpoint of Count filled out with bailiff's soul!

Don Ricardo (*drawing near*).
What are you saying?

Don Matias (*aside to* Don Sancho).
Count, no quarrel here!
(*To* Don Ricardo.)
He was reciting one of Petrarch's sonnets
Unto his lady love.

Don Garcie.
Have you not seen
Among the flowers and women, and dresses gay

Of many hues, a figure spectre-like,
Whose domino all black, upright against
A balustrade, seems like a spot upon
The festival?

DON RICARDO.
Yes, by my faith!

DON GARCIE.
Who is't?

DON RICARDO.
By height and mien I judge that it must be——
The Admiral—the Don Prancasio.

DON FRANCISCO.
Oh, no.

DON GARCIE.
He has not taken off his mask.

DON FRANCISCO.
There is no need; it is the Duke de Soma,
Who likes to be observed. 'Tis nothing more.

DON RICARDO.
No; the Duke spoke to me.

DON GARCIE.
Who then can be
This Mask? But see—he's here.
[*Enter a* Black Domino, *who slowly crosses the back
of the stage. All turn and watch him without
his appearing to notice them.*

DON SANCHO.
If the dead walk,
That is their step.

DON GARCIE (*approaching the* Black Domino).
Most noble Mask——
(*The* Black Domino *stops and turns.* GARCIE *recoils.*)
I swear,
Good Sirs, that I saw flame shine in his eyes.

DON SANCHO.

If he's the devil he'll find one he can
Address.

> [*He goes to the* Black Domino, *who is still motionless.*
> Ho, Demon! comest thou from hell?

THE MASK.

I come not thence—'tis thither that I go.

> [*He continues his walk and disappears at the balus-*
> *trade of the staircase. All watch him with a*
> *look of horrified dismay.*

DON MATIAS.

Sepulchral is his voice, as can be heard.

DON GARCIE.

Pshaw! What would frighten elsewhere, at a ball
We laugh at.

DON SANCHO.
Silly jesting 'tis!

DON GARCIE.
Indeed,

If Lucifer is come to see us dance,
Waiting for lower regions, let us dance!

DON SANCHO.

Of course its some buffoonery.

DON MATIAS.
We'll know

To-morrow.

DON SANCHO (*to* DON MATIAS).
Look now what becomes of him,

I pray you!

DON MATIAS (*at the balustrade of the terrace*).
Down the steps he's gone. That's all.

DON SANCHO.

A pleasant jester he! (*Musing.*) 'Tis strange.

DON GARCIE (*to a lady passing*).
Marquise,

Let us pray dance this time.

> [*He bows and offers his hand.*

THE LADY.
                    You know, dear sir,
My husband will my dances with you all
Count up.

DON GARCIE.
          All the more reason. Pleased is he
To count, it seems, and it amuses him.
He calculates—we dance.
                    [*The lady gives her hand and they exeunt.*

DON SANCHO (*thoughtfully*).
                    In truth, 'tis strange!

DON MATIAS.
Behold the married pair! Now silence all!
          [*Enter* HERNANI *and* DOÑA SOL *hand in hand.* DOÑA
          SOL *in magnificent bridal dress.* HERNANI *in
          black velvet and with the Golden Fleece hanging
          from his neck. Behind them a crowd of Masks
          and of ladies and gentlemen who form their
          retinue. Two Halberdiers in rich liveries follow
          them, and four pages precede them. Everyone
          makes way for them and bows as they approach.
          Flourish of trumpets.*

SCENE 2.—*The Same.* HERNANI, DOÑA SOL, *and retinue.*

HERNANI (*saluting*).
Dear friends!

DON RICARDO (*advancing and bowing*).
                    Your Excellency's happiness
Makes ours.

DON FRANCISCO (*looking at* DOÑA SOL).
                    Now, by James, 'tis Venus' self
That he is leading.

DON MATIAS.
                    Happiness is his!

Don Sancho (*to* Don Matias).

'Tis late now, let us leave.

  [*All salute the married pair and retire—some by the
door, others by the stairway at the back.*

Hernani (*escorting them*).

Adieu!

Don Sancho (*who has remained to the last, and pressing
his hand*).

Be happy!

  [*Exit* Don Sancho.

[Hernani *and* Doña Sol *remain alone. The sound
of voices grows fainter and fainter till it ceases
altogether. During the early part of the following scene the sound of trumpets grows fainter,
and the lights by degrees are extinguished—till
night and silence prevail.*

Scene 3.—Hernani.   Doña Sol.

Doña Sol.

At last they all are gone.

Hernani (*seeking to draw her to his arms*).

Dear love!

Doña Sol (*drawing back a little*).

Is't late?—

At least to me it seems so.

Hernani.

Angel dear,

Time ever drags till we together are.

Doña Sol.

This noise has wearied me. Is it not true,
Dear Lord, that all this mirth but stifling is
To happiness?

Hernani.

Thou sayest truly, Love,

For happiness is serious, and asks

For hearts of bronze on which to 'grave itself.
Pleasure alarms it, flinging to it flowers;
Its smile is nearer tears than mirth.

DOÑA SOL.
                    Thy smile's
Like daylight in thine eyes.
           [HERNANI *seeks to lead her to the door.*
                 Oh, presently.

HERNANI
I am thy slave; yes, linger if thou wilt,
Whate'er thou dost is well. I'll laugh and sing
If thou desirest that it should be so.
Bid the volcano stifle flame, and 'twill
Close up its gulfs, and on its sides grow flowers,
And grasses green.

DOÑA SOL.
            How good you are to me,
My heart's Hernani!

HERNANI.
              Madam, what name's that?
I pray in pity speak it not again!
Thou call'st to mind forgotten things. I know
That he existed formerly in dreams,
Hernani, he whose eyes flashed like a sword,
A man of night and of the hills, a man
Proscribed, on whom was seen writ everywhere
The one word *vengeance.* An unhappy man
That drew down malediction! I know not
The man they called Hernani. As for me,
I love the birds and flowers, and woods—and song
Of nightingale. I'm Juan of Aragon,
The spouse of Doña Sol—a happy man!

DOÑA SOL.
Happy am I!

HERNANI.
           What does it matter now,
The rags I left behind me at the door!

Behold, I to my palace desolate
Come back. Upon the threshold-sill there waits
For me an Angel; I come in and lift
Upright the broken columns, kindle fire,
And ope again the windows; and the grass
Upon the courtyard I have all pluck'd up;
For me there is but joy, enchantment, love.
Let them give back my towers, and donjon-keep,
My plume, and seat at the Castilian board
Of Council, comes my blushing Doña Sol,
Let them leave us—the rest forgotten is.
Nothing I've seen, nor said, nor have I done.
Anew my life begins, the past effacing.
Wisdom or madness, you I have and love,
And you are all my joy!

DOÑA SOL.

How well upon
The velvet black the golden collar shows!

HERNANI.

You saw it on the King ere now on me.

DOÑA SOL.

I did not notice. Others, what are they
To me? Besides, the velvet is it, or
The satin? No, my Duke, it is thy neck
Which suits the golden collar. Thou art proud
And noble, my own Lord. [*He seeks to lead her indoors.*
Oh, presently,
A moment! See you not, I weep with joy?
Come look upon the lovely night.
[*She goes to the balustrade.*
My Duke,
Only a moment—but the time to breathe
And gaze. All now is o'er, the torches out,
The music done. Night only is with us.
Felicity most perfect! Think you not
That now while all is still and slumbering,
Nature, half waking, watches us with love?
No cloud is in the sky. All things like us

Are now at rest. Come, breathe with me the air
Perfumed by roses. Look, there is no light,
Nor hear we any noise. Silence prevails.
The moon just now from the horizon rose
E'en while you spoke to me ; her trembling light
And thy dear voice together reached my heart.
Joyous and softly calm I felt, oh, thou
My lover ! And it seemed that I would then
Most willingly have died.

HERNANI.

     Ah, who is there
Would not all things forget when listening thus
Unto this voice celestial ! Thy speech
But seems a chaunt with nothing human mixed,
And as with one, who gliding down a stream
On summer eve, sees pass before his eyes
A thousand flowery plains, my thoughts are drawn
Into thy reveries !

DOÑA SOL.

    This silence is
Too deep, and too profound the calm. Say, now,
Wouldst thou not like to see a star shine forth
From out the depths—or hear a voice of night,
Tender and sweet, raise suddenly its song?

HERNANI (*smiling*).

Capricious one ! Just now you fled away
From all the songs and lights.

DOÑA SOL.

      Ah yes, the ball !
But yet a bird that in the meadow sings,
A nightingale in moss or shadow lost,
Or flute far off. For music sweet can pour
Into the soul a harmony divine,
That like a heavenly choir wakes in the heart
A thousand voices ! Charming would it be !
   [*They hear the sound of a horn from the shade.*
My prayer is heard.

HERNANI (*aside, trembling*).
          Oh, miserable man!

DOÑA SOL.
An angel read my thought—'twas thy good angel
Doubtless?

          HERNANI (*bitterly*).
          Yes, my good angel! (*Aside.*)
                              There, again!

          DOÑA SOL (*smiling*).
Don Juan, I recognize your horn.

               HERNANI.
                    Is't so?

          DOÑA SOL.
The half this serenade to you belongs?

               HERNANI.
The half, thou hast declared it.

          DOÑA SOL.
                    Ah, the ball
Detestable! Far better do I love
The horn that sounds from out the woods! And since
It is your horn 'tis like your voice to me.
                    [*The horn sounds again.*

          HERNANI (*aside*).
It is the tiger howling for his prey!

          DOÑA SOL.
Don Juan, this music fills my heart with joy.

HERNANI (*drawing himself up and looking terrible*).
Call me Hernani! call me it again!
For with that fatal name I have not done.

          DOÑA SOL (*trembling*).
What ails you?

               HERNANI.
               The old man!

DOÑA SOL.

Oh God, what looks!
What is it ails you?

HERNANI.

That old man who in
The darkness laughs. Can you not see him there?

DOÑA SOL.
Oh, you are wand'ring! Who is this old man?

HERNANI.

The old man!

DOÑA SOL.

On my knees I do entreat
Thee, say what is the secret that afflicts
Thee thus?

HERNANI.

I swore it!

DOÑA SOL.
Swore!
[*She watches his movements with anxiety. He stops
suddenly and passes his hand across his brow.*

HERNANI (*aside*).

What have I said?
Oh, let me spare her. (*Aloud.*)
I—nought. What was it
I said?

DOÑA SOL.
You said——

HERNANI.

No, no, I was disturbed——
And somewhat suffering I am. Do not
Be frightened.

DOÑA SOL.
You need something? Order me,
Thy servant.   [*The horn sounds again.*

Hernani (*aside*).

Ah, he claims! he claims the pledge!
He has my oath. (*Feeling for his dagger.*)
Not there. It must be done!
Ah!——

Doña Sol.

Suff'rest thou so much?

Hernani.

'Tis an old wound
That I thought healed—it has reopened now. (*Aside.*)
She must be got away. (*Aloud.*)
My best beloved,
Now listen; there's a little box that in
Less happy days I carried with me——

Doña Sol.

Ah,
I know what 'tis you mean. Tell me your wish.

Hernani.

It holds a flask of an elixir which
Will end my sufferings.—Go!

Doña Sol.

I go, my Lord.
[*Exit by the door to their apartments.*

Scene 4.

Hernani (*alone*).

This, then, is how my happiness must end!
Behold the fatal finger that doth shine
Upon the wall! My bitter destiny
Still jests at me.
[*He falls into a profound yet convulsive reverie.
Afterwards he turns abruptly.*
Ah, well! I hear no sound.
Am I myself deceiving?——
[*The* Mask *in black domino appears at the balustrade
of the steps.* Hernani *stops petrified.*

SCENE 5.—HERNANI. THE MASK.

THE MASK.
                    "Whatsoe'er
May happen, what the place, or what the hour,
Whenever to thy mind it seems the time
Has come for me to die—blow on this horn
And take no other care. All will be done."
This compact had the dead for witnesses.
Is it all done?

HERNANI (*in a low voice*).
            'Tis he!

THE MASK.
                Unto thy home
I come, I tell thee that it is the time.
It is my hour. I find thee hesitate.

HERNANI.
Well then, thy pleasure say. What wouldest thou
Of me?

THE MASK.
        I give thee choice 'twixt poison draught
And blade. I bear about me both. We shall
Depart together.

HERNANI.
            Be it so.

THE MASK.
                Shall we
First pray?

HERNANI.
        What matter?

THE MASK.
                Which of them wilt thou?

HERNANI.
The poison.

THE MASK.

Then hold out your hand.

[*He gives a vial to* HERNANI, *who pales at receiving it.*

Now drink,

That I may finish.

[HERNANI *lifts the vial to his lips, but recoils.*

HERNANI.

Oh, for pity's sake
Until to-morrow wait! If thou has heart
Or soul, if thou are not a spectre just
Escaped from flame, if thou art not a soul
Accursed, forever lost; if on thy brow
Not yet has God inscribed His "never." Oh,
If thou hast ever known the bliss supreme
Of loving, and at twenty years of age
Of wedding the beloved; if ever thou
Hast clasped the one thou lovedst in thine arms,
Wait till to-morrow. Then thou canst come back!

THE MASK.

Childish it is for you to jest this way!
To-morrow! why, the bell this morning toll'd
Thy funeral! And I should die this night,
And who would come and take thee after me!
I will not to the tomb descend alone,
Young man, 'tis thou must go with me!

HERNANI.

Well, then,

I say thee nay; and, demon, I from thee
Myself deliver. I will not obey.

THE MASK.

As I expected. Very well. On what
Then didst thou swear? Ah, on a trifling thing,
The mem'ry of thy father's head. With ease
Such oath may be forgotten. Youthful oaths
Are light affairs.

HERNANI.

My father!—father! Oh
My senses I shall lose!

THE MASK.
Oh, no—'tis but
A perjury and treason.

HERNANI.
Duke !

THE MASK.
Since now
The heirs of Spanish houses make a jest
Of breaking promises, I'll say Adieu !
[*He moves as if to leave.*

HERNANI.
Stay !

THE MASK.
Then——

HERNANI.
Oh cruel man !   [*He raises the vial.*
Thus to return
Upon my path at heaven's door !
[*Re-enter* DOÑA SOL *without seeing the* MASK, *who is
standing erect near the balustrade of the stair-
way at the back of the stage.*

SCENE 6.—*The Same.* DOÑA SOL.

DOÑA SOL.
I've failed
To find that little box.

HERNANI (*aside*).
Oh God ! 'tis she !
At such a moment here !

DOÑA SOL.
What is't, that thus
I frighten him,—e'en at my voice he shakes !
What hold'st thou in thy hand ? What fearful thought !
What hold'st thou in thy hand ? Reply to me.
[*The* DOMINO *unmasks, she utters a cry in recogniz-
ing* DON RUY.
'Tis poison !

DOÑA SOL WITH THE DEAD BODY OF HERNANI.

Hernani—Act V., Scene 6

HERNANI.

Oh, great Heaven!

DOÑA SOL (*to* HERNANI).

What is it
That I have done to thee? What mystery
Of horror? I'm deceived by thee, Don Juan!

HERNANI.

Ah, I had thought to hide it all from thee.
My life I promised to the Duke that time
He saved it. Aragon must pay this debt
To Silva.

DOÑA SOL.

Unto me you do belong,
Not him. What signify your other oaths?

(*To* DON RUY GOMEZ.)

My love it is which gives me strength, and, Duke,
I will defend him against you and all
The world.

DON RUY GOMEZ (*unmoved*).

Defend him if you can against
An oath that's sworn.

DOÑA SOL.

What oath?

HERNANI.

Yes, I have sworn.

DOÑA SOL.

No, no; naught binds thee; it would be a crime,
A madness, an atrocity—no, no,
It cannot be.

DON RUY GOMEZ.

Come, Duke.

[HERNANI *makes a gesture to obey.* DOÑA SOL *tries to stop him.*

HERNANI.

It must be done.
Allow it, Doña Sol. My word was pledged
To the Duke, and to my father now in heaven!

DOÑA SOL (*to* DON RUY GOMEZ).

Better that to a tigress you should go
And snatch away her young, than take from me
Him whom I love. Know you at all what is
This Doña Sol? Long time I pitied you,
And, in compassion for your age, I seemed
The gentle girl, timid and innocent,
But now see eyes made moist by tears of rage.

[*She draws a dagger from her bosom.*

See you this dagger? Old man imbecile!
Do you not fear the steel when eyes flash threat?
Take care, Don Ruy! I'm of thy family.
Listen, mine Uncle! Had I been your child
It had been ill for you, if you had laid
A hand upon my husband!

[*She throws away the dagger, and falls on her knees
before him.*

At thy feet
I fall! Mercy! Have pity on us both.
Alas! my lord, I am but woman weak,
My strength dies out within my soul, I fail
So easily; 'tis at your knees I plead,
I supplicate—have mercy on us both!

DON RUY GOMEZ.

Doña Sol!

DOÑA SOL.

Oh, pardon! With us Spaniards
Grief bursts forth in stormy words, you know it.
Alas! you used not to be harsh! My uncle,
Have pity, you are killing me indeed
In touching him! Mercy, have pity now,
So well I love him!

DON RUY GOMEZ (*gloomily*).

You love him too much?

HERNANI.

Thou weepest! -

DOÑA SOL.

No, my love, no, no. it must
Not be. I will not have you die. (*To* DON RUY.)

To-day
Be merciful, and I will love you well,
You also.

Don Ruy Gomez.

After him; the dregs you'd give
The remnants of your love, and friendliness.
Still less and less.—Oh, think you thus to quench
The thirst that now devours me? (*Pointing to* Hernani.)
He alone
Is everything. For me kind pityings!
With such affection, what, pray, could I do?
Fury! 'tis he would have your heart, your love,
And be enthroned, and grant a look from you
As alms; and if vouchsafed a kindly word
'Tis he would tell you—say so much, it is
Enough,—cursing in heart the greedy one
The beggar, unto whom he's forced to fling
The drops remaining in the emptied glass.
Oh, shame! derision! No, we'll finish. Drink!

Hernani.

He has my promise, and it must be kept.

Don Ruy Gomez.

Proceed.

   [Hernani *raises the vial to his lips.* Doña Sol
     throws herself on his arm.

Doña Sol.

Not yet. Deign both of you to hear me.

Don Ruy Gomez.

The grave is open and I cannot wait.

Doña Sol.

A moment only—Duke, and my Don Juan,
Ah! both are cruel! What is it I ask?
An instant! that is all I beg from you.
Let a poor woman speak what's in her heart,
Oh, let me speak——

Don Ruy Gomez.

·I cannot wait.

DOÑA SOL.

My Lord,

You make me tremble! What then have I done?

HERNANI.

His crime is rending him.

DOÑA SOL (*still holding his arm*).

You see full well

I have a thousand things to say.

DON RUY GOMEZ (*to* HERNANI).

Die—die

You must.

DOÑA SOL (*still hanging on his arm*).

Don Juan, when all's said indeed

Thou shalt do what thou wilt.   [*She snatches the vial.*

I have it now!

[*She lifts the vial for* HERNANI *and the old man to see.*

DON RUY GOMEZ.

Since with two women I have here to deal,

It needs, Don Juan, that I elsewhere go

In search of souls. Grave oaths you took to me,

And by the race from which you sprang. I go

Unto your father, and to speak among

The dead. Adieu.

[*He moves as if to depart.* HERNANI *holds him back.*

HERNANI.

Stay, Duke. (*To* DOÑA SOL.)

Alas! I do

Implore thee. Wouldst thou wish to see in me

A perjured felon only, and e'erwhere

I go "a traitor" written on my brow?

In pity give the poison back to me.

'Tis by our love I ask it, and our souls

Immortal——

DOÑA SOL (*sadly*).

And thou wilt? (*She drinks.*)

Now take the rest.

Don Ruy Gomez (*aside*).

'Twas then for her!

Doña Sol (*returning the half-emptied vial to* Hernani).
I tell thee, take.

Hernani. (*To* Don Ruy.)
See'st thou,
Oh miserable man!

Doña Sol.
Grieve not for me,
I've left thy share.

Hernani (*taking the vial*).
Oh God!

Doña Sol.
Not thus would'st thou
Have left me mine. But thou! not thine the heart
Of Christian wife! Thou knowest not to love
As Silvas do—but I've drunk first—made sure.
Now drink it, if thou wilt!

Hernani.
What hast thou done,
Unhappy one?

Doña Sol.
'Twas thou who willed it so.

Hernani.
It is a frightful death!

Doña Sol.
No—no—why so?

Hernani.
This philtre leads unto the grave.

Dona Sol.
And ought
We not this night to rest together? Does
It matter in what bed?

Hernani.
My father, thou

Thyself avengest upon me, who did
Forget thee!   (*He lifts the vial to his mouth.*)

DOÑA SOL (*throwing herself on him*).
Heavens, what strange agony!
Ah, throw this philtre far from thee!   My reason
Is wand'ring.   Stop!   Alas! oh, my Don Juan,
This drug is potent, in the heart it wakes
A hydra with a thousand tearing teeth
Devouring it.   I knew not that such pangs
Could be!   What is the thing? 'tis liquid fire.
Drink not!   For much thou'dst suffer.

HERNANI.   (*To* DON RUY.)
Ah, thy soul
Is cruel!   Could'st thou not have found for her
Another drug?   [*He drinks and throws the vial away.*

DOÑA SOL.
What dost thou?

HERNANI.
What thyself
Hast done.

DOÑA SOL.
Come to my arms, young lover, now.
[*They sit down close to each other.*
Does one not suffer horribly?

HERNANI.
No, no.

DOÑA SOL.
These are our marriage rites!   But for a bride
I'm very pale, say am I not?

HERNANI.
Ah me!

DON RUY GOMEZ.
Fulfilled is now the fatal destiny!

HERNANI.

Oh misery and despair to know her pangs!

DOÑA SOL.

Be calm. I'm better.—Towards new brighter light
We now together open out our wings.
Let us with even flight set out to reach
A fairer world. Only a kiss—a kiss!   [*They embrace.*

DON RUY GOMEZ.

Oh, agony supreme!

HERNANI (*in a feeble voice*).

Oh bless'd be Heav'n
That will'd for me a life by spectres followed,
And by abysses yawning circled still,
Yet grants, that weary of a road so rough,
I fall asleep my lips upon thy hand.

DON RUY GOMEZ.

How happy are they!

HERNANI (*in voice growing weaker and weaker*).

Come—come, Doña Sol,
All's dark. Dost thou not suffer?

DOÑA SOL (*in a voice equally faint*).

Nothing now.
Oh, nothing.

HERNANI.

Seest thou not fires in the gloom?*

DOÑA SOL.

Not yet.

HERNANI (*with a sigh*).

Behold—— (*He falls.*)

DON RUY GOMEZ (*raising the head, which falls again*).

He's dead!

---

* Certain poisons are said to produce among their dreadful effects, the appearance of fire when the sufferer is near death.—TRANS.

DoÑa Sol (*dishevelled and half raising herself on the seat*).

     Oh no, we sleep.
He sleeps. It is my spouse that here you see.
We love each other—we are sleeping thus.
It is our bridal. (*In a failing voice.*)
     I entreat you not
To wake him, my Lord Duke of Mendocé,
For he is weary. (*She turns round the face of* HERNANI.)
    Turn to me, my love.
        [*She falls back.*
More near—still closer——

    DON RUY GOMEZ.
     Dead ! Oh, I'm damn'd !
        [*He kills himself.*

THE KING'S DIVERSION.

(LE ROI S'AMUSE!)

A TRAGEDY, IN FIVE ACTS.

(1832.)

TRANSLATED BY FREDERICK L. SLOUS.

(149)

TRANSLATOR'S INTRODUCTION.

 E ROI S'AMUSE " was produced for the first time at the *Théâtre Français* on the 22d of November, 1832, and suppressed next day by ministerial authority.

This unusual interference drew from Victor Hugo an immediate publication of the work; in the Preface to which he expresses not only considerable indignation at so illegal an act, but unbounded surprise that the French government should have interdicted the future progress of his drama, after a first and successful representation.

In my opinion, his astonishment ought to have been greater that "LE ROI S'AMUSE" was allowed to appear before the public at all.

It was not to be expected that so dangerous an attack on the rights and privileges of monarchy could be permitted to receive the nightly plaudits and awaken the republican sympathies of a Parisian audience. Under pretence of placing Francis the First, the sensualist and debauchee, in a well-merited pillory for public execration, a sly opportunity was both afforded and taken, for a pretty plentiful dirt-flinging—not only at Francis in particular, but at royalty and aristocracy in general: and our ingenious author must have wofully deceived himself in imagining that he could so easily elude the jealous vigilance of a government, as yet too insecurely established to bid defiance to the sarcasms of a writer, at once brilliant and powerful.

The political tendency of the tragedy was, I conceive, the sole cause of its suppression. There could be no objection to it on the score of immorality. The French public and the dramatic censor were too much accustomed to the style of the

(151)

romantic school to be startled by "LE ROI S'AMUSE." The well-educated Parisian sups on a dish of horrors—à la Victor Hugo, or à la Alexander Dumas—with as much relish as on the most tempting selections from the carte of the *Trois Frères;* he has no apprehensions that nightmares may result from the one, or indigestion from the other; he is accustomed to, and therefore requires excitement; and if he has any complaint to urge against our talented author, it might be, that his play is too little distinguished by the diableries of the modern school,—that its crimes are all served up *au naturel,* and that it lacks the rich seasoning and high infernal flavor of *Lucrèce Borgie* or *la Tour de Nesle.* The English reader may perhaps object that in this, as in most of Victor Hugo's productions, there is not one really good or noble character—that in scanning the actions of the entire *dramatis personæ,* the eye of the reader, like that of poor TRIBOULET in the text, becomes a-weary with the sight of crime, and that the heart has no single spot of virtue or magnanimity where it may repose awhile from the shocks which the perpetual aspect of vice has inflicted. Alas, it is but too true! Yet notwithstanding this defect, one powerful argument may be advanced in its favor.

Unlike so many of the most favored dramas of the French school, "LE ROI S'AMUSE" contains no attempt to gloss over or inculcate the doctrines of immorality; there is no insidious endeavor to seduce the imagination, or pervert the judgment by making sophistry eloquent, or vice attractive. On the contrary, as the Spartans intoxicated their Helots to make their children abhor drunkenness, so does Victor Hugo exhibit the hideousness of crime to the open detestation of the beholder; and although I am inclined to believe that both Lycurgus and Victor Hugo would have evinced greater wisdom and feeling, had they presented examples of excellence to be revered, rather than depravity to be avoided, still the reader will, I think, agree with me, that it is better that our feelings should be wounded by the thorns, from amidst which we are compelled to gather the roses of poetry and imagination, than that the innocence of youth should be tempted to encounter the serpent, concealed in the basket of flowers.

Of the characters but little need be said. Natural, but not profound, they are the creatures of circumstances, and require no acute critic to render their motive and feelings comprehensible.

Of BLANCHE, the offspring of sorrow, the victim of crime, little can be said in condemnation. The least criminal of the personages in the drama, she is the most severely dealt with ;— a little French Juliet, without the intensity of feeling of Shakespeare, she is a weak-headed, warm-hearted girl of sixteen, and acts accordingly.

FRANCIS THE FIRST, according to history, was a sensualist, a profligate, and a man *sans foi ni loi*, the hero of Marigan, the defeated of Pavia, who, when he lost everything *"fors l'honneur,"* lost all but that which he did *not* possess. History has given us the outlines of his character. Victor Hugo has filled up the sketch with so vigorous a pencil, and so dark a shadowing, that I trust, for the sake of human nature, he may be considered to have slightly exaggerated the foibles of *le Roi des Gentilshommes.* The poor King of the Casket in the Arabian Nights, living and breathing above, was from the waist downwards a mass of black marble. FRANCIS, on the contrary, is gay and animated throughout; with one little exception, his heart, which indeed is marble of the blackest hue.

TRIBOULET—the deformed, the Hunchback, is a being of a different nature from Quasimodo ;* and his character is drawn with a singular mixture of power and inconsistency. He is a cynic, and not a jester—rude, but not witty. His hatred malignant and undignified, and the retribution attendant upon it is more than commensurate with his guilt.

ST. VALLIER is seen but little. His intention of sacrificing his daughter Diana to the embraces of a deformed old Seneschal, abates much of the sympathy that his sorrows would otherwise deserve; and it is matter for regret that he is so soon consigned to oblivion and the Bastille.

With regard to the interest of the piece itself,—which presents a strange mixture of unity and inconsistency—of wonderful beauties, and glaring defects, it may be summed up in a few words.

The plot is simple and unfettered by episode,—increasing in interest throughout, and at length rising in its catastrophe to a

---

* The Hunchback of Notre Dame.

pitch of horrible sublimity, unequalled in any drama I have yet seen.

The incidents also are arranged so as to produce the most striking dramatic effects; but, occasionally, it must be confessed that they depart even from the extreme license of probability, and that the characters are frequently made to do that which mature reflection would not acknowledge as naturally resulting from the situations in which they are placed. On the other hand, the language is so much the language of nature and feeling—of eloquence and sincerity, that the reason forgets for a moment the contradictions of cause and effect. By a sort of verbo-electrotype process, Victor Hugo has showered down a brilliant surface of the purest gold, which entirely conceals the inferiority of the substance beneath, and the mind of the reader, dazzled by the lustre of the thin, though genuine metal, is content to forgive the inconsistent materials, which so splendid a covering invests.

F. L. S.

Note.—It is perhaps necessary to observe that the French drama, more rigid with regard to unity of place than ours, seldom allows more than one *painted* scene to each Act ; and the reader is requested to bear in mind that, according to the French text, when Scene I., II., III., etc., are mentioned, nothing but the entrance of another personage on the stage is understood.

AUTHOR'S PREFACE.*

HE production of this drama on the stage has given rise to a Ministerial action unprecedented.

The morning after its first representation the author received from M. Jouslin de la Salle, stage-manager of the Théâtre Français, the following letter, the original of which he carefully preserves :—

"It is half-past ten o'clock, and I have just received the *order* † to suspend the representation of 'Le Roi s'Amuse.' It is M. Taylor who communicates this command from the Minister.

"*November 23.*"

The first emotion of the author was incredulity. The act was so arbitrary he could not believe in it.

Indeed what is called the *True Charter* says :—"The French have the right to publish——" Observe, the text does not say only the right to print, but clearly and forcibly the *right to publish*. Now the theatre is only one manner of publication, as the press, or engraving, or lithography is. The liberty of the theatre is therefore implied in the Charter with all other freedom of thought. The fundamental law adds :—*Censorship must never be re-established.* Now the text does not say *censorship of journals or of books,* it says *censorship* in general, all censorship, that of the theatre as of writing. The theatre, then, henceforth cannot recognize the legality of censorship.

Besides, the Charter says, *Confiscation is abolished.* Now the suppression of a theatrical piece after its representation is not only a monstrous act of arbitrary censorship, it is a veritable confiscation, a robbery of the theatre and of the author.

* This preface was not translated by Mr. Slous, nor was it included in the original edition of his version, which appeared first in 1843.—ED.

† This word is underlined in the letter.

(155)

Indeed, that all should be clear and unmistakable, and that the four or five great social principles which the French Revolution has moulded in bronze may rest intact on their pedestals of granite, and that the rights of Frenchmen should not be stealthily attacked by the forty thousand notched weapons which in the arsenal of our laws are destroyed by rust and disuse, the Charter in its last article expressly abolishes all which in our previous laws should prove contrary to its text and its spirit.

This is certain. The Ministerial suppression of a theatrical piece, attacks liberty by censorship and property by confiscation. The sense of our public rights revolts against such a proceeding.

The author, not believing in so much insolence and folly, hastened to the theatre. There the fact was confirmed in every particular. The Minister had, indeed, on his own authority, by his divine right of Minister, issued *the order* in question. He gave no reason. The Minister had taken away the author's piece, had deprived him of his rights, and of his property. There only remained that he should send the poet to the Bastille.

We repeat that at the time in which we live, when such an act comes to bar your way and roughly take you by the throat, the first emotion is one of profound astonishment. A thousand questions present themselves to the mind. What is the law? Where is the authority? Can such things happen? Is there, indeed, a something which is called the Revolution of July? It is clear that we are no longer in Paris. In what Pashalic do we live?

Stunned and astonished, the authorities of the Comédie Française took some measures to obtain from the Minister a revocation of his strange decision; but the trouble was wasted. The divan, I should say the Council of Ministers, had assembled in the morning. On the 23d it was only an order of the Minister, on the 24th it was an edict of the Ministry. On the 23d the piece was *suspended;* on the 24th its representation was definitely prohibited. It was even enjoined that from the play-bills should be erased the formidable words *Le Roi s'Amuse.* Besides all this the authorities were even forbidden to make any complaint, or breath a word on the subject. Perhaps it would be grand, loyal, and noble to resist a despotism so Asiatic; but managers of theatres dare not. Fear lest their privileges should be revoked makes them subjects and serfs, to be taxed and controlled at will as vassals, eunuchs, and mutes.

The author will remain and ought to remain aloof from these proceedings of the theatre. He, the poet, depends not on any

Minister. Those prayers and solicitations which his interests, pitifully considered, may perhaps counsel, his duty as an untrammelled writer forbids. To ask permission of power is to acknowledge it. Liberty and property are not things of the ante-chamber. A right is not to be treated as a favor. For a favor sue from the Minister; but claim a right from the country.

It is, then, to the country that he addresses himself. There are two methods of obtaining justice—by public opinion, or the tribunals of the law. He chooses them both.

By public opinion the cause has already been judged and gained. And here the author ought to thank warmly those established and independent personages associated with literature and art, who on this occasion have given so many proofs of sympathy and cordiality. He calculated beforehand on their support. He knows that when he enters on the struggle for freedom of thought he will not be unsupported in the battle.

And let us here observe in passing that power, by a sufficiently contemptible calculation, flattered itself that it should on this occasion find auxiliaries even in the ranks of its opponents in the literary enmities so long aroused by the author. It believed that literary animosity was still more tenacious than political, because the first had its roots in self-love, the second only in interest. But the Government has deceived itself. Its brutal act has proved revolting to honest men in every camp. The author saw rally round him to show a bold front against an arbitrary act of injustice even those who had attacked him the most violently only the day before. If by chance some inveterate enemies remained, they regret now that they gave a momentary support to power. All the loyal and honorable of his foes have stretched out their hands to the author, ready to recommence the literary battle as soon as the political should be finished. In France whoever is persecuted has no longer an enemy except the persecutor.

If now, after having agreed that the Ministerial act is odious, unjustifiable, and impossible to be defended, we descend for a moment to discuss it as a material fact, and seek for some of the elements which may have composed it, the first question which presents itself to every one is this:—"What can be the motive of such a measure?"

We must say it because it is the truth, if the future some day is occupied with our little men and our little things, this will not be the least curious detail of this curious event. It appears that our censors pretend to be shocked at the immorality of *Le Roi s'Amuse;* this piece offends the modesty of the police; the brigade Léotaud considers it obscene; the decider on morals has veiled his face; it has made M. Vidocq blush. In short, the censor's order to the police, and that for some days has been

stammered round about us, is simply *that the piece is immoral.*
Ho, there, my masters ! Silence on that point.

Let us explain ourselves, however, not to the police, to whom
I, an honest man, forbear to speak on these matters, but to the
small number of respectable and conscientious persons who on
hearsay, or after having seen the performance imperfectly, have
been persuaded into an opinion of which, perhaps, the name of the
poet implicated ought to have been a sufficient refutation. The
drama is printed to-day. If you were not present at the representation, read it. If you were there, still read it. Remember
that that representation was less a performance than a battle,
a sort of battle of Montlhéry (let this somewhat ambitious
comparison pass), where the Parisians and the Burgundians
each pretended to have *"pocketed" the victory,* as Matthieu
said.

The piece is immoral ? Think you so ? Is it from its subject ? Triboulet is deformed, Triboulet is unhealthy, Triboulet
is a court buffoon—a threefold misery which renders him evil.
Triboulet hates the king because he is king, the nobles because
they are nobles, and he hates ordinary men because they have
not humps on their backs. His only pastime is to set the nobles
unceasingly against the king, crushing the weaker by the stronger.
He depraves the king, corrupts and stultifies him ; he encourages
him in tyranny, ignorance, and vice. He lures him to the families of gentlemen, pointing out the wife to seduce, the sister to
carry off, the daughter to dishonor. The king in the hands of
Triboulet is but an all-powerful puppet which ruins the lives of
those in the midst of whom the buffoon sets him to play. One
day, in the midst of a fête, at the moment when Triboulet is
urging the king to carry off the wife of M. de Cossé, M. de
Saint-Vallier reaches the presence chamber, and in a loud voice
reproaches the king for the dishonor of Diana de Poitiers. This
father, from whom the king has taken his daughter, is jeered at
and insulted by Triboulet. Then the father stretches forth his
hand and curses Triboulet. It is from this scene the whole play
develops. The real subject of the drama is *the curse of M. de
Saint-Vallier.* Attend. You are in the second act. On whom
has this curse fallen? On Triboulet as the king's fool? No.
On Triboulet as a man, a father who has a heart and has a
daughter. Triboulet has a daughter, all in that is expressed.
Triboulet has but his daughter in the world, and he hides her
from all eyes in a solitary house in a deserted quarter. The
more he spreads in the town the contagion of debauchery and
vice, the more he seeks to isolate and immure his daughter. He
brings up his child in faith, innocence, and modesty. His greatest
fear is that she may fall into evil, for he knows, being himself

wicked, all the wretchedness that is endured by evil-doers. Well, now! The old man's malediction will reach Triboulet through the only being in the world whom he loves, his daughter. This same king whom Triboulet urges to pitiless vice will be the ravisher of Triboulet's daughter. The buffoon will be struck by Providence precisely in the same manner as was M. de Saint-Vallier. And more, his daughter once ruined, he lays a snare for the king by which to avenge her; but it is she that falls into it. Thus Triboulet has two pupils—the king and his daughter—the king, whom he has trained to vice, his daughter, whom he has reared for virtue. The one destroys the other. He intends Madame de Cossé to be carried off for the king, it is his daughter that is entrapped. He wishes to kill the king, and so avenge his child; it is his daughter whom he slays. Punishment does not stop half way; the malediction of Diana's father is fulfilled on the father of Blanche.

Undoubtedly it is not for us to decide if this is a dramatic idea, but certainly it is a moral one.

The foundation of one of the author's other works is fatality. The foundation of this one is Providence.

We repeat expressly that we are not now addressing the police, we do them not so much honor, but that part of the public to whom this discussion may seem necessary. Let us proceed.

If the work is moral in its invention, is it that it was immoral in its execution? The question thus put seems to contradict itself; but let us see. Probably there is nothing immoral in the first and second acts. Is it the situation in the third which shocks? Read this third act, and tell us in all honesty if the impression which results be not profoundly one of chastity and virtuous principle.

Is it the fourth act which is objectionable? But when was it not permitted for a king on the stage to make love to the servant at an inn? The incident is not new either in history or the drama. And more, history shows us Francis the First in a drunken state in the hovels of the Rue du Pelican. To take a king into a viler place is not more new. The Greek theatre, which is the classical, has done it. Shakespeare, whose plays are of the romantic, has done it. The author of this drama has not. He knows all that has been written about the house of Saltabadil. But why represent him to have said what he has not said? Why in a similar case make him overleap a barrier which he has not passed? This Bohemian Maguelonne, so much censured, is assuredly not more brazen than the Lisettes and Marions of the old theatre. The cottage of Saltabadil is a tavern, an hostelry, the pothouse of *The Fir-Cone*, a suspected cut-throat place, we admit, but not still viler. It is terrible, horrible, evil and fearful if you will, but it is not an obscene place.

There remain, then, the details of style. Read. The author accepts for judges of rigid strictness of his style even those persons who are startled at Juliet's nurse, and Ophelia's father, and by Beaumarchais and Regnard, by *L'Ecole des Femmes* and *Amphitryon,* Dandin and Sganarelli, and the grand scene of *Tartuffe* —*Tartuffe,* accused also of immorality in his day. Only there where he has found it necessary to be clear he has thought it his duty to be so at all risks and perils, but always with seriousness and moderation. He desires art to be chaste, but not prudish.

Behold, however, this piece concerning which the Minister has made so many accusations! This immorality, this obscenity— here is the piece laid bare. What a pity! Authority had its hidden reasons, and we shall indicate them presently, for raising against *Le Roi s'Amuse* the strongest prejudice possible. It wished that the public should stifle this piece from a distorted imagination, without hearing or understanding it, even as Othello stifles Desdemona. *Honest Iago!*

But as it finds that Othello has not stifled Desdemona, Iago unmasks and charges himself with the task. The day following the representation the piece is prohibited *by order.*

Certainly if we condescend for a moment to accept the ridiculous fiction that on this occasion it is care for public morality which actuates our rulers, and that shocked at the state of license into which certain theatres have fallen during the last two years, they have chosen at the end, in defiance of all laws and rights, to make an example of a work and an author—certainly if the choice of the work be singular, it must be admitted the choice of the author is not less so. Who is the man whom purblind power controls so strangely? It is a writer so placed that if his talents may be questioned by all, his character cannot be by any one. It is acknowledged that he is an honest man, proved and verified— a thing rare and to be respected just now. He is a poet whom this same licentiousness of the theatre revolted and made indignant from the first; who for the last eighteen months, on the report that the inquisition of theatres was to be equally re-established, has gone in person in the company of many other dramatic authors to warn the Minister against such a measure; and who loudly demanded a law repressive of riot in the theatre, protesting against the censorship in strong language which certainly the Minister has not forgotten. He is an artist devoted to art, who has never courted success by unworthy means, and who has all his life accustomed himself to look the public steadily in the face. He is a moderate and sincere man, who has fought more than one battle for liberty against arbitrary rule; who, in 1829, in the last year of the Restoration, refused all that the Government then offered him

to compensate for the interdict placed on *Marion de Lorme*,* and
who a year later, in 1830, the Revolution of July having taken
place, refused, against his worldly interests, to allow the performance of this same *Marion de Lorme* lest it should be the occasion
of insult and attack upon the deposed king who had prohibited it :
conduct undoubtedly quite natural, and which would have been
that of any man of honor in his place, but which, perhaps, should
have rendered him henceforth safe from censure, and in reference
to which he wrote in August, 1834 :—" The success of political allusions and sought-for scandals he avows pleases him but little.
Such success is short-lived and of little value. Besides, it is pre
cisely when there is no censorship that authors should themselves
be honest, conscientious, severe censors. Thus it is they raise the
dignity of art. When there is perfect liberty, it is becoming to
keep within bounds."

Judge now. On one side you have a man and his works ; on
the other the Minister and his actions.

Now that the pretended immorality of this drama is reduced
to a nonentity ; now that the scaffolding of false and shameful
reasons is thrown down and lies under our feet, it is time to notice
the true motives of the measure, the motive of the ante-chamber,
the motive of the Court, the secret motive which is not told, the
motive that cannot be avowed even to themselves, the motive that
has been so well hidden under a pretext. This motive has already
transpired to the public, and the public has divined correctly. We
shall say no more about it. It may be useful to our cause that
we offer to our adversaries an example of courtesy and moderation.
It is right that a lesson of dignity and good sense should be given
to the Government by an individual, by him who was persecuted
to the persecutor. Besides, we are not of those who think to cure
their own wounds by poisoning the sores of others. It is but too
true that in the third act of this piece there is a line in which
the ill-placed cleverness of some of the intimates of the palace has
discovered an allusion (mark a moment—an allusion !) of which
neither the public nor the author had dreamed until then, but
which, once denounced in this manner, becomes the most cruel
of injuries. It is but too true that this verse sufficed for the
order that in announcements concerning the Théâtre Français the
seditious little phrase of *Le Roi s'Amuse*, should never again be
allowed to satisfy the curiosity of the public. We shall not cite
here this verse, which is as red-hot iron, we shall not even indicate
it, save in a last extremity should they be so imprudent as to drive
us there for our defence. We will not cause the revival of old

---

* In allusion to the offer of Charles the Tenth to grant the author a fresh
pension of 4,000 francs as compensation for the suppression of *Marion de
Lorme*.—TRANS.

historic scandals. We will spare as much as possible a personage in a high position the consequences of this stupidity of courtiers. One may make war generously even on a king. We wish to do thus. Only let the powerful ones reflect on the inconvenience it is to have for a friend the brute who only knows how to crush with the paving-stone of censorship the microscopic allusions which have just been placed before their faces.

We cannot even tell if in this conflict we shall not feel indulgent towards the Minister himself. The whole thing, to speak the truth, inspires us with pity. The Government of July is as yet but new born, it is but thirty months old, and is still in its cradle; it has the little furies of babyhood. Does it deserve that we should spend on it much manly anger? When it is grown up we shall see about that.

However, to look at the question for a moment only from the private point of view, the censorial confiscation of which he complains does more harm, perhaps, to the author of this drama than a like injury could do to any other dramatist. Indeed, during the fourteen years that he has written, not one of his works has escaped the unlucky honor of being chosen on its appearance for a battle-field, and which has not at first, for a longer or shorter period, been obscured by the dust, and the smoke, and the noise of the conflict. Thus, when he produces a piece at the theatre—not being able to hope for a calm audience on the first night—that which concerns him most is a series of representations. If it happens that on the first occasion his voice is drowned in the tumult and his ideas are not comprehended, the following representations may correct first impressions. *Hernani* has been performed fifty-three times, *Marion de Lorme* sixty-one; *Le Roi s'Amuse*, thanks to Ministerial oppression, has only been represented once. Assuredly the wrong done to the author is great. Who can render to him exactly what this third experience—so important to him—might have brought? Who can tell him what might have followed that first performance? Who can restore that public of the next day—a public usually impartial—the public that is without friendships and without enmities, that teaches the poet, and that the poet teaches?

The period of political transition in which we now are is curious. It is one of those moments of general weariness when all acts of despotism are possible, even in a society infiltrated by ideas of emancipation and liberty. France moved fast in July, 1830; she did three days' good work; she made three great advances in the field of civilization and progress. Now in the march of progress many are harassed, many are out of breath, many require to halt. They would hold back those generous, unwearying spirits who do not falter, who still go on. They would wait for the tardy who remain behind, and give them time to join us. There is a singular fear in these of all that advances, of all that stirs, of all that protests, of all who think. A strange frame of mind, easy to comprehend, difficult to define. These are the beings who are afraid of new ideas. It is the league of interests that are ruffled by theories. It is commerce frightened at systems; it is the merchant who wants to sell; it is tumult which terrifies the counting-house; it is the shopkeeper armed to defend himself.

In our opinion Government makes use of this let-alone disposition and fear of revolutionary novelties. It stoops to petty tyrannies. All this is bad for it and for us. If it believes that there is now a feeling of indifference to liberal ideas it deceives itself; there is only a certain weariness. Some day it will be called severely to account for the illegal acts which have accumulated for some time past. What a life it has led us! Two years ago we feared for order, now we tremble for liberty. Questions of free thought, intelligence, and art are imperiously quelled by the viziers of the king of the barricades. It is indeed melancholy to see how the revolution of July is terminating, *mulier formosa superne.*

Certainly if one reflects of how little consequence the work or the author under consideration is, the Ministerial measure against them is of no great importance. It is only a mischievous little blow to literature, which has no other merit than not being too unlike numerous arbitrary acts of which it is the sequel. But if we take a loftier view we shall see that it does not only affect this play and this poet, but, as we said from the first, the rights of liberty and property are both entirely concerned in the question. These are great and serious interests: and though the author is obliged to associate this affair with the simple commercial interests of the Théâtre Français—not being able to attack directly the Minister barricaded behind the plea of being a counsellor of state— he hopes that his cause will appear to every one a great cause on the day when it shall be presented at the bar of the consular tribunal, with liberty on the right hand and property on the left. He will speak himself, if need be, in aid of the independence of his art. He will plead for his rights firmly, with gravity and simplicity, without hatred or fear of any one. He counts on the co-operation of all, on the frank and cordial support of the press, on the justice of public opinion, on the equity of tribunals. He will succeed. He doubts it not. The state of siege will be raised in the city of literature as in the city politic.

When this shall be done, when he shall have brought to his home intact, inviolate, and sacred the liberty of a poet and a citizen, he will again set himself peaceably to the work of his life, from which he has been so violently forced, and from which he would not willingly abstain for a moment. He has his task before him, he knows it, and nothing shall distract him from it. For the moment political work comes to him; he has not sought, but he accepts it. Truly the power which encounters us will not have gained much when we indignant and offended artists quit our conscientious, peaceful, earnest and sacred work—our work of the past and of the future—to mix ourselves with an irreverent and scoffing assembly, who for fifteen years have watched, amid hooting and whistling, the wretched political bunglers who imagined they were building a social edifice because every day, with great trouble, sweating and panting, they wheeled a heap of legal projects from the Tuileries to the Palais-Bourbon, and from the Palais-Bourbon to the Luxembourg!

November 30th, 1832.

PERSONAGES OF THE DRAMA.

FRANCIS THE FIRST.
TRIBOULET, *The Court Jester*.
MONS. ST. VALLIER.
MONS. DES GORDES.
MONS. DE PIENNE.
MONS. DE LATOUR LANDRY.
MONS. DE VIC.
MONS. DE PARDAILLAN.
MONS. DE COSSÉ.
MONS. DE BRION.
MONS. DE MONTMORENCY.
MONS. DE MONTCHENU.
MAÎTRE CLEMENT MAROT, *The Court Poet*.
SALTABADIL, *A Bravo*.

BLANCHE, *Daughter to Triboulet*.
DAME BERARDE, *A Duenna*.
MAGUELONNE, *Sister to Saltabadil*.
MADAME DE COSSÉ.

A Messenger from the Queen.
A Servant of the King.
A Surgeon.
Courtiers, Ladies, Servants.

THE KING'S DIVERSION.

ACT FIRST : MONS. DE ST. VALLIER.

SCENE 1.—*The stage represents a Fête at the Louvre. A magnificent suite of apartments crowded with nobles and ladies of the court in full costume. There are lights, music, dancing, and shouts of laughter. Servants hand refreshments in vessels of porcelain and gold. Groups of guests pass and repass across the stage. The fête draws to an end, daylight peeps through the windows. The architecture, the furniture, and the dresses belong to the style of the Renaissance.*

The KING *as painted by* Titian.—MONS. DE LA TOUR LANDRY.

THE KING.

I'll ne'er relinquish the adventurous chase
Till it give forth the fruit of so much toil.
Plebeian though she be ! of rank obscure,
Her birth unknown, her very name concealed :
What then ? These eyes ne'er gazed on one so fair.

LA TOUR.

And this bright city goddess still you meet
At holy mass ?

THE KING.

        At St. Germain des Prês
As sure as Sunday comes.

LA TOUR.

            Your amorous flame
Dates two months since. You've tracked the game to earth.

THE KING.

Near Bussy's Terrace, where De Cossé dwells,
She lives immured.

LA TOUR.

I think I know the spot,
That is, the outside. Not, perchance, so well
As doth your Majesty the heaven within.

THE KING.

Nay, there you flatter; entrance is denied.
A beldam fierce, who keeps eyes, ears, and tongue
Under her guidance, watches ever there.

LA TOUR.

Indeed !

THE KING.

And then, oh mystery most rare !
As evening falls, a strange unearthly form,
Whose features night conceals, enshrouded close
In mantle dark, as for some guilty deed,
Doth glide within.

LA TOUR.

Then do thou likewise.

THE KING.

Nay.

The house is barred and isolate from all.

LA TOUR.

At least the fair one, with such patience wooed,
Hath shewn some signs of life.

THE KING.

I do confess,
If glances speak the soul, those witching eyes
Proclaim no hatred insurmountable.

LA TOUR.

Knows she a monarch loves ?

THE KING.

Impossible!
A homely garb, a student's woollen dress
Conceals my quality.

LA TOUR.

Oh, virtuous love !

That burns with such a pure undying flame.
I warrant me 'tis some sly Abbé's mistress.
    (*Enter* TRIBOULET, *and a number of courtiers.*)

THE KING.

Hush! some one comes!
    (*Aloud to* TRIBOULET, *as he approaches.*)
                        Silence his lips must seal
Whose love would prosper!—Have I said aright?

TRIBOULET.

To shade the fragile vase, glass lends its veil;
Thus flimsy mystery hides love more frail.

SCENE 2.—*The* KING, TRIBOULET, M. DE GORDES, *and many
    other Gentlemen, superbly dressed.* TRIBOULET *is in the
    dress of the Court Fool, as painted by Bonifacio. The*
    KING *turns to admire a group of Ladies.*

LA TOUR.

Madame de Vendome looks, to-night, divine.

DE GORDES.

Fair D'Albe and Montchevreuil blaze like twin stars.

THE KING.

Now, in my eyes, De Cossé's charming wife
Outshines all three.

DE GORDES (*Pointing to* M. DE COSSÉ, *surnamed* LE BRAN-
    TOME, *one of the four fattest gentlemen of France*).
                        Hush! hush, your majesty!
Unless you mean this for a husband's ear.

THE KING.

Why, for that matter, Count, i'faith I care not.

DE GORDES.

He'll tell the fair Diana.

THE KING.
                        What care I?
[*The* KING *retires to speak to some ladies at the
    back of the stage.*

TRIBOULET (*to* M. DE GORDES).

The King will anger Dian of Poitiers.
For eight long days he holds not converse with her.

DE GORDES.

Will he restore her to her husband's arms?

TRIBOULET.

Indeed, I hope not.

DE GORDES.
            She hath paid in full
A guilty ransom for her father's life.

TRIBOULET.

Ah! apropos, now, of St. Vallier.—
'Tis a most strange and singular old man:
How could he think to join in nuptial bond
His daughter Dian, radiant as the light,
(An angel sent by Heaven to bless this earth),
With an ill-favored hunch-backed seneschal?

DE GORDES.

'Tis an old fool—a pale and grave old man.
When pardon came, I stood beside the block,—
Aye, nearer much than now I do to thee,—
Yet said he nothing, but "God bless the King!"
And now he's quite distraught!

THE KING (*passing across with* MADAME DE COSSÉ).
                  Unkind! so soon?

MADAME DE COSSÉ.

My husband takes me with him to Soissons.

THE KING.

Oh! 'tis a sin! Paris forbids thy flight—
Paris, where wits and courtiers languish all
With melting tenderness and fond desires—
Where duellists and poets ever keep
Their keenest thrusts, their brightest thoughts for thee:
For thee, whose glances, winning every heart,
Warn each fair dame to watch her lover well;
Dazzling our court with such a flood of light.

Thy sun once set, we ne'er shall think 'tis day.
Canst thou abandon kings and emperors,
Dukes, princes, peers, and condescend to shine
(Thou star of town!) in a vile country heaven?

Madame de Cossé.

Be calm.

The King.

As though some sacrilegious hand
Amidst the brightest splendor of the dance
Had from the ball-room torn the chandelier.

Madame De Cossé.

My jealous lord!
(*She points to her husband approaching, and runs away.*)

The King.

The devil claim his soul!
(*Turning to* Triboulet.)
But I have penned a sonnet to his wife.
Has Marot shewn thee those last rhymes of mine?

Triboulet.

I never read your verses,—royal strains
Are always vile.

The King.
Oh, bravo!

Triboulet.

Let the herd
Rhyme love with dove—'tis their vocation thus;
Monarchs, with beauty, take a different course;
Make love, oh sire, and let Marot make verse—
It but degrades a king.

The King.
[*Sees* Madame de Coslin, *to whom he turns, leaving*
Triboulet. (*To* Triboulet.)
I'd have thee whipped,
If fair de Coslin did not tempt me hence.

Triboulet (*aside*).
Another still! Oh, fickle as the wind
That blows thee to her.

DE GORDES (*approaching* TRIBOULET).
     · By the other door
Madame de Cossé comes! I pledge my faith
She drops some token, that the amorous king
May turn to raise it.

TRIBOULET.
          Let's observe awhile.
(MADAME DE COSSÉ *drops her bouquet.*)

DE GORDES.
I said so !

TRIBOULET.
          Excellent !
[*The* KING *leaves* MADAME DE COSLIN, *picks up the
     bouquet, and presents it to* MADAME DE COSSÉ,
     with whom he enters into a lively conversation,
     apparently of a tender nature.*

DE GORDES.
          The bird's re-snared !

TRIBOULET.
Woman's a devil of most rare perfection !
[*The* KING *whispers* MADAME DE COSSÉ—*she laughs.
     Suddenly* M. DE COSSÉ *draws near, coming from
     the back of the stage.* DE GORDES *remarks it to*
     TRIBOULET.

DE GORDES.
Her husband !
[MADAME DE COSSÉ *sees her husband—disengages her-
     self from the* KING, *and runs off.*

MADAME DE COSSÉ.
          Leave me !

TRIBOULET.
                    What a jealous fright
Shakes his fat side, and wrinkles o'er his brow.
(*The* KING *who has been helped to wine comes forward.*)

THE KING.
Oh happy hours ! Why, Jupiter himself,
And Hercules, were two poor senseless fools,

Compared to me! 'Tis woman gilds this earth.
I am all happiness!—and thou? (*To* Triboulet.)

Triboulet.

All joy!
I laugh at balls, pomps, follies, guilty loves;
And sneer whilst you enjoy. Yet both are blest:
You as a King, and as a hunchback I.

The King.

De Cossé damps the fête; but let that pass.
How does he look now, think you?
(*Pointing to* De Cossé, *who is leaving the palace.*)

Triboulet.

Like an ass!

The King.

Nought plagues me save this corpulent old Count;
Mine is the power to do,—to wish!—to have!
Oh, Triboulet, what pleasure 'tis to live!—
The world's so happy!

Triboulet (*aside*).

And the King is drunk.

The King.

Ah, there again! What arms!—what lips!—what eyes!

Triboulet.

Madame de Cossé?

The King (*to* Triboulet).

Take thou charge of me.

The King (*sings*).

"Paris, bright and gay,
Nowhere is thy fellow—
All thy girls are ripe—"

Triboulet (*sings*).

"And all thy men are mellow."

[*Exit* King *and* Triboulet.

Scene 3.—*Enter* Mons. De Gordes, Pardaillan, De Vic,
Maître Clement Marot, *the Poet; after them* M. De
Pienne, *and* De Cossé—(*they salute*).

De Pienne.

Most noble friends, a novelty I bring—
A riddle that would cheat the shrewdest brain;
A something comic, wonderful, sublime;
A tale of love! a thing impossible!

De Gordes.

What is't?

Marot.
What would'st thou, noble Sir?

De Pienne.

Marot, I tell thee, thou'rt a mighty fool.

Marot.

Mighty! I ne'er did think myself in aught.

De Pienne.

I read in your last poem of "Peschére"
These lines on Triboulet: "One marked for scorn—
As wise at thirty as the day when born."
Thou art the fool!

Marot.
May Cupid stop my breath,

If I can take you.

De Pienne.
Hark ye, now, De Gordes,

And you, De Pardaillan, I pray ye, guess,
Something most strange has chanced to Triboulet.

De Pardaillan.

He's become straight.

De Cossé.
Or Constable of France.

MAROT.

Or cooked and served up at the royal table.

De PIENNE.

No!—droller still, he has—(you ne'er can guess—
The thing's incredible).

De PARDAILLAN.

Perhaps an ape
More ugly than himself.

MAROT.

His starving purse
Grown plethoric with gold.

De COSSÉ.

The fitting place
Of turnspit dog.

MAROT.

A billet-doux to meet
The blessed Virgin, up in Paradise.

De GORDES.

Perhaps a soul!

De PIENNE.

Ye ne'er will strike the mark.
The buffoon, Triboulet, uncouth, deformed—
Guess what he has! Come! something monstrous! Guess!

MAROT.

His hump!

De PIENNE.

Nay! nay! ye're dull.—Now listen all!
A mistress!!!   (*All burst into a fit of laughter.*)

MAROT.

Duke, your wit o'ershoots its aim.

De GORDES.

A scurvy joke!

De PIENNE.

I'll swear it, by my soul!
I'll bring you even to the lady's door

Each night he enters, shrouded in his cloak
With air most sombre—like some hungry bard
By happiest chance I spied the quarry out,
Prowling myself hard by De Cossé's gate.
Now keep my secret: I've a scheme to plague him.

MAROT.

A sonnet!—" Triboulet to Cupid changed!
Yet this much I'll engage! should ever more
Another Bedford land on France's shore,
The English foes would dare our arms in vain,
The lady's face would fright them back again."

[*All laugh*—M. DE VIC *drawing near*—DE PIENNE *puts
his finger to his lips.*

DE PIENNE.

Silence, my Lords!

DE PARDAILLAN.

How comes it that the King
Roams every night alone, as though he sought
Some amorous quest.

DE PIENNE (*to* DE VIC).

De Vic will tell us that.

DE VIC.

Just now the wind of his caprice doth sit
To wander forth, in hood and cloak disguised,
That none can know him! If the night's so dark,
He doth mistake some window for a door,
Why (not being married) 'tis no care of mine.

DE COSSÉ.

Ah! who would own a sister, child, or wife?
The King robs others of the joys he takes,
And for his pleasure, makes another's woe.
The laughing mouth has fangs most sharp within.

DE VIC (*to* DE PIENNE *and* MAROT).

He trembles at the King.

DE PIENNE (*aside*).

His pretty wife
Feels no alarm.

Marot (*aside*).
'Tis that which frightens him.

De Gordes (*aloud*).
You're wrong, De Cossé; 'tis a courtier's task
To keep the King kind, liberal and gay.

De Pienne.
Amen, say I :—a melancholy king
Is like long mourning or a backward spring.

Scene 4.—*Enter the* King *and* Triboulet.

Triboulet.
Scholars at Court! Monstrosity most rare!

The King.
Go preach unto my sister of Navarre,
She'd set me round with pedants!

Triboulet.
                          Sire, at least
You'll own I've drunk a somewhat less than you,
And therefore crave I to decide this matter
In all its points, shapes, hues, and qualities.
I've one advantage, nay, I'll reckon two.
First, I am sober, next, I'm not a king.
Rather than summon scholars to the court,
Bring plague and famine!

The King.
                          Yet my sister strives
To fill my court with scholars.

Triboulet.
                          Most unkind
Upon a sister's part.—Believe me, Sire,
There's not in nature's strange menagerie,
Nor hungry wolf, nor crow, nor fox, nor dog,
Nor famished poet, heretic nor Turk,
Nor hideous owl, nor bear, nor creeping sloth
One half so hungry, hideous, filthy, foul,
Puffed with conceits and strange absurdities,

As that same animal, yclept a scholar.
Have you not pleasures, conquests, boundless power,
And (shedding light and perfume over all)
Enchanting woman ?

THE KING.

Marguerite avers
That woman's love may tempt me not for long,
And when it palls—

TRIBOULET.

Oh medicine most strange !
Prescribe a pedant, for a heart that's cloyed.
The Lady Marguerite, 'tis widely known,
Was ever famed for desperate remedies.

THE KING.

I'll have no scholars,—poets might be borne.

TRIBOULET.

Now, were I king, I'd loathe a poet more
Than Beelzebub doth sign of holy cross.

THE KING.

But some half dozen !

TRIBOULET.

'Tis a stable full,—
A whole menagerie. We've quite enough
Of Marot here, without being poison'd quite
With flimsy rhymesters.

MAROT.

Thank you, good buffoon,—
(*Aside*) The fool were wiser had he held his tongue.

TRIBOULET.

Be beauty still your heaven; 'tis the Sun
Whose smiles illumine earth. Ne'er clog your brain
With books.

THE KING.

Nay, by the faith, now, of a gentleman
For books care I as much as fish for apples.

[*Shouts of laughter are heard from a group of courtiers behind.*

Methinks, good fool, they're merry at thy cost.

TRIBOULET (*draws near to the group, listens, and returns*)
Another fool they laugh at!

THE KING.
Aye! whom, then?

TRIBOULET.
The King!!

THE KING.
At me?

TRIBOULET.
Yes, Sire, they call you mean :
Say gold and honors fly into Navarre,
Whilst they get nothing.

THE KING.
Now, I note them well!
Montmorency, Brion, and Montchenû.

TRIBOULET.
Exactly so.

THE KING.
Ungrateful, selfish hounds!
One I made admiral,—constable the next,
And Montchenû my master of the horse;—
Yet they complain!

TRIBOULET.
Why, 'tis not quite enough;
They still deserve something at your hands :—
Best do it quickly, Sire.

THE KING.
Do what?

TRIBOULET.
Hang up all three.

DE PIENNE (*pointing to* TRIBOULET, *and speaking to the three*
Courtiers).
You heard him?

De Biron (*to* De Pienne).
Aye, indeed.

Montmorency (*to* De Pienne).
He smarts for this.

Triboulet (*to the* King).
Your heart methinks must feel a painful void,
Knowing, amongst these yielding fair, not one
Whose eyes invite not, yet whose soul could love.

The King.
What knowest *thou* of this?

Triboulet.
The love of one,
Whose heart hath lost the bloom of innocence,
Is love no longer.

The King.
Art thou then so sure
I have not found one woman who can love?

Triboulet.
Thy rank unknown?

The King (*assenting*).
Unknown!! (*aside*) I'll not betray
My little beauty of De Bussy's Terrace.

Triboulet.
Some city belle!

The King.
Why not?

Triboulet (*with agitation*).
Oh Sire, beware!
Your love runs hazards that it dreams not of;
These citizens, in wrath, are fierce as Romans.
Who takes their goods may leave a life in pledge:
We kings and fools still satisfied should be
With the fair wives and sisters of our friends.

The King.   ·
Methinks De Cossé's wife would suit me well.

TRIBOULET.

Then take her.

THE KING.

Marry, 'tis a hopeless thing;
Easy to say,—to do, impossible ! !

TRIBOULET.

Command it, Sire, this very night 'tis done.

THE KING (*pointing to* DE COSSÉ).

Her jealous Husband,—

TRIBOULET.

Send to the Bastille !

THE KING.

Oh, no !

TRIBOULET.

Well, then, to balance the account,
Create him Duke.

THE KING.

His vulgar jealousy
Might still rebel and trumpet forth his wrongs.

TRIBOULET.

He must be banished then or bought. Yet stay !
[*Whilst* TRIBOULET *is speaking,* DE COSSÉ *comes up
and overhears the rest of the speech.*
There is one method, simple and concise,—
'Tis strange it stepped not first into my mind ;—
Cut off his head ! ! [DE COSSÉ *starts back with affright.*
Involve him in some plot—
Some scheme to help the arms of Spain or Rome.

DE COSSÉ (*coming between*).

Infernal villain !

THE KING (*to* TRIBOULET).

Nay, now, think again ;
Cut off a head like that,—impossible !

TRIBOULET.

What, be a king, yet foiled in a caprice,—
A paltry trifle such as this denied.

DE COSSÉ (*to* TRIBOULET).
I'll have thee beaten.

TRIBOULET.
Nay, I fear thee not:
A war of words on all around I wage,
And care for nothing, whilst my neck doth bear
The sacred head and cap-piece of the fool.
But one thing fear I,—that my hump might fall
And plant itself in front, as thou dost wear it:
'Twould quite disfigure me!

DE COSSÉ (*overcome with rage, draws his sword*).
Ill-manner'd slave!

THE KING.
Be wiser, Count! Come hither, fool, with me!
[*Exeunt* KING *and* TRIBOULET *laughing.*

(*The* COURTIERS *assemble after the* KING *has retired.*)

DE BRION.
Vengeance on Triboulet!

MAROT.
He's too well armed;
How can we strike, or where inflict the blow?

DE PIENNE.
I have it, gentlemen; the wrongs of all
Shall be avenged in full. When evening falls
Meet me, well armed, at Bussy's Terrace wall,
Near to De Cossé's gate; ask nought beside.

MAROT.
I guess thy scheme.

DE PIENNE.
Be silent all; he comes!

TRIBOULET (*aside*).
Whom next to trick?—the King? By Heaven! 'twere
great!
[*Enter a servant in the* KING's *livery, who whispers
to* TRIBOULET.

SERVANT.

Monsieur St. Vallier (an infirm old man
In deepest mourning) asks to see the King.

TRIBOULET.

(*Aside*) The Devil!—(*aloud*) Oh certainly; most glad to
see
Monsieur St. Vallier.   [*Exit Servant.*
(*Aside*) Excellent, by Jove!
This is a joke that makes all others tame—
(*There is a noise and confusion at the door of entrance.*)

VOICE OUTSIDE.

I'll see the King!

THE KING (*stopping short in his attentions to a group of
ladies.*)
Who dares to enter here!

VOICE OUTSIDE.

I'll see the King!

THE KING.

No! no!
[*An old man in deep mourning, with white hair and
beard, bursts through the crowd at the back of
the stage, and confronts the* KING, *gazing steadily upon him.*

SCENE 5.—*The* KING, ST. VALLIER, TRIBOULET *and the*
COURTIERS.

ST. VALLIER.

I will be heard!
Who dare restrain me?

THE KING (*appalled*).
Monsieur St. Vallier!

ST. VALLIER.

'Tis thus I'm named!
[*The* KING *advances angrily towards him, but is
stopped by* TRIBOULET.

TRIBOULET.

Permit *me*, Sire, to speak.
I will so bravely lecture this good man !
[*Puts himself in a theatrical attitude, and addresses*
St Vallier.

TRIBOULET.

Sir ! you once stirred rebellion 'gainst our throne ;
We pardoned, as kind monarch should ; yet now
A stranger, wilder madness takes your mind,—
You seek for offspring from a son-in-law
As hideous as the vilest dwarf e'er known,
Ill-shaped, ill-bred, pale, ghastly, and deformed,
An odious wart upon his monstrous nose,
A shape like that ! (*pointing to* De Cossé)
    An ugly hump like mine !
Who sees your daughter near him, needs must laugh.
(Unless our King had interfered), he might
Have made rare specimens of grandsons for you,
Diseased, unseemly, ricketty, misshaped,
Swoll'n like that gentleman,
   [*pointing to* De Cossé, *who writhes with anger.*
     Or humped like me.
Bah ! he's too ugly ;—now, our noble King
Will give you grandsons, that may be your pride,
To climb your knee and pluck your reverend beard !
   [*The* Courtiers *laugh and applaud* Triboulet.

St. Vallier.

'Tis but one insult more ;—now hear *me*, Sire,
A king should listen when his subjects speak :
'Tis true, your mandate led me to the block,
Where pardon came upon me like a dream ;
I blessed you then, unconscious as I was
That a king's mercy, sharper far than death,
To save a father doomed his child to shame ;
Yes, without pity for the noble race
Of Poitiers, spotless for a thousand years,
You, Francis of Valois, without one spark
Of love or pity, honor or remorse

Did on that night, (thy couch her virtue's tomb,)
With cold embraces, foully bring to scorn
My helpless daughter, Dian of Poitiers.
To save her father's life, a knight she sought,
Like Bayard, fearless and without reproach.
She found a heartless king, who sold the boon,
Making cold bargain for his child's dishonor.
Oh! monstrous traffic! foully hast thou done!
My blood was thine, and justly, tho' it springs
Amongst the best and noblest names of France;
But to pretend to spare these poor gray locks,
And yet to trample on a weeping woman,
Was basely done; the father was thine own,
But not the daughter!—thou hast overpassed
The right of monarchs!—yet, 'tis mercy deemed,
And I, perchance, am called ungrateful still.
Oh, hadst thou come within my dungeon walls,
I would have sued upon my knees for death,
But mercy for my child, my name, my race,
Which, once polluted, is my race no more;
Rather than insult, death to them and me.
I come not now to ask her back from thee;
Nay, let her love thee with insensate love;
I take back nought that bears the brand of shame.
Keep her!—Yet still amidst thy festivals,
Until some father's, brother's, husband's hand,*
('Twill come to pass,) shall rid us of thy yoke,
My pallid face shall ever haunt thee there,
To tell thee, Francis, it was foully done!
And thou shalt listen, and thy guilty pride
Shall shrink abashed before me; would you now
Command the headsman's axe to do its office, ·
You dare not, lest my spectre should return
To tell thee——

* According to ancient writers, St. Vallier's prophecy was terribly fulfilled.
The death of Francis the First affords a melancholy illustration of the morals
of the "good old times." Whether the story be the record of history, or the
invention of slander, we have only to choose between the malignity of the
falsehood, or the infamy of the fact. A sad alternative for the believer in
the supremacy of the past.—F. L. S.

THE KING.

Madness! (*To* DE PIENNE.)

Duke.! arrest the traitor.

TRIBOULET (*sneering at* ST. VALLIER).
The poor man raves.

ST. VALLIER.

Accursed be ye both!
Oh, Sire! 'tis wrong upon the dying lion
To loose thy dog! (*turns to* TRIBOULET)
And thou, whoe'er thou art,
That with a fiendish sneer and viper's tongue,
Makest my tears a pastime and a sport,
My curse upon thee!—Sire, thy brow doth bear
The gems of France!—on mine, old age doth sit;
Thine decked with jewels, mine with these gray hairs;
We both are Kings, yet bear a different crown;
And should some impious hand upon thy head
Heap wrongs and insult, with thine own strong arm
Thou canst avenge them!—GOD AVENGES MINE!

[ST. VALLIER *is led off—the curtain falls.*

ACT SECOND : SALTABADIL.

SCENE 1.—*The scene represents a deserted corner of De Bussy Terrace. On the right a house of decent appearance, with a court-yard in front (surrounded by a wall), which forms a part of the stage. In the court are some trees, and a stone seat. A door opens from the wall into the street. Above the wall is a terrace, with a roof supported by arches. A door from the first floor of the house opens upon this terrace, which communicates with the court by a flight of steps. On the left are the high walls of the De Cossé Palace, and in the background, distant houses and the steeple of St. Severin.*

TRIBOULET, SALTABADIL; *afterwards* DE PIENNE *and* DE GORDES.

[TRIBOULET *is enveloped in his cloak, but without his buffoon's dress—he advances cautiously towards the door in the wall. A man dressed in black, and likewise wrapped in a cloak (from beneath which the point of a sword peeps out), follows him stealthily.*

TRIBOULET (*lost in thought*).
The old man cursed me.

SALTABADIL (*accosting him*).
Sir !

TRIBOULET.
[*Starts, turns round, and searching in his pockets, says angrily,*
I've nothing for you.

SALTABADIL.
And nothing asked I : you mistake !

TRIBOULET (*irritated*).
Then leave me.

SALTABADIL (*bowing and touching his long sword*).
You wrong me, Sir.—By my good sword, I live.

TRIBOULET (*drawing back alarmed*).
A cut-throat!

[*Enter* DE PIENNE *and* DE GORDES, *who remain watching at the back of the stage.*

SALTABADIL (*in an insinuating manner*).
Something weighs upon your mind :
Night after night you haunt this lonely spot—
Confess the truth, some woman claims your care !

TRIBOULET.
That which concerns but me, I tell to none.

SALTABADIL.
But 'tis for your advantage that I speak ;
You'd treat me better if you knew me well.
(*Whispers.*)   Perhaps your mistress on another smiles,—
You're jealous, Sir ?

TRIBOULET.
By all the fiends, what want ye ?

SALTABADIL (*in a low voice, speaking softly and quickly*).
For some broad pieces, by this hand he dies !

TRIBOULET (*aside*).
I breathe again.

SALTABADIL.
I see you deem me now
An honest man.

TRIBOULET.
At least a useful one !

SALTABADIL (*with an assumption of modesty*).
Guard to the honor of our Paris dames.

TRIBOULET.
Name your price to slay a cavalier.

SALTABADIL.
Why that's according to the man we slay,
With some slight guerdon for the skill displayed.

TRIBOULET.

To stab a nobleman?

SALTABADIL.

By Beelzebub !
There's too much risk of a slashed doublet there :
Cunning in fence, and armed, your nobleman
Is dear indeed !

TRIBOULET (*laughing*).

Your nobleman is dear;
And pray, do citizens by your kind aid
Each other slaughter ?

SALTABADIL.

Yes; in truth they do;
But 'tis a luxury—a taste you know
That's scarcely fit, but for the man well born.
Some upstarts are there (being rich forsooth),
That ape the habits of a gentleman,
And force my service,—How I pity them !
I'm paid one half beforehand, and the rest
When the deed's done !

TRIBOULET.

For this you brave the rack ?

SALTABADIL (*smiling*).

Not much ! a tribute paid to the police !

TRIBOULET.

So much per head ?

SALTABADIL.

Just so ! unless indeed—
(What shall I say ?) unless the King were slain !

TRIBOULET.

And how contrive you ?

SALTABADIL.

In the street I slay,
Or else at home !

TRIBOULET.

In a most courteous way ?

SALTABADIL.

If in the street—a sharp keen blade I wear,
And watch my man at night.

TRIBOULET.
                                        And if at home?

SALTABADIL.

Why then my sister Maguelonne assists—
A sprightly girl—that in the streets by night
Doth dance for gain, and, with enticing smiles,
Allures our prey, and draws the game to earth.

TRIBOULET.
I see!

SALTABADIL.

  'Tis managed without noise or stir,
Quite decently! Nay, most respectably.
Now let me crave your patronage, good Sir;
You'll be contented, tho' I keep no shop,
Nor make parade; I am not of that race
Of coward cut-throats, armed from head to heel,
Who herd in bands to take a single life—
Wretches! with courage shorter than their sword.
              [*Drawing an enormously long sword.*
This is my weapon! (TRIBOULET *starts.*)
(*Smiling and bowing to* TRIBOULET.) At your service, Sir!

TRIBOULET.
Just now, indeed, I've no occasion for it.

SALTABADIL.

So much the worse! You'll find me, when you list,
Before the palace of the Duke of Maine.
At noon each day I take my morning's stroll:
My name's Saltabadil!

TRIBOULET.
                        Of gipsy race?

SALTABADIL.
Burgundian too!

DE GORDES (*to* DE PIENNE, *taking out his tablets*).
            A jewel of a man.
Whose name (lest I forget) at once I write.

SALTABADIL.
Sir, you'll not think the worse of me for this?

TRIBOULET.
What for! why should I? every one must live.

SALTABADIL.
I would not be a beggar, idler, rogue!
Then I've four children.

TRIBOULET.
          Whom 'twere barbarous
To leave unfed.   [*Trying to get rid of him.*
Heaven keep you in its love!

DE PIENNE (*to* DE GORDES).
'Tis still too light! Return we here anon.
          [*Exeunt* DE PIENNE *and* DE GORDES.

TRIBOULET (*roughly to* SALTABADIL).
Good day!

SALTABADIL (*bowing*).
Your humble servant, Sir. Adieu!   [*Exit.*

TRIBOULET (*watching him as he retires*).
How much alike his cruel trade to mine;—
His sword is sharp, but with a tongue more keen
I stab the heart! Aye, deeper far than he.

SCENE 2.—TRIBOULET (*alone*).

[SALTABADIL *having departed,* TRIBOULET *gently opens
the door in the wall. He looks anxiously round,
and taking the key out of the lock, carefully shuts
the door on the inside. He then paces the court
with an air of melancholy and abstraction.*

TRIBOULET.
The old man cursed me! even as he spoke
I mocked and taunted him;—and yet, oh shame!
My lip but smiled. His sorrow touched my soul.
Accurst indeed!—   [*he sits down on the stone seat.*

For man with nature leagues
To make me wicked, heartless, and depraved!
Buffoon! Oh heav'n!—deformed, despised, disgraced;
Always that thought, or sleeping or awake,—
It haunts my dreams, and tortures me by day:
The vile buffoon—the wretched fool of court
Who must not, cannot, dare not, for his hire
Do aught but laugh! Oh grief! oh misery!
The poorest beggar, or the vilest slave,—
The very galley convict in his chains,
May weep and soothe his anguish with his tears.
Alas, I dare not! Oh, 'tis hard to feel
Bowed down to earth with sore infirmities;
Jealous of beauty, strength, or manly grace,—
With splendor circled, making me more sad.
In vain my wretchedness would hide from man,—
In vain my heart would sob its griefs alone.—
My patron comes,—the joyous laughing king,
Beloved of women! heedless of the tomb;
Well shapen, handsome, King of France,—and young,
And with his foot he spurns me as I hide;
And, yawning, cries, "Come, make me laugh, buffoon."
Alas, poor fool!—and yet am I a man,
And rancorous hate, and pride, and baffled rage,
Boil in my brain and make my soul like hell.
Ceaseless I meditate some dark design,
Yet, feeling, nature, thought, must I conceal,
And at my master's sign make sport for all.
Abjection base! where'er I move to feel
My foot encumbered with its galling chain.
By men avoided, loathed, and trampled on;—
By women treated as a harmless dog.
Soh! gallant courtiers and brave gentlemen,
Oh, how I hate you!—here behold your foe;
Your bitter sneers I pay you back with scorn,
And foil and countermine your proud desires.
Like the bad spirit, in your master's ear
I whisper death to each aspiring aim,
Scattering with cruel pleasure, leaf by leaf,
The bud of hope—long ere it come to flower.

You made me wicked :—yet what grief to live
But to drop poison in the cup of joy
That others drink!—and if within my breast
One kindly feeling springs, to thrust it forth
And stun reflection with these jingling bells.
Amidst the feast, the dance, the glittering show,
Like a foul demon, seek I to destroy,
For very sport, the happiness of all,
Covering with hollow, false, malignant smile
The venomed hate, that festers at my heart.
Yet am I wretched!   [*He rises from the stone seat.*
                    No, not wretched here!
This door once past, existence comes anew :
Let me forget the world,—no past regret
Shall dim the happiness that waits me here.

                         [*He falls into a reverie.*
The old man cursed me! Why returns that thought?
Forebodes it evil? Pshaw! art mad?—for shame!

    [*He knocks at the door of the house. A young girl
    dressed in white rushes out, and throws herself
    into his arms.*

SCENE 3.—BLANCHE—TRIBOULET ; *afterwards* DAME BERARDE.

TRIBOULET.

My child!   [*He presses her to his bosom with delight.*
               Ah, place your arms around my neck ;
Come to my heart, my child! I'm happy now ;
Near thee all's joy! I live, I breathe again.

               [*He gazes at her with transport.*
More beauteous every day. Blanche, art thou well,—
Quite well? Dear Blanche! come kiss me once again.

BLANCHE.

You are so kind, dear father.

TRIBOULET.

                    No, indeed,
I do but love thee. Thou'rt my life, my blood.
Blanche, if I lost thee!—oh, the thought is death.

HUGO. VOL. V.—13

Blanche (*putting her hand on his forehead*).
What makes you sigh so heavily, my father?
Tell me your sorrows; trust your grief with me.
Have we no kindred? Where are all our friends?

Triboulet.

Daughter, thou hast none.

Blanche.

Tell me then your name.

Triboulet.

Why would'st thou know it?

Blanche.

When at dear Chinon,
The little village where I lived before,
The neighbors call'd me orphan, till you came.

Triboulet.

'Twere far more prudent to have left thee there;
But I could bear my sad, sad life no longer;
I yearned for thee—I wanted one to love me.

Blanche.

Well, if you will not tell me of yourself—

Triboulet (*not listening to her*).

You go not out?

Blanche.

Two months have I been here,
And but eight times to mass gone forth.

Triboulet.

'Tis well.

Blanche.

At least you'll tell me of my mother now?

Triboulet.

No, no, forbear to wake that chord, my child.
Let me not think upon how much I've lost;
Wert thou not here I'd deem it all a dream:
A woman different from all womankind,
Who knew me poor, deserted, sick, deformed,

Yet loved me, even for my wretchedness.
Dying, she carried to the silent tomb
The blessed secret of her sainted love :
Love, fleeter, brighter than the lightning's flash;
A ray from Paradise, illuming Hell.
Oh, earth, press lightly on that angel breast,
Where only did my sorrow find repose.
But thou art here, my child. Oh God, I thank thee !

[He bursts into tears.

Blanche.

Oh, how you weep ! indeed I cannot bear
To see you thus—it makes me wretched too.

Triboulet.

Would'st have me laugh ?

Blanche.

Dear father, pardon me.
Tell me your name,—confide your grief in me.

Triboulet.

I am thy father. Ask me not for more ;
In this great world some hate me—some despise ;
But here at least, where all is innocence,
I am thy father—loved, revered. No name
Is holier than a father's to his child.

Blanche.

Dear father !

Triboulet (*again embracing her*).

Ah, what heart responds like thine ?
I love thee, as I hate all else beside.
Sit thee down by me. Come, we'll talk of this.
Art sure thou lov'st me? Now that we are here
Together, and thy hand is clasped in mine,
Why should we speak of anything but thee?
The only joy that Heaven vouchsafes, my child !
Others have parents, brothers, loving friends,
Wives, husbands, vassals, a long pedigree
Of ancestors, and children numerous—
But I have only thee! Some men are rich,
Thou art my only treasure, Blanche! my all.

Some trust in Heaven : I trust alone in thee.
What care I now for youth, or woman's love,
For pomp or grandeur, dignities or wealth ?
These are brave things, but thou outweigh'st them all ;
Thou art my country, city, family—
My riches, happiness, religion, hope—
My universe ; I find them all in thee.
From all but thee, my soul shrinks, trembling, back.
Oh, if I lost thee ! The distracting thought
Would kill me, if it lived one instant more !
Smile on me, Blanche ! thy pretty, artless smile,
So like thy mother's ; she was artless too.—
You press your hand upon your brow, my child,
Just as she did. My soul leaps forth to thine,
Even in darkness—I can see thee still—
For thou art day, and light, and life to me

BLANCHE.

Would I could make you happy !

TRIBOULET.

Happy ! Blanche !
I am so happy when I gaze on thee—
My very heart seems bursting with delight.
    [*Passes his hand through her hair, and smiles.*
What fine dark hair ! I recollect it once
So very light ! Who would believe it now ?

BLANCHE.

Some day, before the curfew bell has tolled,
You'll let me take a walk, and see the town ?

TRIBOULET.

Oh, never, never ! Thou hast not left home
Unless with Dame Berarde ?

BLANCHE.

Oh, no !

TRIBOULET.

Beware !

BLANCHE.

Forth, but to church, I go !

TRIBOULET.

(*Aside.*) She may be seen,
Perhaps pursued, torn from me, and disgraced.
Hah! were it so! the wretched jester's daughter
There's none would pity. (*Aloud.*) I beseech thee, Blanche,
Stir not abroad.—Thou know'st not how impure,
How poisonous is the Paris air to woman:
How heartless profligates infest the streets,
And courtiers baser still! (*Aside.*) Oh, Heaven, protect,
Watch o'er, preserve her from the damning snares
And touch impure, of libertines, whose breath
Hath blighted flowers pure and fair as she.
Let e'en her dreams be holy!—Here at least
Her hapless father, resting from his woes,
Shall breathe, with grateful heart, the sweet perfume
Of this fair rose of innocence and love!
[*He buries his face in his hands and bursts into tears.*

BLANCHE.

I'll think no more of going out, dear father,
But do not weep.

TRIBOULET.

These tears relieve me, child.
So much I laughed last night:—but I forget,
The hour to bear my hated yoke draws nigh.
Dear Blanche, adieu!

BLANCHE (*embracing him*).

You'll soon be here again.

TRIBOULET.

Alas, I am not master of my will.
Ho! Dame Berarde!—Whene'er I visit here
                              [*An old duenna enters.*
None see me enter?

BERARDE.

Nay, of course not, Sir!
This street's deserted!
[*It is now nearly dark, the KING appears outside the
    wall, disguised in a dark-colored dress. He ex-
    amines the high wall and closed door with
    gestures of impatience and disappointment.*

TRIBOULET.
Dearest Blanche, adieu!
(*to* DAME BERARDE).
The door towards the quay is ever closed?
I know a house more lonely e'en than this,
Near St. Germain! I'll see to it to-morrow.

BLANCHE.
The terrace, father, is so pleasant here,
Above the gardens.

TRIBOULET.
Go not there, my child!
[*He listens.*
Ha! footsteps near!
[*He goes to the gate, opens it, and looks out: the*
KING *slips into a recess in the wall near the door,*
which TRIBOULET *leaves open.*

BLANCHE (*pointing to the terrace*).
But may I not at night
Breathe the pure air?

TRIBOULET.
Alas! you might be seen.
[*Whilst he is speaking to* BLANCHE, *his back towards*
the door, the KING *slips in, unseen by all, and con-*
ceals himself behind a tree.
(*To* DAME BERARDE.)
You let no lamp from out the casement shine.

BERARDE.
Why, gracious powers! what man could enter here?
[*She turns and sees the* KING *behind the tree. Just as*
she is about to cry out, the KING *holds a purse out*
to her, which she takes, weighs in her hand, and
is silent.

BLANCHE (*to* TRIBOULET, *who has been to examine the terrace*
with a lantern.
Why dost thou look?—what fearest thou, my father?

TRIBOULET.
Nought for myself, but everything for thee.
Farewell, my child!

[*He again folds her in his arms ; a ray of light from
the lantern held by* Dame Berarde *falls upon
them.*

The King.

The Devil !—Triboulet ! (*he laughs*).
Triboulet's daughter !—why, the jest's divine.

Triboulet (*returning*).

A thought disturbes me :—when from church you come
Has no one followed thee ?

[*Blanche is confused and casts down her eyes.*

Berarde.

Oh, never, Sir !

Triboulet.

Shriek out for help, if any one molest
Or stop thy path.

Berarde.

I'd scream and call the guard.

Triboulet.

Whoever knocks, keep closed to all the door.

Berarde.

Tho' 'twere the King ?

Triboulet.

Much more if 'twere the King.
[*He embraces* Blanche *again, and goes out, carefully
shutting the door after him.*

Scene 4.—Blanche, Dame Berarde, the King.

(*During the first part of this scene the* King *still remains behind the tree.*)

Blanche.

Yet feels my heart remorse.

Berarde.

Remorse ?—for what ?

BLANCHE.

How sensitive to every fear he seems!
How every shadow darkens o'er his soul!
Ev'n as he left, his eyes were wet with tears.
Dear, good, kind father! should I not have told
How, every Sunday, when we leave the church,
He follows me!—you know!—that fine young man?

BERARDE.

Why speak of that?—already, unprovoked,
Your father's humor sets most fierce and strange;
Besides, of course, you hate this gentleman.

BLANCHE.

Hate him!—Ah, no!—Alas! I shame to say,
His image never fades upon my mind;
But from the hour when first his looks met mine,
Where'er I gaze, methinks I see him there.
Would it were so! Oh! 'tis a noble form!
So gentle, yet so bold! so proud his mien!
Methinks upon a fiery courser's back
He'd look right nobly!
    [*As* DAME BERARDE *stands near the* KING, *he puts a
        handful of gold into her hand.*

BERARDE.

            Well, he charms me too;
He's so accomplished.

BLANCHE.

            Such a man must be——

BERARDE.

Discreet and wise!

BLANCHE.

            His looks reveal his heart;
'Tis a great heart!

BERARDE.

            Oh, wonderful! immense!
    [*At every sentence that* BERARDE *speaks she holds
       out her hand to the* KING, *who puts money in it.*

THE KING AT THE FEET OF BLANCHE.

The King's Diversion.—Act II., Scene 4.

BLANCHE.

Courageous !

BERARDE.

Formidable !

BLANCHE.

Yet so kind !

BERARDE.

So tender !

BLANCHE.

Generous !

BERARDE.

Magnificent !

BLANCHE.

All that can please !

BERARDE.

His shape without a fault,—
His eyes, his nose, his forehead.

[*Holds out her hand for money at each word.*

THE KING (*aside*).

Nay, by Jove,

If she admires in detail, I'm undone :
No purse can long resist, I'm stripped of all.

BLANCHE.

I love to speak of him.

BERARDE.

I know it, child.

THE KING (*aside, giving more money*).

Oil upon fire.

BERARDE.

So tall, kind, handsome, good,
Great-hearted, generous.

KING (*aside*).

There ! She's off again.

BERARDE.

'Tis some great nobleman, his airs so grand,

His glove 1 noted, broidered on with gold.
[*The* King *makes signs when she holds out her hand,*
     that he has nothing left.

BLANCHE.

Oh no! I would not he were rich or great,
But some poor country student; for I think
He'd love me better.

BERARDE.

                    Well, it may be so,
If you prefer it! (*Aside.*) Heavens! what a taste!
These love-sick girls will move by contraries.
          [*Again holding out her hand to the* King.
(*Aloud.*) But this I'm sure, he loves you to despair.
                    [*The* King *gives nothing.*
(*Aside.*) Is he then drained! No money, Sir! no praise!

BLANCHE.

How long it seems till Sunday comes again!
Until I see him, sadness with my soul
Dwells night and day; when on the altar last
My humble gifts I placed, he seemed as though
He would have spoken. How my heart did throb!
Oh I am sure, love hath possessed him too!
My image never, never quits his mind.
Different from other men, his looks sincere
Tell me no woman fills his heart but me;
That, shunning pleasure, solitude he seeks
To think on me.

BERARDE.

[*Making a last effort, holding out her hand to the* King.
I stake my head 'tis true!

THE KING (*taking off a ring and giving it to* BERARDE).
This for *thy* head.

BLANCHE.

                    Oh, how I wish, whene'er
I think of him by day, and dream by night,
He were beside me: I would tell him then,
Be happy; oh be mine, for thee——

[*The* King *comes from behind the tree, and stretches out his arms towards her, going on his knee whilst she has her face turned from him. When she looks round again he speaks, finishing her speech.*

The King.

I love!

Say on; oh, cease not! say thou lov'st me, Blanche:
Love sounds so sweetly from a lip like thine.

Blanche (*frightened, looks round for* Dame Berarde, *who has purposely disappeared*).

Oh! I'm betrayed, alone, and none to help!

The King.

Two happy lovers are themselves a world.

Blanche.

Whence come you, Sir?

The King.

From heaven or from hell,
'Tis of no import—angel, man, or fiend,
I love thee!

Blanche.

Heavens! if my father knew.
I hope none saw you enter! Leave me, Sir!

The King.

Leave thee, whilst trembling in my arms you rest,
And I am thine, and thou art all to me!
Thou lov'st me!

Blanche (*confused*).

Oh, you listened!

The King.

'Tis most true;
What sweeter music could I listen to?

Blanche (*supplicating*).

Well, if you love, leave me for love's own sake.

The King.

Leave thee, when now my fate is linked with thine!

Twin stars, in one horizon, *doubly* bright,*
When heaven itself has chosen me to wake
Within thy virgin breast the dawn of love,
That soon shall blaze like noon! 'Tis the soul's sun;
Dost thou not feel its soft and gentle flame?
The monarch's crown, that death confers or takes,—
The cruel glory of inhuman war;
The hero's name, the rich man's vast domains,—
All these are transient, vain and earthly things.
To this poor world, where all beside doth fade,
But one pure joy remains,—'tis love! 'tis love!
Dear Blanche, such happiness I bring to thee.
Life is a flower, and love its nectared juice.
'Tis like the eagle mated with the dove,—
'Tis trembling innocence with strength allied,—
'Tis like this little hand, thus lost in mine.
Oh let us love! 　　　　　*[He embraces her, she resists.*

BLANCHE.
No! leave me!

BERARDE (*aside, peeping out from the terrace*).
　　　　　　　All goes well!
She's snared!

THE KING.
Oh, tell me thou dost love!

BERARDE.
　　　　　　(*Aside.*) The wretch!

THE KING.
Blanche, say it o'er again,

BLANCHE (*bending down her eyes*).
　　　　　　You heard me once.
You know it.

THE KING.
Then I'm happy!

---

* Victor Hugo's lines run thus:—
　　　"Quand notre double étoile au meme horizon brille!"
But as I cannot find that *double stars* were at all suspected in the days of
Francis the First, I have taken the liberty to avoid the anachronism by a slight
alteration of the text.

BLANCHE.
　　　　　I'm undone!

THE KING.

No, blest with me!

BLANCHE.
　　　　　Alas! I know you not!

Tell me your name.

BERARDE.
　　　　　(*Aside.*) High time to think of that.

BLANCHE.

You are no nobleman, no courtier, sure;
My father fears them.

THE KING.

　　　No, by heaven!—(*Aside.*) Let's see (*he deliberates*).
Godfrey Melune I'm called, a student poor,
So poor!

BERARDE (*who is just counting the money he has given her,
　　　　holds up her hand*).

　(*Aside.*) The liar!

[*Enter* DE PIENNE *and* PARDAILLAN, *they carry a dark
　lantern, and are concealed in cloaks.*

DE PIENNE (*to* PARDAILLAN).
　　　　　Here 'tis, chevalier!

BERARDE (*runs down from the terrace*).
Voices outside I hear.

BLANCHE.
　　　　　Oh, heaven! my father.

DAME BERARDE (*to the* KING).
Leave us!—away!

THE KING.
　　　　　What traitor mars my bliss?
Would that my hands were grasping at his throat!

BLANCHE (*to* BERARDE).
Quick! quick!—Oh, save him! Ope the little gate
That leads towards the quay.

THE KING.

Leave thee so soon!
Wilt love to-morrow, Blanche?

BLANCHE.

And thou?

THE KING.

For ever!

BLANCHE.

Thou may'st deceive: for I've deceived my father.

THE KING.

Never!—One kiss on those bright eyes!

BLANCHE.

No! No!

[*The* KING, *in spite of her resistance, seizes her in
his arms, and kisses her several times.*

BERARDE.

A most infuriate lover, by my soul!

[*Exit the* KING *with* BERARDE.

[BLANCHE *remains for some time with her eyes fixed
on the door through which the* KING *has passed;
she then enters the house. Meanwhile the street
is filled with* Courtiers, *armed and wearing man-
tles and masques.* DE GORDES, DE COSSÉ, DE
BRION, DE MONTMORENCY, DE MONTCHENU, *and*
CLEMENT MAROT, *join* DE PIENNE *and* PARDAIL-
LAN. *The night is very dark—the lanthorns they
carry are closed. They make signals of recog-
nition, and point out* TRIBOULET's *house. A servant attends them bearing a scaling ladder.*

SCENE 5.—BLANCHE—*the* COURTIERS. *Afterwards*
TRIBOULET.

*Blanche comes out on the terrace; she holds a flambeau in
her hand, which throws its light upon her countenance.*

BLANCHE.

Godfrey Melune! Oh, name that I adore,
Be graven on my heart!

DE PIENNE (*to the* Courtiers).
            Messieurs, 'tis she!

DE GORDES.

Some bourgeois beauty; how I pity you,
Who cast your nets amongst the vulgar throng.
        [*As he speaks,* BLANCHE *turns round, and the light
            falls full on her features.*

DE PIENNE.

What think you now?

MAROT.
            I own the jade is fair.

DE GORDES.

An angel,—fairy,—an accomplished grace.

PARDAILLAN.

Is this the mistress of our Triboulet?
The rascal!

DE GORDES.
        Scoundrel!

MAROT.
            Beauty and the Beast!
'Tis just! Old Jupiter would cross the breed.

DE PIENNE.

Enough! we came to punish Triboulet;
We are all here, determined, well prepared,
With hatred armed,—aye, and a ladder too,—
Scale we the walls, and having seized the fair,
Convey her to the Louvre! Our good king
Shall greet the beauty at his morning's levée.

DE COSSÉ.

And straightway seize her, as most lawful prey.

MAROT.

Oh, leave the Devil and Fate to settle that.

DE GORDES. .

'Tis a bright jewel, worthy of a crown.
            [*Enter* TRIBOULET *absorbed in thought.*

TRIBOULET.

Still I return,—and yet I know not why.
The old man cursed me!

> [*In the dark he runs against* DE GORDES.
> Who goes there?

DE GORDES (*runs back to the conspirators, and whispers*).

Messieurs,

'Tis Triboulet!

DE COSSÉ.

Oh, double victory!

Let's slay the traitor!

DE PIENNE.

Nay, good Count,—not so:—
Pray, how, to-morrow, could we laugh at him?

DE GORDES.

Oh, if he's killed, the joke's not half so droll.

DE COSSÉ.

He'll spoil our plans.

MAROT.

No! leave you that to me,—
I'll manage all.

TRIBOULET (*aside*).

Some whispering I hear.

MAROT (*going up to* TRIBOULET).

What! Triboulet!

TRIBOULET (*fiercely*).

Who's there?

MAROT.

Don't eat me up!
'Tis I.

TRIBOULET.

What I?

MAROT.

Marot.

TRIBOULET.

The night's so dark.

MAROT.

Satan has made an inkstand of the sky.

TRIBOULET

Why are you here?

MAROT.

We come (you surely guess):—(*he laughs*)
De Cossé's wife we aim at, for the king.

TRIBOULET.

Ah, excellent!

DE COSSÉ (*aside*).

Would I could break his bones!

TRIBOULET.

How would you enter,—not by open force?

MAROT (*to* DE COSSÉ).

Give me your key. (DE COSSÉ *passes him the key.*)
(*To* TRIBOULET.) This will ensure success.
Feel you De Cossé's arms engraved thereon?

TRIBOULET (*aside, feeling the key*).

Three leaves serrate : I know the scutcheon well,—
There stands his house. What silly fears were mine!
(*returning the key to* MAROT.)
If all you purpose be to steal the wife
Of fat De Cossé—'faith, I'm with you too.

MAROT.

We are all masqued.

TRIBOULET.

Give me a mask as well.
[MAROT *puts on a mask, and ties it with a thick
handkerchief, or bandage, covering both* TRIBOU-
LET'S *eyes and ears.*

MAROT (*to* TRIBOULET).

You guard the ladder.

TRIBOULET.

Are there many here?
I can see nothing.

MAROT.
'Tis so dark a night (*to the* Courtiers).
Walk as you will, and talk without disguise,
The trusty bandage blinds and deafens him.

[*The* Courtiers *mount the ladder, burst open the door
of the terrace, and enter the house. Soon afterwards one returns, and opens the door of the
court-yard from within. Then the whole body
rush out, bearing* BLANCHE, *half-senseless. After
they have left the stage, her voice is heard in the
distance.*

BLANCHE (*in the distance*).
Help! help me, father!

COURTIERS (*in the distance*).
Victory! she's ours!

TRIBOULET (*at the bottom of the ladder*).
How long must I stand doing penance here?
Will they ne'er finish? Soh! I'll wait no more.

[*He tears off the mask, and discovers the bandage.*
Hah! my eyes bandaged!

[*He tears off the mask and bandage. By the light
of a lanthorn left behind, on the ground, he sees
something white, which he takes up, and discovers to be his daughter's veil. He looks
round—the ladder is against his own wall—
the wall-door is open. He rushes into his
house like a madman, and returns dragging out*
DAME BERARDE, *half dressed and scarcely awake.
He looks round in a state of bewilderment and
stupor, tears his hair, and utters some inarticu-
late sounds of agony. At last his voice returns
—he breaks forth into a cry of despair.*

Oh, the curse!—the curse!

[*He falls down in a swoon.*

ACT THIRD: THE KING.

SCENE 1.—*Royal antechamber at the Louvre, furnished in the style of the Renaissance. Near the front of the stage, a table, chair, and footstool. At the back of the scene, a large door richly gilt. On the left, the door of the KING's sleeping apartment, covered with a tapestry hanging. On the right, a beaufet, with vessels of porcelain and gold. The door at the back opens on to a terrace with garden behind.*

THE COURTIERS.

DE GORDES.

'Tis fit we plan the end of this adventure.

DE PIENNE.

Not so; let Triboulet still writhe and groan,
Ne'er dreaming that his love lies hidden here!

DE COSSÉ.

Aye, let him search the world. Yet, hold, my lords!
The palace guard our secret might betray.

DE MONTCHENU.

Throughout the Louvre all are ordered well;
They'll swear no woman came last night within.

PARDAILLAN.

Besides, to make the matter darker still,
A knave of mine, well versed in strategy,
Called at the poor fool's house and told he saw,
At dead of night, a struggling woman borne
To Hautefort's palace.

MAROT (*takes out a letter*).
This last night sent I:

(*He reads.*) " Your mistress, Triboulet, I stole ;
    If her fair image dwells with thee,
    Long may that image fill thy soul :
    But her sweet self leaves France with me."
Signed with a flourish, John de Nivelles.
                    [*Courtiers all laugh vociferously.*

PARDAILLAN.
Gods! what a chase!

DE COSSÉ.
        His grief is joy to me.

DE GORDES.
Aye, let the slave, in agony and tears,
With clenching hands, and teeth that gnash with rage,
Pay in one day our long arrears of hate.
    [*The door of the Royal apartment opens, and the*
    KING *enters, dressed in a magnificent morning*
    dress; he is accompanied by DE PIENNE: *the*
    Courtiers *draw near. The* KING *and* DE PIENNE
    laugh immoderately.

THE KING (*pointing to the distant door*).
She's there!

DE PIENNE (*laughing*).
    The loved one of our Triboulet.

THE KING (*laughing*).
Steal my Fool's mistress!—Excellent, i'faith!

DE PIENNE.
Mistress or wife?

THE KING (*aside*).
        A wife and daughter too!
So fond a fool I ne'er imagined him!

DE PIENNE.
Shall I produce her now?

THE KING.
            Of course, Pardieu!

[De Pienne *leaves the room, and returns immediately,
leading in* Blanche, *closely veiled and trembling.
The* King *sits down in his chair, in a careless
attitude.*

De Pienne.

Enter, fair dame; then tremble as you will.
Behold the King!

Blanche (*still veiled*).

So young!—is that the King?
[*She throws herself at his feet. At the first sound
of* Blanche's *voice, the* King *starts, and then
signs to the* Courtiers *to retire.*

Scene 2.—The King—Blanche.

The King, *when left alone with* Blanche, *takes the veil
from her face.*

The King.

Blanche!

Blanche.

Godfrey Melune! Oh Heav'n!

The King (*bursting into a fit of laughter*).

Now, by my faith!
Whether 'tis chance or planned, the gain is mine.
My Blanche! my beautiful, my heart's delight,
Come to my arms!

Blanche (*rising and shrinking back*).

The King!—forgive me, Sire;
Indeed, I know not what to say.—Good Sir,
Godfrey Melune;—but no! you are the King.
[*She falls on her knees again.*
Whoe'er thou art, alas! have mercy on me!

The King.

Mercy on thee! my Blanche, whom I adore!
Francis confirms the love that Godfrey gave.
I love, thou lovest, and we both are blest.
The name of King dims not the lover's flame.

You deemed me, once, a scholar, clerk,
Lowly in rank, in all but learning poor ;
And now that chance hath made me nobler born,
And crowned me King, is that sufficient cause
To hold me suddenly in such abhorrence ?—
I've not the luck to be a serf—what then ?

> [*The* KING *laughs heartily.*

BLANCHE (*aside*).

Oh, how he laughs !—and I with shame could die !

THE KING.

What fêtes, what sports and pageants, shall be ours !
What whispered love in garden and in grove !
A thousand pleasures that the night conceals !
Thy happy future grafted on mine own—
We'll be two lovers wedded in delight.
Age must steal on, and what is human life ?
A paltry stuff, of mingled toil and care,
Which love with starry light doth spangle o'er ;
Without it, trust me, 'tis a sorry rag—
Blanche, 'tis a theme I've oft reflected on,
And this is wisdom :—honor Heaven above,
Eat, drink, be merry, crowning all with love !

BLANCHE (*confounded and shuddering*).

Oh, how unlike the picture fancy drew !

THE KING.

What did you think me, then, a solemn fool,
A trembling lover, spiritless and tame,
Who thinks all women ready to expire
With melting sympathy, because he sighs
And wears a sad and melancholy face ?

BLANCHE.

Oh, leave me !—(*Aside.*) Wretched girl !

THE KING.

> Know'st who I am ?—

Why, France—a nation—fifteen million souls—
Gold, honor, pleasures, power uncurbed by law,
All, all are mine :—I reign and rule o'er all.

I am *their* sovereign, Blanche, but thou art *mine*—
I am their *King*, Blanche, wilt not be my *Queen?*

BLANCHE.

The Queen! Your wife!

THE KING (*laughing heartily*).

    No! virtuous innocence;
The Queen, my mistress: 'tis the fairer name.

BLANCHE.

Thy mistress! Shame upon thee!

THE KING.

      Hah! so proud?

BLANCHE (*indignantly*).

I'll ne'er be such! My father can protect me!

THE KING.

My poor Buffoon! my Fool! my Triboulet!
Thy father's mine!—my property! my slave!
His will's mine own!

BLANCHE (*weeping*).

Is he, too, yours?   [*She sobs out.*

THE KING (*falling on his knees*).

    Dear Blanche! too dear to me!
Oh, weep not thus! but, pressed against my heart——
      [*He endeavors to embrace her.*

BLANCHE.

Forbear!

THE KING.

Say but again, thou lov'st me, Blanche!

BLANCHE.

No! no!—'tis passed.

THE KING.

    I've pained thee thoughtlessly.
Nay, do not sob! Rather than force from thee
Those precious drops, my Blanche, I'd die with shame,
Or pass before my kingdom and my court
For one unknown to gallantry and fame.
A King,—and make a woman weep! Ye gods!

BLANCHE.

'Tis all a cheat! I know you jest with me!
If you be King, let me be taken home.
My father weeps for me. I live hard by
De Cossé's palace; but you know it well.
Alas! who are you? I'm bewildered!—lost!
Dragg'd like a victim here 'midst cries of joy;
My brain whirls round. 'Tis but a frightful dream!
You, that I thought so kind. (*Weeping.*) Alas! I think
I love you not! (*suddenly starting back*).
              I do but fear you now!

THE KING (*trying to take her in his arms*).
You fear me, Blanche!

BLANCHE (*resisting*).
              Have pity!

THE KING (*seizing her in his arms*).
                        Well, at least
One pardoning kiss!

BLANCHE (*struggling*).
              No! no!

THE KING (*laughing*).
              (*Aside.*) How strange a girl!

BLANCHE (*forces herself away*).
Help! Ah! that door!
    [*She sees the door of the* KING'S *own room, rushes
        in, and closes it violently.*

THE KING (*taking out a little key from his girdle*).
              'Tis lucky I've the key!
    [*He opens the door, rushes in, and locks it behind him.*

MAROT (*who has been watching for some time at the door
        at the back of the stage*).
She flies for safety to the King's own chamber!
Alas! poor lamb! (*He calls to* DE GORDES, *who is outside.*)
              Hey, count!

DE GORDES (*peeping in*).
              May we return?

Scene 3.—Marot—The Courtiers—Triboulet.

All the Courtiers come in except De Pienne, *who remains watching at the door.*

Marot (*pointing to the door*).
The sheep seeks refuge in the lion's den!

Pardaillan (*overjoyed*).
Oh ho! poor Triboulet!

De Pienne (*entering*).
Hush! hush! he comes!
Be all forewarned; assume a careless air.

Marot.
To none but me he spoke, nor can he guess
At any here.

Pardaillan.
Yet might a look betray.

[*Enter* Triboulet. *His appearance is unaltered. He has the usual dress and thoughtless deportment of the Jester,* only he is very pale.

[De Pienne *appears to be engaged in conversation, but is privately making signs and gestures to some of the young nobles, who can scarcely repress their laughter.*

Triboulet (*advancing slowly to the front of the stage*).
They all have done this! guilt is in their looks:—
Yet where concealed her?—It were vain to ask—
But to be scoffed at!
[*He goes up to* Marot *with a gay and smiling air.*
Ah, I'm so rejoiced
To see you took no cold last night, Marot.

Marot.
Last night!

Triboulet (*affecting to treat it as a jest*).
The trick, I own, was neatly played.

Marot.
The trick!

TRIBOULET.
Aye! well-contrived!

MAROT.
Why, man, last night,
When curfew tolled, ensconced between the sheets
I slept so soundly, that the sun was high
This morn when I awoke.

TRIBOULET (*affecting to believe*).
I must have dreamed.
[TRIBOULET *sees a white handkerchief upon the table,
and darts upon it; he examines the initials.*

PARDAILLAN (*to* DE PIENNE).
See, Duke, how he devours my handkerchief!

TRIBOULET (*with a sigh*).
Not hers!

DE PIENNE (*to the young* Courtiers, *who cannot control
their laughter*).
Nay, gentlemen, what stirs your mirth?

DE GORDES (*pointing to* MAROT).
'Tis he, by Jupiter!

TRIBOULET.
They're strangely moved.
Sleeps the King yet, my lord? (*advancing to* DE PIENNE.)

DE PIENNE.
He doth, good Fool.

TRIBOULET.
Methinks I hear some stir within his room.
[*He attempts to approach the door.*

DE PIENNE (*preventing him*).
You'll wake his Majesty!

DE GORDES (*to* PARDAILLAN).
Viscount, hear this:——·
Marot (the rascal) tells a pleasant tale,
How the three Guys, returning Heaven knows whence,
Found each, last night,—what sayest thou, Buffoon?—
His loving wife with a gallant!

MAROT.
Concealed!

TRIBOULET.

Ah, 'tis a wicked world in which we live!

DE COSSÉ.

Woman's so treacherous!

TRIBOULET.
My Lord, take heed!

DE COSSÉ.

Of what?

TRIBOULET.
Beware! the case may be your own;

Just such a pleasant tale of you they tell;
E'en now there's something peeps above your ears.
[*Makes a sign of horns.*

DE COSSÉ (*in a fury*).

Hah!

TRIBOULET (*speaking to the* COURTIERS, *and pointing to*
DE COSSÉ).
'Tis indeed an animal most rare;

When 'tis provoked, how strangely wild its cry!
Hah! (*mimicking* DE COSSÉ).
[*The* COURTIERS *laugh at* DE COSSÉ.

Enter a GENTLEMAN *bearing the Queen's livery.*

DE PIENNE.
Vandragon! what now?

GENTLEMAN.
Her Majesty

Would see the King, on matters of import.
[DE PIENNE *makes signs that it is impossible.*

GENTLEMAN.

Madame de Brezé is not with him now!

DE PIENNE (*angrily*).

The King still sleeps!

GENTLEMAN.
How, Duke!—a moment past
You were together!

DE PIENNE (*makes signs to the* Gentleman, *who will not understand him, and which* TRIBOULET *observes with breathless
attention*).
He has joined the chase.

GENTLEMAN.
Indeed! without a horse or huntsman, then,
For all his equipages wait him here.

DE PIENNE.
Confusion! (*Then in a rage to the messenger.*)
Now, Sir, will you understand?
The King sees nobody to-day.

TRIBOULET (*in a voice of thunder*).
She's here!
She's with the King! (*The* Courtiers *are alarmed.*)

DE GORDES.
What she?—I'faith he raves.

TRIBOULET.
Ah, gentlemen, well know you what I mean;
Nor shall you fright me from my purpose now.
She, whom last night you ravished from my home—
Base cowards all!—Montmorency, Brion,
De Pienne, and Satan (for with fiends you're leagued),
She's here,—She's mine!

DE PIENNE.
What then, my Triboulet?
You've lost a mistress! Such a form as thine
Will soon find others.

TRIBOULET (*in a loud voice*).
Give me back my child!

COURTIERS (*appalled*).
His child!

TRIBOULET.
My daughter! Do you taunt me now?

Why, wolves and courtiers have their offspring too,
And why not I? Enough of this, my lords;
If 'twere a jest, 'tis ended now! You laugh,—
You whisper! Villains! 'twas a heartless deed.
I'll tear her from you. Give me back my child!
She's there!

> [*He rushes to the door of the* KING'S *room. All
> the* Courtiers *interpose and prevent him.*

MAROT.

His folly has to madness turned.

TRIBOULET.

Base courtiers! demons! fawning race accurst!
A maiden's honor is to you as nought—
A king's fit prey—a profligate's debauch.
Your wives and daughters (if they chance to please),
Belong to him. The virgin's sacred name
Is deemed a treasure, burthensome to bear:
A woman's but a field—a yielding farm
Let out to royalty. The rent it brings,
A government, a title, ribbon, star!
Not one amongst ye give me back the lie.
'Tis true, base robbers! you would sell him all!
  (*to* DE GORDES)—Your sister, sir!
        (*to* PARDAILLAN)—Your mother!
            (*to* DE BRION)—You!—Your wife!
Who shall believe it?—Nobles, dukes, and peers;
A Vermandois from Charlemagne who springs;
A Brion from Milan's illustrious duke;
A Gordes Simiane; a Pienne; a Pardaillan
And you, Montmorency! What names are these
Who basely steal away a poor man's child?
O never from such a high and ancient race,
Such blazons proud, sprung dastards such as ye,
But from some favored lacquey's stolen embrace:
You're bastards all!

DE GORDES.

Bravo, Buffoon!

TRIBOULET.

              How much

Has the King given for this honored service?
You're paid,—I know it.   [*Tears his hair.*
                      I, who had but her,—
What can the King for me! He cannot give
A name like yours, to hide me from mine own:
Nor shape my limbs, nor make my looks more smooth.
Hell!—he has taken all! I'll ne'er go hence
Till she's restored! Look at this trembling hand,—
'Tis but a serf's; no blood illustrious there;—
Unarmed you think, because no sword it bears,—
But with my nails I'll tear her from ye all!

> [*He rushes again at the door—all the* Courtiers *close
> upon him; he struggles desperately for some
> time, but at length, exhausted, he falls on his
> knees at the front of the stage.*

All! all combined against me! ten to one!

                      (*turning to* Marot).
Behold these tears, Marot!—Be merciful;
Thine is a soul inspired. Oh, have a heart!
Tell me she's here! Ours is a common cause,
For thou alone, amidst this lordly throng,
Hast wit and sense. Marot!—Oh, good Marot!

                      (*turns to the* Courtiers).
Even at your feet, my Lords, I sue for grace;
I'm sick at heart; alas, be merciful!
Some other day I'll bear your humors better;
For many a year, your poor mis-shaped Buffoon
Has made you sport—aye, when his heart would break.
Forgive your Triboulet, nor vent your spleen
On one so helpless; give me back my child—
My only treasure—all that I possess!
Without her, nothing in this world is mine.
Be kind to me! another night like this
Would sear my brain, and whiten o'er my hair.

> [*The door of the* King's *room opens, and* Blanche,
> *agitated and disordered, rushes out, and, with a
> cry of terror, throws herself into her father's arms.*

BLANCHE.

My father, ah! (*She buries her head in her father's bosom.*)

TRIBOULET.

My Blanche! my darling child!
Look ye, good Sirs, the last of all my race.
Dear angel!—Gentlemen, you'll bear with me—
You'll pardon, I am sure, these tears of joy.
A child like this, whose gentle innocence
Even to look on makes the heart more pure,
Could not be lost, you'll own, without a pang.
(*to* BLANCHE).
Fear nothing now; 'twas but a thoughtless jest,
Something to laugh at.—How they frightened thee!
Confess it, Blanche. [*Embraces her fondly.*
But I'm so happy now,
My heart's so full, I never knew before
How much I loved. I laugh, that once did weep
To lose thee; yet to hold thee thus again,
Is surely bliss.—But thou dost weep, my child?

BLANCHE (*covering her face with her hand*).
Oh, hide me from my shame!

TRIBOULET (*starting*).
What mean'st thou, Blanche?

BLANCHE (*pointing to the* Courtiers).
Not before these; I'd blush and speak, alone.

TRIBOULET (*turns in an agony to the* KING'S *door*).
Monster!—She too!

BLANCHE (*sobbing and falling at his feet*).
Alone with thee, my father!

TRIBOULET (*striding towards the* Courtiers).
Go, get ye hence! And if the King pretend
To turn his steps this way,
(*to* VERMANDOIS) You're of his guard!
Tell him he dare not!—Triboulet is here!

DE PIENNE.
Of all the fools, no fool e'er equalled this.

DE GORDES.
To fools and children sometimes must we yield,
Yet will we watch without.
[*Exeunt all the* Courtiers *but* DE COSSÉ.

TRIBOULET.

Speak freely to me, Blanche. [*He turns and sees* DE COSSÉ.
(*In a voice of thunder.*) You heard me, Sir?

DE COSSÉ (*retiring precipitately*).
These fools permit themselves strange liberties.

SCENE 4.—TRIBOULET—BLANCHE.

TRIBOULET (*gravely and sternly*).
Now, speak!

BLANCHE (*with downcast eyes, interrupted by sobs*).
Dear father, 'twas but yesternight
He stole within the gate—— (*She hides her face.*)
I cannot speak.
[TRIBOULET *presses her in his arms, and kisses her
forehead tenderly.*
But long ago, (I should have told you then.)
He followed me, yet spoke not, and at church,
As sure as Sunday came, this gentleman——

TRIBOULET (*fiercely*).
The King!

BLANCHE.
——Passed close to me, and, as I think,
Disturbed my chair, that I might look on him.
Last night he gained admittance.

TRIBOULET.
Stop, my child;
I'll spare thy shame the pang of telling it;
I guess the rest. (*He stands erect.*)
Oh, sorrow, most complete!
His loathsome touch has withered on thy brow
The virgin wreath of purity it wore,
And in its stead has left the brand of shame!
The once pure air that did environ thee
His breath has sullied. Oh, my Blanche! my child!
Once the sole refuge of my misery,
The day that woke me from a night of woe,
The soul through which mine own had hopes of Heaven,

A veil of radiance, covering my disgrace,
The haven still for one by all accurst,
An angel left by God to bless my tears,
The only sainted thing I e'er did trust!
What am I now? Amidst this hollow court,
Where vice, and infamy, and foul debauch,
With riot wild, and bold effrontery, reign;
These eyes, aweary with the sight of crime,
Turned to thy guileless soul to find repose;
Then could I bear my fate, my abject fate,
My tears, the pride that swelled my bursting heart,
The witty sneers that sharpened on my woes—
Yes, all the pangs of sorrow and of shame
I could endure, but not thy wrongs, my child!
Aye, hide thy face and weep; at thy young age
Some part of anguish may escape in tears;
Pour what thou canst into a father's heart.

(*Abstractedly.*)

But now, enough. The matter once dispatched,
We leave this city,—aye, if I escape!

[*Turning with redoubled rage to the* King's *chamber.*
Francis the First! May God, who hears my prayer,
Dig in thy path a bloody sepulchre,
And hurl thee down, unshrived, and gorged with sin!

BLANCHE (*aside*).
Grant it not, Heaven! for I love him still.

DE PIENNE (*speaking outside*).
De Montchenû, guard hence to the Bastille
Monsieur St. Vallier, now your prisoner.

Enter ST. VALLIER, MONTCHENU, *and* Soldiers.

ST. VALLIER.
Since neither Heaven doth strike, nor pitying man
Hath answered to my curse on this proud King,
Steeped to the lip in crime,—why, then 'tis sure
The monarch prospers, and my curse is vain.

TRIBOULET (*turning round, and confronting him*).
Old man, 'tis false! There's *one shall* strike for thee?

ACT FOURTH : BLANCHE.

SCENE 1.—*The scene represents the Place de la Grève, near la Tournelle, an ancient gate of the City of Paris. On the right is a miserable hovel, which purports, by a rude sign, to be house of entertainment, or auberge of the lowest description. The front of the house is towards the spectators, and is so arranged, that the inside is easily seen. The lower room is wretchedly furnished. There is a table, a large chimney, and a narrow staircase leading to a sort of loft or garret above, containing a truckle bed, easily seen through the window. The side of the building to the left of the actor has a door which opens inwards. The wall is dilapidated, and so full of chinks and apertures, that what is passing in the house may be witnessed by an observer outside. The remainder of the stage represents the Grève. On the left is an old ruined wall and parapet, at the foot of which runs the river Seine. In the distance beyond the river is seen the old City of Paris.*

TRIBOULET—BLANCHE *outside*—SALTABADIL *inside the house.*

[*During the whole of this scene, TRIBOULET has the appearance of one anxious and fearful of surprise. SALTABADIL sits in the Auberge, near the table, engaged in cleaning his belt, and not hearing what is passing without.*

TRIBOULET.

Thou lov'st him still?

BLANCHE.

For ever!

TRIBOULET.

Yet I gave
Full time to cure thee of this senseless dream.

BLANCHE.

Indeed, I love him.

TRIBOULET.

Ah, 'tis woman's heart!
But, Blanche, explain thy reasons—why dost love?

BLANCHE.

I know not.

TRIBOULET.

'Tis most strange!—incredible!

BLANCHE.

Not so!—It may be 'tis for that I love—
Say that a man doth risk his life for ours,
Or husband bring us riches, rank and fame,
Do women *therefore* love?—In truth, I know,
All he hath brought me are but wrongs and shame,
And yet I love him, tho' I know not why.
Whate'er is linked with him ne'er quits my mind.
'Tis madness, father! Canst thou pardon still?
Though he hath wronged, and thou art ever kind,
For him I'd die as surely as for thee.

TRIBOULET.

I do forgive thee.

BLANCHE.

Then he loves me too.

TRIBOULET.

Insensate!—No!

BLANCHE.

He pledged his faith to me,
And with a solemn oath confirmed his vows,
Such loving things!—with such resistless grace
He speaks, no woman's heart his truth can doubt.
His words, his looks, so eloquent, so kind,
'Tis a true King, a handsome and a brave!

TRIBOULET.

'Tis a cold, perjured, and relentless fiend!
Yet 'scapes he not my vengeance.

BLANCHE.

                Dearest father,
You once forgave him.

TRIBOULET.

                Till the snare was spread
For his dark villainy, I dared not strike.

BLANCHE.

'Tis now a month—(I tremble as I speak)—
You seemed to love the King.

TRIBOULET.

                    'Twas but pretence ;
Thou shalt have vengeance !

BLANCHE.

              Father, spare your child !

TRIBOULET.

Thy senseless passion might be turned to hate,
If he deceived thee.

BLANCHE.

          He ! I'll ne'er believe it !

TRIBOULET.

What if those eyes, that plead his cause with tears,
Beheld his perfidy—would'st love him still ?

BLANCHE.

I cannot tell. He loves me ! nay, adores.
'Twas but last night——

    TRIBOULET (*interrupting her, sneeringly*).
                What time ?

BLANCHE.

                About this hour.

TRIBOULET.

Then witness here, and, if thou canst, forgive !
    [*He draws her to the house, and directs her gaze
        through one of the apertures in the wall, where
        all that passes within may be seen.*

BLANCHE.

Nought but a man I see.

TRIBOULET.

Look now!

[*The* KING, *dressed as an Officer, appears from a
door which communicates with an apartment
within.*

BLANCHE (*starting*).

Oh, father!

[*During the following scene,* BLANCHE *remains, fixed
as a statue, against the fissure in the wall, observing what is passing within, inattentive to
all else, and only agitated from time to time
with a convulsive shudder.*

SCENE 2.—BLANCHE—TRIBOULET *outside.*—SALTABADIL—
THE KING—MAGUELONNE *inside.*

THE KING (*striking* SALTABADIL *familiarly on the shoulder*).
Two things at once—your sister and a glass!

TRIBOULET (*aside*).
The morals of a King by grace divine;
Who risks his life in low debaucheries,
And doth prefer the wine that damns his sense,
If proffered by some tavern Hebe's hand!

THE KING (*sings*).
" Changeful woman, constant never,
He's a fool who trusts her ever,
For her love the wind doth blow,
Like a feather, to and fro." *

[SALTABADIL *goes sullenly to the next room, returning with a bottle and glass, which he places on
the table. He then strikes twice on the floor
with the handle of his long sword, and at this
signal a young girl, dressed in the Gipsy dress,
bounds quickly down the stair. As she enters,
the* KING *tries to seize her in his arms, but she
slips away.* SALTABADIL *re-commences cleansing
his belt.*

---

* The reader's attention is requested to these verses. They are made the
means of producing, in the Fifth Act, a most startling dramatic effect.

THE KING (*to* SALTABADIL).

My friend, thy buckle would be brighter far
Cleaned in the open air.

SALTABADIL (*sullenly*).

I understand.

[*He rises, salutes the* KING *awkwardly, opens the
door and comes out. He sees* TRIBOULET. *and
comes cautiously towards him.* BLANCHE *sees
nothing but the young Gipsy girl, who is dancing
round the* KING.

SALTABADIL (*in a low voice to* TRIBOULET).

Shall he die now?

TRIBOULET.

Not yet!—return anon.

[TRIBOULET *makes signs to him to retire.* SALTABADIL
*disappears behind the parapet wall. Meantime
the* KING *endeavors to caress the young Gipsy.*

MAGUELONNE (*slipping away*).

No, no!

THE KING.

Thou offerest too much defence.
A truce! Come hither! (*The girl draws nearer.*)
                               'Tis a week ago,
At Triancourt's Hotel, (Ah, let me see,
Who took me there?—I think 'twas Triboulet,)
There first I gazed upon that beauteous face.
'Tis just a week, my goddess, that I love thee,
And thee alone.

MAGUELONNE.

And twenty more besides;
To me, a most accomplished rake you seem.

THE KING.

Well, well! I own some hearts have ached for me.
True, I'm a monster!

MAGUELONNE.

Coxcomb!

THE KING.
'Tis most true!
But, tempter, 'twas your beauty lured me here,
With most adventurous patience to endure
A dinner of the vilest;—and such wine!
Your brother's hang-dog looks have soured it:
An ugly wretch! How dares he shew his face
So near those witching eyes and lips of bliss!
It matters not. I stir not hence to-night.

MAGUELONNE (*aside*).
He courts the snare! (*to the* KING, *who tries to embrace her*).
Excuse me!

THE KING.
Why resist?

MAGUELONNE.
Be wise!

THE KING.
Why this is wisdom, Maguelonne,
Eat, drink, and love; I hold exactly there
With old King Solomon.

MAGUELONNE (*laughing*).
Ha! ha! I think
Thou lov'st the tavern better than the church.

THE KING (*stretching out his arms to catch her*).
Dear Maguelonne!

MAGUELONNE (*runs round behind the table*).
To-morrow!

THE KING (*seizing the table with both hands*).
Say again
That odious word, thy fence I'll overthrow;
The lip of beauty ne'er should say to-morrow.

MAGUELONNE (*comes suddenly round and sits by the* KING).
Well, let's be friends!

THE KING (*taking her hand*).
Ah, what a hand is thine!
So soft, so taper!—'twere a Christian's part,

Without pretence to over sanctity,
To court thy blow, and turn his cheek for more.

MAGUELONNE (pleased).

You mock me.

THE KING.
Never !

MAGUELONNE.
But I am not fair.

THE KING.

Unkind to me, and to thyself unjust !
Queen of inexorables, know'st thou not
How tyrant love doth rule the soldier's heart?
" And if bright beauty doth our suit approve,
Though 'twere 'midst Russia's snows, we blaze with love."

MAGUELONNE (bursting into a fit of laughter).

I'm sure you've read that somewhere in a book.

THE KING (aside).

Quite possible ! (Aloud.) Come, kiss me !

MAGUELONNE.
Sir, you're drunk !

THE KING.

With love !

MAGUELONNE.

I know you do but jest with me,
And couch your wit against a silly girl.

> [*The* KING *succeeds in giving her a kiss, and tries
> a second time, which she refuses.*

Enough !

THE KING.

I'll marry thee.

MAGUELONNE (laughing).
You pledge your word.

> [*The* KING *clasps her round the waist, and whispers
> in her ear.* BLANCHE, *unable to bear the scene
> any longer, turns round, and totters towards her
> father.*

TRIBOULET (*after contemplating her for some time in silence*).
What think'st thou now of vengeance, my poor child?

BLANCHE.

Betrayed! ungrateful!—Oh, my heart will break!
He hath no soul, no pity, kindness—none!
Even to that girl, who loves him not, he says
The same fond words that once he said to me.
                    [*Hides her head in her father's bosom.*
And oh, that shameless creature!

TRIBOULET.
                              Hush! no more!
Enough of tears, leave now revenge to me!

BLANCHE.
Do as thou wilt.

TRIBOULET.
I thank thee.

BLANCHE.
                              Yet, alas!
Father, I tremble when I read thy looks.
What would'st thou do?

TRIBOULET.
                    I pray thee, ask me not!
All is prepared!—Now to our house, my child;
There quick disguise thee as a cavalier,
Mount a swift steed, and store thy purse with gold;—
Hie thee to Evreux, stop not on the road,
And by to-morrow's eve I'll join thee there.
Beneath thy mother's portrait stands a chest—
Thou know'st it well—the dress lies ready there.
The horse stands saddled. Do as I have said,
But come not here again; for here shall pass
A deed most terrible. Go now, dear Blanche!

BLANCHE.
You'll surely come with me?

TRIBOULET.
                    Impossible!

BLANCHE (aside).

My heart feels sick and faint.

TRIBOULET.

Now, fare thee well!
Remember, Blanche, do all as I have said.

[Exit BLANCHE.

[During this scene, the KING and MAGUELONNE continue laughing and talking in a low voice. As
soon as BLANCHE is gone, TRIBOULET goes to the
parapet and makes a sign for SALTABADIL who
appears from behind the wall. Night draws on;
the stage becomes darker.

SCENE 3.—TRIBOULET—SALTABADIL outside:—THE KING—
MAGUELONNE (inside the house).

TRIBOULET (counting out the gold to SALTABADIL).
You ask for twenty,—here are ten in hand.
Art sure he stays the night?

[He stops in the act of giving him the money.

SALTABADIL (goes to examine the appearance of the night).
The storm comes on.
In one short hour, the tempest and the rain
Shall aid my sister to detain him here.

TRIBOULET.
At midnight I return.

SALTABADIL.
No need of that.
Thank Heaven. I've strength enough, unhelped, to throw
A corpse into the Seine.

TRIBOULET.
That triumph's mine.
These hands alone shall do it.

SALTABADIL.
As for that,
Even as you please; 'tis no affair of mine.

I balk no fancies. In a sack concealed,
Your man shall be delivered you to-night.

> TRIBOULET (*gives him the gold*).

'Tis well !—At midnight, and the rest are thine.

> SALTABADIL.

It shall be done ! How call you this gallant ?

> TRIBOULET.

Would'st know his name ?—Then hear mine own as well,
For *mine* is *chastisement,* and *his* is *crime !*

> [*Exit* TRIBOULET.

SCENE 4.—SALTABADIL—THE KING—MAGUELONNE.

[SALTABADIL, *alone outside, examines the appearance of
the sky, which is becoming gradually more overcast.
It is almost night. The lightning flashes, and
thunder is heard in the distance.*

> SALTABADIL.

The storm o'erhangs the city,—aye, that's well.
This place will soon be lonely as the grave.
'Tis a strange business this, and, by my head !
I cannot fathom it. These people seem
Possessed with something that I can't divine.

> [*He examines the sky again. During this time the
> KING is laughing with MAGUELONNE. He en-
> deavors to embrace her.*

> MAGUELONNE (*repulsing him*).

My brother's coming !

> THE KING.
>> Sweetest one, what then ?

SALTABADIL *enters, closing the door after him. A loud
peal of thunder.*

> MAGUELONNE.

Hark, how it thunders !

> SALTABADIL.
>> Listen to the rain.

THE KING.

Well, let it rain ! 'tis our good pleasure here
To stop this night.

> [*Slapping* SALTABADIL *on the shoulder.*

MAGUELONNE (*laughing at him*).

'Tis our good pleasure ! Well !
This is a King indeed ! Your family
May be alarmed.

> [SALTABADIL *makes signs to her not to prevent him.*

THE KING.

Nor wife nor child have I.
I care for none.

SALTABADIL (*aside*).

There's Providence in that.

> [*The rain falls heavily. The night becomes quite dark.*

THE KING.

Thou, fellow, may'st go sleep, e'en where thou wilt.

SALTABADIL (*bowing*).

Most happy.

MAGUELONNE (*in an earnest whisper, while lighting the lamp*).

Get thee hence !

THE KING (*laughs and speaks aloud*).

In such a night !
I'd scarcely turn a poet out of doors.

SALTABADIL (*aside to* MAGUELONNE, *showing the gold*).

Let him remain. I've ten good crowns of gold—
As much more when 'tis done !

> (*To the* KING) Most proud am I
To offer my poor chamber for the night.

THE KING.

Beshrew me now, 'tis some infernal den,
Where summer bakes one, and December's snows
Freeze every vein.

SALTABADIL.

I'll show it, with your leave.

THE KING.

Lead on :

[SALTABADIL *takes the lamp; the* KING *goes to* MAGUE-
LONNE, *and whispers something in her ear. Then
both mount the narrow staircase,* SALTABADIL *pre-
ceding the* KING.

MAGUELONNE (*she looks out at the window*).

Ah, poor young man !

How dark without.

[*The* KING *and* SALTABADIL *are seen through the window of the room above.*

SALTABADIL (*to the* KING).

Here is a bed, a table, and a chair !

THE KING (*measuring them*).

Three, six, nine feet in all. Thy furniture
Hath surely fought at Marignan, my friend,
'Tis chopped, and cut, and hacked so wondrous small.

[*He examines the window, in which there is no glass.*

How healthy 'tis to sleep i' the open air :
No glass—no curtains ! sure the gentle breeze
Was ne'er more courteously received than here.
Good night, good fellow !

SALTABADIL (*descending the stairs*).

Heaven preserve you, sir !

THE KING.

In truth, I'm weary, and would sleep awhile.—

[*He places his hat and sword on the chair, takes off
his boots, and throws himself on the bed.*

'Tis a sweet girl !—that Maguelonne, so gay,
So fresh, so young. I trust the door's unbarred.

[*He gets up and tries the lock.*

Ah, 'tis all right !

[*Throws himself again on the bed, and is soon fast
asleep.*

[MAGUELONNE *and* SALTABADIL *are sitting down below.
The tempest rages. Thunder, lightning, and rain
incessant.* MAGUELONNE *sits with some needle-
work.* SALTABADIL, *with a nonchalant air, is
emptying the bottle of wine the* KING *has left.
Both seem lost in thought.*

MAGUELONNE (*after a pause of some duration*).
Methinks this Cavalier
Most prepossessing!

SALTABADIL.
Faith, I think so, too—
He fills my purse with twenty crowns of gold!

MAGUELONNE.
How many?

SALTABADIL.
Twenty.

MAGUELONNE.
Oh, he's worth much more!

SALTABADIL.
Go up, pert doll! and if his sleep be sound,
Bring down his sword!

[MAGUELONNE *obeys. The storm rages violently. At
this moment* BLANCHE *enters from the back of
the stage, dressed as a man, in a black riding
habit, boots and spurs.—She advances slowly to
the crevice in the wall. Meanwhile* SALTABADIL
continues to drink; and MAGUELONNE, *with a
lamp in her hand, bends over the sleeping* KING.

MAGUELONNE.
He sleeps. Alas! poor youth.
[*She brings down his sword to* SALTABADIL.

SCENE 5.—THE KING *asleep in the upper room.* SALTABADIL
and MAGUELONNE *in the room below.* BLANCHE *outside.*

BLANCHE (*walking slowly in the dark, guided by the flashes of
lightning. Thunder incessant*).
A deed most terrible!! Is reason fled?
There's something more than nature buoys me up:—
Even in this dreadful house he stops to-night!
Oh, pardon, Father, pardon my return—
My disobedience! I could bear no more
The agony of doubt that racked my soul—

I, who have lived, till now, unknowing all
The tears and sorrows of this cruel world
Midst peace and flowers!—now am hurled at once
From happy innocence to guilt and shame!
Love tramples on the ruined edifice
Of virtue's temple, that his torch has seared!
His fire's extinct—the ashes but remain :—
He loves me not! Was that the thunder's voice?
It wakes me from my thoughts! Oh, fearful night!
Despair has nerved my heart—my woman's heart
That once feared shadows!

      [*Sees the light in the upper window.*
       Ah, what is't they do?
How my heart throbs! They would not slay him, sure?
       [*Noise of thunder and rain.*

SALTABADIL (*within*).
Heaven growls above as though 'twere married strife—
One curses,—t' other drowns the earth with tears.

BLANCHE.
Oh, if my father knew his child were here!

MAGUELONNE (*within*).
Brother!

    BLANCHE (*startled*).
Who spoke?

    MAGUELONNE (*louder*).
      Why, brother?

    SALTABADIL.
       Well, what now?

    MAGUELONNE.
Thou canst not read my thoughts?

    SALTABADIL.
      Not I!

    MAGUELONNE.
       But guess!

    SALTABADIL.
The fiend confound thee!

MAGUELONNE.

     Come! this fine young man—
So tall! so handsome!—who lies wrapped in sleep
As thoughtless and as trusting as a child!—
We'll spare his life!

    BLANCHE.
    Oh, heaven!

   SALTABADIL.

     Take thou this sack,
And sew these broken seams.

    MAGUELONNE.

     What would you do?

   SALTABADIL.
E'en place therein thy handsome, tall gallant,
When my keen blade hath dealt with him above,
And sink his carcase, garnished with yon stone,
Deep in the river's bed.

    MAGUELONNE.
    But—

   SALTABADIL.

     Silence, girl!
Urge me no more.

    MAGUELONNE.
    Yet—

   SALTABADIL.

     Wilt thou hold thy peace?
Wert thou consulted, no one would be slain.
On with thy work.

    BLANCHE.
    What dreadful pair are these!
Is it on hell I gaze?

    MAGUELONNE.
    Well, I obey:
But you must hear me.

    SALTABADIL.
    Umph!

THE DESERTED WHARF OF THE TOURNELLE.

The King's Diversion.—Act IV., Scene 5.

MAGUELONNE.

You do not hate
This gentleman.

SALTABADIL.

Not I. I love the man
That bears a sword. 'Tis by the sword I live.

MAGUELONNE.

Why stab a handsome youth, to please, forsooth,
An ugly hunchback, crooked as an S!

SALTABADIL.

Hark ye awhile, the simple case I'll state.
A hunchback gives, to slay a handsome man—
I care not whom,—ten golden crowns in hand,
And ten besides, whene'er the deed is done.
Of course—he dies!

MAGUELONNE.

Why not the old man slay
When he returns to pay thee o'er the gold?
'Twere all the same.

BLANCHE.

My father!

SALTABADIL (*with indignation*).

Hark ye now :—
I'll hear no more of this. Am I a thief,—
A bandit, cut-throat, cheat? Would'st have me rob
The client who employs and pays my sword?

MAGUELONNE.

Couldst thou not place this log within the sack?
The night's so dark, the cheat he could not tell.

SALTABADIL.

Ha! ha! Thy trick would scarce deceive the blind.
There's something in the clammy touch of death
That baffles imitation.

MAGUELONNE.

Spare his life!

SALTABADIL.

I say—he dies!

MAGUELONNE.

I'll scare him from his sleep:—
Save and protect him hence.

BLANCHE.

Good, generous girl!

SALTABADIL.

My twenty crowns!

MAGUELONNE.

'Tis true!

SALTABADIL.

Hear reason, then:
He must not live.

MAGUELONNE

I say he shall not die!
[*She places herself in a determined attitude at the
foot of the stairs;* SALTABADIL, *fearing to wake
the* KING, *stops in his purpose, apparently thinking how to compromise the affair.*

SALTABADIL.

Hear me:—At midnight comes my patron back;
If any stranger chance to pass this way,
And claim our shelter, ere the bell shall toll,
I'll strike him dead,—and offer, in exchange,
His mangled body for thy puppet yonder.
So that the corse he throws into the Seine,
He cannot guess the change. But this is all
That I can do for thee.

MAGUELONNE.

Gramercy, brother,—
In the fiend's name, whoe'er can pass this way?

SALTABADIL.

Nought else can save his life!

MAGUELONNE.

At such an hour!

Blanche.

Oh God! thou temptest me! Thou bid'st me die
To save a perjured life! Oh, spare me yet!
1 am too young. Urge me not thus, my heart!
                                        [*Thunder rolls.*
Oh, agony! Should I go call the guard?
No, all is silence! darkness reigns around :—
Besides, these demons would denounce my father; .`
Dear father, I should live to thank thy love,—
To cherish and support thy failing years.
Only sixteen!—'tis hard to die so young ;—
To feel the keen, sharp dagger at my heart!
Ah me! how cold the plashing rain comes down!
My brain seems fire—but my limbs are ice!
            [*A clock in the distance strikes one quarter.*

Saltabadil.

'Tis time!   [*The clock strikes two more quarters.*
        Three-quarters past eleven now!
Hear'st thou no footsteps? Ere the midnight hour,
It must be done.   [*He puts his foot on the first stair.*

MAGUELONNE (*bursts into tears*).
            Oh, brother, wait awhile!

Blanche.

This woman weeps, yet *I* refuse to save.
He loves me not! Have I not prayed for death?
That death would save him, but my heart recoils.

SALTABADIL (*attempting to pass* MAGUELONNE).
I'll wait no longer.

Blanche.

            If he'd strike me dead
With one sharp sudden blow! not gash my face,
Or mangle me. How chilling falls the rain!
Oh, it is horrible to die so cold.
        [SALTABADIL *again attempts to pass* MAGUELONNE.
        BLANCHE *gradually drags herself round to the
        door, and gives a feeble knock.*

Maguelonne.

A knock.

SALTABADIL.

'Tis but the wind.

MAGUELONNE (BLANCHE *knocks again*).

                    Again!—a knock!
[*She runs to the window, opens it, and looks out.*

SALTABADIL (*aside*).

'Tis passing strange!

MAGUELONNE.

          Who's there?
(*Aside* to SALTABADIL.)   A traveller!

BLANCHE (*faintly*).

A night's repose!

SALTABADIL (*aside*).

          A sound eternal sleep!

MAGUELONNE (*aside*).

Aye, a long night indeed!

BLANCHE.

                    Haste! haste!—I faint!

SALTABADIL.

Give me the knife!

MAGUELONNE.

          Poor wretch! his hand hath struck
Upon the portal of his tomb!
(*Aside to* SALTABADIL.) Be quick!

SALTABADIL.

Behind the door, I'll strike him as he comes.

MAGUELONNE (*opening the door to* BLANCHE).
Come in!

BLANCHE (*shuddering*).
I dare not!

MAGUELONNE (*half dragging her in*).
          'Tis too late for that!
[*As she passes the threshold,* SALTABADIL *strikes.*
                    [*The Curtain falls.*

ACT FIFTH: TRIBOULET.

SCENE 1.—*The Stage represents the same scene as the Fourth Act; but the house of* SALTABADIL *is completely closed. There is no light within. All is darkness.*

[TRIBOULET *comes slowly from the back of the stage, enveloped in his mantle. The storm has somewhat diminished in violence. The rain has ceased; but there are occasional flashes of lightning, and distant thunder is heard.*

TRIBOULET.

Now is the triumph mine! The blow is struck
That pays a lingering month of agony.
'Midst sneers and ribald jests, the poor Buffoon
Shed tears of blood beneath his mask of smiles.
                    [*Examines the door of the house.*
This is the door—oh vengeance exquisite!—
Thro' which the corse of him I hate shall pass.
The hour has not yet tolled; yet am I here
To gaze upon thy tomb! Mysterious night!   [*Thunder.*
In heaven a tempest; murder upon earth!
Now am I great indeed. My just revenge
Joins with the wrath of God. I've slain the King!!
And such a king!—upon whose breath depends
The thrones of twenty monarchs; and whose voice
Declares to trembling millions, peace or war!
He wields the destinies of half mankind,
And falling thus, the world shall sink with him.
'Tis I that strike this mighty Atlas down!
Through me, all Europe shall his loss bewail.
Affrighted earth, e'en from its utmost bounds,
Shall shriek! Thy arm hath done this, Triboulet.

Triumph, Buffoon !—exult thee in thy pride ;
A fool's revenge the globe itself doth shake !
    [*The storm continues. A distant clock strikes twelve.*
The hour !!   [*He runs to the door, and knocks loudly.*

Voice (*from within*).
Who knocks ?

TRIBOULET.
                        'Tis I ! admit me ! haste !

Voice (*within*).
All's well ; but enter not !
    [*The lower half of the door is opened, and* SALTABA-
    DIL *crawls out, dragging after him an oblong-
    shaped mass, scarcely distinguishable in the
    darkness of the night.*

Scene 2.—Triboulet—Saltabadil.

SALTABADIL.
                        How dull a load.
Lend me your aid awhile ; within this sack
Your man lies dead !

TRIBOULET.
                        I'll look upon his face.
Bring me a torch !

SALTABADIL.
                        By all the saints, not I.

TRIBOULET.
What, canst thou stab, yet fear to look on death ?

SALTABADIL.
The guard I fear !—the archers of the night ;
You'll have no light from me. My task is done.
The gold !
    [TRIBOULET *gives it to him, then turns to gaze on
                the dead body.*

TRIBOULET.
'Tis there ! (*Aside.*)—So hatred hath its joys !

SALTABADIL.

Shall not I help you to the river's side?

TRIBOULET.

Alone I'll do it.

SALTABADIL.

Lighter 'twere for both.

TRIBOULET.

'Tis a sweet load; to me 'tis light indeed!

SALTABADIL.

Well, as you will; but cast it not from hence.
          [*Pointing to another part of the wall.*
The stream runs deepest there. Be quick. Good-night.
          [*He re-enters the house, closing the door after him.*

SCENE 3.—TRIBOULET *alone, his eyes fixed on the body.*

TRIBOULET.

There lies he! dead! Would I could see him now.
                    [*He examines the sack.*
It matters not, 'tis he!—his spurs peep forth.
Yes! yes! 'tis he!
          [*He rises up and places his foot on the body.*
                    Now, giddy world, look on!
Here see the Jester! There, the King of Kings,
Monarch o'er all, unrivalled, Lord supreme!
Beneath my feet I spurn him as he lies,
The Seine his sepulchre, this sack his shroud.
Who hath done this? 'Tis I—and I alone.
Stupendous victory! When morning dawns
The slavish throng will scarce believe the tale,
But future ages, nations yet unborn
Shall own, and shudder at, the mighty deed.
What, Francis of Valois, thou soul of fire,
Great Charles's greater rival, King of France,
And God of battles! at whose conquering step
The very battlements have quaked for fear!

Hero of Marignan, whose arm o'erthrew
Legions of soldiers, scattered like the dust
Before the impetuous wind ! whose actions beamed
Like stars o'ershining all the universe,
Art thou no more?—unshrived, unwept, unknown,
Struck down at once ! In all thy power and pride,
From all thy pomps, thy vanities, thy lusts,
Dragged off and hidden like a babe malformed ;
Dissolved, extinguished, melted into air :
Appeared and vanished like the lightning's flash.
Perhaps to-morrow,—haggard ! trembling ! pale !
And prodigal of gold--thro' every street
Criers shall shout to wond'ring passers by,
Francis the First—Francis the First is lost !
'Tis strange !

> (*After a short silence.*)

But thou, my poor long-suffering child,
Thou hast thy vengeance. What a thirst was mine
That craved for blood ! Gold gave the draught ! 'Tis
          quench'd !

[*He bends over the body in a fit of ungovernable rage.*
Perfidious monster ! Oh, that thou couldst hear !
My child, more precious than a monarch's crown,
My child, who never injured aught that breathed,
You foully robbed me of, and gave her back
Disgraced and shamed ; but now the triumph's mine.
With well dissembled art I lured thee on,
And bade thy caution sleep, as if the woe
That breaks a father's heart could e'er forgive !
'Twas a hard strife, the weak against the strong :
The weak hath conquered ! He who kissed thy foot
Hath gnawed thy heartstrings. Dost thou hear me now,
Thou King of Gentlemen ! The wretched slave,
The Fool, Buffoon, scarce worth the name of man—
He whom thou calledst dog—now gives the blow !

> [*He strikes the dead body.*

'Tis vengeance speaks, and at its voice the soul,
How base soe'er, bursts from its thralling sleep.
The vilest are ennobled, changed, transformed :
Then from its scabbard, like a glittering sword,

The poor oppressed one, draws his hatred forth,
The stealthy cat's a tiger, and the Fool
Becomes the executioner of kings.
Would he could feel how bitterly I hate!
But 'tis enough. Go seek thou in the Seine
Some loyal current that against the stream
May bear thy mangled corse to *Saint Denis.*
Accursed Francis!

> [*He takes the sack by one end, and drags it to the
> edge of the wall: as he is about to place it on
> the parapet* MAGUELONNE *comes out, looks round
> anxiously, and returns with the* KING, *to whom
> she makes signs that he may now escape unseen.*

> *At the moment that* TRIBOULET *is about to throw the
> body into the Seine, the* KING *leaves the stage in
> the opposite direction, singing carelessly,—*

THE KING.
" *Changeful woman!—constant never!*
  He's a fool who trusts her ever! "

TRIBOULET (*dropping the body on the stage*).
              Hah! what voice was that?
Some spectre of the night is mocking me!

> [*He turns round, and listens in a state of great agi-
> tation. The voice of the* KING *is again heard
> in the distance.*

THE KING.
" *For her love the wind doth blow,*
  Like a feather, to and fro."

TRIBOULET.
Now, by the curse of Hell! This is not he!
Some one hath saved him!—robbed me of my prey!—
Betrayed! betrayed!

> [*Runs to the house, but only the upper window is open.*
              Assassins!—'Tis too high!
What hapless victim has supplied his place—
What guiltless life?—I shudder!   (*Feels the body.*)

'Tis a corpse!
But, who hath perished? 'Tis in vain to seek—
From this abode of hell—a torch to break
The pitchy darkness of this fearful night!
I'll wait the lightning's glare!

> [*He waits some moments, his eyes fixed on the half-
> opened sack, from which he has partly drawn
> forth the body of* BLANCHE.

SCENE 4.—TRIBOULET—BLANCHE.

A flash of lightning! TRIBOULET *starts up with a frenzied
scream.*

TRIBOULET.
                    Oh, God! My child!
Hah, what is this? My hands are wet with blood—
My daughter! Oh, my brain!—some hideous dream
Hath seized my senses! 'Tis impossible!
But now she left me! Heaven be kind to me!
'Tis but a maddening vision—'tis not she!

> [*Another flash of lightnign.*

It is my child—my daughter! Dearest Blanche!
These fiends have murdered thee! Oh, speak, my child!
Speak to thy father! Is there none to help?
Speak to me, Blanche! My child! My child! Oh, God!

> [*He sinks down exhausted.*

BLANCHE.
(*Half dying, but rallying at the cries of her father—In
a faint voice—*)
Who calls on me?

TRIBOULET (*in an ecstasy of joy*).
                    She speaks! She grasps my hand!
Her heart beats yet! All-gracious Heaven, she lives!

BLANCHE.
> [*She raises herself to a sitting position. Her coat has
> been taken off, her shirt is covered with blood, her
> hair hangs loose; the rest of her body is concealed.*

Where am I?

TRIBOULET.

Dearest, sole delight on earth,
Hear'st thou my voice? Thou know'st me now?

BLANCHE.

My father!

TRIBOULET.

Who hath done this? What dreadful mystery!
I dare not touch, lest I should pain thee, Blanche.
I cannot see, but gently guide my hand.
Where art thou hurt?

BLANCHE (*gasping for breath*).

The knife—has reached—my heart.
I felt—it pierce me.

TRIBOULET.

Who has struck the blow?

BLANCHE.

The fault's mine own, for I deceived thee, father!
I loved too well! And 'tis for him—I die.

TRIBOULET.

Oh, retribution dire!—the dark revenge
I plotted for another falls on me!
But how?—what hand?—Blanche, if thou canst, explain!

BLANCHE.

Oh, ask me not to speak!

TRIBOULET (*covering her with kisses*).

Forgive me, Blanche!
And yet to lose thee thus!

BLANCHE.

I cannot breathe!
Turn me this way!—Some air!

TRIBOULET.

Blanche, Blanche! my child!
Oh, do not die! (*Turns round in despair.*)
Help, help! Will no one come? .
Will no one help my child? The ferry bell

Hangs close against the wall. An instant now
I'll leave thee, but to call assistance here,
And bring thee water.
                    [BLANCHE *makes signs that it is useless.*
                    Yet I must have aid.
                    (*Shouts for help.*)
What, ho!—Oh, live to bless your father's heart!
My child, my treasure, all that I possess
Is thee, my Blanche!—I cannot part with thee!
Oh, do not die!

            BLANCHE (*in the agony of death*).
                    Help, father!—Raise me up!
Give me some air!

            TRIBOULET.
                    My arm hath pressed on thee.
I am too rough. I think 'tis better now.
Thou hast more ease, dear Blanche!—For mercy's sake,
Try but to breathe till some one pass this way
To bring thee succor.—Help! Oh, help my child!·

            BLANCHE (*with difficulty*).
Forgive him, father!   •
            [*She dies. Her head falls back on his shoulder.*

            TRIBOULET (*in an agony*).
                    Blanche!—She's dying;—Help!
[*He runs to the ferry-bell, and rings it furiously.*
Watch! murder! help!   [*He returns to* BLANCHE.
                    Oh, speak to me again.
One word—one, only one. In mercy speak!
                    [*Essaying to lift her up.*
Why wilt thou lie so heavily, my child?
Only sixteen!—so young! Thou art not dead.
Thou would'st not leave me thus. Shall thy sweet voice
Ne'er bless thy father more? Oh, God of Heaven!
Why should this be? How cruel 'twas to give
So sweet a blessing. Yet forbear to take
Her soul away ere all its worth I knew.
Why didst thou let me count my treasure o'er?

Would'st thou had died an infant! aye, before
Thy mother's arms had clasped thee! or that day
(When quite a child) thy playmates wounded thee,
I could have borne the loss. But, oh, not now,
My child! my child!

> [*A number of people, alarmed by the ringing of the
> bell, now come in, being present during the lat-
> ter part of the foregoing speech.*

A Woman.

His sorrow wrings my heart!

Triboulet.

So ye are come at last!—indeed, 'twas time!

> [*Turning to a* Waggoner, *and seizing him by the arm.*

Hast thou a horse, my friend?—a loaded wain?

Waggoner.

I have—(*aside*) How fierce his grasp!

Triboulet.

Then take my head,
And crush it 'neath thy wheels!—my Blanche! my child!

Another Man.

This is some murder! Grief has turned his brain:
Better to part them.   [*They drag* Triboulet *away.*

Triboulet.

Never!—here I'll stay.
I love to look upon her, though she's dead.
I never wronged ye—why then treat me thus?
I know ye not. Good people, pity me! (*To the* Woman.)
Madam, you weep—you're kind. In mercy beg
They drag me not from hence.

> [*The* Woman *intercedes; they let him come back to
> the body of* Blanche. *He runs wildly to it, and
> falls on his knees.*

Upon thy knees—
Upon thy knees, thou wretch, and die with her!

The Woman.

Be calm—be comforted. If thus you rave
You must be parted!

TRIBOULET (*wild with grief*).

No! no! no!

[*Seizes her in his arms, and suddenly stops in his
       grief—his senses are evidently wandering.*

I think

She breathes again. She wants a father's care!
Go some one to the town, and seek for aid :
I'll hold her in my arms.—I'm quiet now.

[*He takes her in his arms and holds her as a mother
          would an infant.*

X   No! she's not dead, God will not have it so,
He knows that she is all I lov'd on earth.
The poor deformed one was despised by all,
Avoided, hated. None were kind to him
But she! she loved me, my delight, my joy :
When others spurned, she loved and wept with me.
So beautiful, yet dead! Your kerchief, pray,
To smooth her forehead. See, her lip's still red.
Oh, had you seen her, as I see her still,
But two years old : her pretty hair was then
As fair as gold !   [*Presses her to his heart.*

Alas! most foully wronged,
My Blanche, my happiness, my darling child !
When but an infant, oft I've held her thus :
She slept upon my bosom just as now—
And when she woke, her laughing eyes met mine,
And smiled upon me with an angel's smile.
She never thought me hideous, vile, deformed.
Poor girl! she loved her father. Now she sleeps !
Indeed, I know not what I feared before—
She'll soon awaken ! Wait awhile, I pray,
You'll see her eyes will open ! Friends ! you hear
I reason calmly. I'm quite tranquil now ;
I'll do whate'er you will, and injure none,
So that you let me look upon my child.

[*He gazes upon her face.*

How smooth her brow, no early sorrows there
Have marked the fair entablature of youth.
(*Starting.*) Ha ! I have warmed her little hand in mine.
(*To the people.*) Feel how the pulse returns !

(*Enter* a Surgeon.)

THE WOMAN (*to* TRIBOULET).

The Surgeon's here.

TRIBOULET.

Look, Sir, examine, I'll oppose in nought.
She has but fainted, is't not so?

SURGEON (*after feeling her pulse, says coldly*).

She's dead!

[TRIBOULET *starts up convulsively, the* Surgeon *goes on examining the wound.*

The wound's in her left side. 'Tis very deep.
Blood must have flowed upon the lungs. She died
By suffocation.

TRIBOULET (*with a scream of agony*).

I have slain my child!

[*He falls senseless on the ground.*

FREDERICK L. SLOUS.

RUY BLAS:

A TRAGEDY IN FIVE ACTS.

(1838.)

Translated by Mrs. Newton Crosland.

AUTHOR'S PREFACE.

THREE sorts of spectators compose what we are accustomed to call the play-going public. Firstly, women; secondly, thinkers; and thirdly, the general crowd. That which the last-named chiefly requires in a dramatic work is action; what most attracts women is passion; but what the thoughtful seek above all else is the portrayal of human nature. If one studies attentively these three classes of spectators this may be remarked; the crowd is so delighted with incident, that often it cares little for characters and passions.* Women, whom action likewise interests, are so absorbed in the development of emotion, that they little heed the representation of characters. As for the thoughtful, they so much desire to see characters, that is to say living men, on the scene, that though they willingly accept passion as a natural element in a dramatic work, they are almost troubled by the incidents. Thus what the mass desires on the stage is sensational action; what the women seek is emotion; and what the thoughtful crave is food for meditation. All demand pleasure, —the first, the pleasure of the eyes; the second, the gratification of the feelings; the last, mental enjoyment. Thus on our scene are three distinct sorts of work; the one common and inferior, the two others illustrious and superior, but all supplying a want: melodrama for the crowd; tragedy which analyzes passion for the women; and for the thinkers, comedy that paints human nature.

Let us say, in passing, that we do not lay down an infallible law, and we entreat the reader to make for himself the restric-

---

* That is to say, style. For if action can in many cases express itself by action alone, passions and characters, with few exceptions, are expressed by speech. Now the words of the drama—words fixed and not fluctuating—form style.

Let the personage speak as he should speak, *sibi constet*, says Horace. All is in that.

tions which our opinions may contain. Rules always admit of exceptions; we know well that the crowd is a great body, in which all qualities are to be found,—the instinct for the beautiful and the taste for mediocrity, love of the ideal and liking for the matter-of-fact. We know also that every great intellect ought to be feminine on the tender side of the heart ; and we are aware that, thanks to that mysterious law which attracts the sexes to each other, as well mentally as bodily, very often a woman is a thinker. This understood, and after again beseeching the reader not to attach too rigid a meaning to our statement, there only remains for us to proceed.

To every man who considers seriously the three sorts of spectators we have just indicated it will be evident that all are to be justified. The women are right in wishing to have their hearts touched; the thinkers are right in desiring to be taught; and the crowd is not wrong in wishing to be amused. From these established facts the laws of the drama are deduced. In truth, that fiery barrier called the footlights separates the world of reality from that ideal world where the dramatist's art is to create, and make live in conditions combined of art and nature, characters, that is to say, and we repeat it, men; into these men and these characters to fling the passions which develop some and modify others ; and at last, in the conflict of these characters and these passions with the great laws of Providence to show human life, that is to say events, great and small, pathetic, comic, and terrible, which prove for the heart what we call interest, and for the mind what may be considered the truths of moral philosophy; such is the aim of the drama. One sees that the drama is tragedy by its illustration of the passions, and comedy by its portrayal of characters. The mixed drama is the third great form of the art, comprising, encircling, and making fruitful the two others. Corneille and Molière would remain independent of each other if Shakespeare were not between them, giving to Corneille his left hand, and to Molière his right. In this manner the two opposite electric forces of comedy and tragedy meet, and the spark struck out is the drama.

In explaining, as he understands them, and as he has already often stated, the laws and the end of the drama, the author is not ignorant of the limitation of his own powers. He defines now—and let it be so understood—not what he has done, but what he has endeavored to do. He shows what his aim was. Nothing more.

We can but write a few lines at the beginning of this book ; we have not space for necessary details. Let us then be permitted to pass on, without dwelling otherwise on the transition from the general ideas which we have just indicated, and which in our opinion, the conditions of the ideal being maintained, rule the entire art, to some of the special reflections which this drama, *Ruy Blas*, will suggest to the attentive mind.

And first, to take only one side of the question, from the point of view of the philosophy of history, what is the spirit of this drama? Let us explain. At the moment when a monarchy is about to fall several phenomena may be observed. First, the nobility has a tendency to break up, and in dissolving divides after this fashion :—

The kingdom totters, the dynasty destroys itself, law decays: political unity crumbles away by the action of intrigue; the best born of society are corrupt and degenerate; a mortal enfeeblement is felt on all sides without and within; great purposes of the state fall low, and only little ones stand forth—a mournful public spectacle: more police, more soldiers, more taxes; every one divines the end has come. Hence among all there is the weariness of expectancy and fear of the future, distrust of all men, and general discouragement, with profound discontent. As the malady of the State is in the head, the nobility, who are the nearest, are the first attacked. What becomes of them then? One party, the least worthy and the least generous, remains at court. All will soon be engulfed, there is no time to be lost, men must hasten to enrich and aggrandize themselves and profit by circumstances. Each thinks only of himself. Without pity for the country each man acquires a little private fortune in some department of the public evil. He is courtier and minister, and hastens to be prosperous and powerful. He is clever and unscrupulous, and he succeeds. Offices of the state, honors, places, money, they take all, and covet all, and pillage everywhere; they live only for ambition and cupidity. They hide the evils which human infirmity may engender, under a grave exterior. And as this debased life, given up to the excitements of the vanities and pleasures of pride, has for its first condition oblivion of all proper sentiments, a man is made ferocious by leading it. When the day of misfortune arrives some monstrous quality is developed in the fallen courtier, and the man becomes a fiend.

The desperate state of the kingdom drives the other half of the nobility, the best and best born, into another mode of living. They retire to their palaces, their estates and country houses. They have a horror of public affairs, they can do nothing, the end of the world is at hand, what use is it to lament? They must divert themselves, and shut their eyes, live, drink, love, and be merry. Who knows? Have they not yet perhaps a year before them? This said, or even simply thought, the gentleman takes the thing in earnest, multiplies his establishment tenfold, buys horses, enriches women, orders fêtes, pays for orgies, flings away, gives, sells, buys, mortgages, forfeits, devours, gives him-

self up to money lenders, and sets fire at the four corners to all
he has. One fine morning a misfortune happens to him. It is
that, though the monarchy goes down hill at great speed, he
himself is ruined before it. All is finished, all is burnt. Of this
fine blazing life there remains not even the smoke that has passed
away; some ashes, nothing more. Forgotten and deserted by all
except his creditors, the poor gentleman then becomes what he
may,—a little of the adventurer, a little of the swash-buckler, a
little of the Bohemian. He sinks and disappears in the crowd,
that great, dull, black mass, which until this day he has scarcely
noticed, from afar off, under his feet. He plunges therein and
takes refuge there. He has no more gold, but there remains to
him the sun, that wealth of those who have nothing. At first
he dwelt in the highest society: see, now that he herds with the
lowest, and accommodates himself to it, he laughs at his ambitious relative who is rich and powerful; he becomes a philosopher,
and compares thieves to courtiers. For the rest he is good
natured, brave, loyal and intelligent; a mixture of poet, prince
and scamp; laughing at everything; making his comrades to-day
thrash the watch, as formerly he bade his servants, but not doing
it himself; combining in his manner, with some grace, the assur-
ance of a marquis with the effrontery of a gipsy; soiled outside,
but wholesome within: and having nothing left of the gentleman
but his honor which he guards, his name which he hides, and his
sword which he shows.

If the double picture we have just drawn is a faithful representation of the state of all monarchies at a given moment, it
is especially and in a striking manner true of that of Spain at
the close of the seventeenth century. Thus, if the author has
succeeded in executing this part of his plan, which he is far
from assuming, in the drama before the reader, the first half of
the Spanish nobility of that period is depicted in Don Salluste,
and the second half in Don Cæsar; the two being cousins, as is
seemly.

Here, as throughout, let it be well understood that in sketch-
ing our outline of the Castilian nobles towards 1695 we would
wish to reserve rare and revered exceptions. Let us continue.

Always in examining this monarchy and this epoch, below
the nobility thus divided—and which up to a certain point may
be personified in the two men just named—one sees trembling
in the shade something great, gloomy, and unrecognized. It is
the people. The people for whom is the future but not the
present; the people orphans, poor, intelligent and strong, placed
very low, and aspiring very high; bearing on their backs the
marks of servitude, and in their hearts the premonitions of
genius; the people serfs of the great lords, in their abject misery,

in love with the only form which in this decaying society represents for them in divine radiance authority, charity, and fertility. The people should be represented in the character of Ruy Blas.

Now above these three men, who thus considered should make move and be apparent to the spectator three facts, and in these facts all the Spanish monarchy of the seventeenth century,—above these men, we say, is a pure and luminous creature, a woman, a queen. Unhappy as wife, because she is as if she had not a husband; unhappy as queen, because she lives as if without a king; inclining towards those beneath her by royal pity, and also perhaps by womanly instinct, looking downwards, while Ruy Blas—personification of the people—looks up.

In the author's opinion, and without wishing to slight what the accessory characters may contribute to the truthfulness of the entire work, those four personages, so grouped, comprise the leading principles which present themselves to the philosophical historian of the Spanish Monarchy as it was a hundred and forty years ago.* To those four personages we might add a fifth, namely, Charles the Second. But in history, as in the drama, Charles the Second of Spain is not a figure, but a shadow.

Now let us hasten to say that what has just been stated is not an explanation of *Ruy Blas*. It is only one of the aspects. It is the impression which, if the drama be worth studying seriously and conscientiously, would be produced on the mind from the point of view of the philosophy of history.

But, small as it may be, this drama, like everything in the world, has many aspects, and it can be looked at in many other ways. One can take many views of an idea, as of a mountain. It depends on our position. Let pass, for the sake of making ourselves clear, a comparison that is infinitely too presumptuous. Mont Blanc seen from the Croix-de-Fléchères does not resemble Mont Blanc seen from Sallenches. It is, however, always Mont Blanc.

In the same manner, to descend from a very great thing to a very little one, this drama, of which we have just indicated the historical meaning, presents quite another aspect if we look at it from a still more elevated point of view, that is to say the purely human. Then Don Salluste would be the personification of absolute egotism, anxiety without rest; Don Cæsar, his opposite in all respects, would be regarded as the type of generosity and thoughtless carelessness; and Ruy Blas would express the spirit and passion of the community, and springing forth the

---

* Written in 1838.

higher in proportion to the violence of their compression; the queen would exemplify virtue undermined by wearying monotony.

Simply from the literary point of view the aspect of this design, such as it is, entitled *Ruy Blas*, would again change. The three governing forms of the art would appear there personified and summed up. Don Salluste would be the mixed drama; Don Cæsar, comedy; and Ruy Blas, tragedy. The drama provides action, comedy confuses it, and tragedy decides it.

All these aspects are just and true, but not one of them is complete. Absolute truth is only to be found in the entire work. If each finds therein what he seeks, the poet, who does not flatter himself about the remainder, will have attained his end. The philosophical motive of *Ruy Blas* is a people aspiring to a higher state; the human subject is a man who loves a woman; the dramatic interest is a lackey who loves a queen. The crowd who flock every night to witness this work, because in France public attention never fails to be directed to mental efforts, whatever they may be besides, the crowd, we say, see only in *Ruy Blas* the last, the dramatic subject, the lackey; and they are right.

And what we have just said of *Ruy Blas* seems to us applicable to every other production. The old renowned works of the masters are even more remarkable in that they offer more facets to study than others. Tartuffe makes some laugh, and others tremble. Tartuffe is the domestic serpent—the hypocrite; or rather, hypocrisy. He is sometimes a man, and sometimes an idea. Othello is for some but a black man who loves a fair woman; for others he is an upstart who has married a patrician; for some he is a jealous man; for others the personification of jealousy. And this diversity of opinion takes nothing from the fundamental unity of the composition. We have said so elsewhere; there are a thousand branches and one trunk.

If in this work the author has particularly insisted on the historical significance of *Ruy Blas,* it is that in his opinion, by its historical meaning—and it is true by that alone—*Ruy Blas* is allied to *Hernani.* The grand fact of the condition of the nobles is shown in *Hernani,* as in *Ruy Blas,* by the side of existing royalty. Only in *Hernani,* as an absolute monarchy was not yet established, the nobility still struggled with the king, here by haughtiness, there by the sword, in a mixture of feudalism and rebellion. In 1519 the great lord lived far from court, in the mountains as bandit like Hernani, or in patriarchal state like Ruy Gomez. Two centuries later the position is changed. The vassals have become courtiers, and if from circumstances the noble has still occasion to conceal his name, it is not to escape from the king, but to elude his creditors. He does not become a bandit, he turns Bohemian. One feels that royal despotism has passed during these long years over the noble heads, bending some and crushing others.

And, if we may be permitted this last word between *Hernani* and *Ruy Blas*, two centuries of Spanish life are framed; two great centuries, during which the descendants of Charles the Fifth were permitted to rule the world; two centuries of a state which Providence—and it is a remarkable thing—would not prolong another hour, for Charles the Fifth * was born in 1500, and Charles the Second died in 1700. In 1700 Louis the Fourteenth inherited from Charles the Fifth, as in 1800 Napoleon inherited from Louis the Fourteenth. These great dynastic apparitions, which from time to time illuminate history, are for the author a beautiful and pathetic spectacle to which his eyes often turn. He tries at times to transfer something of their interest to his works. Thus he has striven to show *Hernani* in the bright light of an aurora, and to cover *Ruy Blas* with the gloom of twilight. In *Hernani* the sun of the House of Austria was rising; in *Ruy Blas* it was setting.

PARIS, *November 25th*, 1838.

* Charles the Fifth of Germany and First of Spain.

PERSONAGES OF THE DRAMA

RUY BLAS.
DON SALLUSTE DE BAZAN.
DON CÆSAR DE BAZAN.
DON GURITAN.
THE COUNT DE CAMPOREAL.
THE MARQUIS DE SANTA-CRUZ.
THE MARQUIS DEL BASTO
THE COUNT D'ALBE.
THE MARQUIS DE PRIEGO.
DON MANUEL ARIAS.
MONTAZGO.
DON ANTONIO UBILLA.
COVADENGA.
GUDIEL.

A Lackey.
An Alcaid.
An Usher.
An Alguazil.
A Page.

DOÑA MARIA DE NEUBOURG, Queen of Spain.
THE DUCHESS D'ALBUQUERQUE.
CASILDA.
A DUENNA.

Ladies, Lords, Privy Councillors, Pages, Duennas, Alguazils,
Guards, and Gentlemen Ushers.

MADRID, 169—.

RUY BLAS.

ACT FIRST: DON SALLUSTE.

[*The Hall of Danaé in the King's palace at Madrid. Magnificent furniture in the half-Flemish Style of Philip IV.
At the left, a large window with small squares of glass
set in gilt frames. On each side a low door leading to
some interior apartments. At the back, a large glass
partition with gilt frames opens by a glass door on a
long corridor. This corridor, which stretches all along
the stage, is concealed by wide curtains that fall from
top to bottom of the glass partition. A table with
writing materials, and an easy chair.*

DON SALLUSTE *enters by the little door at the left, followed
by* RUY BLAS, *and by* GUDIEL, *who carries a cash-box
and other packages as if in preparation for a journey.*
DON SALLUSTE *is dressed in black velvet, in the fashion
of the Court of Charles II., and wears the Golden
Fleece. Over his black dress he has a rich mantle of
light velvet embroidered with gold and lined with black
satin. A sword with a large hilt. A hat with white
feathers.* GUDIEL *is in black and wears a sword.* RUY
BLAS *is in livery—leggings and undercoat brown; over-
coat turned up with red and gold. Bareheaded and
without a sword.*

SCENE 1.—DON SALLUSTE DE BAŻAN, GUDIEL;
RUY BLAS *at intervals.*

DON SALLUSTE.

That window open, Ruy Blas—and shut
The door.

[RUY BLAS *obeys, and then, at a sign from* DON
SALLUSTE, *goes out by the door at the back.*
DON SALLUSTE *walks to the window.*
            All here still sleep. 'Tis nearly dawn.
        (*He turns suddenly towards* GUDIEL.)
It is a thunderbolt ! Ah, yes, my reign
Is over, Gudiel ! Exiled and disgraced,
All lost in but a day. At present, though,
The thing is secret—speak not of it, pray.
Yes, only for a little love affair,
—At my age senseless folly I admit—
And with a nobody—a serving maid
Seduced—ill luck ! because she was about
The Queen, who brought the girl from Neubourg here.
This creature wept, complained of me, and dragg'd
Into the royal chambers her young brat ;
Then was I ordered to espouse the girl,
And I refused. They banished me. Me—me
They exiled ! After twenty years of work
So difficult, engaging day and night,
Years of ambition. I, the President,
Abhorr'd by all the Court Alcaids, who named
Me but with dread. Chief of the house Bazan
That is so proud ; my credit, power, and all
I did, and had, and dreamed, honors and place
One moment sweeps away, amid the roars
Of laughter of the crowd.

                    GUDIEL.
                        None know it yet,
My Lord.

            DON SALLUSTE.
        Ah, but to-morrow ! 'Twill be known
To-morrow ! We shall then be on our way.
I will not fall. No, no, I'll disappear.
        (*He hastens to unbutton his doublet.*)
You always fasten me as if I were
A priest. You strain my doublet ; and oh, now
I stifle.
        (*He sits down.*)

Ah, with th' air of innocence
I'll dig a deep, dark mine! Chased—chased away!
(*He rises.*)

GUDIEL.

Whence came the blow, my Lord?

DON SALLUSTE.

'Twas from the Queen.
Oh, Gudiel, I will be revenged. Thou know'st,
Thou understandest me—whom thou hast taught
And aided well for twenty years in things
Long past. Thou know'st where turn my darken'd
thoughts,
As a skill'd architect can at a glance
Measure the depth of wells that he has sunk.
I will set out for my Castilian lands,
Estates of Finlas, there to brood and plan.
All for a girl! Thou must—for time is short—
Arrange for our departure. First I'd speak
A word at any risk unto the scamp
Thou know'st. It may be that he proves of use.
I know not. But till night I'm master here.
I will have vengeance—how I cannot tell;
But I will make it terrible. Go now,
At once get ready—hasten—silent be!
You shall go with me—hasten.

[GUDIEL *bows and exit.* DON SALLUSTE *calls.*
Ruy Blas!

RUY BLAS (*appearing at the door at the back*).
Excellency?

DON SALLUSTE.

Within the Palace walls
I sleep no more; thus shutters should be closed
The keys be left.

RUY BLAS.

My Lord, it shall be done.

DON SALLUSTE.

Listen, I beg. In two hours will the Queen,
In coming back from mass unto her room

Of state, pass through the corridor; you must
Be there.

Ruy Blas.

I will, my Lord.

Don Salluste (*at the window*).

                See you that man
I' the square—a paper to the guard he shows
And passes? Sign to him without a word
That he may enter by the back stair way.

[Ruy Blas *obeys.* Don Salluste *continues, pointing*
      to the little door on the right.

Before you go look in the guard room there—
See if three Alguazils on duty are
As yet awake.

Ruy Blas (*he goes to the door, half opens it, and*
      comes back).

      My Lord, they sleep.

Don Salluste.

                Speak low.
I shall be wanting you, so go not far
Away. Keep watch that we be not disturbed.

[*Enter* Don Cæsar de Bazan. *Hat staved in. A
ragged cloak, which conceals all his dress except
stockings that hang loose, and shoes that are split
open. Sword of a brawler.*

As he enters, he and Ruy Blas *glance at each other
from opposite sides with gestures of surprise.*

Don Salluste (*observing them, aside*).

Looks were exchanged! Can they each other know!

                [*Exit* Ruy Blas.

Scene 2.—Don Salluste—Don Cæsar.

Don Salluste.

So, bandit, you are here!

Don Cæsar.

           Yes, cousin, yes.
Behold me.

DON SALLUSTE.

Great the pleasure 'tis to see

A beggar!

DON CÆSAR (*bowing*).

I delighted am.

DON SALLUSTE.

                    We know

Your doings, sir.

DON CÆSAR (*graciously*).

        Which you approve?

DON SALLUSTE.

                  Oh yes,

They're mighty meritorious. Don Charles
De Mira but the other night was robb'd.
They took from him his sword with scabbard chased,
And shoulder belt. As 'twas near Easter Eve,
And he a knight of bless'd St. James, the band
Let him retain his cloak.

DON CÆSAR.

           Just heaven, why?

DON SALLUSTE.

Because upon it was embroidered plain
The order. Well, what say you to all this?

DON CÆSAR.

The devil! I but say we live in times
Most dreadful. Oh, what will become of us
If thieves pay court to good St. James, and count
Him of themselves?

DON SALLUSTE.

        You were with them.

DON CÆSAR.

                Well, yes;

If I must speak, I was. But your Don Charles
I did not touch. I only gave advice.

DON SALLUSTE.

Worse still. Last night, just when the moon had set,
A crowd of low riff-raff,—all sorts of men,

Shoeless and ragged, rushed out from their dens
Pell-mell unto the Mayor Square, and then
Attacked the guard. There you were.

DON CÆSAR.

Cousin, yes,
'Tis true. But always I disdain to fight
The mere thief-catchers. There I was—that's all;
For during all the row, I walked apart
Beneath th' Arcade, verse making. Ah, they knock'd
Each other about finely.

DON SALLUSTE.

. That's not all.

DON CÆSAR.

Well, what is it?

DON SALLUSTE.

'Mong other things, in France
They say that you, with rebels like yourself,
Did force the lock of the strong money box
Of the Excise

DON CÆSAR.

Oh, I deny it not,
France is the country of an enemy.

DON SALLUSTE.

Again, in Flanders, meeting with Don Paul
Barthélemy, who then had just received
The product of a vineyard he was charged
To carry to Mons' noble Chapter, you
Laid hands upon it, though the gold belonged
E'en to the clergy.

DON CÆSAR.

In Flanders, was it?
It might be so, for I have travelled much.
And is that all?

DON SALLUSTE.

The sweat of shame, Don Cæsar,
To my forehead mounts whene'er I think of you.

DON CÆSAR.

Well, let it mount.

DON SALLUTE.
Our family——

DON CÆSAR.
No, stay;
For only unto you in all Madrid
My real name is known. So do not speak
Of family.

DON SALLUSTE.
Only the other day,
A marchioness, when leaving Church, spoke thus:
Who is that brigand there below, who struts
With nose turned up, and eyes upon the watch,
Squaring himself with arms a-kimbo set?
More tatter'd far than Job, and prouder he
Than a Braganza—covering his rags
With arrogance—handling his big sword-hilt
Beneath his sleeve, that's all in slits, the while
The blade about his heels hangs as he steps
With masterful air, his cloak in dented gaps
Resembling saws, his stockings all awry.

DON CÆSAR (*glancing at his own attire*).
And then, of course, you promptly answered her,
It is dear Zafari !

DON SALAUSTE.
No, Sir, I blush'd.

DON CÆSAR.
Ah, well, the lady had her laugh. I like
To make a woman laugh.

·DON SALLUSTE.
Your comrades are
Swashbucklers infamous.

DON CÆSAR.
Mere learners they—
Scholars—each one as gentle as a sheep.

DON SALLUSTE.

You everywhere are seen with women vile.

DON CÆSAR.

Oh Love's bright radiance! Oh sweet Isabels!
What fine things now one hears of you! A shame
It is to treat you thus—beauties with sly
And laughing eyes, to whom I tell at night
The sonnets I have made at morn.

DON SALLUSTE.

In short,
The friend you are of Matalobos, that
Galician thief who desolates Madrid,
Defying our police.

DON CÆSAR.

If you will deign
I beg you let us reason. Without him
Bare-backed I should have been—that would have looked
Unseemly. Seeing me without a coat,
Though it was winter time, he felt for me.—
That amber-perfumed fop, the Count of Albe,
Was robbed but lately of his doublet fine,
His silken one——

DON SALLUSTE.

Well?

DON CÆSAR.

I it is who have it,
Matalobos gave it me.

DON SALLUTE.

The Count's pelisse!
And you are not ashamed?

DON CÆSAR.

I'm ne'er ashamed
Of wearing a good coat, 'broidered, galloon'd,
That keeps me warm in winter—makes me smart
In summer time. Look, here it is, quite new.

[*He half opens his cloak, and shows a superb doub-*
let of rose-colored satin embroidered in gold.

By scores, love-letters written to the Count
Are cramm'd i' the pockets. Oft, when poor, love-sick,
With nought to eat, a steaming vent hole I
Discover, from the which comes up the smell
Of cooking, cheating then by turns my heart
And stomach, I can sit me down to read
The Count's sweet letters, revelling there alike
I' the scent of feasting, and a dream of love.

DON SALLUSTE.

Don Cæsar——

DON CÆSAR.

Cousin, now a truce, I beg,
Unto reproaches. A grandee I am,
And of your kindred. Cæsar is my name,
The Count Garofa, but upon my birth
'Twas folly crown'd me. Lands and palaces
I had, and well I paid the Cólimènes.
Pshaw! Scarcely twenty years I knew before
The whole had vanished, only there remained
Of my good fortune—true or false—a pack
Of creditors to howl about my heels.
Good faith! I took to flight and changed my name.
Now am I but a boon companion found,
Zafari, whom none know by other name
Save you. No money, Master, give you me;
I do without. At night, with head upon
The stones, before the ancient palace walls
Of Tevé, there these nine years past I've stopp'd.
I slumber with the blue sky overhead,
And happy thus. 'Tis a fine fortune, mine!
The world believes me to the Indies gone,
Or to the devil—dead. The fountain near
Supplies my drink, and afterwards I walk
With air of glory. My own palace, whence
My money flew, is tenanted to-day
By the Pope's Nuncio, Espinola. Well,
When I by chance am there, I give advice
Unto the Nuncio's workmen—occupied
In sculpturing a Bacchus o'er the door.—
But will you lend me just ten crowns?

DON SALLUSTE.

> Hear me——

DON CÆSAR (*crossing his arms*).
Now, what is't you would say?

DON SALLUSTE.

> I sent for you ·
That I might serve you. I, childless and rich,
And much the elder, see you, Cæsar, now
With sorrow and regret to ruin dragged,
And fain would save you. Bully that you are,
You are unfortunate. I'll pay your debts,
Restore your palace—place you at the Court,
And make of you again a lady-killer.
Let then Zafari be extinguished now,
And Cæsar newly born. I wish that you
Henceforth should, at your will, my fortune use
Fearless, and taking with both hands, nor care
For future needs. When we have relatives
We must support them, and be pitiful.

> [*While* DON SALLUSTE *is speaking* DON CÆSAR'S *countenance takes more and more the expression of astonishment, joyous and hopeful. At last he bursts out.*

DON CÆSAR.
You always had a devil's wit, and what
You've said just now's most eloquently put.
Go on.

DON SALLUSTE.

> Yes, Cæsar, I will do all this
On one condition. I'll explain it all
A moment hence. First take my purse.

DON CÆSAR (*weighing the purse, which is full of gold*).

> This is
Magnificent!

DON SALLUSTE.

> And I intend for you
Five hundred ducats.

DON CÆSAR (*bewildered*).
Marquis!

DON SALLUSTE.

From to-day.

DON CÆSAR.

By Jove, I'm yours to order. Now then tell
Conditions—name them. On a brave man's faith
My sword is at your service to command.
Your slave I am, and, if you wish it so,
I'll cross blades with the Don Spavento, who
A captain is that comes from hell.

DON SALLUSTE.

No, not
Your sword can I accept, for reasons good.

DON CÆSAR.

What then? Right little else have I.

DON SALLUSTE (*drawing nearer and lowering his voice*).

You know,
And in this case 'tis lucky, all the rogues
About Madrid.

DON CÆSAR.

You do me honor.

DON SALLUSTE.

You
Can always in your train bring all the pack;
You could raise up a tumult if need be.
I know it. All this may be useful now.

DON CÆSAR.

Upon my word it seems you would invent
An opera. What part am I to take?
Shall I compose the verse, or symphony?
Command, I for a frolic row am good.

DON SALLUSTE (*gravely*).

'Tis to Don Cæsar that I speak, and not
Zafari (*lowering his voice more and more*). List! 'Tis
for a stern result

I need that some one should in secret work
And aid me with his skill to bring about
A great event. Not mischievous am I,
But times there are when without any shame
One the most delicate turns up his sleeves
And sets to work. Thou shalt be rich, but thou
Must help me silently to spread a net
As in the night bird-catchers do. A web
That's strong, but hid by shining glass, a snare
Such as is set for lark or girl. The plan,
It must be terrible and wonderful.
I think you are not very scrupulous.—
Avenge me.

DON CÆSAR.

You avenge!

DON SALLUSTE.

Yes, me.

DON CÆSAR.

On whom?

DON SALLUSTE.

A woman.

DON CÆSAR (*drawing himself up and looking haughtily at* DON SALLUSTE).

Halt! and say no more of this
To me. Now, Cousin, on my soul I'll speak
My mind to you. He who can claim the right
A sword to bear, and yet by stealthy means
Takes vengeance basely—on a woman, too,—
Who, born patrician, acts the bailiff's part,
Were he grandee of Old Castile, and did
A hundred clarions follow him, and sound
Their din, were he with orders harness'd, were
He Marquis, Viscount, or the lineal heir
Of blameless, noble sire—for me he'd be
Only a scoundrel of the deepest dye,
Whom for such villainy I'd gladly see
Upon the gallows, hanging by four nails.

DON SALLUSTE.

Cæsar!——

DON CÆSAR.

Add not a word, outrageous 'tis.

[*He throws the purse at the feet of* DON SALLUSTE.

There—keep your secret and your money, too.
Ah, I can comprehend a theft, a stroke
That's murderous, or in darkness of the night
The forcing prison doors—hatchet in hand,
And with a hundred desperate buccaneers,
With howl and thrust, to slaughter jailers there,
Claiming, we bandits, for an eye an eye,
And tooth for tooth—men against men. That's well.
But stealthily a woman to destroy,
And dig a trap beneath her feet—perchance
Abuse her, for who knows what chance may be?—
To take this poor bird in some hideous snare—
Oh, rather than accomplish such dishonor,
And be at such a price, my noble Lord,
So rich and great—I say before my God,
Who sees my soul, much sooner would I choose—
Than reach such odious infamy—that dogs
Should gnaw my bones beneath the pillory.

DON SALLUSTE.

Cousin——

DON CÆSAR.

Your benefits I shall not need,
So long as I shall find in my free life
Fountains of water—in the fields fresh air,
And in the town a thief who me provides
With winter raiment; in my soul shall be
Forgetfulness of past prosperity,
When, Sir, before your palace's great doors,
At noon I lay me down, my head in shade
And feet in sunshine, without thought for what
May be on waking. So adieu;—'tis God
Can judge between us. Now, Don Salluste, you
I leave with people of the Court, who are
Of your own sort; I with the scamps will stay.
I herd with wolves, but not with serpents.

DON SALLUSTE.

Hold
An instant——
DON CÆSAR.

Now, my master, cease. Let us
Cut short this visit; if 'twas meant to trap
And send me off to prison—do it quick.

DON SALLUSTE.

I thought you, Cæsar, much more hardened. Ah,
My trial of you has succeeded well.
I now am satisfied. Your hand, I pray.

DON CÆSAR.

How—what?

DON SALLUSTE.

'Twas but in jest I spoke to you.
All that I said just now was but a test,
And nothing more.

DON CÆSAR.

You've set me dreaming, though,
About a woman, vengeance, and a plot——

DON SALLUSTE.

A trap—imagination, that was all.

DON CÆSAR.

Ah, well and good!—But how about my debts?
Is paying them imagination, too?
And the five hundred ducats promised me?

DON SALLUSTE.

I'm going now to fetch them.
     [*He goes towards the door at the back, and makes
          a sign to* RUY BLAS *to come in.*

DON CÆSAR (*aside, at the front, and looking across to*
          DON SALLUSTE).

Hum! The face
A traitor's is. And when the mouth says yes,
The look implies, perhaps.

Don Salluste (*to* Ruy Blas).
> Ruy Blas, stay here.
(*to* Don Cæsar).

I'm coming back.

> [*Exit by little door at left. As soon as he is gone,*
> Don Cæsar *and* Ruy Blas *approach each other*
> *eagerly.*

Scene 3.—Don Cæsar—Ruy Blas.

Don Cæsar.
> No, I was not deceived;

Upon my faith, 'tis thou, Ruy Blas!

Ruy Blas.
> 'Tis thou,

Zafari! But how comest thou within
The palace?

Don Cæsar.
> Oh, by chance. But soon I take

Myself away. I am a bird, and like
Free space. But thou? this livery? is it worn
For a disguise?

Ruy Blas (*bitterly*).
> No, I'm disguised when I

Am otherwise.

Don Cæsar.
> What is it that you say?

Ruy Blas.
Give me thy hand to press again, as in
The happy time of joy and wretchedness.
When without home I lived, hungry by day
And cold at night, when I at least was free!
Then when thou knew'st me, I was still a man;
Born of the people both of us—alas!
It was life's morn!—So much alike we were
That many thought us brothers, and from dawn
Of day we caroll'd—and at night we slept
Before our God, our Father and our Host,
Beneath starr'd heaven sleeping side by side.

Yes, we shared all things—but at last there came
The day—the mournful hour when we were forced
To go our different ways, but now unchanged,
After four years I find thee still the same;
As joyous as a child, and free as are
The gipsy folk. Always Zafari, rich
Though poor, who never had, and never aught
Desired! But as for me, what change! What can
I say, my brother? Orphan boy, brought up
From charity at College! nursed in pride
And science, it but proved a mournful boon.
Instead of skilful workman I was made
A dreamer. Thou hast known me well. My thoughts
And aspirations lifted I to heav'n
In strophes wild. Against thy railing laugh
I brought a hundred answers. Knowing then
That strange ambition fired my soul, what need
Had I to work? But towards an end unseen
I moved; I thought dreams true and possible,
And hoped all things from fate.—And since I am
Of those who pass long, idle days in thought
Before some palace gorged with wealth—and watch
The Duchesses go in and out—one day,
When torn by hunger in the street, I picked
Up bread where I could find it;—brother, 'twas
By ignominious sluggishness. Oh, when
I was but twenty, full of confidence
In my own powers, I barefoot walked, but lost
In meditations on humanity;
I built up many plans, a mountain made
Of projects. Pitying the ills of Spain
I thought, poor soul, that by the world myself
Was needed. Friend, the issue see—behold,
I am a lackey!

DON CÆSAR.

Yes, I know full well
That want is a low door, which, when we must
By stern necessity pass through, doth force
The greatest to bend down the most. But fate
Has ever ebb and flow. So hope, I say.

Ruy Blas (*shaking his head*).
My master is the Marquis of Finlas.

Don Cæsar.
I know him. Is it, then, that you reside
Within this palace?

Ruy Blas.
No! until to-day,
Just now, I never have the threshold cross'd.

Don Cæsar.
Ah, is it so? Your master from his place,
His duties, must live here himself?

Ruy Blas.
Oh yes,
The Court may want him any hour. But he
A little secret dwelling has—where perhaps
In daylight he has never yet been seen.
An unobtrusive house, a hundred steps
Beyond the palace; brother, there I live;
And by the secret door, of which alone
He has the key, sometimes at night he comes
Followed by men whom he lets in. These men
Are masked and speak in whispering tones. They are
Shut in together, and none ever knows
What passes then. Of two black mutes I am
The master and companion. But my name
They know not.

Don Cæsar.
Yes, 'tis there that he receives
His spies, as Chief of the Alcaids. 'Tis there
He plans his many snares. Subtle is he,
And holds all in his hand.

Ruy Blas.
'Twas yesterday
He said "you must be at the palace ere
The dawn; and enter by the golden grill."
I came, and then he made me don this suit,
This odious livery which you see me in,
And which to-day I for the first time wear.

DON CÆSAR.

Sill hope !

RUY BLAS.

I hope ! But you know nothing yet.
To breath 'neath this degrading garb, to lose
The joy and pride of life—all this is naught.
To be a slave and vile, what matters that !
But listen, brother, well. I do not feel
This servile dress, for at my heart there dwells
A hydra, with the fangs of flame, that binds
Me in its fiery folds. If the outside
Has shock'd you—what would be could you but look
Within?

DON CÆSAR.

What can you mean ?

RUY BLAS.

Invent—suppose—
Imagine—search your mind for all strange things
Unheard of, mad, and horrible—a fate
Bewildering ! Yes, compose a deadly draught,
And dig a pit more black than crime, more dull
Than folly, still my secret thou wilt not
Approach. Thou canst not guess it ! Ah, who could,
Zafari ? In the gulf where destiny
Has plunged me—plunge thine eyes ! I love the queen !

DON CÆSAR.

Good heavens !

RUY BLAS.

Beneath a splendid canopy,
Adorned at top with the Imperial globe,
There is in Aranjuez, or may be
In the Escurial—or sometimes here—
A man that scarce is looked on from below,
Or named, except with dread—before whose eyes
We all of equal meanness seem, as if
That he were God. A man that men gaze on
With trembling, serving him on bended knee.
To in his presence stand with cover'd head
Is token of high honor. If he will'd

Our heads should fall, a sign would be enough.
His every whim is an event. He lives
Alone—superb—encased in majesty,
So bulwark'd and profound, its weight is felt
Through half the world. Well, now thou understand'st
That I the lackey—ah, yes even I
Am jealous of that man—yes, of the king!

Don Cæsar.

You jealous of the king!

Ruy Blas.
          Undoubtedly,
Because I love his wife!

Don Cæsar.
          Unhappy one!

Ruy Blas.
Listen: each day I watch to see her pass,
And like a madman am. And oh, the life
Of this poor thing is one long weariness.
Each night I dream of her. Oh, think what 'tis
For her to live in this dull court of hate,
And base hypocrisies,—married to one
Who in the chase spends all his time! A king—
A fool—an imbecile! at thirty years
Already old—and less than man—unfit
Alike to live or reign. And of a race
That's dying off. His father could not hold
A parchment, so debilitated he!
What misery for her, so young and fair,
Thus to be wedded to the second Charles!
Unto the sisters of the Rosary
She goes each eve—thou know'st it—traversing
The Ortaleza street,—I cannot tell
How 'twas this madness grew within my heart,
But judge! She loves a little azure flower
Of Germany—I go each day a league
To Caramanchel, where alone I find
It grows. I have sought for it everywhere.
I pluck the finest, and a posy make.

Oh, but I tell you now these foolish things !—
At midnight like a thief I scale the wall
Around the royal park, and place the flowers
Upon her favorite bench. Even last night
I dared to put a letter 'mid the flowers—
Truly a letter ! Brother, pity me !
At night to reach this bank I have to mount
The wall where bristle iron spikes. I know
Some time that I shall leave my flesh thereon.
Now will she find my flowers—my letter too ?
I know not—but you see how mad I am.

DON CÆSAR.

It is the devil ! Now take care—thy game
Is dang'rous. There's the Count Oñate, he loves
Her also, and keeps guard as Chamberlain
As well as lover. On some night a trooper
Unpitying might despatch you with one blow,
Before your flowers were faded nailing them
Unto your heart. Oh th' idea, I say,
Is quite preposterous—loving thus the queen !
And why ? It is a devil's scrape you're in.

RUY BLAS (*with energy*).

Do I not know it ! I myself ! My soul
Is given over, I would sell it might
I thus become like one of those young Lords
That from this window I behold—who are
A live offence, entering with plumèd hats
And haughty brows. Yes, if I could but break
My chain, and could, as they, approach the queen
In garments not degrading. But—oh ! rage,
To thus appear to her, and unto them !
To be for her a lackey ! pity me,
Oh God !   [*Approaching* DON CÆSAR.
        But I must recollect myself.
Ask'st thou not when and why I loved her thus ?
One day—but what's the good of this ? 'Tis true
My desperate madness I've made known to thee
And all my thousand tortures made you share,
In showing you my agony—but ask

Not how—or wherefore! only I love her—
Insanely love her, that is all.

DON CÆSAR.
There now,
Don't fret.

RUY BLAS (*pale and overcome, falling into the arm-chair*).
No—no—I suffer—pardon me,
Or rather fly from me, my brother. Go,
And leave the wretched madman who but knows
With horror that beneath the lackey's coat
There rage the passions of a king!

DON CÆSAR (*laying his hand on the shoulder of* RUY BLAS).
Leave thee!
What, I! who have not suffer'd thus because
I have not loved. Like a poor bell am I
Without a clapper—beggar who e'en begs
For love he knows not where. To whom from time
To time fate throws some paltry coin. With heart
Extinguished—drawn within itself, as from
The tatter'd play-bill of the yester night.
Seest thou that for this all absorbing love
I envy quite as much as pity thee!
Oh, Ruy Blas!
[*A moment of silence, while with clasped hands
they look at each other sorrowfully, but with
confiding friendship.*

Enter DON SALLUSTE. *He advances softly, looking at*
DON CÆSAR *and* RUY BLAS *with profound attention,
they not perceiving him. In one hand he holds a hat
and a sword, which on entering he places on an
arm-chair, and in the other a purse which he lays
on the table.*

DON SALLUSTE (*to* DON CÆSAR).
Here is the money.
[*At the voice of* DON SALLUSTE, RUY BLAS, *suddenly
aroused, starts up, and with eyes looking down,
assumes an attitude of respect.*

DON CÆSAR (*aside, and looking sideways at* DON SALLUSTE).
Ah,

The devil has me! At the door no doubt
The artful one has listened. After all
What matter—Pshaw! (*aloud to* DON SALLUSTE).
Don Salluste, thanks.

[*He opens the purse—spreads the money on the table,
handling the ducats delightedly. Then he ar-
ranges them in two piles on the velvet cover.
While he is counting them,* DON SALLUSTE *goes
to the back, looking behind him to be sure that*
DON CÆSAR *is not observing him. He opens the
little door at the right. At a sign from him
three Alguazils, armed with swords and dressed
in black, appear.* DON SALLUSTE *points out*
DON CÆSAR *to them in a mysterious manner.*
RUY BLAS *stands upright and motionless as a
statue by the table, neither seeing nor hearing
anything.*

DON SALLUSTE (*in a low tone to the* Alguazils).
You see

That man who counts the money—follow him
When he goes hence, and seize him silently,
And without violence. And then embark
By shortest way to Denia.
[*He gives them a sealed parchment.*
Here is writ

The order by my hand. And afterwards,
Without attending to his statements, all
Chimerical, you'll sell him on the sea
To corsairs there will be from Africa;
A thousand piastres for you—but be quick.
[*The three Alguazils bow and exeunt.*

DON CÆSAR (*finishing the arrangement of his ducats*).
Surely there's nothing more amusing than
To equally divide the crowns that are
One's own.
(*He makes two equal piles and turns to* RUY BLAS.)
Here, brother, is thy share.

RUY BLAS.
                              How—what!

DON CÆSAR (*pointing to one of the heaps of gold*).
Come—take, be free!

DON SALLUSTE (*aside, looking at them from the back*).
                    The devil!

RUY BLAS (*shaking his head in sign of refusal*).
                              No—the heart
It is that has to be delivered. No,
My lot is here. I must remain.

DON CÆSAR.
                    Well—well
Have thine own way. Art thou the crazy one?
And am I wise? God knows.
          [*He gathers the money into the bag and puts it in
              his pocket.*

DON SALLUSTE (*from the back, watching them*).
                              How near alike
They are in mien and face!

DON CÆSAR (*to* RUY BLAS)
                    Adieu!

RUY BLAS.
                              Thy hand!
[*They press hands. Exit* DON CÆSAR *without noticing* DON SALLUSTE, *who has kept himself apart*

SCENE 4.—RUY BLAS. DON SALLUSTE.

DON SALLUSTE.
Ruy Blas!

RUY BLAS (*turning quickly*).
My Lord?

DON SALLUSTE.
                    I am not confident
Whether 'twas fully daylight when you came
This morning—tell me.

RUY BLAS.

Excellency, no,

Not quite. I gave your pass without a word
To the door-keeper, then came up.

DON SALLUSTE.

Wore you

A cloak?

RUY BLAS.

I did, my Lord.

DON SALLUSTE.

In that case then

None in the Castle yet has seen on you
This livery?

RUY BLAS.

Nor person of Madrid.

DON SALLUSTE (*pointing to the door by which* DON CÆSAR *had
gone out*).

That's well. Go, close the door. Take off this coat.

[RUY BLAS *takes off his livery-coat and throws it on
a chair.*

I think your writing's good. Write now for me.

[*He makes a sign to* RUY BLAS *to seat himself at
the table where there are writing materials.*
RUY BLAS *obeys.*

My secretary you must be to-day,
And first a love-letter must write; you see
I nothing hide from you—my queen of love
Is Doña Praxedis—a witch that's come,
I think, from paradise. There—I'll dictate.
" A danger terrible environs me;
My queen alone can stay the tempest's force
By coming to my house this night. If not,
I'm lost. My life, my heart, my reason now
I lay before the feet I kiss."

[*He laughs, interrupting himself.*

Danger,

A turn well put to draw her on. I am
Expert. Women like much to save just those
Who fool them most. Add now, " Come to the door

That's at the end of the Avenue—at night
You'll not be recognized. And one who is
Devoted will be there to ope the door."
'Tis perfect, on my word.—Sign now.

RUY BLAS.
Your name,
My Lord?

DON SALLUSTE.
Not so—sign Caesar. 'Tis the name
in such adventures I adopt.

RUY BLAS (*after having obeyed*).
Unknown
Will be the writing to the lady?

DON SALLUSTE.
Pshaw!
The seal will be enough. Oft thus I write.
I go away at night-fall, Ruy Blas,
And leave you here. I'm planning for you as
A friend sincere. Your state shall change, but then
You must obey me in all things. In you
I've found a servant faithful and discreet.

RUY BLAS (*bowing*).
My Lord!

DON SALLUSTE.
To better your condition here
I wish.

RUY BLAS (*showing the letter he has just written*).
How should the letter be addressed?

DON SALLUSTE.
I will attend to that.
[*Approaching* RUY BLAS *in a significant manner.*
I wish your good.
[*Silence for a few moments. Then he makes a sign
for* RUY BLAS *to seat himself again at the table.*
Write thus. "I, Ruy Blas, the serving man
Of the most noble Lord the Marquis of
Finlas, engage to serve him faithfully

On all occasions as a servant true
In public or in secrecy." (RUY BLAS *obeys*.)
                        Now sign
Your name. The date. That's well. Give it to me.
        [*He folds and puts into his portfolio the letter and
        the paper which* RUY BLAS *has just written.*
Just now they brought me in a sword.—Ah, there
It is upon the chair.
        [*He looks towards the arm-chair on which he had
        placed the sword and hat—goes to it and takes
        up the sword.*
                        The tie's of silk,
Painted and 'broidered in the newest style—
                [*He makes* RUY BLAS *admire it.*
Take it. What say you to this foil, Ruy Blas?
The hilt is workmanship of Gil the famed
Engraver, he who chisels out a box
For sweetmeats in a sword's hilt, to amuse
The pretty girls.
        [*He passes the scarf to which the sword is attached
        over the shoulders of* RUY BLAS.
                Now put it on—I want
To see the effect on you. I do declare
You look a noble every inch. (*Listening.*)
                        They come—
Ah yes, 'tis almost time the queen were here—
The Marquis Basto !—
        [*The door at the end of the corridor opens.* DON
        SALLUSTE *unfastens his cloak and hastily throws
        it over the shoulders of* RUY BLAS, *just at the
        moment when the* MARQUIS DEL BASTO *appears;
        then he goes up to the* MARQUIS, *drawing after
        him* RUY BLAS *in a stupefied state.*

SCENE 5.—DON SALLUSTE, RUY BLAS, DON PAMFILO D'AVALOS,
MARQUIS DEL BASTO,—*afterwards the* MARQUIS DE SANTA-
CRUZ, *then the* COUNT D'ALBE *and all the Court.*

        DON SALLUSTE (*to the* MARQUIS DEL BASTO).
                        Let me to your grace

Present my cousin—the Don Cæsar—Count
Of Garofa, near to Velalcazar.

> RUY BLAS (*aside*).

Oh heav'ns !

> DON SALLUSTE (*aside to* RUY BLAS).
> Silence !

> MARQUIS DEL BASTO (*to* RUY BLAS).
> Sir, I am charm'd——

[*He puts out his hand, which* RUY BLAS *takes in a
confused manner.*

> DON SALLUSTE (*in a whisper to* RUY BLAS).

Let be—
Salute him.   [RUY BLAS *bows to the* MARQUIS.

> MARQUIS DEL BASTO (*to* RUY BLAS).
> Ah, I loved your mother much.
> (*Aside to* DON SALLUSTE.)

How changed ! I scarcely would have known him

> DON SALLUSTE (*speaking low to the* MARQUIS).

Ah !
Ten years away !

> MARQUIS DEL BASTO (*in the same manner*).
> Indeed !

> DON SALLUSTE (*slapping* RUY BLAS *on the shoulder*).
> At last come back !

You recollect the prodigal he was ?
And how he squander'd the pistoles ? Each night
A dance or fête—a hundred instruments
Of music on Apollo's fish-pond raged.
Concerts and masquerades, and wildest pranks
Dazzled Madrid with sudden scenes. Ruin'd
In just three years ! Truly a lion he.—
He came from India in the galleon.

> RUY BLAS (*confused*).

My Lord——

> DON SALLUSTE (*gaily*).
> Oh, call me cousin—such we are.

We, the Bazans, are an old family,

Our ancestor was Iniguez d'Iviza ;
His grandson, Pedro de Bazan, was wed
To Marianne de Gor. Their son was Jean ;
Under King Philip he was admiral.
Jean had two sons, who on our ancient tree
Grafted two stocks for blazonry : I am
The Marquis of Finlas, and you the Count
Of Garofa, each equal in degree.
And by the women, Cæsar, 'tis the same.
'Tis Aragon you claim, I Portugal.
Your branch as lofty is as ours. I am
The fruit of one, and of the other you
The offspring are.

RUY BLAS (aside).

Where is he dragging me ?

[*Whilst* DON SALLUSTE *was speaking the* MARQUIS
DE SANTA-CRUZ, DON ALVAR DE BAZAN Y BENA-
VIDES, *an old man with a white moustache and a
thick wig was approaching them.*

MARQUIS DE SANTA-CRUZ (to DON SALLUSTE).

You make it clear. If he your cousin is
Mine is he too.

DON SALLUSTE.

True, Marquis—for we come

Of the same stock.

[*He presents* RUY BLAS *to the* MARQUIS DE SANTA-CRUZ.
Don Cæsar.

MARQUIS DE SANTA-CRUZ.

I opine

It is not he whom we thought dead ?

DON SALLUSTE.

It is.

MARQUIS DE SANTA-CRUZ.

He has come back then ?

DON SALLUSTE.

From the Indies.

MARQUIS DE SANTA-CRUZ (*looking at* RUY BLAS).
Ah,
Indeed !

DON SALLUSTE.
You then remember him ?

MARQUIS DE SANTA-CRUZ.
By Heav'ns,
I recollect his birth.

DON SALLUSTE (*aside to* RUY BLAS).
Half blind he is—
The good man will not own it. 'Tis to prove
His eyes are good he recognizes you.

MARQUIS DE SANTA-CRUZ (*extending his hand to* RUY BLAS).
Your hand, my cousin.

RUY BLAS (*bowing*).
My Lord——

MARQUIS DE SANTA-CRUZ (*in a low tone to* DON SALLUSTE,
and pointing to RUY BLAS).
He could not look
Better. (*To* RUY BLAS.) Charmed again to see you.

DON SALLUSTE (*in a low tone and taking the* MARQUIS *aside*).
His debts
I mean to pay. I think that you can serve him,
In your position, if some place at court
Should vacant be—about the king or queen——

MARQUIS DE SANTA-CRUZ (*in a low tone*).
A charming youth he is ; I will not fail
To think of it ; for he a kinsman is.

DON SALLUSTE.
At the Castilian council board I know
You're powerful, I recommend him to you.
> [*He quits the* MARQUIS DE SANTA-CRUZ, *and goes to
> other nobles to whom he presents* RUY BLAS.
> *Among them is the* COUNT D'ALBE *very superbly
> dressed,* DON SALLUSTE *introduces* RUY BLAS *to
> him.*

My cousin, Cæsar, Count of Garofa,
Near to Velalcazar.

> [*The nobles gravely exchange bows with* RUY BLAS,
> *who is abashed.* DON SALLUSTE *to the* COUNT DE
> RIBAGORZA.

                        You missed last night
The Atalanta ballet? Lindamiro
Did dance divinely.

> [*He goes into ecstasies at the doublet of the* COUNT
> D'ALBE.

                    Count, this is splendid!

COUNT D'ALBE.

Ah, I had one was richer—rose-colored
Satin with golden braid. Matalobos
Stole it.

AN USHER OF THE COURT (*from the back*).

          The Queen is coming. Gentlemen,
Arrange yourselves.

> [*The large curtains at the glazed side of the corridor
> open. The nobles fall into line near the door.
> The guards line a passage.* RUY BLAS, *breathless
> and beside himself, comes to the front as if to
> take refuge there.* DON SALLUSTE *follows him.*

DON SALLUSTE (*in a low voice to* RUY BLAS).

              Are you not 'shamed that with
Expanding fortunes, thus your heart should shrink?
Awake. I quit Madrid. My little house
Near to the bridge, where you reside, I leave
For you to use, nothing reserving save
The secret keys. I leave the mutes with you.
Some other orders you will soon receive.
Obey, and I will make your fortune. Rise,
Fear nothing, for the time is opportune.
The Court's a territory where one moves
With little light. Walk you with bandaged eyes.
I'll see for you, my man!

USHER (*in a loud voice*).
                    The Queen!

Ruy Blas.

Queen! oh!

[*The* Queen *appears magnificently attired and surrounded by ladies and pages, and under a canopy of scarlet velvet supported by four gentlemen of the chamber bare headed.* Ruy Blas, *bewildered, gazes as if absorbed by this resplendent vision. All the* Grandees *of Spain cover, the* Marquis del Basto, *the* Count d'Albe, *the* Marquis de Santa-Cruz, Don Salluste. Don Salluste *moves rapidly to the arm-chair, takes from it the hat, which he carries to* Ruy Blas *and puts on his head.*

Don Salluste.

What giddiness has seized you? Cover now,
Cæsar, you are grandee of Spain.

Ruy Blas (*absent, low to* Don Salluste).

And next,
My lord, what is't you order me to do?

Don Salluste (*indicating the* Queen, *who is slowly passing along the corridor*).

To please that woman, and her lover be.

ACT SECOND: THE QUEEN OF SPAIN.

A Saloon next to the Queen's bedchamber. At the left a little door opening into that room. At the right, in an angle of the wall, another door opening to the external apartments. At the back large open windows. It is the afternoon of a fine day in summer. The face of a saint richly enshrined is against the wall; beneath it is read, " Holy Mary in slavery." On the opposite side is a Madonna, before which a golden lamp is burning. Near to the Madonna is a full length portrait of Charles the Second.

At the rising of the curtain the QUEEN DOÑA MARIA OF NEUBOURG *is in one corner seated beside one of her ladies, a young and pretty girl. The* QUEEN *is in a white dress of cloth of silver. She is embroidering, but interrupts herself from time to time to chat. In the opposite corner is seated, in a high-backed chair, the* DOÑA JUANA DE LA CUEVA, DUCHESS D'ALBUQUERQUE, *first lady of the Chamber, with tapestry in her hand, an old woman in black. Near to the* DUCHESS *a table where several ladies are engaged in feminine work. At the back stands* DON GURITAN COUNT D'OÑATE, *the Chamberlain, a tall, thin man of about fifty-five years of age, with gray moustache, looking the old soldier though dressed with exaggerated elegance, wearing ribbons down to his shoes.*

SCENE 1.—THE QUEEN, THE DUCHESS D'ALBUQUERQUE, DON GURITAN, CASILDA, DUENNAS.

THE QUEEN.

He's gone, however! And I ought to be
At ease. Ah well, I am not, though! this man,
The Marquis of Finlas, weighs on my soul,
He hates me so.

CASILDA.
According to your wish

Is he not exiled?

THE QUEEN.
That man hates me.

CASILDA.
Oh

Your majesty——

THE QUEEN.
'Tis true, Casilda. Strange
This man for me is like an angel bad.
One day—'twas on the morrow he must leave—
He came as usual to kiss hands. The rest,
All the grandees, approach'd the throne in file;
I gave my hand—was sorrowful, and still,
Observing vaguely in the hall's dim light
A battle picture painted on the wall,
When, suddenly it was, my eyes looked down
Near to the table and perceived this man,
So dreaded, was advancing unto me.
Soon as I saw him nothing more I saw.
Slowly he moved, and fingered all the while
His poignard's sheath, so that at times the blade
I saw. Grave was he, yet he dazzled me
With looks of flame. Sudden he bent, and like
A creeping thing——and then upon my hand
I felt his serpent-mouth!

CASILDA.
He render'd you
His homage;—do not we the same?

THE QUEEN.
His lips
Were not like other lips. 'Twas the last time
I saw him. Often since I've thought of him.
'Tis true that I have other troubles, yet
I tell myself that hell is in that soul.
Only a woman am I to that man.
In dreams of night I meet again this fiend,

And feel his frightful kiss upon my hand;
I see his eyes shine out with hatred's glare;
And as a deadly poison runs from vein
To vein, so e'en within my freezing heart
I feel the shudder of that icy kiss!
What sayest thou to this?

CASILDA.

Madam, they are
But phantoms!

THE QUEEN.

Ah, indeed—sorrows I know
That are more real. (*Aside*). Oh, but I must hide
That which torments me. (*To* CASILDA.) Those poor
  mendicants
Who dare not to approach—tell me——

CASILDA (*going to the window*).

Madam,
I know. They still are in the square.

THE QUEEN.

Here then,
Throw them my purse.
[CASILDA *takes the purse and throws it from the window.*

CASILDA.

Oh Madam, you who give
Your alms so sweetly,
  [*Pointing to* DON GURITAN, *who, standing erect and
    silent at the back of the stage, looks at the
    QUEEN with an expression of mute adoration.*
Will you nothing throw
In pity to the Count Oñate—a word,
Only a word. A brave old man is he,
With love beneath his armor, and a heart
More soft than hard the rind!

THE QUEEN.

So tiresome he!

CASILDA.

I know it. Yet I pray you speak to him.

The Queen (*turning towards* Don Guritan).
Good day unto you, Count.

> [Don Guritan, *making three bows, approaches the
> Queen, sighing, to kiss her hand, which with
> an indifferent and absent manner she allows him
> to do. Afterwards he returns to his place be-
> side the chair of the* Duchess.

Don Guritan (*in retiring to* Casilda).
                    How charming is
The Queen to-day !

Casilda (*looking at him retreating*).
                    Oh ! the poor heron ! near
The stream that tempts, he stays. After a day
Of quiet waiting, he but snatches up
A "good day" or "good night," often a dry
Cold word, and goes away delighted with
This little morsel in his beak.

The Queen (*with a sorrowful smile*).
                    Be still !

Casilda.
He only needs for happiness to see
The Queen. To see you means delight for him !

> [*Looking with ecstasy at a box on a round table.*
Oh, what a lovely box !

The Queen.
                    I have the key.

Casilda.
This box of calambac is exquisite.

The Queen (*giving her the key*).
Now open it and see. I've had it fill'd,
My dear, with relics, and 'tis my intent
To send it on to Neubourg—well I know
My father will be greatly pleased with it.

> [*She muses for a moment. Then suddenly forces
>   herself out of her reverie.*
I will not think ! That which is in my mind
I wish to drive from it. (*To* Casilda.) Go to my room

And fetch me thence a book.—— What foolishness!
I don't possess a German book! they all
Are Spanish! And the king is at the chase;
Always away. What weariness! Near him,
In six months, I have only pass'd twelve days.

CASILDA.

Who'd wed a king if she must live this way!
> [*The* QUEEN *again falls into reverie—and again
> rouses herself by a violent effort.*

THE QUEEN.

I wish to go out now.
> [*At these words, pronounced imperiously by the
> QUEEN, the* DUCHESS D'ALBUQUERQUE, *who till
> this moment had remained motionless in her
> chair, lifts up her head, then rising makes a
> low curtsey to the* QUEEN.

DUCHESS D'ALBUQUERQUE (*in a hard, curt manner*).
It needs before
The Queen goes out—it is the rule—that all
The doors should opened be by some grandee
Of Spain who has the right to bear the keys;
Now at this hour not one of them remains
Within the palace.

THE QUEEN.

Then you shut me up!
Duchess, in short, they wish that I should die!

THE DUCHESS (*with another curtsey*).

I am duenna of the chamber, so
I must fulfil my duty (*reseats herself*).

THE QUEEN (*lifting her hands to her head despairingly,
aside*).
Well, then, now
To dream again! But no! (*Aloud.*) Ladies, be quick!
A table—let us play at lansquenet!

THE DUCHESS (*to the ladies*).

Ladies, stir not (*rising and curtseying to the* QUEEN).
Your Majesty cannot,

According to the ancient law, play cards,
Except with kings or with their relatives.

THE QUEEN (*with an air of command*).
Well, then, go bring to me these relatives.

CASILDA (*looking at the* DUCHESS).
Oh this duenna!

THE DUCHESS (*making the sign of the Cross*).
To the King who reigns
God has not given, Madam, any kin.
The Queen his mother's dead. He's now alone.

THE QUEEN.
Let them, then, serve me a collation.

CASILDA.
Yes,
That were amusing.

THE QUEEN.
I invite you now
To it, Casilda.

CASILDA (*aside, looking at the* DUCHESS).
Oh, you proper—prim
Old grandmother!

THE DUCHESS (*making a reverence*).
When absent is the King,
The Queen eats quite alone (*reseats herself*).

THE QUEEN (*her patience at an end*).
Oh God! what is 't
That I can do? Not take fresh air, nor play
A game, nor even eat at mine own will!
Most truly I've been dying all the year
That I've been Queen.

CASILDA (*aside, looking at her with compassion*).
Oh the poor woman! thus
To pass her days in weariness in this
Insipid Court! with no distraction, save
To see at border of this sleepy swamp
(*looking at* DON GURITAN)

An old, but love-sick Count, that stands upon
One leg to dream.

THE QUEEN (to CASILDA).

                    Think now of something; say,
What shall we do?

CASILDA.

                    Ah, hold ! The King away,
'Tis you who rule. Just for amusement's sake
Summon the Ministers.

THE QUEEN (shrugging her shoulders).

                    A pleasure that!
To see eight gloomy countenances ranged
For talk with me concerning France, and its
Declining king, of Rome,—they'd also tell
About the portrait of the Archduke which
They bear about at Burgos, 'mid the show
Of cavalcades, beneath a canopy
Of cloth of gold upheld by four Alcaids!
Oh, think of something else!

CASILDA.

                              Well, now, 'twould be
Amusing if some youthful equerry
I made come up.

THE QUEEN.
Casilda !

CASILDA.

                              Oh, I want
So much to look at some young man. Madam,
This venerable Court is death to me.
I think that through the eyes old age comes on,
That we, by always looking at the old,
Ourselves age all the sooner.

THE QUEEN.

                              Foolishness !
There comes a time the heart asserts itself.
As it wakes up from sleep, it loses joy.

(Thoughtfully.)

My only happiness—ah, that is in
The corner of the park, where I'm allowed
To go alone.

CASILDA.

Fine happiness, indeed!
A charming place! where snares are set behind
The marble forms—and where one nothing views.
The walls around are higher than the trees.

THE QUEEN.

Oh, how I wish I could go out sometimes!

CASILDA (*in a low voice*).

Go out? Well, Madam, listen. Let us, though,
Speak softly. In such a prison's gloomy shade
Nought is there so worth search and finding as
One precious sparkling jewel that is called
The key o' the fields. I have it! And whene'er
You wish, in spite of foes, I'll let you out
At night, and through the town we both can go.

THE QUEEN.

Heavens! never! Silence!

CASILDA.

'Tis quite easy.

THE QUEEN.

Peace!

(*She draws a little away from* CASILDA, *and falls into reverie.*)

Oh would that I, who fear the grandees here,
Were still in my good Germany, beside
My parents, as when with my sister dear
I rambled freely through the fields; and when
We met the peasants trailing their rich sheaves,
We talked to them. 'Twas charming. But alas!
One night a man arrived who said—and he
Was dressed in black, I holding by the hand
My sister, sweet companion—"Madam, you
Are to be Queen of Spain."—My father was
All joyous, but my mother wept. Now they
Both weep.—I mean to send in secret soon
This box unto my father, he'll be pleased.

See you how everything disheartens me.
My birds from Germany all died.

> [CASILDA *looks across to the* DUCHESS, *and makes a
> sign of wringing the birds' necks.*

                   And then
They would not let me have the flowers that grew
In mine own country. Never on mine ear
Doth vibrate now a word of love. A Queen
I am to-day. But formerly I knew
What freedom was. Truly thou say'st this park
At eve is dreary—with its walls so high,
One cannot see beyond.—Oh weariness !

> [*Singing afar off is heard.*

What is that sound ?

CASILDA.

              The laundrywomen, they
Are singing, as they pass the heather through.

> [*The singers approach. The words are heard. The*
> QUEEN *listens eagerly.*

SONG FROM OUTSIDE.

Why should we listen
    To birds that rejoice ?
The bird the most tender
    Sings now in thy voice.

Let God show or veil
    The stars in the skies,
The purest of stars
    Shines now in thine eyes.

Let April renew
    All the blossoms around,
The loveliest flower
    In thy heart will be found.

The passionate bird song,
    The day star above,
And the flower of the soul
    But call themselves love !

THE QUEEN (*musing*).
Love—love ! Ah, they are happy ! And their song.
Their voices, do me harm as well as good.

THE DUCHESS (*to the ladies*).

These women with their song annoy the Queen,
Drive them away!

THE QUEEN (*eagerly*).
How, Madam! scarcely can
I hear them; 'tis my will that they, poor things,
Should pass in peace.
(*To* CASILDA, *pointing to a casement at the back.*)
The trees are here less thick,
This window opens to the country; come
Let us now try to look at them.

[*She goes towards the window with* CASILDA.

THE DUCHESS (*rising and curtseying*).
Spain's Queen
Must not look out of window.

THE QUEEN (*stopping and retracing her steps*).
Oh, what next!
The lovely sunset filling all the vales,
The golden dust of evening rising o'er
The way, the far-off songs to which all ears
May listen,—these for me exist no more,
Unto the world I've said adieu. Not e'en
May I regard the nature made by God!
E'en others' freedom I may not behold!

THE DUCHESS (*making signs to the assistants to leave*).
Go now. To-day is sacred to the Saints,
Th' Apostles.
[CASILDA *goes towards the door. The* QUEEN *stops her.*

THE QUEEN.
What! You leave me?

CASILDA (*pointing to the* DUCHESS)..
Madam, we
Are ordered out.

THE DUCHESS (*curtseying to the ground*).
'Tis right that we the Queen
To her devotions leave.
[*All go out with profound reverence.*

SCENE 2.

THE QUEEN (*alone*).

To her devotions?
Say rather to her thoughts! How can I flee
Now from them? All have left me, and alone
I am, poor soul, without a torch to light
My dusky way! (*Musing.*) That bleeding hand whose
    print
Was on the wall! Oh, God, and could it be
That he was hurt? If so it was his fault.
Why would he climb the wall so high? And all
To bring me flowers which they refuse me here;
For such a little thing to venture thus!
Doubtless his wounds were from the iron spikes—
A scrap of lace hung there. A drop of blood
Shed for me claims my tears. (*Losing herself in reverie.*)
    Each time I go
Unto the bench, to seek the flowers, I say
To God—whose help forsakes me—that I will
No more return. And yet I still go back.—
But he! Behold three days have pass'd and he
Has not been there.—And wounded!—Oh, young man,
Unknown, whoever thou may'st be, who thus
Dost see me lonely, and afar from them
Who cherish'd me, who without recompense,
Or even hope of aught, comes to me thus
-'Mid perils never counted—thou who shed'st
Thy blood, and risk'st thy life to give a flower
Unto the Queen of Spain, whoever thou
May'st be—the friend whose shadow follows me—
Since unto law inflexible my heart
Submits, may'st thou be by thy mother loved,
And bless'd by me!
    [*Energetically, and pressing her hand on her heart.*
        But oh, his letter burns!
    (*Falling again into reverie.*)
And he that other! the implacable
Don Salluste! I by destiny am now

Afflicted and protected too. At once
An angel follows me, and spectre dread.
And without seeing them I feel a stir
Amid the gloom that is perchance about
Moments supreme to bring, in which a man
Who hates me will come near to him who loves.
Shall I by one be from the other saved?
I know not. Oh my fate seems but the sport
Of two opposing winds. To be a Queen
How weak and poor a thing! Ah, I will pray.
        (*She kneels before the Madonna.*)
Oh Blessèd Lady, help me! For mine eyes
I dare not raise to look on you! (*She interrupts herself.*)
        Oh, God!   thee

The lace, the letter, and the flowers are fire!

> [*She puts her hand to her bosom and takes out a
> crumpled letter, some little dried blue flowers, and
> a morsel of lace stained with blood which she
> throws on the table; then she again kneels.*

Oh Virgin, thou the star o' the sea! the hope
Of martyrs! help me now! (*Interrupting herself.*) That
        letter!

> [*Turns half round to the table.*

                        Ah!
'Tis that distracts me. (*She kneels again.*) Not again I'll
        read
The letter. Queen of sweet compassion! you
Who wert bestowed on all afflicted souls
For sister! Come, I call you!

> [*She rises, advances towards the table, then pauses, but
> at last grasps the letter as if yielding to an irre-
> sistible impulse.*

                        Yes, I will
Re-read it one last time, and after that
Destroy it. (*With a sad smile.*) For a month, alas! 'tis this
I've said!   [*She unfolds the letter resolutely and reads.*

        "Madam, in dull obscurity
Beneath your feet, and hidden in the shade,
A man there is who loves you! he the worm
That suffers, loving thus a star; who would

For you give up his soul, if so must be ;
And who lies depths below, while you must shine
On high."　　　　　　　[*She places the letter on the table.*
　　　　　　When souls are thirsty they must drink,
Though it be poison !
　　　　　　　　[*She puts the letter and the lace in her bosom.*
　　　　　　　　　　Nought on earth have I.
Ah, but I need some one to love.　The King
I would have truly loved, had he so will'd it.
But me he leaves alone, of love bereft.
　　　　[*The great folding doors open.　An* USHER *of the*
　　　　　　Chamber in full dress enters.

　　　　　THE USHER (*in a loud voice*).
A letter from the King !

THE QUEEN (*as if suddenly awakened, with a joyful cry*).
　　　　　　　　　From him !　I'm saved !

SCENE 3.—THE QUEEN, THE DUCHESS D'ALBUQUERQUE, CASILDA,
DON GURITAN, Ladies in Waiting, Pages, RUY BLAS.

All enter with solemnity, the DUCHESS *at their head, followed by
the women.　* RUY BLAS *remains at the back of the chamber.
He is magnificently dressed.　His cloak falls over his left
arm and hides it.　Two pages, carrying the* KING's *letter on
a cushion of cloth of gold, kneel before the* QUEEN *at a few
paces distant.*

　　　　　RUY BLAS (*at the back—aside*).
Where am I now ?—How beautiful she is !
Oh, for what purpose am I here ?

　　　　　　THE QUEEN (*aside*).
　　　　　　　　　　　'Tis aid
From heaven !　(*Aloud.*)　Give it me—be quick !
　　　　　　　　[*Turning to the portrait of the* KING.
　　　　　　　　　　My thanks
Your majesty !　(*To the* DUCHESS.)　Whence comes this
　　letter, say ?
　　　　　　THE DUCHESS.
From Aranjuez, Madam, where the King
Now hunts.

THE QUEEN.

And from my soul I thank him. He
Has understood my need of words of love
From him, in my lone weariness. Come then,
Now give it me.

THE DUCHESS (*curtseying and pointing to the letter*).
I must inform you that
The custom is, that whatsoe'er it be
I first must open it and read.

THE QUEEN.
Again !—
Ah well, then read.
[*The* DUCHESS *takes the letter and slowly unfolds it.*

CASILDA.
Let's hear the lines of love.

THE DUCHESS (*reading*).
" Madam, the wind is high, and I have killed
Six wolves. Signed, Charles."

THE QUEEN (*aside*).
Alas !

DON GURITAN (*to the* DUCHESS).
And is that all?
THE DUCHESS.
Yes, Count.

CASILDA (*aside*).
Six wolves he's killed ! How this excites
Th' imagination ! Tender is your heart,
Exacting, weary, sick. Six wolves he's killed !

THE DUCHESS (*to the* QUEEN, *presenting the letter to her*).
If that your Majesty ?——

THE QUEEN (*pushing it away*).
Oh no.

CASILDA (*to the* DUCHESS).
And this
Is really all?
THE DUCHESS.
Undoubtedly. What more

Should be? Our king is hunting; on the way
He writes declaring all he's killed, and states
The weather he has had. All this is well.

              [*Examining the letter again.*
He writes—ah no, he dictates.

THE QUEEN (*snatching the letter and examining it herself*).
                   Then, in short,
'Tis not his hand, only his signature.

    [*She examines it with more attention, and seems
          struck with stupor. (Aside.)*
Is it delusion? the handwriting's just ˙
The same as that o' the letter!

    [*She indicates with her hand the letter she has just
         hidden in her bosom.*
                      Oh, what's this?

          (*To the* DUCHESS.)
Who, then, conveyed the letter?

      THE DUCHESS (*pointing to* RUY BLAS).
                    He is there.

     THE QUEEN (*half turning towards* RUY BLAS).
That young man?

          THE DUCHESS.
           'Twas he himself who brought it.
He's a new equerry his Majesty
Has given to the Queen. A noble whom,
As from the King, my Lord of Santa-Cruz
Has introduced to me.

         THE QUEEN.
           His name?

         THE DUCHESS.
                He is
The noble Cæsar de Bazan—the Count
Of Garofa. If rumor be believed
He is the most accomplish'd gentleman
That can be found.

         THE QUEEN.
        That's well. I'll speak to him;

(*To* Ruy Blas.)

Sir——

Ruy Blas (*aside, trembling*).

Ah, she sees—she speaks to me. Oh God!
I, tremble.

The Duchess (*to* Ruy Blas).

Count, approach.

Don Guritan (*aside, and looking sideways at* Ruy Blas).

I did not dream
Of this,—that young man! he an equerry!

[Ruy Blas, *pale and troubled, slowly advances.*

The Queen.

You come from Aranjuez?

Ruy Blas.

Yes, Madam.

The Queen.

The king is well?

[Ruy Blas *bows, she points to the royal letter.*

This letter was by him
Dictated?

Ruy Blas.

He on horseback was when he

[*Hesitates a moment.*

To one of his attendants did the lines
Dictate.

The Queen (*aside, looking at* Ruy Blas).

His looks so pierce me that I dare
Not ask to whom. (*Aloud.*) 'Tis well, you may depart.
Ah!—

[Ruy Blas, *who had stepped back a few paces, turns
again towards the* Queen.

Many nobles were assembled there? (*Aside.*)
Why am I stirr'd on seeing this young man?

[Ruy Blas *bows and she continues.*

Who were they?

Ruy Blas.

Names I do not know. I was

But there a few short moments, for Madrid
I quitted but three days ago.

THE QUEEN (*aside*).
Three days!
[*She looks at* RUY BLAS *with a troubled expression.*

RUY BLAS (*aside*).
Another's wife! Oh frightful jealousy!
Of whom? A gulf has opened in my heart.

DON GURITAN (*approaching* RUY BLAS).
You are an equerry unto the Queen.
One word with you. Know you your duty? You
To-night must in the next room stay to be
In readiness to open to the king
Should he arrive.

RUY BLAS (*trembling, aside*).
I open to the king!
(*Aloud.*)
But——he is absent now.

DON GURITAN.
Yet may he not,
Though unexpectedly, return?

RUY BLAS (*aside*).
Ah—how!

DON GURITAN (*aside, observing* RUY BLAS).
What ails him?

THE QUEEN (*who has heard all and is looking at* RUY BLAS).
Oh, how pale he grows!
[RUY BLAS, *tottering, leans his arm on a great chair.*

CASILDA (*to the* QUEEN).
Madam,
This young man's ill!

RUY BLAS (*supporting himself with difficulty*).
I—I—oh, no! But strange
It is, how that—the sun—fresh air—the length
Of road—— (*Aside.*) To open to the King!

[*He falls fainting on to the arm-chair. His cloak
slips aside and shows his left hand to be bound
up in blood-stained linen.*

CASILDA.
·Great God,
He's wounded, Madam, in the hand !

THE QUEEN.
A wound !

CASILDA.
He's losing consciousness ! Quick, make him breathe,
Some essence.

THE QUEEN (*feeling in her ruff*).
Here's a flask of mine contains
An extract.
[*At this moment her glance falls on the ruffle* RUY
BLAS *wears on his right arm. Aside.*
'Tis the self-same lace !
[*When she took the flask from her bosom, she in her
trouble drew out the morsel of lace which was
hidden there.* RUY BLAS, *whose eyes were fixed
on her, saw and recognized it.*

RUY BLAS (*distracted*).
Oh—oh !
[*The eyes of the* QUEEN *and* RUY BLAS *meet. Silence.*

THE QUEEN (*aside*).
'Tis he !

RUY BLAS (*aside*).
Upon her heart !

THE QUEEN (*aside*).
'Tis he !

RUY BLAS (*aside*).
Grant, God,
That now I die !
[*In the confusion of the women pressing round* RUY
BLAS, *no one had remarked what passed between
the* QUEEN *and him.*

CASILDA (*holding the flask for* RUY BLAS *to inhale from*).
How were you injured, say ?

Was it just now? Ah no! The wound I see
Must have reopened on the way. And why,
How happened it, that you were made to bear
The message from the King?

THE QUEEN.

                    I hope that soon
You'll finish questioning.

THE DUCHESS (*to* CASILDA).

                    What's this, my dear,
Unto the Queen?

THE QUEEN.

                    Since it was he who wrote
The letter, it was well he brought it me,
Was it not so?

CASILDA.

                    But he has never said
He wrote it.

THE QUEEN (*aside*).

        Oh! (*To* CASILDA.)   Be still!

CASILDA (*to* RUY BLAS).

                    How is your Grace?
Are you now better?

RUY BLAS.

            I'm restored!

THE QUEEN (*to the Ladies*).

                    'Tis time
That we retire. To his apartments let
The Count be led. (*To the* Pages *at the back.*)
                    You know the King will not
Come back to-night. He will remain away
Through all the hunting season.

        [*She retires with her attendants to her apartments.*

CASILDA (*watching her go out*).

                    Ah, the Queen
Has something on her mind.

        [*She goes out by the same door as the* QUEEN, *carry-
            ing the little casket of relics.*

Ruy Blas (*remains alone*).

[*He seems as if listening for some time with deep
    joy to the last words of the* Queen, *and lost in
    reverie. The morsel of lace which the* Queen
    *had let fall in her trouble had remained on the
    ground. He picks it up, looks at it with emo-
    tion and covers it with kisses. Then he raises
    his eyes to heaven.*

                                    Mercy, oh God!
Make me not mad!

            (*Looking at the morsel of lace.*)
                            'Twas surely near her heart!

[*He hides it in his bosom.—Enter* Don Guritan *by
    the door of the room into which he had followed
    the* Queen. *He walks slowly towards* Ruy Blas
    *When close to him, he, without saying a word,
    half draws his sword, and compares its appear-
    ance with that of* Ruy Blas'. *They are not
    alike. He puts back his sword into the scab-
    bard.* Ruy Blas *looks at him with surprise.*

Scene 4.—Ruy Blas—Don Guritan.

Don Guritan (*again pushing back his sword*).
I will bring two that are of equal length.

                    Ruy Blas.
What mean you, Sir?——

                    Don Guritan (*gravely*).
                                    I was most deep in love
In sixteen hundred and fifty. Then I dwelt
In Alicante. There a young man was,
As handsome as the loves; he looked too near
Upon my mistress, passing every day
Beneath her balcony, before the old
Cathedral; he was prouder than a Captain
Of an Admiral's ship; Vasquez his name, and though
Bastard he was ennobled. Him I killed.

[Ruy Blas *tries to interrupt him; but* Don Guritan
    prevents him by a gesture, and continues.

And after that—it was towards sixty-six—
Gil, Count of Iscola,—a splendid knight,
Sent to my beauty, named Angelica,
A loving letter which she showed, and a slave
Named Grifel of Viserta. Him I had
Despatched, and slew myself the master.

RUY BLAS.

Sir !

DON GURITAN (*continuing*).

And later—near the year eighty—I had cause
To think I was deceived by beauty, one
Of easy ways, through Tirso Gamonal,
One of those youths whose haughty faces charm,
And go so well with splendid feathers. 'Twas
The time when mules were shod with purest gold.
I slew Don Tirso Gamonal.

· RUY BLAS.

But what,

Sir, means all this ?

DON GURITAN.

It means to show you, Count,

That if you draw, there's water in the well,
And that to-morrow morn the sun will rise
At four o'clock; that there's a lonely spot
Behind the chapel, far from any road,
Convenient for men of spirit. You
They call Cæsar, I am named Don Gaspar
Guritan Tassis y Guevarra, Count
Of Oñate.

RUY BLAS (*coldly*).

Well, Sir, I will be there.

[*A few moments before,* CASILDA, *out of curiosity, had
entered softly by the little door at the back, and
had listened to the last words without having been
seen by the speakers.*

CASILDA (*aside*).

A duel ! I must tell the Queen.

[*She disappears by the little door.*

Don Guritan (*still imperturbable*).

               If, Sir,
It pleases you to study and to know
My tastes, for your instruction I will say
I never much admired a coxcomb, or
A ladies' man with curled moustache, on whom
The women like to look, who sometimes are
All lackadaisical, and sometimes gay.
Who in the house speak with their eyes, and fall
In charming attitudes upon arm-chairs,
Just fainting at some little scratches.

Ruy Blas.

                              But
I do not understand.

Don Guritan.

               You understand
Quite well. We both desire the same good things,
And in this palace one of us is one
Too many. You are equerry, in short,
And I the Chamberlain. And so our rights
Are equal. I am ill-provided, though.
Our shares are not the same. I have the right
Of age, and you of youth. This frightens me.
At table where I fast, I see sit down
A hungry youth, with strong terrific teeth
And flaming eyes, and air of conqueror;
This troubles me; for vain contention were
Upon love's territory—that fine field,
Which always trembles with mere trifles,—I
Should make th' assault but badly. I've the gout.
Besides, I am not such an arrant fool
As for the heart of a Penelope
To wrestle with a spark so prompt to faint.
Because your handsome, tender, winning, 'tis
That I must kill you.

Ruy Blas.

               Well, then, pray try.

Don Guritan.

                           Count
Of Garofa, to-morrow morn at hour

Of sunrise, at the place that's named, without
A servant or a witness, if you please,
We'll slaughter one another gallantly,
With sword and dagger, like true gentlemen
Of houses such as ours.

> [_He extends his hand to_ Ruy Blas, _who takes it._

Ruy Blas.

No word of this?

(_The_ Count _makes a sign of assent._)
Until to-morrow.   [_Exit_ Ruy Blas.

Don Guritan (_alone_).

No—no tremor in

His hand I found. To know he'll surely die,
And be thus calm, proves him to be a brave
Young fellow.

> [_Noise of a key in the little door of the_ Queen's _room._
> Some one surely's at that door?
> [_The_ Queen _appears and walks briskly towards_ Don
> Guritan, _who is surprised and delighted to see
> her. She holds the little casket in her hands._

Scene 5.—Don Guritan—The Queen.

The Queen (_smiling_).

'Twas you I sought to find!

Don Guritan.

What brings to me

This honor?

The Queen (_placing the casket on the round table_).

Oh, 'tis nothing—or, at least,

A small affair, my Lord (_she laughs_). Just now 'twas
  said,
'Mong other things—you know how foolish are
The women—and Casilda said, maintained
That you, for me, aught that I asked would do.

Don Guritan.

And she was right.

THE QUEEN (*laughing*).
                But I the contrary

Declared.

DON GURITAN.
Then, Madam, you were wrong.

THE QUEEN.
                                    She said
That you for me would give your soul—your life——

DON GURITAN.
Casilda spoke right well in saying that.

THE QUEEN.
But I said No.

DON GURITAN.
                And I say yes, all things
I for your Majesty would do.

THE QUEEN.
                            All things?

DON GURITAN.
Yes all.

THE QUEEN.
            Well let us see!—swear now that you
To please me will this instant do the thing
I ask you.

DON GURITAN.
            By the venerated King
My patron saint, King Gaspar, I do swear!
Command, and I obey or die!

THE QUEEN (*taking up the casket*).
                            Well then,
You will set out and leave Madrid at once,
And carry straight this box of calambac
To Neubourg, to my father th' Elector.
Take it.

DON GURITAN (*aside*).
I'm caught, indeed! (*Aloud*). What! to Neubourg!

THE QUEEN.
To Neubourg.

Don Guritan.

Ah! six hundred leagues from here!

The Queen.

Five hundred 'tis and fifty,—

[*pointing to the silken cover of the box.*

Pray take care

That on the road the blue fringe does not fade.

Don Guritan.

When shall I start?

The Queen.

This instant.

Don Guritan.

Let it be

To-morrow!

The Queen.

No, I cannot yield.

Don Guritan (*aside*).

Entrapp'd

I am. (*Aloud.*) But——

The Queen.

Now set off.

Don Guritan.

But why is this?——

The Queen.

You've promised me.

Don Guritan.

Affairs——

The Queen.

Impossible.

Don Guritan.

The object is so frivolous——

The Queen.

Be quick!

Don Guritan.

One day alone!

The Queen.
No, not a moment.

Don Guritan.
                    For——

The Queen.
Now do my bidding.

Don Guritan.
          I——

The Queen.
          No.

Don Guritan.
                    But——

The Queen.
                              Set off.

Don Guritan.
If—if——

The Queen.
          Yes, I will kiss you!
[*She puts her arms round his neck and kisses him.*

Don Guritan (*vexed and yet delighted*).
                              I resist
No more. I will obey you, Madam. (*Aside.*) God
Made Himself man; so be't. As woman 'tis
The devil comes!

The Queen (*pointing to the window*).
                    A carriage there below
Is waiting for you.

Don Guritan.
          All then is prepared!
[*He writes hurriedly a few words on a piece of
    paper and rings a little bell. A Page enters.*
Page, take unto Don Cæsar de Bazan
This letter, and without one moment lost.
          (*Aside.*)
This duel must be taken up again
When I return. I shall come back! (*Aloud.*) I go
At once to satisfy your Majesty.

THE QUEEN.

Now I'm contented.

[*He takes the casket, kisses the* QUEEN'S *hand,
    makes a low bow and exit. The next minute
    the sound of wheels is heard.*

THE QUEEN (*falling into a chair*).
He shall not be kill'd !

ACT THIRD: RUY BLAS.

The Council Chamber of the KING'S *palace at Madrid. At the
back a large door above some steps. In the angle to the
left an opening closed by tapestry of a raised warp. In
the opposite angle a window. To the right a square
table with a green velvet cover around which are placed
stools for eight or ten persons, corresponding to the
number of desks placed on the table. At the side of
the table which faces the audience is a large arm-chair,
covered with cloth of gold, and surmounted by a canopy
of the same material, with the arms of Spain and the
royal crown emblazoned. A chair at one side of it.
When the curtain rises the Privy Council of the* KING
is about to sit.

SCENE 1.—DON MANUEL ARIAS, PRESIDENT OF CASTILE; DON
    PEDRO VELEZ DE GUEVARRA, COUNT DE CAMPOREAL,
    Knight-Counsellor of the Chief Exchequer. DON FER-
    NANDO DE CORDOVA Y AGUILAR MARQUIS DE PRIEGO *of
    the same quality.* ANTONIO UBILLA, *Chief Secretary of
    the Revenue.* MONTAZGO, *Counsellor of the Black Robe
    for India.* COVADENGA, *Chief Secretary for the Isles.
    Many other Counsellors. Those of the Robe in black.
    The others in Court Dress.* CAMPOREAL *has the cross of
    Calatrava on his mantle,* PRIEGO *the Golden Fleece at
    his neck.* DON MANUEL ARIAS, *President of Castile,
    and the* COUNT DE CAMPOREAL *chat together in low tones
    at the front. The others form groups here and there in
    the Hall.*

DON MANUEL ARIAS.

Behind such fortune lurks a mystery.

COUNT DE CAMPOREAL.

He has the Golden Fleece. Behold him made
Chief secretary—minister—and now
Duke d'Olmedo he is !

DON MANUEL ARIAS.
All in six months.

COUNT DE CAMPOREAL.

In some strange secret way he has been raised.

DON MANUEL ARIAS (*mysteriously*).
The Queen !

COUNT DE CAMPOREAL.
In fact, the king an invalid,
Insane at heart, lives at his first wife's tomb.
He abdicates the throne, shut up within
Th' Escurial, and leaves the Queen alone
To govern all things.

DON MANUEL ARIAS.
Dear Camporeal,
She reigns o'er us—Don Cæsar over her.

COUNT DE CAMPOREAL.

His way of life is quite unnatural.
In the first place, he never sees the Queen ;
They seem to shun each other. You may doubt
My word, but for six months I've watched them well,
For reasons good, and of it I am sure.
Then, from morose caprice, his dwelling is
A little lodge that's near th' Hôtel Tormez,
With shutters ever closed—where negroes two
Guard well the close-shut doors—Lackeys who could
Tell much, if only that they were not dumb.

DON MANUEL ARIAS.
Mutes, then ?

COUNT DE CAMPOREAL.
Yes, mutes. His other servitors
Remain in those apartments which he has
Within the palace.

Don Manuel Arias.

It is strange, indeed.

Don Antonio Ubilla (*who joined them a few moments before*)
He comes of an old family,—enough
That is.

Count de Camporeal.

The strange thing seems that he pretends
To be an honest man.

(*To* Don Manuel Arias.)

Cousin he is
Unto the Marquis Salluste, who last year
Was banished—therefore 'twas that Santa-Cruz
Befriended him.—In former years, this man,
Don Cæsar, who to-day our master proves,
Seemed but the greatest fool the moon saw born—
A hare-brained dolt—we know the people well
Who knew him. He for revenue consumed
His fortune—changed his loves, his carriages
Each day. His fancies had ferocious teeth,
That could have eaten in a year Peru.
One day he ran away, 'twas not known where.

Don Manuel Arias.

But time has made of this gay fool a sage
Severe.

Count de Camporeal.

Frail women prudish grow when aged.

Ubilla.

I think the man is honest.

Count de Camporeal (*laughing*).

Simpleton,
Ubilla! to be dazzled thus by such
A probity! (*in a significant tone*). The household of the
Queen,
Civil and ordinary (*looking at some papers*), almost costs
Seven hundred thousand golden ducats now
In yearly charges. Here's assuredly
A shady calm Pactolus, where one might
In safety throw a very certain net:
The water trouble, and the fish is there.

"GOOD APPETITE, GENTLEMEN!"

Ruy Blas—Act III., Scene 2.

Marquis de Priego (*coming forward*).
Ah, that does not displease you. But unwise
Are you to speak thus freely. Let me say,
My late grandfather, he who was brought up
With the Count-Duke, did oft advise that we
Should gnaw the king—but kiss the favorite.
Now let us, gentlemen, engage ourselves
With public business.

> [*They sit round the table; some take up pens, others
> turn over the papers. The remainder are idle.
> A brief silence.*

Montazgo (*whispering to* Ubilla).
                    I have asked from you,
Out of the money meant for purchasing
Of relics, just a sum enough to buy
The post of Alcaid that my nephew wants.

Ubilla (*whispering*).
You—you—you said you'd shortly give the place
Of bailiff o' the Ebro to my cousin
Melchior of Elva.

Montazgo (*exclaiming*).
                    Only just now
We dowered your daughter. The festivities
O' the nuptials still proceed.—Without a pause
I am assailed. . . .

Ubilla (*whispering*).
                    The Alcaid's post is yours.

Montazgo (*whispering*).
And yours the bailiff's.   [*They press hands.*

Covadenga (*rising*).
                    Gentlemen, we are
Castilian counsellors, and needful 'tis,
In order that each keeps within his sphere,
To regulate our rights and take our shares.
The revenue of Spain is scatter'd when
A hundred hands control it. We need now
To end this public evil. Some acquire

Too much, the others do not have enough.
The farming of tobacco goes to you,
Ubilla. Indigo and musk belong
To Marquis de Priego. Camporeal
Receives the taxes of eight thousand men,
The import dues, the salt, a thousand sums,
And five per cent. on gold, on jet, and on
The amber.

(To MONTAZGO.)

You who with a restless eye
Regard me, you have managed for yourself
To have the tax on arsenic, and the rights
Of snow. You have dry docks, and cards, and brass,
The ransoms of the citizens that should
Be punished with the stick—the ocean tithes,
And those on lead and rosewood. Nothing, Sirs,
Have I. Decree me something.

COUNT DE CAMPOREAL (bursting out laughing).
Oh, the old

Devil! Of all he takes the largest share
Of profits. If the Indies we except,
He has the islands of both seas. What spread
Of wings! He holds Majorca in one claw,
And with the other clutches Teneriffe!

COVADENGA (growing angry).

I say I've nothing!

MARQUIS DE PRIEGO (laughing).
He the negroes has.
[They rise, all speaking at once and quarrelling.

MONTAZGO.

I should long since have made complaint. I want
The forests.

COVADENGA (to the MARQUIS DE PRIEGO).
Let me have the arsenic, then

The negroes unto you I will give up.

[A few moments before RUY BLAS had entered by the
door at the back, and had witnessed this scene
without having been observed by the speakers. He

*is dressed in black velvet, with a mantle of scarlet
velvet; he has a white feather in his hat, and
wears the Golden Fleece at his neck. At first he
listened to them in silence, but suddenly he advances with soft steps and appears in their midst
at the height of the quarrel.*

Scene 2.—The Same—Ruy Blas.

Ruy Blas (*bursting on them*).
I wish you joy!
    [*All turn round. Silence of surprise and uneasiness.
    Ruy Blas puts on his hat, crosses his arms, and
    continues looking them full in the face.*
            Oh faithful ministers!
And virtuous counsellors! Behold your mode
Of working, servants you who rob the house!
And without shame the dark hour choose, when Spain
Weeps in her agony!—caring for nought
Except to fill your pockets—afterwards
To flee away! Branded you are before
Your country sinking into ruin. Oh,
Her grave you've dug, and robbed her in it too.
But look—reflect—and have some shame. The worth
Of Spain, her virtue and her greatness pass
Away. Since the Fourth Philip's time we've lost
Not only Portugal and the Brazils
Without a struggle made, but in Alsace
Brisach; Steinfort in Luxembourg, and all
The Comté to its last small town; Rousillon,
Ormuz and Goa, five thousand leagues of coast
And Pernambuc, and the blue mountains' range.
But see—from western shores unto the east
Europe, which hates you, laughs at you as well.
As if your King a phantom only were,
Holland and England share his states, and Rome
Deceives you; half an army is the most
You dare to risk in Piedmont; though supposed
A friendly country, Savoy and its Duke

Abound in subtle dangers. France awaits
The hour propitious to attack and take.
And Austria also watches you. And then
Bavaria's Prince is dying—that you know.
As for your viceroys—your Medina, fool
Of love, fills Naples with such tales as are
A scandal; Milan's sold by Vaudémont,
Legañez loses Flanders. What for this
The remedy? The state is indigent,
The state is drained of troops and money both.
Upon the sea—where God his anger shows—
We have already lost three hundred ships
Without our counting galleys. And you dare!——
Ye Sirs, for twenty years the People—think
Of it—and I have reckoned it is thus—
Have borne the burden under which they bend
For you—your pleasures and your mistresses;—
The wretched people whom you still would grind,
Have sweated for your uses, this I say,
More than four hundred millions of their gold!
And this is not enough for you! and still
My masters!—— Ah, I am ashamed! At home
The spoilers, troopers, traverse all the land
And fight, the harvest burning. Carbines too
Are pointed at each thicket, just as 'twere
The war of princes; war is there between
The convents, war between the provinces,
All seeking to devour their neighbors poor,
Eaters o' the famished on a vessel wreck'd!
Within your ruined churches grows the grass,
And they are full of adders. Many great
By ancestry, but workers none. Intrigue
Is all, and nothing springs from loyalty.
A sewer is Spain, to which th' impurity
Of all the nations drains.—In his own pay
Each noble has a hundred cut-throats, who
Do speak a hundred tongues. The Genoese,
Sardinian, Flemish.—Babel's in Madrid.
The magistrates, so stern to poverty,
Are lenient to the rich. When night comes on

There's murder, then each one cries out for help!
But yesterday they robb'd me, yes, myself,
Near the Toledo bridge. One-half Madrid
Now robs the other half, judges are bribed,
No soldier gets his pay. Old conquerors
O' the world—the Spaniards that we are—see now
What army have we? It but barely shows
Six thousand men who barefoot go; a host
Made up of beggars, Jews and mountaineers,
Who, armed with daggers, dress themselves in rags.
And every regiment plies a double trade.
When darkness falls disorder reigns, and then
The doubtful soldier changes to a thief.
The robber Matalobos has more troops
Than any Baron. One of his followers
Made war upon the king of Spain. Alas!
The country peasantry, unshamed, insult
The carriage of the king. And he, your lord,
Consumed by grief and fear, stays all alone
Within the Escurial, with but the dead
He treads upon, and stoops his anxious brow
From which the empire crumbles fast! Behold,
Alas! all Europe crushing 'neath its heel
This land, once purpled—which is now in rags.
The state is ruined in this shocking age;
And you dispute among yourselves who shall
The fragments take! The Spanish nation, once
So great, lies in the shadow enervate,
And dies while you upon it live—mournful
As a lion that to vermin is a prey!—
Oh, Charles the Fifth, in these dread times of shame
And terror, oh, what dost thou in thy tomb,
Most mighty Emperor? Arise,—come, see
The best supplanted by the very worst;
This kingdom, now in agony—that was
Constructed out of Empires—near its fall.
It wants thine arm! Come to the rescue, Charles!
For Spain is dying, blotted out, self-slain!
Thy globe, which brightly shone in thy right hand,
A dazzling sun that made the world believe

That thenceforth at Madrid the day first dawn'd,
Is now a dead star, that in the gloom grows less
And less—a moon three quarters gnaw'd away,
And still decreasing ne'er to rise again
But be effaced by other nations! Oh,
Thy heritage is now put up for sale.
Alas! they make piastres of thy rays,
And soil thy splendors! Giant! can it be
Thou sleepest? By its weight thy sceptre now
They sell! A crowd of dwarfs deformed cut up
Thy royal robes to make their doublets, while
Th' Imperial Eagle, which beneath thy rule
Covered the world, and grasped its thunderbolts
And darted flame, a poor unfeather'd bird
Is cooking in their stew-pan infamous!

> [*The* Counsellors *are silent in their consternation. But the* MARQUIS DE PRIEGO *and the* COUNT DE CAMPO-REAL *raise their heads and look angrily at* RUY BLAS. *Then* CAMPOREAL, *after having spoken to* PRIEGO, *goes to the table and writes a few words on a piece of paper which they both sign.*

COUNT DE CAMPOREAL (*pointing to the* MARQUIS DE PRIEGO *and presenting the paper to* RUY BLAS).
In both our names, your Grace, I tender you
The resignation of our posts.

RUY BLAS (*taking the paper calmly*).
                              Thanks. You
Will with your family retire,
              (*To* PRIEGO.)
                              You, Sir,
To Andalusia.
              (*To* CAMPOREAL.)
                    You, Count, unto
Castile. To his estates each one. Set out
To-morrow.

> [*The two nobles bow and exeunt haughtily wearing their hats.* RUY BLAS, *turning to the other counsellors.*

Whosoe'er declines to go

My road, can follow now those gentlemen.

> [*Silence for awhile.* Ruy Blas seats *himself in a*
> *chair with a back, placed by the side of the royal*
> *chair, and begins to open letters. While running*
> *his eyes over them one after another,* Covadenga,
> Arias, *and* Ubilla *exchange a few words in low*
> *tones.*

Ubilla (*To* Covadenga, *indicating* Ruy Blas).
A master we have found, my friend. This man
Will rise to greatness.

Don Manuel Arias.
Yes, if he has time.

Covadenga.
And if he does not lose himself at view
Of all too near.

Ubilla.
He will be Richelieu!

Don Manuel Arias.
Unless 'tis Olivarez * that he proves!

Ruy Blas (*after having run over in an excited manner a letter*
he had just opened).
A plot! what's this? Now, Sirs, what did I say?
(*Reading.*)
" Duke d'Olmedo must watch. A snare there is
Preparing to remove a personage,
One of the greatest of Madrid." (*Examining the letter.*)
They say
Not whom. But I will watch.—Anonymous
The letter is.

Enter a Court Usher, *who approaches* Ruy Blas *with a*
profound bow.
How now—what's this?

---

* Gaspar Guzman, Count d'Olivarez, Minister of Philip the Fourth of Spain.
For a time he seemed the redresser of abuses, but commerce and agriculture declined under his sway, and his foreign policy was disastrous. He was ultimately
banished from Court and died in disgrace.—Trans.

USHER.

Unto
Your Excellence, th' Ambassador of France
I now announce.

RUY BLAS.

Ah, Harcourt! at this time
I cannot see him.

USHER (*bowing*).

And the Nuncio
Imperial waits in the saloon of honor
To see your Excellence.

RUY BLAS.

Oh, at this hour
It is impossible.

[*The* Usher *bows and exit. A few moments pre-
viously a* Page *dressed in a livery of pinkish-
gray and silver, had entered and approached*
RUY BLAS.

RUY BLAS (*perceiving him*).

My Page, to none
Whatever am I visible just now.

THE PAGE (*in a low voice*).

The Count de Guritan, who has return'd
From Neubourg——

RUY BLAS (*with a gesture of surprise*).

Ah!—Page, show to him my house
I' the suburb, saying that to-morrow he
Will find me there—if it should please him.   Go.

[*The* Page *exit*.

(*To the* Counsellors.)

We shall have work together soon to do.
In two hours, gentlemen, return.

[*All exeunt, bowing low to* RUY BLAS.

[RUY BLAS *is alone, and walks a few steps, absorbed
in deep reverie. Suddenly in the corner of the
room the tapestry is raised, and the* QUEEN *appears. She is dressed in white, with a crown
on her head. She seems radiant with joy, and*

looks at Ruy Blas *with an expression of
respect and admiration. She holds back the
tapestry with one arm, behind which is percep-
tible a dark recess, in which a little door can be
distinguished.* Ruy Blas, *in turning round, sees
the* Queen, *and remains as if petrified by the
apparition.*

SCENE 3.—RUY BLAS—THE QUEEN.

THE QUEEN.
                    Oh, thanks!
              RUY BLAS.
Oh, Heaven!
              THE QUEEN.
              You have done well to speak them thus.
I can refrain no longer, Duke. I must
Press now that loyal hand so strong and true.
    [*She walks quickly towards him and takes his hand,
        which she presses before he can prevent her.*

              RUY BLAS (*aside*).
To shun her for six months, and then at once
Thus suddenly behold her!
              (*Aloud.*) Madam, you
Were there?——
              THE QUEEN.
              Yes, Duke, and I heard all you said,
Yes, I was there, and listened with my soul!

    RUY BLAS (*pointing to the hiding-place*).
I never thought——Madam, that hiding-place——

              THE QUEEN.
It is unknown to all. A dark recess
That the Third Philip hollowed in the wall,
By means of which the master heard all things
While, spirit-like, invisible. And oft
From there have I beheld the Second Charles,
Mournful and dull, attend the Councils where
They pillaged him and sacrificed the State.

RUY BLAS.

And what said he?

THE QUEEN.
He nothing said.

RUY BLAS.

Nothing!

What did he, then?

THE QUEEN.
He to the hunting field
Went off. But you! Your threatening words still ring
Upon mine ear. Oh! in what haughty ways
You treated them, and how superbly right
You were! The border of the tapestry
I raised and saw you. Yes, your flashing eyes
With lightning overwhelmed them, and without
Fury. Unto them everything was said.
You seemed to me the only upright one!
But where, then, have you learn'd so many things?
How comes it that you know effects and cause?
That everything you know? Whence cometh it
That your voice speaks as tongues of kings should speak,
Why, then, were you like messenger of God,
So terrible and great?

RUY BLAS.
Because—because
I love you! I whom all these hate. Because
I know full well that what they seek to crush
Must fall on you! Because there's nothing can
Dismay a reverent passion so profound.
Therefore to save you I would save the world!
Unhappy man, who loves you with such love.
Alas! I think of you as think the blind
Of day. Oh, Madam, hear me. I've had dreams
Uncounted. I have loved you from afar,
From the deep depths of shade; I have not dared
To touch your finger-tips. You dazzled me
As sight of angel might. I've suffered much,
Truly I have. Ah, Madam, if you knew!
Six months I hid my love—but now I speak.

I fled—I shunned you, but I tortured was.
I am not thinking of these men at all.
I love you! And, oh God! I dare to speak
The words unto your Majesty. Now say,
What I must do? Should you desire my death,
I'll die. Oh, pardon me—I'm terrified!

THE QUEEN.

Oh, speak! enchant me! Never in my life
Such words I've heard. I listen. 'Tis thy soul
That speaking overwhelms me quite. I need
Thy voice, thine eyes. Oh, if thou knewest! I
It is who suffered! Ah, a hundred times
When in the last six months your eyes shunn'd mine——
But no, I must not say these things so fast——
I'm most unhappy. Silent let me be.
I am afraid!

RUY BLAS (listening with rapture).
Oh, Madam, finish. You

With joy fill up my heart.

THE QUEEN.
Well, listen, then.
[Raising her eyes to heaven.

Yes, I will tell him all. Is it a crime?
So much the worse! But when the heart is torn
One cannot help but show what there was hid.
Thou fled'st the Queen? Ah, well, the Queen sought thee.
Each day she came there to that secret place,
And listened to thee, gathering up thy words.
Silent, in contemplation of thy mind,
Which judged, and resolutely willed. Thy voice
Enthralled me, and gave interest to all.
To me thou seem'dst the real king, the right
True master. I it was that in six months—
Perchance thou doubtest—made thee mount unto
The summit; where by fate thou should'st have been,
A woman placed thee. All that concerned me
Thou hast considered. First it was a flower,
But now an Empire. Ah, I reverence thee.
At first I thought thee good—but afterwards

I found thee great. My God, 'tis this that wins
A woman! If I now do ill, oh why
Was I incarcerated in this tomb,
As in a cage they put a dove, deprived
Of hope, of love, without one gilded ray?
—Some day, when we have time, I'll tell thee all
That I have suffered, I, ever alone,
As if forgot! humiliated too
Most constantly. Now judge. 'Twas yesterday,——
My chamber I disliked; you know—for you
Know all things—rooms there are where we feel more
Depressed than in some others. Mine I wished
To change. Now see what chains are ours, they would
Not let me. Thus a slave am I. O Duke,
It must have been that Heaven sent thee here
To save the tottering state, and from the gulf
To draw the people back--the working ones,
And love me who thus suffer. Ah I tell
Thee all at random, in my simple way.
You must, however, see that I am right.

　　　　RUY BLAS (*falling on his knees*).
Madam.——
　　　　　　THE QUEEN (*gravely*).
　　　　　　Don Cæsar—I to you give up
My soul. The Queen for others, I to you
Am but a woman. By the heart to you
It is that I belong. And I have faith
To know your honor will respect mine own.
Whenever you shall call me I will come.
Ready I am. Sublime thy spirit is,
Oh Cæsar. And be proud, for thou art crown'd
By genius. (*She kisses his forehead.*)
　　　　　　Adieu! [*She raises the tapestry and exit.*

　　　　SCENE 4.—RUY BLAS (*alone*).

　　[*He is as if absorbed in seraphic contemplation.*
　　　　　　Before mine eyes
'Tis heav'n I see! In all my life, oh God,
This hour stands first. Before me is a world,

A world of light, as if the paradise
We dream about had open'd wide and fill'd
My being with new life and brilliancy!
In me, around me, everywhere is joy,
Intoxication, mystery, and delight,
And pride, and that one thing that on the earth
Approaches most divinity, love—love,
In majesty and power. The Queen loves me!
Oh heavens, it is true—me—me—myself!
Since the Queen loves me I am more than King!
Oh, it is dazzling. Conqueror, happy, loved.
Duke d'Olmedo am I—and at my feet
Is Spain. I have her heart. That angel, whom
Upon my knees I contemplate and name,
Has by a word transfigured me and made
Me more than man. But in my star-lit dream
Do I move waking! Yes, I'm very sure
'Twas she herself who spoke—quite sure 'twas she.
A little diadem of silver lace
She wore; and I observed the while she spoke
—I think I see it still—an eagle 'graved
Upon her golden bracelet. She confides
In me, has told me so.—Poor Angel! Oh,
If it be true that God in granting love
Does by a miracle within us blend
That which can make man great with that which can
His nature soften, I who nothing fear
Since I am loved by her, I, who have power,
Thanks to her choice supreme, I, whose full heart
Might well the envy be of kings, declare—
Before my God who hears me—without fear,
And with loud voice, that Madam you may trust
In me,—unto my arm as Queen, unto
My heart as woman,—for devotion, pure
And loyal, dwells i' the depth of my great love.
Ah, fear thou nothing!

> [*During this speech a man had entered, by a door at
> the back, wrapped in a large cloak and with a
> hat gallooned in silver. He advances slowly to-
> wards* RUY BLAS *without being seen, and at the*

moment when RUY BLAS, *intoxicated with ecstasy and happiness, raises his eyes to heaven, this man slaps him on the shoulder.* RUY BLAS *turns, startled as if awakening from a dream. The man lets fall his cloak, and* RUY BLAS *recognizes* DON SALLUSTE. DON SAL-LUSTE *is dressed in a pinkish-gray livery gallooned with silver, like that of the page of* RUY BLAS.

SCENE 5.—RUY BLAS, DON SALLUSTE.

DON SALLUSTE (*placing his hand on the shoulder of* RUY BLAS).
Ah, good day.

RUY BLAS (*aside*).
Great God!
I'm lost! It is the Marquis that is here!

DON SALLUSTE.
I wager now you did not think of me.

RUY BLAS.
Indeed your lordship did surprise me.
(*Aside.*) Oh,
My misery is resumed. When turned towards
An angel, 'twas a demon came!
[*He hurries to the tapestry which conceals the little hiding place, and bolts the door inside. Then he returns trembling to* DON SALLUSTE.

DON SALLUSTE.
Well now,
How are you?

RUY BLAS (*his eyes fixed on* DON SALLUSTE *who is imperturbable, and as if himself incapable of gathering together his ideas*).
Why this livery?

DON SALLUSTE (*still smiling*).
I desired
To find an entrance to the palace. This
Admits me everywhere. I have assumed
Your livery, and find it suits me well.
[*He puts on his hat.* RUY BLAS *remains bareheaded.*

RUY BLAS.

But I'm alarmed for you.

DON SALLUSTE.

Alarmed! What was
That word so ludicrous?

RUY BLAS.

Exiled you were!

DON SALLUSTE.

You think so? Possibly.

RUY BLAS.

If it should be
That in the palace you were recognized
In the broad daylight?

DON SALLUSTE.

Nonsense! Happy folks,
Who are about the Court, would waste their time,
The time that flies so fast, remembering
A face that's in disgrace. Besides, who looks
Upon a lackey's profile?

(*He seats himself in the arm-chair.* RUY BLAS *remains
standing.*)

By the bye,
And if you please, what's this that in Madrid
They say? Is't true, that, burning with a zeal
Extravagant, and only for the sake
Of public funds, you've exiled a grandee,
That dear Priego? You've forgotten quite
That you're relations, for his mother was
A Sandoval—yours also. What the deuce!
A Sandoval doth bear on field of "or"
A bend of "sable." Look to your blazonry,
Don Cæsar, it is very clear. Such things,
My dear, between relations should not be.
The wolves that fight with other wolves, make they
Good leaders? Open wide your eyes for self,
But shut them for the others. For himself
Each one.

RUY BLAS (*recovering himself a little*).
    However, Sir—permit me, pray.
The Marquis de Priego, of the State
A noble, does great wrong in swelling now
Th' expenses of the kingdom. Soon we shall
Have need to put an army in the field;
We have not money, yet it must be done.
Bavaria's Prince is at the point of death;
And yesterday the Count d'Harcourt, whom well
You know, said to me in the Emperor's
His master's name, that if the Archduke should
Assert his claim, war would break out——

DON SALLUSTE.
                                The air
Seems rather chill—will you be good enough
To close the casement?
        [RUY BLAS, *pale with shame and despair, hesitates*
        a moment; then by an effort he goes slowly to
        the window, and shuts it. He returns to DON
        SALLUSTE, *who is still seated in the arm-chair,*
        watching him in an indifferent manner.

RUY BLAS (*continuing his endeavor to convince* DON
        SALLUSTE).
                        Deign, I beg, to see
How very difficult a war will prove :
What without money can we do? Listen,
My Lord. Spain's safety in her honor lies.
For me—I've to the Emperor said, as if
Our arms were ready, I'd oppose him——

DON SALLUSTE (*interrupting him, and pointing to his hand-*
        kerchief, which he had let fall on entering).
                                Stay,
        Pick up my handkerchief.
        [RUY BLAS, *as if tortured, again hesitates; then*
        stoops and takes up the handkerchief, giving it
        to DON SALLUSTE.

DON SALLUSTE (*putting the handkerchief in his pocket*).
                        You did observe?——

RUY BLAS (*with an effort*).

Yes, Spain is at our feet; her safety now
And public interest demand that each
Forgets himself. The nation blesses those
Who would release her. Let us dare be great,
And strike and save the people. Let us now
Remove the mask from knaves, and let in light
Upon intrigue.

DON SALLUSTE (*with indifference*).

First let me say all this
Is wearying,—it of the pedant smacks,
His petty way of making monstrous noise
Concerning everything. What signifies
A wretched million, more or less, devoured,
That all these dismal cries are raised about?
My boy, great Lords are not the pedant class,
Freely they live—I speak without bombast.
The mien of them who would redress abuse
Is pride inflated and with anger red!
Pshaw! now you want to be a famous spark
Adored by traders and by citizens.
'Tis very droll. Have newer fancies, pray.
The public good! First think now of your own.
Spain's safety is a hollow phrase; the rest
Can shout, my boy, as well as you can do.
And popularity? a rattling noise
Thought glory. Oh, what charming work to prowl
Like barking dog about the taxes! But
I know conditions better. Probity?
And faith? and virtue? faded tinsel, used
Already from the time of Charles the Fifth.
You are no fool. Must you be cured of all
This sentiment? You were a sucking child
When we did gaily and without remorse
By pin-pricks, or a kick, burst all at once
Your fine balloon, and amidst roaring mirth
Let out the wind from all these crotchets.

RUY BLAS.

But

My Lord, however——

DON SALLUSTE (*with icy smile*).
                    You're astonishing.
Let us be serious now.
          (*In an abrupt and imperious manner.*)
                    To-morrow, all
The morning you will wait at home for me,
Within the house I lent you. What I do
Now nears the end. Only retain the mutes
To wait upon us. In the garden have,
But hidden by the trees, a carriage, well
Appointed, horses, all prepared for use.
I will arrange relays. Do all I wish.
—You will want money, I will send it you.—

                    RUY BLAS.
I will obey you, Sir. I will do all.
But first, oh, swear to me that with this work
The Queen has nought to do.

DON SALLUSTE (*playing with an ivory knife on the table,*
                    turns half round).
                    With what are you
Now meddling?

RUY BLAS (*trembling and looking at him with terror*).
          Oh, you are a fearful man!
My knees beneath me tremble.—;—Towards a gulf
Invisible you drag me. Oh, I feel
That in a hand most terrible I am!
You have some monstrous scheme. Something I see
That's horrible.——Have mercy upon me!
Oh, I must tell you,—judge alas! yourself
You knew it not. I love that woman!

                    DON SALLUSTE.
                              Yes.
I knew it.

                    RUY BLAS.
          Knew it?

                    DON SALLUSTE.
                    What, by heaven, can
That signify?

Ruy Blas (*leaning for support against the wall, and as if speaking to himself*).

> Then for mere sport he has,
> The coward! this torture practiced upon me!
> Ah, this affair will be most horrible!

[*He raises his eyes to heaven.*

> Oh, God all-powerful! who tries me now,
> Spare me, oh God!

Don Salluste.

> There, that's enough—you dream!
> Truly you think in earnest that you are
> A personage, but 'tis buffoonery.
> I to an end move on which I alone
> Should know, an end that happier is for you
> Than you can guess. But keep you still. Obey.
> I have already said, and I repeat
> I wish your good. Proceed, the thing is done.
> And after all, what are the woes of love?
> We all go through them—troubles of a day.
> Know you, an Empire's destiny's concerned?
> What's yours beside it? Willingly I'd tell
> You all; but have the sense to comprehend.
> Your station keep. I'm very good and kind.
> A lackey though, of coarse clay or of fine,
> Is but an instrument to serve my whims.
> With your sort, what one wishes one can do.
> Your master did disguise you as his plan
> Required, and can unmask you at his will.
> I made you a great Lord—fantastic part—
> But for the instant—and you have complete
> The outfit. But forget not that you are
> My servant. You pay court unto the Queen—
> An incident—like stepping up behind
> My carriage. Therefore reasonable be.

Ruy Blas (*who has listened distracted, as if he could not believe his ears*).

> Oh God—oh God! the just! the merciful!
> Oh, of what crime is this the punishment?
> What have I done? Oh, Thou our Father art,

And wouldst not that a man despair. Behold,
Then, where I am!—And willingly, my Lord,
And without wrong in me—only to see
A victim agonized, in what abyss
You've plunged me! torturing thus a heart replete
With love and faith, to serve alone as means
For vengeance of your own!

(As if speaking to himself.)

For vengeance 'tis!

The thing is certain. I divine too well
It is against the Queen! What can I do?
Go tell her all? Great Heaven! become to her
An object of disgust and horror! Knave
With double face! A Crispin! Scoundrel base
And impudent, such as they bastinade
And drive away! Never!—I grow insane,
My reason totters!

(A pause. He ponders.)

God! behold what things

Are done! To build an engine silently,
To arm it hideously with frightful wheels
Unnumber'd, then to see it work, upon
The stone to throw a livery'd one, a thing,
A serving man, and set in motion all—
And suddenly to watch come out, beneath
The wheels, some muddy, blood-stained rags, a head
All broken, and a warm and steaming heart,
And not to shudder then to find, despite
The name they call him, that the livery was
But outward covering of a man.

(Turning towards Don Salluste.)

But oh,

There still is time! Truly, my Lord, as yet
Th' horrible wheel is not in motion.

(Throws himself at his feet.)

Oh,

Have pity on me! Mercy! Pity her!
You know that I a faithful servant am,
You often said it. See how I submit!
Oh, grace!

DON SALLUSTE.

The man will never understand.
This wearies me!

RUY BLAS (*trailing at his feet*).
Oh, mercy!

DON SALLUSTE.

Let us now
Have done.
(*He turns towards the window.*)
You badly closed the window there,
I'm sure. A draught comes thence.
(*He goes to the casement and shuts it.*)

RUY BLAS (*rising*).

It is too much!
At present I'm Duke d'Olmedo, and still
Th' all-powerful minister! I raise my head
From 'neath the foot which crushes me.

DON SALLUSTE.

What's that
You say? Repeat the phrase. Is Ruy Blas
Indeed Duke d'Olmedo? Your eyes are bound.
'Twas only on Bazan that thou wast raised
To be Olmedo.

RUY BLAS.

I will order you
To be arrested.

DON SALLUSTE.

I'll say who you are.

RUY BLAS (*excitedly*).
But——-

DON SALLUSTE.

You'll accuse me? I've risked both our heads.
That was foreseen. Too soon do you assume
The air of triumph.

RUY BLAS.

I'll deny it all.

DON SALLUSTE.
Pshaw! you're a child.

RUY BLAS.
                    You have no proof!

DON SALLUSTE.
                                        And you
No memory. I'll do just what I say,
And you had best believe me. But the glove
Are you, I am the hand.
        (*Lowering his voice and approaching* RUY BLAS.)
                        If thou obey'st
Me not, if thou to-morrow do not stay
At home preparing what I wish, if thou
Should'st speak a single word of all which now
Is passing, if by look or gesture thou
Betray—first she, for whom thou fearest, shall,
By this thy folly, in a hundred spots
Be publicly defamed, and ruined quite,
And afterwards she shall receive—in this
There's nought obscure—a paper under seal
Which in a place secure I keep; 'twas writ
Thou wilt remember by what hand? and signed
Thou knowest how? These are the words her eyes
Will read : "I, Ruy Blas, the serving-man
Of the most noble Lord the Marquis of
Finlas, engage to serve him faithfully
On all occasions as a servant true
In public or in secrecy."

        RUY BLAS (*crushed, and in husky voice*).
                        Enough.
I will, my Lord, do what you please.
        [*The door at the back opens.* *One sees the members
        of the Privy Council re-entering.* DON SALLUSTE
        hastens to wrap his cloak round him.

        DON SALLUSTE (*in a low voice*).
                                They come.
        (*Aloud, and bowing low to* RUY BLAS.)
I am your humble servant, my Lord Duke.   [*Exit.*

ACT FOURTH: DON CÆSAR.

A small, gloomy, but sumptuous room. Old-fashioned wainscot and furniture, with old gilding. The walls covered with old hangings of crimson velvet pressed down in places, and at the back of the arm-chairs, and gathered by shining gold galloon into vertical bands. At the back folding doors. At the left angle of the wall, a large corner chimney with sculpture of the time of Philip the Second, and an escutcheon of wrought iron inside. At the opposite angle a little door leading to a dark closet. A single window at the left, placed very high, has bars across it, and an inside splay like the windows of prisons. On the walls are some old portraits smoke-begrimed and half defaced. A chest for clothes and a Venetian looking-glass. Large arm-chairs in the fashion of Philip the Third's time. A highly ornamented cup-board against the wall. A square table with writing materials on it. A little round table with gilt feet in a corner. It is morning.
When the curtain rises* Ruy Blas, *dressed in black without his mantle and without the Fleece, is seen walking about the room greatly agitated. At the back stands his* Page *motionless, as if awaiting orders.*

SCENE 1.—RUY BLAS. THE PAGE.

RUY BLAS (*aside, as if speaking to himself*).
What is it can be done? She must be saved!
Before all else! Nothing but her to be
Considered! Should my brains from on a wall
Spurt out, or should the gibbet claim, or should
Hell seize me, rescued she must be! But how?
To give my blood, my heart, my soul, all that
Were nothing—it were easy. But to break
This web! To guess, for guess one must, what schemes
This man constructing has combined! Sudden

He comes from out the shadow, and therein
Replunges. Lone in darkness what does he?
When I remember that at first to him
For self I pleaded ! Oh, 'twas cowardice !
Moreover it was stupid ! This is why—
He is a wretch.—The thing has olden date,
No doubt.—How could I think, that when he held
His prey but half devoured, the demon would,
In pity for his lackey, leave the Queen !
Can we subdue wild beasts ? Oh misery !
I yet must save her ! I, the cause of this !
At any price it must be done. All—all
Is ended. Now behold my fall ! From height
So great so low ! Have I then dream'd ?—Yet oh !
She must escape ! But he ! By what door will
He come—and by what trap, oh God, will he,
The traitor black, proceed ? As of this house,
So of my life, he is the lord. He can
The gilding all strip off. He has the keys
Of all the locks. Enter and leave he can,
Approaching in the dark to tread upon
My heart as on this floor. Yes, this my dream !
Such fate confuses thought i' the rapid tide
Of things so quickly done. I am distraught.
No one thought have I clear. My mind—of which
I was so vain—oh God ! is now in such
A hurricane of rage and fear 'tis like
A reed storm-twisted !—Oh what can I do ?
Let me reflect. At first to hinder her
From stirring from the palace. Yes, 'tis that
Undoubtedly that is the snare. Around
Myself the whirlpool is, and darkness dense.
I feel the mesh but see it not. Oh, how
I suffer !—'Tis decided. To forewarn—
Prevent her going from the palace—this
At once to do. But how ? No one I have !

  [*He reflects earnestly. Suddenly, as if struck with an
   idea, and having a ray of hope, he raises his head.*

Don Guritan ! Ah, yes, he loves her well,
And he is loyal !

(He signs to the Page *to approach, then speaks low.)*
     Page, this instant go
Unto Don Guritan. Make him from me
Apologies; and beg him then without
Delay to seek the Queen, and pray her in
My name, and in his own, that whatsoe'er
May happen or be said, on no account
To leave the palace for three days. To stir
Not out. Now run. *(Recalling the* Page.)
      Ah!
(He takes a leaf and a pencil from his note case.)
      Let him give these words
Unto the Queen,—and watch!
   (He writes on his knee rapidly.)
       " Believe what says
Don Guritan, as he advises do."
    [*He folds the paper and gives it to the* Page
As for the duel, tell him I was wrong,
That I am at his feet, that I have now
A trouble, beg of him to pity me,
And take my supplication to the Queen
On th' instant. Tell him that I will to him,
In public, make apologies. And say
There is for her a danger imminent.
She must not venture out for quite three days
Whate'er occurs.—— Exactly do all this;
Go, be discreet, and nothing let appear.

      Page.
I am to you devoted—for you are
A master good.
      Ruy Blas.
    Run fast, my little Page,
Hast thou well understood?

      Page.
     Oh yes, my lord,
Be satisfied.   [*Exit* Page.

  Ruy Blas (*alone, falling into an arm-chair*).
    My thoughts grow calmer now.
Yet I forget, and feel things all confused

As were I mad. Ah yes, the means are sure.
Don Guritan.—— But I myself? Is there
The need to wait Don Salluste here? Wherefore?
Oh no, I will not wait, and that perchance
Will paralyze him for a day. Within
A church I want to pray. I'll go—I've need
Of help, and God will me inspire!

> [*He takes his hat from a side table, and shakes a*
> *little bell placed on the table. Two negroes*
> *dressed in pale green velvet brocaded with gold,*
> *jackets plaited into great lappets, appear at the*
> *door at the back.*

                                                    I leave.
But very soon a man will hither come—
And by an entrance known to him. May be,
When in the house, as if he were indeed
The master, he will act. Let him so do.
And if some others come——

> (*After hesitating a moment.*)

                                        My faith, why then
You'll please to let them enter.

> [*By a gesture he dismisses the negroes who bow in*
> *token of obedience and exeunt.*

                                Now I go!   [*Exit.*

> [*At the moment the door closes on* RUY BLAS *there*
> *is heard a great noise in the chimney, from which*
> *suddenly falls a man wrapped in a tattered*
> *cloak. It is* DON CÆSAR *who throws himself*
> *into the room.*

SCENE 2.—DON CÆSAR.

DON CÆSAR (*scared, out of breath, stupefied, disordered,*
with an expression of mingled joy and anxiety).
'Tis I! So much the worse!

> [*He rises, rubbing the leg on which he has fallen, and*
> *comes into the room hat in hand and bowing low.*

                                Your pardon, pray!
But heed me not. I don't attend—go on
With your discourse, continue I entreat,

I enter rather rudely Sirs, for that
I'm sorry !
(*He stops in the middle of the room, perceiving he is alone.*)
                    No one here ?—When on the roof
Just now I perched, I thought I heard the sound
Of voices.—No one, though !
            (*Seats himself in an arm-chair.*)
                              That's very well.
Let me now gather up my thoughts. And good
Is solitude. Oh, what events !—Marvels
With which I'm charged, just as a wetted dog
Who shakes off water. First those Alguazils
Who seized me in their claws, and that absurd
Embarkment ; then the corsairs, and the town
So big where I was beaten sorely. Then
Temptations of that sallow woman ; next,
Departure from the prison : travels, too,
And at the last return to Spain. And then—
Oh, what a tale !—The day that I arrived,
Those self-same Alguazils the first I met.
My desperate flight, and their enraged pursuit ;
I leaped a wall, and then I saw a house
Half-hidden by the trees ; I thither ran ;
None saw me, so I nimbly climbed from shed
To roof ; at last I introduced myself
Into the bosom of a family
By coming down a chimney, where I tore
To rags my newest mantle, that now hangs
About my heels. By heav'n, Cousin Salluste,
You are a braggart rogue !
(*Looking at himself in a little Venetian glass placed on
            the sculptured chest.*)
                              My doublet here
Has kept to me through these disasters all.
It struggles yet.
        [*He takes off his mantle and admires in the glass
            his rose-colored doublet, now torn and patched ;
            then he puts his hand sharply to his leg, with a
            look at the chimney.*
                    But in my fall my leg

Has suffer'd horribly!

[*He opens the drawers of the chest. In one of them
he finds a mantle of light-green velvet embroidered with gold. The mantle given by* DON SAL-
LUSTE *to* RUY BLAS. *He examines it and compares it with his own.*

It seems to me
This mantle is more decent than my own.

[*He puts on the green mantle, and leaves his own
in the chest, after having carefully folded it up.
He adds his hat, which he crushes under the
mantle with a blow of his fist. Then he shuts
the drawer, and struts about proudly draped in
the fine mantle embroidered with gold.*

'Twill do. Behold me now return'd. All is
Proceeding well. Ah, cousin very dear,
You wished to send me off to Africa,
Where man is mouse unto the tiger! Ah,
I'll be revenged on you most savagely,
My cursèd cousin, when I've breakfasted.
In my right name I'll go to you, and drag
With me a troop of rogues, such as can smell
The gibbet a league off—and more, I will
Deliver you alive, thus to appease
The appetites of all my creditors,
These followed by their little ones.

[*He perceives in the corner a pair of splendid boots
trimmed with lace. He takes off his shoes in a
leisurely manner, and, without scruple, puts on
the new boots.*

But first
Now let me see where all his perfidies
Have led me.

(*After looking all round the room.*)

A mysterious dwelling, fit
For tragedies. Closed doors and shutters barr'd,
A dungeon quite. Into this charming place
One enters from the top, just as there comes
The wine into the bottles.   (*With a sigh.*)

Ah, good wine
Is very good.

[*He notices the little door at the right, opens it, and hastily enters the closet with which it communicates, and then comes back with a gesture of astonishment.*

     Oh wonders, wonders more !
Where everything is closed, a little room
Without the means of egress !

  [*He goes to the door at the back, half-opens it, and looks out; he lets it close and comes to the front.*

        Not a soul !—
Oh, where the deuce am I ?—At any rate,
I've managed to escape the Alguazils.
What matters all the rest ? Need I be scared
And take a gloomy view, because I ne'er
Before beheld a house like this ?

(*He seats himself in the arm-chair, and yawns, but soon gets up again.*)

        Come, though,
I feel the dullness here is horrible !

  (*Perceiving a little corner cupboard in the wall.*)
Let's see, this looks to me a little like
A bookcase.

(*He opens it and finds it to be a well-furnished larder.*)

     Ah ! 'tis just the thing.—A pie,
A water-melon, and some wine. A cold
Collation for emergency. By Jove !
I'd prejudices 'gainst this house.

  (*Examines the flagons one after the other.*)

        All good.—
Come now ! This place is worthy of great praise.

  [*He goes to the corner, and brings thence to the front a little round table, on which he places the contents of the larder—bottles, dishes, etc. He adds a glass, plate, fork, etc. Then he takes up one of the bottles.*

Let's read this one the first.

  (*He fills the glass, and drinks off the wine.*)

        A work that is
Most admirable. The production fine
Of that so famous poet called the sun !

Xérès-des-Chevaliers can nothing show
More ruby-like.
>   (*He sits and pours out another glass of wine.*)
>   What book's worth this? Find me
Something that is more spiritual!
>   (*He drinks.*)
>   Ah!
This comforts! Let us eat.
>   · (*He cuts the pie.*)
>   I have outstripp'd
Those dogs of Alguazils. They've lost the scent.
>   (*He begins eating.*)
The king of pies! and as for him who is
The master here, should he drop in——
> (*He goes to the sideboard, and brings thence a glass
>   and a plate.*)
>   Why, him
I now invite, if that he does not come
To drive me hence. Let me be very quick.
>   (*He takes large mouthfuls.*)
My dinner done, I'll look about the house.
Who can inhabit it? Maybe, he is
A jolly fellow. This place can but hide
Some feminine intrigue. Pshaw! What's the harm
That here I do? What is it, I beseech?
Nought but this worthy's hospitality
After the ancient way,
> (*He half kneels, surrounding the table with his arms.*)
>   Embracing thus
The altar. (*He drinks.*)
>   Firstly though, this wine is not
A bad man's wine. And then if any one
Should come, I'd certainly declare myself.
How you would rage, my old accursèd coz!
What, that low fellow, that Bohemian!
That beggarly black sheep Zafari? Yes,
Don Cæsar de Bazan, the cousin he
Of the Don Salluste! What a fine surprise!
And what a hubbub in Madrid! When was't
That he return'd? This morning, or this night?

What tumult everywhere at such a bomb,
The great forgotten name that all at once
Again is heard! Don Cæsar de Bazan!
Yes, if you please, good Sirs. Nobody thought—
Nobody spoke of him,—then he's not dead!
He lives, my dames and gentlemen! The men
Will cry: The deuce! The women they will say,
Indeed! Aye, aye! Soft sound that mingles with
The barking of three hundred creditors
As you go home! Fine part to play! Alas!
I'm wanting money for it.
          (*A noise is heard at the door.*)
                              Some one comes!
No doubt t' expel me like a vile buffoon.—
No matter though. Cæsar, do nought by halves!
     [*He wraps himself in his cloak up to the eyes. The
      door at the back opens. A* Lackey *in livery
      enters bearing a great courier's bag on his back.*

SCENE 3.—DON CÆSAR.   A LACKEY.

DON CÆSAR (*scanning the* LACKEY *from head to foot*).
Whom seek you here, my friend? (*Aside.*)
                              I must assume
Great confidence—the peril is extreme.

THE LACKEY.
Don Cæsar de Bazan?

DON CÆSAR (*lowering his mantle from his face*).
                    Don Cæsar! That's
Myself! (*Aside.*)
        Here is the wonderful!

THE LACKEY.
                    You are,
My Lord, Don Cæsar de Bazan?

DON CÆSAR.
                    By heav'n
I have the honor so to be. Cæsar,
The true and only Cæsar! Count of Gar——

THE LACKEY (*placing the bag on the arm-chair*).
Now deign to see if the amount be right.

DON CÆSAR (*dazed—aside*).
Some money! Oh, it is too wonderful!
(*Aloud.*)
My man——

THE LACKEY.
You'll condescend to count. It is
The sum that I was told to bring you.

DON CÆSAR (*gravely*).
Ah!
'Tis well, I understand. (*Aside.*)
The devil now
I wish—— But there we must not disarrange
This admirable story. In the nick
Of time it comes. (*Aloud.*)
Now want you a receipt?

THE LACKEY.
Not so, my Lord.

DON CÆSAR (*pointing to the table*).
Put there the money bag.
[*The* LACKEY *obeys.*
Whom comes it from?

THE LACKEY.
My Lord knows very well.

DON CÆSAR.
Undoubtedly, but still——

THE LACKEY.
This money here—
And this is what is needful that I add—
Now comes for purpose that you know, from him
You know.

DON CÆSAR (*satisfied with the explanation*).
Ah!

THE LACKEY.
Both of us must careful·be—
Hush!.

Don Cæsar.

Hush!—This money comes—— The phrase is most
Magnificent! Repeat it once again.

The Lackey.

This money——

Don Cæsar.

All explains itself. It comes
From him I know——

The Lackey.

For purpose that you know.
We must——

Don Cæsar.

The pair of us!

The Lackey.

Be guarded now.

Don Cæsar.

It is quite clear.

The Lackey.

I do not understand,
I but obey.

Don Cæsar.

Pshaw—pshaw!

The Lackey.

But you, I know,
Do comprehend.

Don Cæsar.

The deuce!

The Lackey.

Sufficient 'tis.

Don Cæsar.

I take it and I understand, my boy,
Receiving money always easy is.

The Lackey.

Hush!

Don Cæsar.

Hush! Deuce take it—ah, we must not now
Imprudent be!

THE LACKEY.
Count it, my Lord!

DON CÆSAR.
For what,
Pray, do you take me?
[*Admiring the rotundity of the bag on the table.*
Oh! the fine paunch!

THE LACKEY (*insisting*).
But——
DON CÆSAR.
I do confide in thee.

THE LACKEY.
The gold is in
Broad quadruples, that weigh their full seven drachms
And six and thirty grains, or good doubloons,
The silver in cross-maries.
[DON CÆSAR *opens the great bag and takes from it
several small bags full of gold and silver, which
he opens and empties on to the table admiringly;
then he digs his hand into the bags of gold and
draws out handfuls, filling his pockets with quadruples and doubloons.*

DON CÆSAR (*pausing, with majesty. Aside.*)
Now behold
My fine romance,—the crown of fairy-dreams
Is dying for love of a fat million.
[*He continues filling his pockets.*
Oh joy! I take in like a galleon!
[*One pocket filled, he passes to another. He seeks
everywhere for pockets and seems to have for-
gotten the Lackey.*

THE LACKEY (*who looks at him calmly*).
And now I wait your orders.

DON CÆSAR (*turning round*).
What to do?

THE LACKEY.
To promptly execute without delay

A something which you know, but I do not,
A thing of great importance——

Don Cæsar (*interrupting him as if understanding*).
                                        Public 'tis
And private——

THE LACKEY.
                Which this instant should be done.
I say what I was told to say. .

    Don Cæsar (*slapping him on the shoulder*).
                                        And I
Applaud thee for it—faithful servant thou !

        THE LACKEY.
That nothing be delayed my master sends
Myself to help you.

        DON CÆSAR.
                Acting in accord,
Let us do what he wishes. (*Aside.*) Hang me now
If I know what to tell him. (*Aloud.*) Galleon,
Come here, and first (*He fills the other glass with wine*),
            Drink this !

        THE LACKEY.
                        Indeed, my Lord——

        DON CÆSAR.
Drink this.
    [*The* Lackey *drinks, and* DON CÆSAR *again fills the glass.*
            'Tis wine of Oropesa !
(*He makes the* Lackey *sit down, and plies him with wine.*)
                                        Now
Let's chat.
    (*Aside.*) His eyes already sparkle.
    (*Aloud, and stretching himself on his chair.*)
                                        Man
Is nought, dear friend, but black smoke that proceeds
From out the passions' fire. Pshaw ! I declare
        (*Pours wine for him to drink*)
'Tis rubbish this I'm telling thee. At first
The smoke, unto blue heav'n recalled, comports
Itself in manner different from when

'Tis in a chimney.   It mounts gaily, while
We tumble down.
               (*He rubs his leg.*)
               Only vile lead is man.
               (*He fills the two glasses.*)
Let's drink.   All thy doubloons are of less worth
Than is a passing drunkard's song.
(*Approaching nearer to him in a mysterious manner.*)
                              But see,
Be prudent.   The o'erloaded axle breaks ;
The wall without foundation suddenly
Gives way.—My mantle's collar please to hook.

               THE LACKEY (*haughtily*).
My lord, I'm not a valet.
(*Before* DON CÆSAR *can prevent him, he rings the little bell
on the table.*)

               DON CÆSAR (*aside—terrified*).
                    Oh, he rings !
The master, perhaps, will come himself.   I'm caught !
     [*Enter one of the* Negroes.   DON CÆSAR, *a prey to the
     greatest anxiety, turns towards the opposite side,
     as if not knowing what to do.*

               THE LACKEY (*to the* Negro).
Fasten my Lord's clasp.
     [*The* Negro *gravely approaches* DON CÆSAR, *who looks
     at him as if stupefied.   Then he fastens the mantle,
     bows, and goes out, leaving* DON CÆSAR *petrified.*

     DON CÆSAR (*rising from the table—aside*).
                    On my word of honor !
Beelzebub's abode this is !
               (*He comes to the front, and strides about.*)
                    My faith !
Now let things drift, and take what comes.   At least,
I'll stir the crowns ; a coffer full of them.
The money I have got !   What shall I do
With it ?
(*Turning towards the* Lackey, *who is still at the table, drinking,
     and who begins to reel in his chair.*)
               Your pardon—stop.

(*Musing—aside.*)
Now, let me see,—

If I should pay my creditors?—for shame!
—At least, to calm their minds that are so prompt
At turning sour,—if I should water them
With something on account? What good is it
To water flowers so villainous? How now
The devil did I think of such a' thing?
Nothing there is like money to corrupt
A man, and fill him up unto the throat
With all mean sentiments! E'en if he were
From Hannibal himself descended, him
Who conquer'd Rome! To see me paying debts
I owe! what would they say? Ah, ah!

THE LACKEY (emptying his glass).
What now

Do you command of me?

DON CÆSAR.
Let be—I am

Reflecting. Drink, while waiting.

    [*The* Lackey *begins drinking again.* DON CÆSAR *con-
tinues to muse; then suddenly strikes his forehead,
as if he had found an idea.*

Yes!

(To the Lackey.)
Get up

Immediately. See now what must be done.
Thy pockets fill with gold.

    [*The* Lackey *rises, stumbling, and fills the pockets of
his coat,* DON CÆSAR *helping him as he continues.*

Go thou unto

The lane which leads from out the Mayor Square,
Enter at Number Nine. A narrow house;
A pleasant dwelling, if it did not hap
The glass panes at the right were paper patched.

THE LACKEY.

A one-eyed house?*

DON CÆSAR.
Oh no, it only squints,*

---

* *Maison borgne*—French slang for a disreputable house; and *louche*, for a
suspicious one.—TRANS.

One might be crippled mounting up the stairs,
So take you care.

THE LACKEY.

A ladder is't?

DON CÆSAR.

Almost,

But steeper. Up above, a beauty dwells,
Easy to know—beneath a threepenny cap
Thickish disordered hair. She's rather short
And red—a charming woman, though. My boy,
You'll be respectful, she my dear love is,
Lucinda fair, with eyes like indigo,
Once she; who danced fandango for the Pope
At eve to see. Count out and give to her
A hundred of the ducats, in my name.
Then, in a hovel near, you'll see a stout
And red-nosed devil, with an old felt hat
Dragged down upon his eyebrows, and a plume,
A feather brush, that tragically hangs
Astonished from it; rapier at his side,
And rags upon his back. Give next, from me,
Unto this creature six piastres.—Then
Go further, thou wilt find a hole, black like
An oven, 'tis a tavern at cross roads;
There smokes and drinks i' the porch, a frequenter,
A gentle-manner'd man who leads a life
That's elegant, a gentleman from whom
An oath ne'er dropp'd, my heart's friend he; his name
Is Goulatromba. Give him thirty crowns!
And tell him for thanksgiving he alone
Must drink them quick, and he shall have some more.
Give to these rascals in the biggest coins,
And do not wonder at the eyes they'll ope.

THE LACKEY.

And afterwards?

DON CÆSAR.

Why, keep the rest. And then

At last——

THE LACKEY.

What would my Lord?

DON CÆSAR.

Then surfeit thou
Thyself, thou scamp. Break many pots, and make
Much noise, and not until to-morrow, in
The night, go home.

THE LACKEY.

Enough, my Prince.
[*He moves towards the door in a zigzag way.*

DON CÆSAR (*aside—observing his walk*).

He is
Abominably drunk!
(*Recalling the other, who turns back.*)

Ah, now—when out
Thou goest, idle folks will follow thee.
Do honor to the drink thou'st had. Try thou
To bear thyself in noble fashion. If
By chance some crowns from out thy stocking drop,
Then let them fall,—and if assayers, clerks,
Some scholars, or the beggars that one sees
Pass by, should pick them up, let them do so.
Don't be a mortal fierce, that they would dread
T' approach.—And e'en if from thy pocket some
They take—be thou indulgent. They are men
As we. And, as you see, it is a law
For us, in this world full of misery,
To give sometimes a little joy to all
Who live.
(*With melancholy.*)

Perchance they will be hang'd some day!
Show, then, the kindness to them which is due!
Go, now.
[*The Lackey goes out. Left alone, DON CÆSAR sits
down again, and leans his elbow on the table,
appearing to be plunged in deep thought.*

It is the duty of the sage
And Christian having money that he use
It well. For eight days at the very least
I have enough. These will I live. And should
A little money still remain, I will
Employ it piously. But I must not

Be over confident. Undoubtedly
'Tis all a blunder, and from me it will
Be taken, ah, the thing will all become
Misunderstood. A fine scrape this of mine. . . .

> [*The door at the back opens. Enter an old gray-
> haired* Duenna *in black dress and mantle, and
> with a fan.*

Scene 4.—Don Cæsar. A Duenna.

The Duenna (*at the threshold of the door*).
Don Cæsar de Bazan?

> [Don Cæsar, *absorbed in his meditations. turns his head
> suddenly.*

Don Cæsar.

Now then, what is it ? (*Aside.*)
A woman ! Oh !

> [*Whilst the* Duenna *makes a low respectful curtsey at
> the back he comes to the front wonder-struck.*

The devil or Salluste
Must be mixed up in this ! Next I expect
To see my cousin here. Duenna, oh !
(*Aloud.*)
'Tis I, Don Cæsar, tell your business, pray.
(*Aside.*)
Most commonly it is a woman old
That ushers in a young one.

The Duenna (*bowing and making sign of the Cross*).
I, my Lord,
Salute you, on this fast day, in the name
Of Him o'er whom there's nothing can prevail.

Don Cæsar (*aside.*)
A galant ending that begins devoutly.
(*Aloud.*)
Amen. Good day.

The Duenna.
May God maintain you, e'er
In happiness. (*Mysteriously.*)
Know you of some one who

Has sent me now, with whom you've plann'd to-night
A secret meeting? .

DON CÆSAR.
Oh, I'm capable
Of such a thing.

THE DUENNA (*who takes from her farthingale a folded letter which she shows to him, but without allowing him to take it*).
Then you indeed it is,
Galant discreet, who've just addressed to one
'Who loves you, for to-night a message,—one
Whom you know well?

DON CÆSAR.
It must be I.

THE DUENNA.
Good—good.
The lady married to some dotard old
Is forced, no doubt, to careful be. I was
Desired to hither come. Her I know not,
But you know her—it was her waiting-maid
Who told me about things. That was enough,
Without the names.

DON CÆSAR.
Excepting mine.

THE DUENNA.
'Tis plain,
Th' appointment for the lady has been made
By her soul's friend,—but fearing there may be
Some 'snare, and knowing too much caution ne'er
Spoiled aught, she sends me here from your own mouth
To have the confirmation——

DON CÆSAR.
Oh the old
And surly thing! What fuss about a sweet
Love letter! Yes, 'tis I myself, I tell
You so.

THE DUENNA (*placing on the table the folded letter, which DON CÆSAR looks at with curiosity*).
In that case then, if you it be,

The one word, *Come,* upon the letter you
Will write—but not by your own hand—that so
There may be nothing compromised.

DON CÆSAR.

Indeed!

From mine own hand! (*Aside.*)

A message well conveyed!

[*He puts out his hand to take the letter; but it has
been resealed and the* Duenna *will not let him
touch it.*

THE DUENNA.

You must not open. You will recognize
The fold.

DON CÆSAR.

By Heaven! (*Aside.*)

I who burn to see!——

But let me play my part!

[*He rings the little bell. One of the* Negroes *enters.*

Know'st thou to write?

[*The* Negro *nods an affirmative sign. Astonishment
of* DON CÆSAR. (*Aside.*)

A sign! (*Aloud.*) Art thou then dumb, thou rascal?

[*Again the* Negro *makes the sign of affirmation.
Fresh stupefaction of* DON CÆSAR. (*Aside.*)

Well!

Continue! Mutes appear the latest thing!

[*To the* Mute, *showing him the letter which the old
woman holds down on the table.*

Write there : *Come.*

[*The* Mute *writes.* DON CÆSAR *signs to the* Duenna
to take back the letter, and to the Mute *to go.
Exit the* Mute.

Ah! he is obedient!

THE DUENNA (*with an air of mystery again placing the letter in
her farthingale, and approaching nearer to* DON CÆSAR).

To-night you'll see her. Is she very fair?

DON CÆSAR.

Oh, charming!

THE DUENNA.

'Twas the cunning waiting-maid

Who managed it. At sermon-time aside

She took me. Oh, how beautiful was she!
With angel's profile and a demon's eye.
Knowing in love affairs she seemed to be.

> DON CÆSAR (*aside*).
I'd be contented with the maid!

> THE DUENNA.
>   We judge—
For always beauty makes the plain afraid,—
So with Sultana and her slave, and with
The master and his man. Most certainly
Your love is very beautiful.

> DON CÆSAR.
>   I'm proud,
Indeed, to think so!

THE DUENNA (*making a curtsey and about to withdraw*).
>   Sir, I kiss your hand.

> DON CÆSAR (*giving her a handful of doubloons*).
I'll grease thy palm. Old woman, stop.

> THE DUENNA (*pocketing them*).
>   Ah, youth
Is gay to-day!

> DON CÆSAR (*dismissing her*).
>   Now go.

> THE DUENNA (*curtseys*).
>   If you have need——
I'm named Dame Oliva. Saint Isidro,
The Convent,——

> [*She goes out. Afterwards the door re-opens and
>   her head appears.*
>   Always at the right I sit
Of the third pillar entering the church.

> [DON CÆSAR *turns round with impatience. The door
>   closes; again it half opens and the old woman
>   re-appears.*
To-night you'll see her! In your prayers, my Lord,
Remember me.

> DON CÆSAR (*driving her away angrily*).
>   Ah!

> [*The* Duenna *disappears and the door closes.*

DON CÆSAR (*alone*).

Now I'm resolved, my faith,
At nothing more to be at all surprised.
I'm in the moon. Behold a love affair
Now comes; I am about to satisfy
My heart, after long hunger. (*Musing.*) Oh all this
To me just now seems mighty good. But ah!
Beware the end!

[*The door at the back opens. DON GURITAN appears
with two long naked swords under his arm.*

SCENE 5.—DON CÆSAR—DON GURITAN.

DON GURITAN (*at the back*).
Don Cæsar de Bazan?

DON CÆSAR (*turning and perceiving DON GURITAN with the
two swords*).
And now! Well, well! Events were fine enough,
But better still they are. A dinner good,
Then money; and an assignation—now
A duel! Cæsar in his natural state
Again am I!

[*He greets DON GURITAN gaily, with demonstrative
salutations; DON GURITAN looks at him impatiently, and advances to the front with a firm step.*

Here is he, my dear Lord.
And will you please to enter—take a chair.

(*He places an arm-chair—DON GURITAN remains standing.*)

Be seated, pray;—without formality.
As if at home. I'm charm'd to see you, Sir;
There, let us chat a moment. Tell me now
What's doing in Madrid? A charming place!
I nothing know; but I suppose that still
They wonder at the Matalobos, and
The Lindamere! As for myself, I'd fear
The stealer of our hearts as peril more
Than stealer of our money bags. Oh, Sir,
The women! Sex possessed! My brain is crack'd
Where they're concern'd, they so enslave me. Speak,
And tell me what is doing nowadays;

DON CÆSAR—"BAH! ONE OF US DEAD! I DEFY YOU TO KILL DON CÆSAR."

Ruy Blas—Act IV., Scene 5.

I am but half alive—an ox—a thing
Absurd—with nought that's human left in him,
A dead man risen, an hidalgo true
Of old Castile. They've robbed me of my plume,
And I my gloves have lost. I come from lands
Most wonderful.

DON GURITAN.

You come, dear Sir? Ah well,
I've just arrived from farther off than you!

DON CÆSAR (*brightening up*).
From what distinguished shore?

DON GURITAN.

Down yonder, in
The north.

DON CÆSAR.
And I from farther in the south.

DON GURITAN.
I'm furious!

DON CÆSAR.
Is it so? I am enraged!

DON GURITAN.
Twelve hundred leagues I've travelled!

DON CÆSAR.
I have done
Two thousand! Women fair, black, yellow, brown
I've seen. To places bless'd by heaven I've been.
Algiers the happy town, and fair Tunis
Where one may see—such pleasant ways have Turks—
People impaled hooked up above the doors.

. DON GURITAN.
I have been played a trick.

DON CÆSAR.
And I've been sold.

DON GURITAN.
Almost exiled I was.

DON CÆSAR.
I almost hang'd!

DON GURITAN.

To Neubourg cunningly they sent me off,
To bear these few words written in a box:
"Keep this old fool as long as possible."

DON CÆSAR (*bursting out laughing*).
And who did this?

DON GURITAN.
But I will wring the neck
Of Cæsar de Bazan.

DON CÆSAR (*gravely*).
Ah!

DON GURITAN.
And to crown
His insolence, he just now sent to me
A lackey to excuse himself, he said,
A serving man, but I refused to see
The varlet, and I made them lock him up.
Now to the master, Cæsar de Bazan,
I come! This most audacious traitor knave!
See now, I'll kill him! Where is he?

DON CÆSAR (*still gravely*).
I'm he.

DON GURITAN.
You!—You are joking, Sir?

DON CÆSAR.
I am Don Cæsar.

DON GURITAN.
What! This again!

DON CÆSAR.
Undoubtedly again!

DON GURITAN.
Leave off this play, you greatly weary me,
E'en if you think that you are droll.

DON CÆSAR.
And you
Amuse me much. You have to me the air

Of jealousy. Exceedingly, dear Sir,
I pity you. The ills that come to us
From our own vices are more hard to bear
Than those which hap to us from others' sins.
I'd rather be—and so I've often said—
Quite poor than miserly, and be deceived
Rather than jealous. You are both. And now,
Upon my soul, I do to-night expect
Your wife.

DON GURITAN.

My wife!

DON CÆSAR.

Oh yes, your wife!

DON GURITAN.

Come now!

I am not married.

DON CÆSAR.

Yet you have stirr'd up
This riot! And you're not a married man!
For the last quarter of an hour you have
Assumed the husband's roar, or else the air
Of weeping tiger, so efficiently
That in simplicity I've given you
A heap of precious counsel seeming fit!
But if not married, why, by Hercules,
Have you thus made yourself ridiculous?

DON GURITAN.

Do you know, Sir, that you exasperate me?

DON CÆSAR.

Pooh!

DON GURITAN.

This is too much.

DON CÆSAR.

Truly?

DON GURITAN.

Oh, but you
Shall pay for this!

DON CÆSAR (*looking in a jeering manner at* DON GURITAN'S *feet,
which are covered by waves of ribbon, according to the
new fashion*).

In days gone by it was
That on the head were ribbons worn. I mark
That now—and 'tis an honest mode—they're placed
Upon the boot, and feet are thus adorned.
A charming thing!

DON GURITAN.

I see that we must fight!

DON CÆSAR (*with indifference*).

You think so?

DON GURITAN.

You're not Cæsar, that concerns
Myself; but I'll commence with you.

DON CÆSAR.

Good, good!
Take care with me to finish.

DON GURITAN (*presenting one of the swords to him*).

Fop! At once.

DON CÆSAR (*taking the sword*).

Immediately. When I've a chance to fight
I do not lose it!

DON GURITAN.

Where?

DON CÆSAR.

Behind the wall.
This street's deserted.

DON GURITAN (*trying the point of his sword on the floor*).

As for Cæsar, ah!
I'll kill him afterwards.

DON CÆSAR.

Indeed?

DON GURITAN.

Most surely!

DON CÆSAR (*also making his sword bend*).

Pshaw! One of us dead, you I then defy
To kill Don Cæsar.

Don Guritan.

Let us out!

[*They go out. The sound of their retreating steps is heard. A little concealed door opens in the right wall, and* Don Salluste *enters by it.*

Scene 6.

Don Salluste (*dressed in a dark green coat, almost black. He appears anxious and pre-occupied. He looks about, and listens uneasily*).

There's nought

Prepared! (*Noticing the table covered with dishes.*)
What means all this?

(*Hearing the noise of* Cæsar's *and* Guritan's *steps.*)

What noise is that?

(*He walks about in reverie.*)

This morning Gudiel saw the Page go out
And followed him.—Unto Don Guritan
He went.—I see not Ruy Blas. This Page——
Oh Satan! 'Tis some countermine! some word
Of faithful counsel, with the which he charged
Don Guritan for her!—And from the mutes
One can learn nothing! It is that! I had
Not counted on Don Guritan at all.

[*Enter* Don Cæsar. *In his hand he carries the bare sword, which, on entering, he throws upon an arm-chair.*

Scene 7.—Don Salluste—Don Cæsar.

Don Cæsar (*from the threshold of the door*).
Ah, I was very sure! I see you then,
Old fiend!

Don Salluste (*turning round petrified*).
Don Cæsar!

Don Cæsar (*crossing his arms and bursting out laughing*).
You are weaving now
Some frightful scheme! But have I not disturb'd
It all just now, by sprawling heavily
Into the midst of it?'

Don Salluste (*aside*).
Oh, all is lost!

Don Cæsar (*laughing*).
Through all this morning have I come across
Your spider webs. Not one of all your plans
Is now unspoilt. I flung myself on them
At hazard; and the whole demolished I.
This is delightful!

Don Salluste (*aside*).
Demon! What can he
Have done?

Don Cæsar (*laughing louder and louder*).
The man you sent with money-bag
For purpose that you know, to whom you know.
(*He laughs.*)
What a good joke!

Don Salluste.
What then?

Don Cæsar.
I made him drunk.

Don Salluste.
About the money that he had?

Don Cæsar.
With it
I presents made to divers persons. Well,
We all have friends.

Don Salluste.
You wrongly me suspect——

Don Cæsar (*rattling the money in his pockets*).
I first my pockets filled, you will believe.
(*Laughs again.*)
You understand? the lady!

Don Salluste.
Oh!

Don Cæsar (*remarking his anxiety*).
You know,—

[DON SALLUSTE *listens with redoubled anxiety.* DON
CÆSAR *proceeds, laughing.*

She sent an old duenna—fearful wretch,
With sprouting beard and drunkard's ruddy nose——

DON SALLUSTE.

What for?

DON CÆSAR.

To quietly inquire if it
Were true—from prudence—that Don Cæsar here
Expected her to-night——

DON SALLUSTE (*aside*).
                    Good Heavens!   (*Aloud.*)
                                    And what
Didst thou reply?

DON CÆSAR.
            My master, I said yes!
That I awaited her.

DON SALLUSTE (*aside*).
                It may be all
Is not yet lost!

DON CÆSAR.
            At last your swordsman fine,
Your Captain, on the field he gave his name—
'Twas Guritan. .(DON SALLUSTE *starts.*)
                This morning prudently
He would not see the lackey that was sent
With message from Don Cæsar, and he came
To me demanding satisfaction——

DON SALLUSTE.
                        Well,
And what didst thou?

DON CÆSAR.
            I killed the goose-cap.

DON SALLUSTE.
                                Ah!
Indeed?

DON CÆSAR.
Yea, 'neath the wall he's dying now.

DON SALLUSTE.

Art sure he'll die?

DON CÆSAR.

I fear so.

DON SALLUSTE (*aside*).

Oh, again

I breathe! By Grace of heaven! nothing he
Has yet disturbed! Quite otherwise. But let me
Be rid of him, this rough assistant, now!
The money—as for that, 'tis nought. (*Aloud.*)

Your tale
Is very strange. And have you seen none else?

DON CÆSAR.

No soul. But soon I shall. I shall go on.
My name will cause sensation through the town.
I'll make a frightful scandal, you may rest
Assured.

DON SALLUSTE (*aside*).

The devil!

(*Eagerly, and approaching* DON CÆSAR.)

Money you may keep,
But leave this house.

DON CÆSAR.

Ah, yes, one knows your ways;
You'd have me followed! Then I should return—
Delightful destiny—to contemplate
Thy blue, oh sea Mediterranean!
Not I.

DON SALLUSTE.

Believe me.

DON CÆSAR.

No. Besides, within
This palace-prison some one is, I feel,
A prey to your dark treachery. All plots
Of Courts have double ladders. On one side
Arms tied, and gloom, and troubled looks. By one
Ascends the suff'rer, by the other mounts
The executioner.—Now you must be
The headsman——of necessity.

Don Salluste.
> Oh! oh!

Don Cæsar.
For me! I pull the ladder, and crack—down
It goes!

Don Salluste.
> I swear——

Don Cæsar.
> I will to spoil it all
Stay through th' adventure. Oh, I know you sharp
Enough, my subtle cousin, puppets two
Or three to hang up by one cord. Hold, now,
I'm one! and I will here remain!

Don Salluste.
> Hark, now——

Don Cæsar.
To rhetoric! Ah, me you sold away
To Afric's pirates! Here you fabricate
Some Cæsar false! And thus you compromise
My name!

Don Salluste.
> Mere chance it was.

Don Cæsar.
> Mere chance! Excuse
That dish that rogues prepare for fools to gulp;
No chance was it. The worse for you if plans
Break through. But I intend to succor those
Whom you'd destroy. I shall cry out my name
From the house-tops.

(He climbs on the window supports and looks out.)
> Now wait! Here is good luck!
The Alguazils are 'neath the window now.

(He passes his arm through the bars and shakes them,
*   crying out)*
Halloa!

Don Salluste *(aside, and terrified, at the front of the stage).*
> All's lost if he be recognized!

> [*The* Alguazils *enter, preceded by an* Alcaid. Don Sal-
> luste *appears in great perplexity.* Don Cæsar
> *goes towards the* Alcaid *with an air of triumph.*

SCENE 8.—THE SAME, AN ALCAID, AND THE ALGUAZILS.

DON CÆSAR (*to the* Alcaid).
You, in your warrant, will take down——

DON SALLUSTE (*pointing to* DON CÆSAR).
That this
Man is the famous robber Matalobos!

DON CÆSAR (*amazed*).
How!

DON SALLUSTE (*aside*).
All I gain, if I but gain a day.
(*To the* Alcaid.)
This man in shining daylight dares to come
Into our houses.—Seize the thief.
[*The* Alguazils *seize* DON CÆSAR *by the collar.*

DON CÆSAR (*furious, to* DON SALLUSTE).
Pardon!
You lie outrageously!

THE ALCAID.
Who was it, then,
That called us?

DON SALLUSTE.
It was I.

DON CÆSAR.
By heaven, now!
That's bold!

THE ALCAID.
Be still! I think he's right.

DON CÆSAR.
But list,
I am Don Cæsar de Bazan himself!

DON SALLUSTE.
Don Cæsar! If you please, examine now
His mantle—you will find that Salluste's writ
Beneath the collar. 'Tis a mantle which
Just now he stole from me.
[*The* Alguazils *snatch off the mantle, and the* Alcaid
examines it.

THE ALCAID.

                    Quite right—'tis so.

DON SALLUSTE.

The doublet that he wears——

                    DON CÆSAR (*aside*).

                    Accursèd Salluste !

DON SALLUSTE (*continuing*).

Belongs to the Count d'Albe ; it was from him
He stole it,
(*showing an escutcheon embroidered on the facing of the
                    left sleeve*)
                    And whose 'scutcheon you behold !

                    DON CÆSAR (*aside*).

Bewitched he must be !

          THE ALCAID (*examining the blazon*).

                    Ah, yes—yes ; here are
The castles two, in gold——

          DON SALLUSTE.

                    Also you'll see
Two cauldrons, Henriquez and Guzman.
          [*In struggling,* DON CÆSAR *has let fail some doub-
          loons from his pockets.* DON SALLUSTE *points out
          to the* Alcaid *the manner in which they were filled.*
                    There !
Is that the way that money's borne about
By honest men?

          THE ALCAID (*shaking his head*).
                    Ahem !

          DON CÆSAR (*aside*).
                    I'm caught !

          THE ALCAID.
                    Here are
Some papers.

          DON CÆSAR (*aside*).
          Ah, they're found ! Oh, oh, the poor
Love-letters saved through all my scrapes !

THE ALCAID (*examining the papers*).

                               Letters——

What's this?—in different hands are they——

DON SALLUSTE (*making him observe the directions*).

                               But all

Directed to the Count.

THE ALCAID.
Yes.

DON CÆSAR.
              But——

THE ALCAID (*tying his hands*).

                           Caught now !

What luck !

AN ALGUAZIL (*entering to the* Alcaid).

              Outside, my Lord, a man has just

Been killed.

THE ALCAID.
Who is the murderer ?

DON SALLUSTE (*pointing to* DON CÆSAR).

                        'Tis he.

DON CÆSAR (*aside*).
The duel ! Oh, that senseless freak !

DON SALLUSTE.
                         Ah, when

He entered, in his hand he had a sword,
And there it is.

THE ALCAID (*examining the sword*).

                And blood upon it ! Ah !

              (*To* DON CÆSAR.)

There—go with them.

DON SALLUSTE (*to* DON CÆSAR, *whom the* Alguazils *are taking away*).

                  To Matalobos now

Good evening.

DON CÆSAR (*making a step towards him and looking at him fixedly*).

Earth's vilest scoundrel you !

ACT FIFTH : THE TIGER AND THE LION.

The same room. It is night. A lamp is on the table. At the
rising of the curtain RUY BLAS *is alone. He is dressed in*
a long black robe, which conceals his other vestments.

SCENE 1.

RUY BLAS (*alone*).

'Tis ended now. The dream—the vision—all
Has passed away. All day till eve I've walked
Haphazard through the streets. Just now I've hope.
I'm calm. At night the head is less disturb'd
By noise, and one reflects the better then.
Nought too alarming in these darkened walls
I see ; the furniture is 'ranged ; the keys
Are in the locks ; the mutes sleep overhead ;
The house is truly very still. Oh yes,
There is no reason for alarm. All things
Proceed quite well. My Page all faithful is.
Don Guritan is sure to stir himself
For her. Oh, God ! May I not thank Thee now,
Just God, for suff'ring that advice to reach
Her ears. Thou, gracious God, hast aided me.
'Tis Thou hast helped me to protect and save
This angel, and defeat Don Salluste. Oh
May she have nought to fear, and nought, alas,
To suffer ; and may she be ever saved !
And oh, that I may die !

[*He draws from his bosom a little vial which he*
places on the table.

Yes, perish now,

Despised ! and sink into the grave ! Yes, die
As one should die, who seeks to expiate
A crime ! Die in this dwelling, wretched, vile,
And lone !

[*He throws open the black robe, under which is seen*
the livery which he wore in the first act.

Die with thy livery beneath
Thy winding-sheet! Oh, if the demon comes
To see his victim dead,
        [*He pushes a piece of furniture to barricade the*
            secret door.
                he shall at least
Not enter by this horrid door! [*He comes back to the table.*
                        'Tis sure
The Page has spoken to Don Guritan.
It was not eight o'clock this morn. [*He gazes on the vial.*
                        For me
I have condemned myself, and now prepare
My execution,—on my head I shall
Myself let fall the tomb's so heavy lid.
At least I have the comfort certainly
To know there is no help. My fall must be.
                [*Sinking into the arm-chair.*
And yet she loved me! Oh God, help me now!
I've not the courage!   [*He weeps.*
                Oh! he might in peace
Have left us! [*He hides his face in his hands and sobs.*
        Oh, my God!
        [*Raising his head, as if distraught, and looking at*
            the vial.
                    The man who sold
Me this asked me what day o' the month it was.
I could not tell. My head's confused. Oh, men
Are cruel. You may die, and none will care.
I suffer.—Me she loved!—To know things past
Can never be restored! And to behold
Her nevermore! Her hand that I have press'd!
Her lips that touch'd my brow—— Angel adored!
Poor angel! There is need to die, and die
Despairing! Oh, her dress, the folds of which
Each one had grace, her footstep that had power
To stir my soul when it pass'd by, her eyes
That did intoxicate mine own still all
Irresolute, her smile, her voice —— and I
Shall see her, hear her never more. Is this
Then possible? Oh, never!

[*In anguish he stretches out his hand to the vial; at the moment when he seizes it convulsively the door at the back opens. The* QUEEN *appears dressed in white, with a dark mantle, the hood of which having fallen back on her shoulders, shows her pale face. She carries in her hand a dark lantern which she places on the floor and walks rapidly towards* RUY BLAS.*

SCENE 2.—RUY BLAS—THE QUEEN.

THE QUEEN (*entering*).
Don Cæsar!

RUY BLAS (*turning round with a frightened gesture, and closing hurriedly the robe which had hidden his livery*).
Oh God! 'tis she! In a most horrid snare
She's taken. (*Aloud.*) Madam!——

THE QUEEN.
Cæsar! What a cry
Of fright——

RUY BLAS.
Who was it told you to come here?

THE QUEEN.
Thyself.

RUY BLAS.
Oh, how?

THE QUEEN.
I have received from you——

RUY BLAS (*breathless*).
Speak, quick!

THE QUEEN.
A note.

RUY BLAS.
From me!

THE QUEEN.
By your own hand
Indited.

RUY BLAS.
This is but to dash one's brow
Against the wall! But oh, I have not writ——
Of that I'm very sure!

THE QUEEN (*drawing from her bosom a letter, which she gives him*).

Read—read it then.

[RUY BLAS *takes the letter eagerly, and bends towards the lamp to read it.*

RUY BLAS (*reading*).

" A danger terrible environs me ;
My Queen alone can stay the tempest's force——
    [*He looks at the letter as if in a stupor and unable to read further.*

THE QUEEN (*continuing, and pointing with her finger to the lines as she reads*).

" By coming to my house this night. If not,
I'm lost."

RUY BLAS (*in a stifled voice*).

What treason ! Oh, that letter !

THE QUEEN (*continuing to read*).
                                                " Come
To the door that's at the end of th' Avenue ;
At night you'll not be recognized. And one
Who is devoted will be there to ope
The door."

RUY BLAS (*aside*).

This note I had forgotten.
    [*To the* QUEEN, *in a terrible voice.*
                                                Go
Away !

THE QUEEN.

I'll go, Don Cæsar. You are cruel !
My God ! What have I done ?

RUY BLAS.
                                        Good heavens ! What ?
You ruin and destroy yourself !

THE QUEEN.
                                        But how ?

RUY BLAS.
Explain I cannot. Fly—fly quick.

THE QUEEN.
                                        This morn

I for your safety did precaution take,
And a duenna sent——

RUY BLAS.

Oh God ! but now

As from a heart that bleeds, I feel your life
In streams is running out.—Go—go !

THE QUEEN (*as if struck by a sudden idea*).

Inspired

I am by that devotion which my love
Suggests. Oh, you approach some dreadful hour,
And would remove me from the danger now !
But I remain !

RUY BLAS.

Oh, what sublimity !

What thoughtfulness !—Oh God ! to thus remain
At such an hour in such a place !

THE QUEEN.

From you

The letter really came. And thus——

RUY BLAS (*raising his arms to heaven in despair*).

Oh Power

Divine !

THE QUEEN.

You wish me gone.

RUY BLAS (*taking her hands*).

Oh, understand !

THE QUEEN.

I do. Upon the moment's spur you wrote,
And after——

RUY BLAS.

Unto thee I have not writ.

I am a demon. Fly ! Ah it is thou,
Poor child, who lead'st thyself into the snare !
Ah, it is true, and hell on every side
Besieges thee ! Then nothing can I find
That will persuade thee ? Listen—understand ;
I love thee well, thou know'st. To save thy mind

From what is imaged, I would pluck my heart
From out my body. Go thou !

THE QUEEN.
Don Cæsar——

RUY BLAS.
Go—go. But I remember, some one must
Have opened to you ?

THE QUEEN.
Yes.

RUY BLAS.
Oh Satan ! Who ?

THE QUEEN.
One in a mask—and hidden by the wall.

RUY BLAS.
What said the man ? what was his figure—say ?
Oh, was he tall ? Who was he ? Speak, I wait !
[*A man in black, and masked, appears at the door at
the back.*

THE MASKED MAN.
'Twas I.
[*He takes off his mask. It is* DON SALLUSTE. *The*
QUEEN *and* RUY BLAS *recognize him with terror.*

SCENE 3.—THE SAME, DON SALLUSTE.

RUY BLAS.
Great God ! Fly, Madam, fly !

DON SALLUSTE.
There is
No longer time. Madame de Neubourg now
Has ceased to be the Queen of Spain.

THE QUEEN (*horrified*).
Don Salluste !

DON SALLUSTE (*pointing to* RUY BLAS).
That man's companion you henceforth must be.

THE QUEEN.

Great God! ah yes, it is indeed a snare!
Don Caesar——

RUY BLAS (*despairingly*).
Madam, what, alas! is it
You've done?

DON SALLUSTE (*moving slowly towards the* QUEEN).
I hold you here.—But I will speak
Without offence unto your Majesty,
For without wrath am I.—I find you here—
Now listen, do not let us make a stir—
At midnight, in Don Caesar's room alone.
This fact, if public—for a queen—would be
Enough at Rome the marriage to annul,
And promptly would the Holy Father be
Informed of it.—But by consent the thing
Could be concealed.

[*He draws from his pocket a parchment, which he
unrolls and presents to the* QUEEN.

Sign me this letter then
Unto His Majesty our King. I will
Send it by hand of the grand equerry
To the chief notary, and afterwards—
A carriage, where I've placed a heap of gold
(*Pointing outside.*)
Is there—set out the two of you at once.
I help you. Be not anxious, you can go
Toledo way by Alcantare—so
Reach Portugal. Go where you will—to us
It is the same. We'll shut our eyes.—Obey.
I swear that I alone as yet am 'ware
Of the adventure; but if you refuse,
Madrid to-morrow shall know everything.
Let us be calm. I hold you in my hand.

[*Pointing to the table on which is an ink-stand.*
Madam, for writing, what you need is there.

THE QUEEN (*overwhelmed, falling into an arm-chair*).
I'm in his power!

DON SALLUSTE.
From you I only ask

This acquiescence signed, for me to send
To the king.
> [*Whispering to* RUY BLAS, *who listens motionless
> and thunderstruck.*

Let me alone, it is for thee
I work. (*To the* QUEEN.) Sign now.

THE QUEEN (*aside, trembling*).

What can I do?

DON SALLUSTE (*leaning over her, whispering in her ear, and
presenting a pen*).

There now!

What is a crown? You happiness will gain,
Though you may lose a throne. My people all
Remain outside. They nothing know of this,
All passes here between us three.
> [*Trying to put the pen between the* QUEEN'S *fingers,
> she neither taking nor rejecting it.*

Well now,
> [*The* QUEEN, *distraught and undecided, looks at him
> with anguish.*

If you sign not you strike the blow yourself—
The scandal and the cloister!

THE QUEEN (*overwhelmed*).

Oh, my God!

DON SALLUSTE (*pointing to* RUY BLAS).

Don Cæsar loves you. He is worthy you;
Upon my honor he is nobly born;
Almost a prince. Lord of a donjon keep
With walls embattled, holding fee of lands,
He is the Duke d'Olmedo—Count Bazan,
Grandee of Spain——
> [*He pushes to the parchment the hand of the* QUEEN,
> *who, trembling and dismayed, seems ready to sign.*

RUY BLAS (*as if suddenly awakening*).

My name is Ruy Blas,
And I a lackey am!
> [*Snatching the pen from the hand of the* QUEEN, *and
> the parchment, which he tears.*

Madam, sign not!—
At last!—I suffocate!

THE QUEEN.

Oh, what says he?

Don Caesar!

RUY BLAS (*letting his robe fall, and showing himself in livery
without a sword*).

Yes, my name is Ruy Blas.
I am the servant of that man! (*Turning to* DON SALLUSTE.)
I say
There's been enough of treason, and that I
Refuse my happiness!—Oh thanks!—you thought
That you did well to whisper in my ear!
I say that it is time, that I at last
Should waken, though I'm strangled in your web
Of hideous plots—and I no further step
Will go. I say we two together make,
My Lord, a pair that's infamous. I have
The clothing of a lackey—you the soul!

DON SALLUSTE (*to the* QUEEN *coldly*).
This man indeed my servant is.
(*To* RUY BLAS, *with authority*).
Not one
Word more.

THE QUEEN (*letting a cry of despair escape her, and wringing
her hands*).
Just heav'n!

DON SALLUSTE (*continuing*).
Only he spoke too soon.
[*He crosses his arms, and holds himself up, speaking
with a voice of thunder.*
Well—yes! now 'tis for me to tell it all.
It matters not, my vengeance in its way
Is all complete.
(*To the* QUEEN.)
What think you? On my word,
Madrid will laugh! You ruined me! and you
I have dethroned. You banished me, and now
I boast of driving you away. Ha, ha!
You offered me for wife your waiting-maid!
(*Bursting into laughter.*)
My lackey I for lover give to you.

You can espouse him certainly.   The King
Sinks fast !—A lover's heart will be your wealth.
(*He laughs.*)
You will have made him Duke, that you might be
His Duchess !
(*Grinding his teeth.*)
Ah, you blighted, ruined me.
And trampled me beneath your feet, and yet—
And yet you slept in peace !   Fool that you were !
[*Whilst he has been speaking,* RUY BLAS *has gone to
the door at the back and fastened it; then he has
approached him by soft steps from behind, with-
out having been perceived.   At the moment when*
DON SALLUSTE *finishes, fixing his eyes full of
hatred and triumph on the annihilated* QUEEN.
RUY BLAS *seizes the sword of the* MARQUIS *by the
hilt, and draws it out swiftly.*

RUY BLAS (*with the sword of* DON SALLUSTE *in his hand*).
I say you have insulted now your Queen !
[DON SALLUSTE *rushes towards the door.*   RUY BLAS
bars the way.
—Oh, go not there !   'tis not worth while ; long since
I fastened it.   Marquis, until to-day,
Satan protected thee ; but if he will
From my hands pluck thee, let him show himself.
—'Tis my turn now !—When we a serpent meet,
It must be crush'd.   No one can enter here.
No, not thy people, and not hell.   Beneath
Mine iron heel I hold thee foaming now !
—This man spoke insolently to you, Madam !
I will explain.   He has no human soul.
A monster he.   With jibings yesterday
He suffocated me.   He crush'd my heart,
For his mere pleasure.   Oh, he bade me close
A window, and he martyrized me then !
I prayed—I wept—I cannot tell you all.
(*To the* MARQUIS.)
In these last moments you have counted o'er
Your wrongs.   I shall not answer your complaints.
Besides, I comprehend them not.   But you.
Oh wretch ! you dare your Queen to outrage now

—Woman adorable—whilst I am by!
Hold! for a clever man, in truth you much
Astonish me! And you imagine, too,
That I shall see you do it, and say nought!
But listen,—whatsoe'er his sphere, my Lord,
When a vile, trait'rous, tortuous scoundrel strange
And monstrous acts commits, noble or churl,
All men have right, in coming on his path,
To splutter out his sentence to his face,
And take a sword, a knife, a hatchet——Oh,
By Heav'n! to be a lackey! When I should
The headsman be!

THE QUEEN.

You do not mean to kill

This man?

RUY BLAS.

Madam, I am ashamed, indeed,

That I my duty must accomplish here;
But this affair must all be stifled now.

   (*He pushes* DON SALLUSTE *towards the closet.*)
'Tis settled. Go you there, my Lord, and pray.

DON SALLUSTE.

It is assassination.

RUY BLAS.

Think you so?

DON SALLUSTE (*unarmed, and looking around him with rage*).
Nothing upon these walls! No arms!

(*To* RUY BLAS.)

A sword,

At least!

RUY BLAS.

Marquis, you jest! What! Master! is't

That I'm a gentleman? a duel! fie!
One of thy servants am I, in galloon
And red, a knave to be chastised and whipp'd,
And one who kills! Yes, I shall kill you, Sir——
Believe you it?—as villain infamous!
As craven! as a dog!

THE QUEEN.

Have mercy on him!

RUY BLAS (*to the* QUEEN, *and seizing the* MARQUIS).
Madam, each one takes vengeance for himself.
The demon cannot any longer be
Saved by an Angel!

THE QUEEN (*kneeling*).
Mercy!

DON SALLUSTE (*calling for help*).
Murder! help!

RUY BLAS (*raising the sword*).
How soon will you have done?

DON SALLUSTE (*throwing himself on* RUY BLAS).
Demon! I die
By murder!

RUY BLAS (*pushing him into the closet*).
No, in rightful punishment!
[*They disappear in the cabinet, the door of which*
closes on them.

THE QUEEN (*alone, and falling half dead into the arm-chair*).
Oh heavens!
[*A moment of silence.* RUY BLAS *re-enters, pale.*
and without the sword.

SCENE 4.—THE QUEEN—RUY BLAS.

RUY BLAS *totters a few steps towards the* QUEEN, *who remains*
motionless and as if frozen. Then he falls on both knees,
his eyes fixed on the ground, as if he dared not raise
them to her.

RUY BLAS (*in a grave low voice*).
Now, Madam, must I speak to you.
But I will not come near. I frankly speak.
I'm not as guilty as you think I am.
I know my treason, as to you it seems,
Must horrible appear. Oh, to explain
It is not easy. Yet not base my soul,—
At heart I'm honest. 'Tis this love which has
Destroyed me. Not that I defend myself,
For well I know I should have found some means
T' escape. The sin is consummated now!
But all the same, I've loved you truly well.

THE QUEEN—"THIS HORRIBLE FLUID IS NOT POISON? SPEAK!"

Ruy Blas—Act V., Scene 4.

THE QUEEN.

Sir——

RUY BLAS (*still on his knees*).

Fear not. I will not approach. Yet would
I to your Majesty from step to step
The whole declare. Believe I am not vile!
To-day—all day I paced about the town
Like one possessed. Often the people looked
At me. And near the 'spital that by you
Was founded, vaguely did I feel, athwart
My brain delirious, that silently
A woman of the crowd did wipe away
The sweat from off my brow. Have mercy, God!
My heart is broken!

THE QUEEN.
What is't that you wish?

RUY BLAS (*joining his hands*).
That, Madam, you would pardon me!

THE QUEEN.
Never.

RUY BLAS.
Never! [*He rises, and walks slowly towards the table.*
Very sure?

THE QUEEN.
No, never—never!

RUY BLAS (*he takes the vial that was placed on the table,
carries it to his lips, and empties it at one draught*).
Sad flame, extinguished be!

THE QUEEN (*rising and rushing to him*).
What have you done?

RUY BLAS (*showing the vial*).
Nothing. My woes are ended. Nothing. You
Curse me—and I bless you. There—that is all.

THE QUEEN (*overcome*).
Don Cæsar!

RUY BLAS.
When I think, poor angel, that
You loved me!

THE QUEEN.

Oh, what was that philtre strange?
What have you done? Speak—answer—tell to me.
I do forgive and love thee, Cæsar.   I
Believe in thee.

RUY BLAS.

My name is Ruy Blas.

THE QUEEN (*throwing her arms round him*).
I do forgive thee, Ruy Blas. But speak,
Say what it is you've done? 'Tis my command!
That frightful draught—it was not poison? Say?

RUY BLAS.

Yes; it was poison. But my heart is glad.
[*Holding the* QUEEN *in his arms and raising his
eyes to heaven.*
Permit, oh God,—the Sovereign Justice Thou—
That the poor lackey pours out blessings on
This Queen, who did console his tortured heart
By—in his life—her love, and pity gives
In death.

THE QUEEN.

Poison! Oh God! 'tis I—'tis I
Have killed thee! Ah, I love thee! If I had
But pardoned!

RUY BLAS (*sinking*).

I had done the same.
[*His voice fails. The Queen supports him.*
I could
No longer live! Adieu! (*Pointing to the door.*)
Fly hence, and all
Will secret be. I die. (*He falls.*)

THE QUEEN (*throwing herself on his body*).
Ruy Blas!

RUY BLAS (*at the point of death, rousing himself at his
name pronounced by the* QUEEN).
I thank thee!

THE END.

www.ingramcontent.com/pod-product-compliance
Lightning Source LLC
Chambersburg PA
CBHW030822110726
47900CB00006B/1714